ETERNAL CURSE

"Have ye any last words?"

Rachel glared at the judge, focusing onto this one man her entire lifetime's store of anger, misery, and suffering.

"I tell ye all this. I curse this man! May the Lord in Heaven smite him and all the liars who have brought me to this untimely end."

She caught sight of John Saunders in the crowd as, with down-turned face, he glanced at her.

"None of ye shall escape the cleansing Fire! Do you hear me? And I say this: after I am gone, if this property ever leaves the hands of my daughters — or *her* daughter — then I beseech the Lord in Heaven to smite with just retribution whomever is living in my house! Let them burn in the agony of hellfire!"

She took a deep breath and held it. "That is all," she said at last glancing down at the men who held the ladder.

The two men pulled the ladder away from the branch, and Rachel Parsons fell until the rope caught her up and snapped her neck. For a long moment, the crowd watched in awed silence as her body swung slowly back and forth. twitching as though in a wild dance.

RICK HAUTALA

DARK SILENCE

ZEBRA BOOKS
KENSINGTON PUBLISHING CORP.

Dedication:

This one is for Matti,
who carries sunshine in a smile.

ZEBRA BOOKS

are published by

Kensington Publishing Corp.
475 Park Avenue South
New York, NY 10016

First printing: October, 1992

Printed in the United States of America

ACKNOWLEDGMENTS

First up for big "thank yous" this time is Dr. Russell Collett, who gave me invaluable (and at times stomach-churning) information that made the medical aspects of this novel fall into place like a neatly set bone. Without his open and genuine enthusiasm for his own work, I would never have gotten started on mine.

Robert LeFebvre, Fire Chief for Gorham, Maine, answered a whole slew of questions about fire fighting, all of which added a solid "backbone" to this story.

Roberta Grossman and Wendy McCurdy, at Zebra, brainstormed on this book with me from the beginning, and I greatly value their suggestions and ideas for directions the story could take.

And, as always, I have to thank Dominick Abel, for continuing to show faith in me and my work; Matt Costello, Mike Kimball, Joe Citro, Chris Fahy, and Mike Feeney for listening and *listening;* and Bonnie and the boys, for putting up with some rather erratic mood swings while I was working on this book.

Finally, and most importantly, I want to thank you, the reader, for buying and reading my books. I hope this one won't disappoint.

Thanks again, everyone!

CONTENTS:

PART THREE: The 'Old Witch Lady's' House

Prologue

November 1694

". . . the wrong doing of one generation lives into the successive ones, and . . . becomes a pure and uncontrollable mischief."

— Hawthorne
The House of the Seven Gables

Prologue: November 1694
A Hanging

The wind came in off the distant ocean, carrying with it a cold drizzle that lashed like a whip against the small group of people who had gathered beneath the wide-spanning, leafless oak tree. Thin, gray clouds raced to the west as though fleeing the tossing waves of the Atlantic. A lone seagull spiralled high overhead, no more than a white speck against the sky. Its lonely cry punctuated the slick whistling of the wind that beat down the yellowed grass and brown weeds covering the slope along the boulder-strewn shore of the Saco River.

In the clearing beneath the oak, a tall, bearded man wearing a long black cloak that flapped like a raven's wing in the wind, stood in front of an aged woman. She wore a plain, gray linen dress and had a dark wool shawl thrown over her frail shoulders against the autumn chill. Her white hair hung in a loose tangle down to her shoulders. She was supported by two burly men who grasped her roughly by the upper arms. Behind her back, a thick hempen rope dug into her wrists as she struggled against her bonds. Mist sprinkled her face like the sweat of one in the grips of a fever as she looked at the hard glint in the man's pale blue eyes. She never had — and now knew she never would — find an ounce of mercy in the eyes of Judge William Talmadge.

"Ye have heard the charges laid against thee, Rachel Par-

11

sons," Judge Talmadge said in a deep, sonorous voice, "and ye have heard the sentence as decreed by the court. Have ye any last words?"

For the span of several heartbeats, Rachel Parsons was silent. Her gaze darted from face to face in the crowd as she tried to understand how these, her friends and neighbors for nearly two decades, could turn on her like this. Last month, many of them had been at the mockery of justice that had been called her "trial" for the crime of witchcraft. A few had testified against her, specifying particular instances and incidents where she had worked her evil against them and their kin. John Saunders, whose son was betrothed to Elizabeth Hull, had testified how last spring Rachel had put a curse on his milk cow which she said she wouldn't lift until he brought her a load of firewood for the winter. And Ester Hull, her nearest neighbor, had told the court that many a full moon night over the past ten years she had seen Rachel leave her house at midnight in the form of a black cat, and go into the forest to revel with Satan and his Dark Legion.

Behind her, Rachel was aware of the looming presence of the large, leafless oak tree. She could imagine that the lashing branches reached high into the heavens and were shredding the rain clouds, tearing them to windblown ribbons. She could hear the dull creaking of the rope that hung from one of the lower branches as it swayed back and forth in the wind. Within minutes, that rope was to be looped around her neck and she would be hanging, lifeless and cold, in the drizzling rain.

"If ye have no more to say, then gaolers, prepare to carry out the sentence," Judge Talmadge said.

Unmindful of the agony it caused, the two men fairly lifted her by the arms. Then climbing up ladders perched on either side of her, they hustled her up the middle ladder that leaned against the branch around which the rope had been tied. While one of them held up her wet hair, the other slipped the noose around her neck and pulled it snugly tight. The thick rope pinched the skin at the back of Rachel's neck like the stinging bite of a serpent. Rachel winced with pain as the two men scurried back down safely to the ground and removed their ladders.

"Yea—I do have something to say," Rachel said in a voice that strained to be heard above the hissing wind.

In the distance, through the trees, she could see the swift, silver band that was the Saco River. The whispering crowd grew hushed with expectation. Stepping forward, Judge Talmadge looked up at her, his mouth a hard, lipless line.

"Be brief, Dame Parsons," he said. "The Lord in heaven—or your Dark Master in hell below—awaits to embrace your eternal soul."

The deep trembling in Rachel's chest made it difficult for her to speak. Words and images, fragments of thoughts raced through her mind. Memories of her life in England, of the dangerous passage to the colonies, of the hard work she and Thomas, her husband, now long dead, had endured, carving out a life for themselves in the rich lands on the north shore of the Saco River in the Province of Maine. The joy and pain of childbirth, and the grief of losing all but one of her six children before they turned twelve. Rage and pain threatened to burst out of Rachel like the raging wind that rattled the branches of the Gallows Tree overhead.

"This is *my* land," Rachel said in a tremulous voice that threatened to break on every syllable. "This oak tree, which soon will bear my lifeless body like some unrighteous fruit, is on *my* property!"

"I prithee, be brief," Judge Talmadge said, glaring up at her harshly.

Rachel eyed him coldly as her anger fanned all the higher.

"Then hear me out, Judge Talmadge! I have a daughter—Nancy, who lives in Winnisquam, New Hampshire, with her husband, William, and her daughter, Elizabeth. In my will, which Parson Wells has writ down for me and duly recorded, I bequeath my house and property to her. And I know—"

For a moment, her voice broke as hot, red anger filled her. Rachel struggled to free her hands so she could shake her clenched fists at the storm-tossed sky.

13

"—I know, Judge Talmadge, that ye have long coveted this land which Thomas and I have cleared and made fertile. But I tell ye this: the land now belongs to my daughter, Nancy, and no one else!"

Her voice trembled as it rose higher so the entire assembly could hear her.

"And I tell ye all this. I curse this man! May the Lord in heaven smite him and all the liars who have brought me to this untimely end!"

She caught sight of John Saunders in the crowd as, with downturned face, he glanced at her from beneath the brim of his wide, black hat.

"None of ye shall escape the cleansing fire of the Lord's judgment! Do ye hear me? And I say this: after I am gone, if this property ever leaves the hands of my daughter—or *her* daughter—then I beseech the Lord in heaven to smite with just retribution whomever is living in my house! Let them and all their kin burn in the agony of hellfire!"

Smiling thinly, Judge Talmadge said, "Your words condemn you all the more, Dame Parsons, and do but convince me further that we have acted justly in the name of the Lord."

Rachel glared at the judge, focusing onto this one man her entire lifetime's store of anger, misery, and suffering. Lowering her voice, she said, "My soul is as pure, Judge, as I know thine is black. I go now to heaven, with all the innocence and purity of a child. But heed ye my words! Heed them well!" She took a deep breath and held it. "That is all," she said at last, glancing down at the men who held the ladder upon which she stood. "I am at peace."

Without waiting for an order from the judge, the two men pulled the ladder away from the branch, and Rachel Parson fell until the rope caught her up and snapped her neck. For a long moment, the crowd watched in awed silence as her body swung slowly back and forth, twitching as though in a wild dance. Above the low whistle of the wind, the only sound was the steady creaking of the rope, which sounded like the runners

14

of an old rocking chair on a wooden floor.

"Stand ye back!" Judge Talmadge suddenly shouted to the two jailers. A dark stain spread across the lap of Rachel's linen dress, and then a thin stream of urine dripped to the ground with a loud splatter. Carried by a gust of wind, a few drops sprinkled the judge's forehead. He feverishly wiped his face clean with the flat of his hand before turning to face the crowd, but he was unable to ignore the foreboding presence suspended from the tree, dangling above his left shoulder like a lowering, black cloud.

"Heed ye *not* her words!" he shouted, although his voice trembled, and not just from the cold wind. "These were the words of a servant of Satan and thus have no power over the righteous!"

With that, the crowd silently began to move away, leaving behind only the two gaolers, whose orders were to guard the body until sunset, at which time they were to cut down the witch's body and bury her in a shallow, unmarked grave on the hill beneath the oak. Then they were told to chop down the oak tree and burn it to ashes, which they were to scatter over the grave.

Part One:

Another Fall

Autumn 1963

"Blood asketh blood, and death must death requite."

— Thomas Norton and Thomas Sackville
Gorboduc

Chapter One
Retard

"You gonna pay for it?"

"What do you mean, am I gonna *pay* for it? Are you crazy? Of *course* I ain't gonna pay for it!"

"But you *gotta* pay for it! We'll be in deep shit if you get caught stealing that!"

"We'd be in even deeper shit if I tried to pay for it, now, wouldn't we? Seems to me as though either way we're gonna be in deep—"

"Hey! Can I help you boys with somethin'?"

Herb LaPointe was slouched behind the cash register at the back of LaPointe's Newsstand in a chair that looked entirely too small for his bulk. His head was wreathed with cigar smoke as he scanned the sports page of the *Portland Press Herald*. His eyes narrowed as he stared over the edge of the newspaper at twelve-year-old Eddie Fraser and his buddy, Ray Saunders, as they huddled in front of the magazine display, their backs turned to him. Both boys were dressed in jeans and faded T-shirts. Eddie, who was the smaller of the two, wore his hair a bit longer than Ray. Their arms and necks were tanned a deep, nut-brown, and their hair had been bleached almost blond by the summer sun.

"Uhh no—no sir," Ray said without turning around. He ran the flat of his hand over the stubble of his crewcut. His eyes were wide with apprehension as he glanced sidelong at Eddie.

"Yeah, I was just—just looking for the new issue of *Mad* for my brother. Did that come in this week?" Eddie asked.

"Hey, if you don't see it, it ain't come in yet, all right?" Herb replied. "So either get the hell out of my store, or else buy something and *then* get the hell out of my store. This ain't the goddamned library, you know." He rustled the pages of his newspaper as if he'd gone back to his reading, but both boys could feel his gaze crawling like a cold snake up their backs.

Ray snickered beneath his breath and said, "Yeah, but I'll bet the library'll never carry something like *this!*" His hands were slick with sweat as he clutched the rolled-up issue of this month's *Playboy* close to his chest. He'd grabbed it off the top shelf when Herb's back had been turned. Just thinking about the cover copy made Ray's throat go desert dry.

September 1963
EUROPE'S NEW SEX SIRENS
A 14 PAGE COLOR PORTFOLIO.

Last week, when Herb had gone out back to the stockroom for something, Ray had sneaked a peak inside the magazine. That quick glimpse of fleshy treasures had left him thirsting for more. He had to *own* this magazine; but even if he'd had the necessary seventy-five cents—God, almost two weeks' allowance—he knew darn-right well that he didn't have the guts to actually *buy* it. Herb LaPointe, or "Farty," as most of the kids called him because of his unselfconscious habit of letting farts rip whenever he wanted to, would be on the phone within minutes to both boys' parents. Ray knew there was no other alternative. He *had* to steal this magazine—today!—because he *had* to own it . . . especially the picture on page 145! He had been counting on Eddie to cover for him, to create some kind of diversion so he could slip the magazine into his three-ring binder, but their plans were being

20

foiled.

"Cripes, come on. *Do* something, will ya!" Ray whispered between clenched teeth.

"Do what? My idea was to get him to check out back for the new issue of *Mad*."

"Then think of something else."

"Hey, what are you guys doin' over there, tradin' government secrets or something?" Herb snarled.

"Uhh — no, no," Eddie replied, glancing at Farty. "I was just — I wanted to get a roll of Lifesavers, and I was just reminding Sandy, here, about that twenty-five cents he owes me from yesterday. Re-*mem*-ber that, knuckle head?"

Ray's usual nickname was "Sandy," but because his father gave him a crewcut every September before school started, a crewcut which really amounted to shaving the boy's head, Eddie teased his friend by calling him "knuckle head" because, he said, at least for one month out of the year, Ray's head looked like a big knuckle.

"I don't owe you no twenty-five cents," Ray said, appearing for a moment to take Eddie seriously. "And don't go calling me *knuckle head*, either!"

"Sure thing, *knuckle head*," Eddie said as he rapped the back of his friend's head with his clenched fist and made a hollow knocking sound with his tongue. "And now that I think about it, it wasn't twenty-five cents; it was *fifty* cents you owed me. So — are you gonna cough it up, or am I going to have to beat it out of you."

"Not in *my* store, you don't" Herb said calmly. "I just had the floor waxed last week. I don't want you messin' it up with his blood."

"Oh, good! Real good!" Ray said, glancing over his shoulder at Farty and rolling his eyes. "Thanks a *lot* for your concern." He'd finally caught on that Eddie was just pouring it on heavy to distract Farty, but he didn't take very kindly to the threat of being beaten up. Actually, if it came right down to it, he knew that since he was a bit taller and heavier than Eddie, he could take him, easily. Then again, best friends

21

didn't beat up best friends, even if they did say stupid things about you to other people . . . especially when they were helping steal the latest issue of *Playboy*.

"Well, then," Eddie said with a forced nonchalance, "I suppose I could give you another day or two to come up with the dough before I have to give 'Fat Tony' a call and ask him to break your kneecaps or something."

Slipping one hand into his pants pocket, he moved over to the counter, picked up a roll of Five Flavor Life Savers, and said, "I guess I'll have one of these."

Just as Herb was leaning forward in his seat to ring in the sale, the bell at the front of the store jingled. Eddie cursed under his breath when he turned and saw Mikie, his younger brother, walking toward them. A wide smile split Mikie's face as he waved his hands excitedly over his head and called out, "Hi, Eddie! Hi, Sandy!"

His voice carried a high lilt to it that made Eddie cringe. *Damnit!* he thought. *Why'd he have to show up? He's gonna blow it!*

Catching Ray's attention with a quick glance, Eddie placed the roll of candy on the counter and then gave it a little push. It rolled to the edge of the counter and then, before Herb could stop it, dropped to the floor behind the cash register. Sighing heavily, Herb heaved himself forward to retrieve it. As soon as his head was down below counter level, Ray snapped open his notebook, tucked the magazine inside, and then clutched the notebook tightly to his chest. He nearly fainted, knowing that Mikie must have seen what he had done, but he nailed the younger boy with a hostile stare that screamed, *Shut-the-hell-up-don't-say-a-damned-thing-or-else!*

"That'll be a nickel," Farty said. "Think you can manage that, Mr. Hot-shot, High-finance?"

"Yeah—sure," Eddie said with a cockiness he didn't really feel as he dug a nickel out of his pocket and handed it to Herb. His hand was clammy and shaking, but he hoped the old fart didn't notice.

22

"Well, all right," Herb said. He held the coin up in front of his eyes and studied it for a moment before dropping it into the cash drawer. "A whole nickel!" He ran the cash drawer shut with a loud clang. "Now I can *finally* afford that Florida retirement home I've always dreamed about."

"Eddie, I — uh, you know, I ought to get going," Ray said in a voice that sounded higher, more constricted than normal. He started bouncing up and down on his toes like he had to go the bathroom *real* bad. "My dad's expecting me to get my chores done before dark." All the while, he was casting nervous glances between Farty and Mikie.

"Hey, what's that you got there?" Mikie said.

At the same instant, Ray and Eddie both blurted, "Nothing." Then Eddie turned to his brother and, holding the Life Savers up temptingly, said, "Oh, do you mean these?"

Mikie shook his head in denial and looked like he was going to say something more, but Eddie moved over to him quickly and, like a hypnotist, danced the candy in front of his brother's face. Mikie's smile widened as he licked his lips and said, "Yeah, can I have one?"

Milking the moment, and wishing to God that Ray would hurry up and start for the door, Eddie peeled the wrapper back and pried out a piece of candy. He made a move as if he was going to give it to Mikie, but then he popped it into his own mouth, smacking his lips loudly as he savored the flood of orange taste for a moment. "Umm-umm, that's *s-o-m-e* good!" he said. "Are you sure you want one?" he asked, offering the opened package to Mikie.

"Yeah, really . . . I do," Mikie said, nodding his head eagerly.

"Hey, didn't I tell you kids to get the hell out of here?" Farty shouted. He shook his head as though disgusted, then took an angry puff on his cigar and blew a billowing cloud of blue smoke in Eddie's direction. Eddie coughed into his fist as he waved his hand holding the Life Savers in front of him. Then he spun around on his heel, and he and Ray headed toward the exit. When Ray passed by Mikie, he paused and, leaning close, whispered, "I swear to God, if you tell him what you saw, I'll *kill* you!"

Then, side by side, Eddie and Ray stepped out into the warm afternoon. As soon as the door swung shut behind them, they both let out their withheld breaths and laughed nervously.

"God, that was close!" Ray said as they started down the sidewalk at a fast clip, heading through town. It was a beautiful late summer afternoon. The sun bathed their faces with warmth, and there was a clean, sweet smell in the air that felt more like mid-August than September. Summer just didn't seem to want to let go. The boys had just finished suffering through their third day of the new school year, but they were elated because — finally — the weekend was here and they had a brand new copy of *Playboy*.

"So tell me, *knuckle head,*" Eddie said, as they walked past the Summerfield Public Library. "Is that a roll of Life Savers in your pocket, or are you just happy to finally have your magazine?"

"Shut up, will you?" Ray said. His voice trembled slightly as he cast a nervous glance over his shoulder just to make sure Farty wasn't coming after them with a shotgun. "I think he saw me do it."

"Who, Farty?"

Ray snorted. "No, your dimwit brother. I'm positive he did. He was looking right at me." He swallowed noisily. "Do you think he'll say anything to Farty?"

"Naw. Not a chance," Eddie said, waving his hand dismissively. "And I doubt Farty will even notice there's an issue missing; but even if he does, he'll never connect it with us."

"Not unless your retard brother tells him."

"He's not a retard," Eddie said, bristling for a moment. "So don't worry, okay? Mikie wouldn't say anything if he knew it would get me in trouble."

Ray sniffed with nervous laughter. "That's what I'm afraid of — that he won't know the difference. After all, he *is* a retard."

"He is not!" Eddie snapped.

Ray almost kept the argument going but fell silent as they continued down Main Street.

"Hey, come on, Sandy," Eddie said at last. "Let's duck out behind the post office. I want to see this month's foldout and that European 'sex siren' you've been babbling about all week." He grabbed at Ray's notebook and almost pulled it from his hands.

"Hey, cut it out, will yah?"

"What do you mean, cut it out? I helped you get the damned thing. I want to take a look at it."

"Not *now!*" Ray said, his voice edging tight and shivery. "I meant what I said. I gotta get my butt home and get the chickens fed and the coop cleaned out, or else my old man will *whop* me a good one."

Eddie stopped short, caught Ray up by the shirt sleeve, and spun him around. "Well, *I'll* whop you a good one, too, if you don't at least let me take a peek at this month's Playmate." He clenched one fist and waved it threateningly in front of Ray's nose. He knew he would never in the world *really* start a fight with Ray — he'd probably get the tar knocked out of him; he was just hoping his best friend would see reason.

"You know where it'll be," Ray said as he pulled away and started walking again to increase the distance between them and LaPointe's Newsstand. There was still no sign of Farty giving chase to reclaim his stolen magazine, but Ray wanted to keep moving — fast. "I'll see you out there first thing tomorrow morning just like we agreed, okay?"

"Hey, wait a minute! Sandy! That's horse crap, and you know it!" Eddie shouted, but he didn't give chase. He just stood there, watching helplessly as Ray hurried away from him.

"Couldn't you at least let me — "

"No way," Ray called back over his shoulder. "I'll see yah tomorrow." Then he broke into a run, turned the corner onto Chestnut street, and was gone.

"Yeah, sure—" Eddie said softly as he shook his head. "Thanks a whole lot, pal!"

" 'Scuse me," Mikie said, "but did the new issue of *Mad* come in yet?"

Herb looked up from his paper and saw the look of excited expectation lighting the boy's clear, blue eyes as he stood in front of the newsstand counter. His hands were thrust deep into his jeans pockets, making his shoulders sag forward, like he was caught in a permanent shrug. A shock of dark hair hung like a wet wing over his forehead, making his face look unusually pale for this late in the summer.

Maybe it's just the lighting, Herb thought, *or else the poor kid just didn't get to the beach all that much this summer.*

Herb placed his cigar in the ashtray on the counter and smiled up at Mikie. He'd always liked the boy, had always felt a warm spot in his heart for him. He told himself it wasn't just because he felt sorry when he saw how the kids in town, especially the older ones, treated him; and it wasn't just because Mikie reminded him, quite a bit, actually, of his own son, Jeffrey, who had died of leukemia more than ten years ago.

Ten years? Herb thought. God, it can't have been *that* long ago, can it? In some ways it seemed like just yesterday!

Herb folded his newspaper in half and placed it onto the counter, smoothing it with the flat of his hand. He stroked his flabby jowls for a moment as though trying hard to place a memory; then, smiling and nodding like Santa Claus, he said, "Oh, yeah, I think maybe it might've come in with this morning's shipment. You know, I just ain't had time to put it out yet. What, were you looking for a copy?"

Mikie's smile widened, exposing the narrow gap between his teeth.

"You know, I kinda had a hunch you'd be in here today," Herb said. He reached underneath the counter and produced a fresh copy of the magazine, holding it out to the boy's eager hands. Before Mikie took it, Herb glanced at the cover and chuckled to himself, thinking how — especially when Mikie was excited — he looked a little bit like the goofy-looking kid on the cover.

"Aww, great!" Mikie said. He wedged the magazine under his arm while he dug into his pocket to produce a handful of change along with a few shreds of pocket lint. "I want a roll of Life Savers, too, like my brother just got." He picked up a roll of candy from the display case and held it up high like a lit candle.

Herb took the handful of pennies and nickels from him and started counting the change carefully into the cash drawer, dropping each coin so it landed with a satisfying clink.

"Hey! Looks to me like you're a bit light, here, son," he said. "Actually, you're three cents short for the magazine, not to mention the candy."

"Oh, no! Really?" Mikie said, his expression suddenly darkening with a look of near terror. Herb saw the watery glaze that began to fill the boy's eyes. "Aww, Jeeze, I really wanted it." He glanced over his shoulder at the front door. "I — I don't wanna have to do what Ray did."

Herb wasn't exactly sure what the boy meant, but he chuckled as he shut the cash drawer by nudging it with his belly.

"Well, then," he said, "I guess that there roll of Life Savers is just gonna have to be on the house, huh?"

In an instant, Mikie's smile brightened his face again. He stood there for a moment, shifting nervously from one foot to the other and staring at Herb as though he didn't quite believe what he had just heard.

"Ah-ah — thanks. Thank you very much, Far — I mean, Mr. LaPointe. I — uh, I really appreciate it." He was halfway to the door but then turned back and shouted. "I get my allowance every Friday. I can pay you back next week, I promise."

"Hey, don't worry about it," Herb said. "I don't think eight cents is gonna bust me." He picked up his newspaper, shook it out, and settled back in his chair to continue reading. "Someday when you're rich and famous, you can pay me back double, okay?"

"Sure thing! It's a deal," Mikie said; then he turned on his heel and left the store, whistling an off-key tune between his teeth.

The abandoned Hollistown Lumber Mill was located four miles from downtown Summerfield on the north bank of the Saco River, about two miles north of where Stackpole Creek joins the river in its southeasterly flow. The only approach to the mill was from the south, along a long-unused dirt road that runs parallel to the river. The road was overgrown with tall grasses, scrub brush, and saplings, mostly birch and maple. Canoeists on the Saco could easily see the antique building, a weathered, gray hulk that stood out against the sky like an ancient, brooding castle, but a series of rapids prevented all but the most intrepid adventurers from attempting to land there.

The building itself had withstood almost three-quarters of a century of disuse quite well, considering the abuse it had taken since closing its doors to business back in 1927. All of the windows had been broken out long ago by barrages of stones thrown by local kids. On the first floor inside the mill, the wide-planked floors and walls had been stripped clean of anything and everything of value. All that remained in the echoing, empty rooms were scatterings of stones that had taken out the windows, shards of glass and splintered wood, and fifty years of accumulated debris — mostly dried leaves, old newspapers, mouse and bird droppings, and litter left behind by careless visitors. Age had dried out and weakened the floorboards, which creaked and threatened to break whenever anyone walked on them. On the riverside, a gaping square hole in the floor marked where the sawing frame and cutting bed had once been. In the center of the opening was a long, metal shaft which still had a rusted saw blade attached to it.

Not much light entered the building, especially the cellar, where narrow windows lined the mill's stone foundation at ground level, front and back. Inside, the basement was a warren of small, interconnected rooms, some of which still contained an assortment of junk no one had bothered to carry away—rotting barrels and supply boxes, piles of unwanted lumber and debris, rusted tools and equipment, and literally hundreds of cans and broken bottles—soda, beer, and liquor—littered the floor along with old food wrappers. Some of the cellar's interior dividing walls, also made of granite blocks, had caved in, leaving piles of rubble that looked like gigantic dominoes had spilled. Beneath the gaping hole of the sawing frame was a huge mound of rotting sawdust which, over the decades, had become home for a colony of rats. The dark holes of their burrows made the sawdust pile look like a huge chunk of spoiled Swiss cheese. At the front of the building, beneath the ruins of a large landing, a set of stone stairs led down into the cellar from outside, but most of the kids who came out here were adept at squeezing through the narrow windows or dropping down from the first floor, either through the small trapdoor near the front door of the mill or else through the gap of the sawing frame.

Generation after generation of Summerfield boys and girls had come out to the mill to explore and test their bravery by entering some of the darker, narrower recesses of the cellar or by going up into the echoing, dust-filled attic. Although there were the usual stories that the place was haunted, there had never been any officially recorded incidents of anyone entering the mill and never coming out. Of course, there were rumors, and tall tales told by older kids to frighten the younger ones, but even those exaggerated stories didn't stop many of the area's youngsters from visiting the site and from using it as an unofficial hangout.

The only extensive damage to the mill had occurred in two places. Some years ago, the peaked roof on the riverside had collapsed inward, looking—at least to the canoeists on the Saco River—as though a huge-fisted giant had punched in the top of the building. Over the years, rain and snow had poured into the mill, speeding the deterioration of the walls and floor on that side of the building. The other area of damage was on the backside of the building where a small L-shaped extension—some say it had once been the lumber mill managers' office—had burned flat to the ground, leaving nothing but a pile of blackened, broken timbers covering the foundation hole. The side of the building had also suffered some damage before the fire had been put out; but because the mill was no longer in operation, no attempt had ever been made to restore it.

On this particular Saturday morning, three boys were huddled together in the basement, near the pile of rubble in the corner where a stairway had once led up to the first floor. Two of them—Eddie Fraser and Charlie "Fish-eyes" Costello—were standing behind Ray, who was seated on a makeshift bench made out of an old, charred timber. A cigarette dangled from Ray's mouth as he slowly, almost religiously turned the pages of his stolen issue of *Playboy.* Narrow beams of dusty sunlight filtered through the cracks in the walls and floor, turning the cigarette smoke into bright blue spikes. The air was cool and moist, thick with the smell of rotting wood and damp soil. The beam of the flashlight Eddie was holding darted like a dragonfly across the glossy pages.

"Oh, my God—my *God!*" Charlie shouted as he did an excited little dance. He'd gotten his nickname years ago because of the Coke-bottle thick glasses he had to wear. He was the smallest of the three boys, with arms and legs as thin as rails. He reached forward and slapped the magazine, almost knocking it out of Ray's hands. "Jesus Christ! Look at the ba*zoo*bas on *that* one!"

"I want to see the foldout again."

"No, no—keep going, Sandy. Maybe there's something even better."

30

"Just *look* at her *titties!*"

"I wish they'd show the *real* thing, if you know what I mean?"

"Yeah, some *pussy!* I wanna see some *real* pussy!"

Eddie leaned his head back and made a yowling cat sound that elicited frowns from the other two boys.

"I saw the real thing once — some real tit, anyway," Charlie said.

"Yeah, but your sister doesn't count!"

The boys had plans to go swimming at the Nickerson's Quarry just as soon as they finished checking out Ray's stolen treasure; but for right now, none of them were thinking about what a beautiful September morning was wasting away outside.

"I don't see why you have to stash it way the heck out *here*, though," Charlie said, using that high-pitched, whiny voice of his that drove *everybody* nuts.

"Why?" Ray replied. "Because my old man'd *kill* me if he ever found something like this in my bedroom. *That's* why!"

"Naw . . . he'd just keep it for himself to jerk off with," Eddie said. A thin blue stream of cigarette smoke draped over Ray's shoulder and drifted into Eddie's face. Eddie waved it away vigorously with one hand. For some reason, the smell of something burning made him nervous — especially in a closed, confined space like this. Maybe it had something to do with one of the stories his mother had told him about the mill.

"Remember what happened when he found that copy of *Gem* we had stashed up in the rafters of the chicken coop?" Ray said.

"Yeah, but *that* one didn't even show any *nipple!*" Charlie said, sounding ultimately disappointed.

"I thought it was funny as *shit* the way you couldn't say a word when he caught you," Eddie said, chuckling with the memory. "You kept stammering so bad, I thought you were gonna have a permanent stutter."

"Can something like that really happen?" Charlie asked.

31

"Sure thing," Eddie replied. "If someone hits you on the back while you're stuttering, you'll never be able to stop."

"Ever — ?"

"That's right," Ray said with a chuckle. "Never! And I heard if you jerk off too much, hair will grow in the palm of your hand . . . or else you'll go blind."

"For *real?*" Charlie asked.

"*You* tell us, Fish-eyes," Eddie said. "Check your own hand . . . or better yet, check Sandy's." He sneered as Ray's cigarette smoke wafted into his face.

"You guys have gotta be putting me on, right?"

" 'Course we are," Eddie said, "those are just . . . just old witch's tales, or whatever the hell you call them." In truth, he had no idea what could or couldn't make someone a stutterer or grow hair on the palm of their hands. "Come on," he said, indicating the magazine. "Keep turning the pages."

They spent the next ten minutes exclaiming over the full color photos of naked women, hurrying past the articles, cartoons, and stories, none of which any of them would ever read, although Eddie thought the story by a guy named Ray Bradbury looked sort of interesting. During a moment of silence, they all became aware of a faint voice chattering away outside the building. They listened for a moment, then realized that it was getting closer. At first, they caught only snatches of what was being said.

". . . unless I tell them . . . how far it's gone . . . last night, but I don't want it to happen again . . ."

"Who the hell is that?" Charlie asked, his eyes rounding wide behind his thick glasses.

Ray's expression was one of surprise, almost panic. "Oh, *shit!* What if Farty found out that we're out here?"

"Everybody ditch it 'till we find out," Eddie said. Without another word, he snapped off the flashlight, and all three boys blended into the dark corners of the basement. They waited in silence as the voice grew steadily louder, the footsteps crackling in the dried leaves and grass outside.

"Can't tell . . . never know when it'll happen . . . without warning now that they're so close . . . should've told someone else."

"It's gotta be Dougie, late as always," Charlie whispered.

"Christ, yes. He was 'spozed to meet us out here half an hour ago," Eddie said, glancing at his wristwatch.

"Dougie Dog-shit will be late for his own damned funeral," Ray added, but all three boys remained where they were until they could find out for sure who it was.

"No—wait a minute," Eddie said.

As the voice grew steadily clearer, he moved out from his hiding place. Standing on tiptoes, he peered out through one of the narrow, glassless basement windows. The bright sunlight stung his eyes. "I think it sounds more like—"

Before he could say the name, a thin figure with a pale, round face topped by a shock of dark brown hair appeared on the road, heading toward the far side of the building. The boy had a curiously blank, almost detached expression as he shaded his eyes with his hand and surveyed the mill. A long-handled shovel was slung over one shoulder like a rifle. A large, flat black leather carrying case dangled from his belt, bouncing against his leg with every other step he took.

Ray skittered over beside Eddie and, looking outside, snickered softly. "Ahh, shit—it's just the retard."

"Don't you go calling my brother *that!*" Eddie said, backing away from the window and clenching both hands into fists.

Ray shrugged. "Well, that's what he is. What should I call him?"

"How about his real name? *Mike!*"

"You mean *Mikie?* . . . *Mental Mikie? Mikie the Mental Midget?* He *is* a retard, though, ain't he?"

"Is *not!*"

"Is *so!*"

While this heated whispered exchange was going on, Mikie—obviously unaware of the boys in the basement—angled off to the right, heading around to the back of the building where the extension had burned down so many

33

years ago. He kept mumbling senselessly to himself, interspersing his comments with an off-key rendition that might have been the Davy Crockett theme song. His voice faded away when he rounded the corner of the building.

"I say we check out what the retard's up to," Ray said, glancing at the other boys to gauge their reactions.

"Let's just stash the magazine and leave," Eddie countered. "I thought we were heading out to Nickerson's, anyway."

Charlie just stood there, staring back and forth between them. Then, with a touch of menace in his voice, Ray said, "I say we've *got* to see what he's up to." He gave Charlie a leering look. "We don't want him to find my *Playboy* while he's out here poking around, now, do we?"

That got to Charlie, who shifted closer to Ray, obviously taking sides.

"Hey, he saw me take it yesterday," Ray said, giving Eddie an earnest stare. "If he tells Farty about it, and then finds it out here, you're gonna get in just as much trouble as me."

Eddie shifted back and forth on his feet, feeling both nervous and frustrated as he looked at his friends. He'd realized for years that unofficial leadership of their group had always been hazily divided between himself and Ray. He always got nervous whenever there was a direct conflict because, while he was the "brains" of the group, Ray was definitely the muscle; he had the courage to *act*. He was the one who had stolen the magazine.

"Besides," Ray added, meanly eying Eddie, "we don't want *anyone* coming out here without *our* permission . . . right?"

"You're forgetting one thing," Eddie said, fighting to still the low tremor in his voice. "The mill's on my mother's property, so Mikie has every right in the world to come out here."

"Oh, yeah?" Ray said, curling his upper lip into a sneer, "So what? And anyway, don't you think we ought to watch out for him? I mean, he shouldn't be out here all alone! Why, he might fall down and hurt himself. We've got to keep an eye on him, right? I mean, what if he—"

"What if *nothing!*" Eddie said. "I say we leave him alone and just head on out to the quarry and—"

"Come on, Fish-eyes," Ray snapped. "Are you with me or not?"

He stood up and slid the *Playboy* under one of the old barrels; then he turned quickly on his heel and, waving once over his shoulder, started climbing up the rocks and debris that were piled beneath the trap door. He quickly scaled them and then, grunting loudly, jumped up, grabbed the edge of the opening, and hoisted himself up onto the first floor. Charlie followed close behind. Before boosting himself up through the trapdoor, he turned back to Eddie and, waving to him, said, "Come on! Are you with us or not?"

"Screw you, Fish-eyes," Eddie replied, but Charlie was gone.

From outside, Eddie heard the thumping of footsteps as Ray and Charlie, having jumped out the open doorway at the back of the building, ran around to the front. A cold, hard knot twisted in his stomach as he balanced his loyalty to his friends and his retarded brother. Then, nodding to himself, he moved slowly and followed Ray and Charlie up to the first floor and out into the bright sunshine.

As he followed the overgrown road through the woods to the old mill, Mike Fraser squinted up at the sunlight which skimmed like white fire through the autumn-tinged trees. It was a little past nine o'clock in the morning, and already the temperature was close to sixty degrees. All around him, the woods flickered and rippled with flashes of light and quivering shade. Dappled shadows slid like splotches of dark water across his face and bare arms. On his left, through the trees, the Saco River sparkled with reflected sunlight, looking cool and inviting. Mike pushed aside any thoughts of going swimming. Besides being well aware that he should never go swimming alone, he was afraid of the river, especially this close to the mill, where it ran fast, turning into a bubbling, white-capped froth that looked to him like curdled milk. No, sitting in the shallow end of Nickerson's quarry — in what his brother's friends teasingly called the "Baby End" — was more than enough swimming for him.

But summer and swimming were over, and as beautiful as the day was, Mike found it difficult, almost impossible to be happy. He knew he should be happy because he was finally doing *something* about what had been bothering him for so long. At last, he had a plan; and he was proud that he was doing more than most people were doing these days. Ever since last year — last October, to be exact, when President Kennedy had blockaded those Russian ships loaded with nuclear missiles on their way to Cuba — Mike had wondered and worried and fretted about what he could do to help protect himself and his family. Just last night — at last — he had gotten the idea to build a bomb shelter; and the old, deserted lumber mill was the *perfect* place to do it!

"But you know *damn* right well—" he said, then stopped himself. Smiling nervously, he glanced around to see if anyone was nearby and might have heard him swear. He chuckled to himself and went on, "You know *damn-damn-damn* right well that when the time comes, *everyone's* gonna want to use it!" He sniffed loudly and wiped his nose with the back of his wrist. "Oh, yeah — sure, sure! They'll *all* wanna *use* it! The whole town will! But I won't let 'em in. No-sir-ee! I won't! Just me and my family . . . and maybe not even Eddie! Not unless he gives me some of his Life Savers."

Through the screen of trees, the old mill came gradually into view, its weathered gray sides looking like a steep, granite mountain against the pale blue sky. Mike shivered as he drew to a stop, wiped his forehead on his bare arm, and swung the shovel to his other shoulder. He had no idea how long it would take him to do what he planned to do. As far as he was concerned, he should stay out here until he was finished — work right up until lunchtime. He was positive he wouldn't be done by the time his mother rang the cowbell to signal him to come home for lunch. At the very least, he'd have to come back this afternoon and work until dark. Maybe all night, if he had to. With luck — and plenty of hard work — maybe he'd have everything done by tomorrow morning.

" 'N maybe I won't even go home for lunch," he said. "No one knows I'm out here . . . not unless I tell them. I probably wouldn't even hear the cowbell, anyway. I — I just wish people could see how far it's gone. How bad it is. I shouldn't have gotten so scared last night, but I don't want it to happen again, so I've gotta do this. I've *gotta* do this! *Damn-damn-damn!*"

Gritting his teeth, he started walking again. His fingers hurt from the tight grip he maintained on the shovel handle.

"I can't tell anyone, though. Of *course* not! Because you never know when it'll happen. The Russians could attack without warning now that they're so close, with their missiles there in Cuba. I'll bet they didn't even take them all out, either. They're just trying to trick the president. Maybe I should've told someone else so I would have had some help out here."

Nervousness coiled like a dry snake in his stomach as he broke out of the woods and started up the dusty road that led to the mill. What used to be the loading yard was now overgrown with weeds and thin grass. A gentle breeze blew dust like hazy, yellow smoke up into the air. The sunlight hurt his eyes, and the heat of the day wrapped around him like a heavy blanket. For an instant, he thought he detected a shifting of motion inside one of the basement windows, but he knew from experience that it was better to ignore everyone and everything he saw out here. If someone wanted to talk to him, they would talk to him when they were ready. He knew he shouldn't go looking for them, expecting them to show themselves. They didn't want to be seen. It was unnerving, though, the way they would always talk to him and *never* let him see them. Sometimes it was kind of creepy, the way they'd just whisper to him — and to themselves — in the echoing darkness of the mill.

No, Mikie told himself, the only thing to do right now was

simply to decide where to begin and get to work. He crossed the weed-choked loading yard and entered the soft, blue shadow cast by the building, grateful for the relief the shade gave him from the heat. Wandering out back, he started to whistle "Davy Crockett," all the while scanning the sides of the deserted building, looking for a likely spot to enter. He shivered again, thinking that he could feel cold eyes staring at him through the broken windows on the top floor. The wind whistled around the corner of the building with a high, steady hiss that sounded like a snake, hissing . . . or *almost* like those whispering voices . . . almost . . .

Mikie paused a moment to listen, to see if they had anything to say to him. He couldn't stop wondering if the voice he had heard last night, suggesting that he build his bomb shelter out here today, was one of the same voices he heard at the mill from time to time. That voice last night hadn't *sounded* like one of his friends from out here; but then again, even though he thought he knew everyone's voice well enough to recognize them, one of them could have disguised his voice — or else it could have been someone else . . . someone he hadn't met yet.

"But what if — what if it's someone . . . *bad*," Mike said, shivering wildly as he looked up at the building. The hair on his arms prickled as though electrified. His gaze fixed on the flattened ruins of the small building attached to the back of the mill. "Or what if the Russians are broadcasting radio messages only I can hear, trying to control me? What if this is a trap and they're *making* me do this?"

Another wild shiver shook his shoulders, and his teeth chattered in spite of the day's heat pressing down on him.

Someone is watching me!

He dropped the shovel to the ground and fumbled to open the leather case at his side. His hands were slick with sweat, and he almost dropped the camera as he unfolded the lens and raised it to his eye. Squinting into the viewfinder, he swept it back and forth and then aimed it at the burned-out building. The world was curiously distorted through the lens.

"Squeeze . . . squeeze slowly, now," he cautioned himself, aware that his hands were trembling.

The shutter clicked, and then the mechanism inside his camera started churning. Mike watched as the gray sheet of film slid slowly out the side of the camera. He tore off the print and started counting out loud to sixty while he collapsed the camera and put it back into its carrying case. His voice was trembling with repressed agitation as he waited for the picture to develop. When he was done counting, he peeled off the protective gray covering and looked at the snapshot.

His aim had been bad, and he had jiggled the camera just as he had clicked it. The picture was tilted to one side and blurred, but it had caught most of the charred timbers of the flattened building as well as a corner of the smoke-blackened side of the mill. The trees in the background were nothing more than an out-of-focus riot of shadow and light, but there was something in the foreground, something behind the burned timbers that caught Mike's attention. He shielded the photo from the glare of the sun with his body and brought it up close to his face, trying to see whether or not that really was what he thought it was—someone's face, peering at him from underneath the pile of burned rubble. It certainly *looked* like a face!

"Do you want me to make it in there?" he whispered with a tight trembling in his voice. "Is—is that what you're trying to tell me . . . that I can build my fallout shelter in the cellar? Under the burned part?"

His eyes jerked from the photo to the reality. He wasn't at all surprised that there was no longer even a hint of a face in the pile of rubble. Lots of things he saw and heard out here had a way of being there and then disappearing.

"So you—you don't mind if I'm out here, then, huh? Do you?" he shouted, almost choking on his words as he looked up at the tall, smooth side of the building. His voice rebounded with a dull echo from inside the abandoned mill, and he tried not to think about the flutter of motion he thought he saw behind one of the broken windows in the cellar. Even the birds and the breeze seemed hushed as he cocked his head to one side as though waiting for a reply.

"It's just that I . . . I have something I want to do," he shouted. "Something I *have* to do. I thought maybe you were the ones who told me to do it."

Still, there was no reply, so Mike picked up his shovel and, after making sure his camera was fastened securely to his belt, started walking around to the front of the mill. He was trembling inside as he approached the doorless front entryway. He paused a moment to look up at the towering, gray side of the building. A wave of nausea swept through him. Shuddering wildly, he forced himself to ignore the many pairs of eyes he sensed were watching him from the surrounding shadows as he walked up to the doorway and entered the old mill.

"What the hell is he up to?" Charlie whispered.

He and Ray were crouching outside the mill, peering into the basement through one of the windows out front. Eddie had his arms folded across his chest and was leaning back against the side of the building with one foot supporting him. The sun was beating down hard on his face, and he could feel a sheen of sweat beneath his T-shirt.

"You didn't tell him we were coming out here, did you, Eddie?" Charlie whispered, casting a suspicious glance at his friend.

"Looks to me like he's trying to set up house down there or something," Ray said. Then, turning to Eddie, he asked pointedly, "Is that what the *retard's* up to? Playing house? Or did your old lady finally give up on him and kick him out for good?"

Eddie scowled but said nothing.

"I just don't like the way he's moving crap around down there," Ray said nervously. "I left the *Playboy* under that barrel. What if he picks it up?"

"What's the big sweat?" Charlie said. "If he finds it, you can take it away from him and tell him never to mention it. Stop worrying about it. And anyway, he wouldn't know what to do with it if he did find it."

"And *you* would?" Eddie said, snickering.

"Up your ass, Buzz-saw!"

"I want to get my magazine," Ray said, sounding almost desperate. "How the hell am I gonna get in there without him seeing me?"

"Who the hell cares if he sees you? What's he gonna do to you, huh?"

"He almost blew it yesterday, and if he sees me with it again, he might say something to Farty or someone. I dunno. I just don't like him being down there."

"Cool your heels, will you?" Eddie said. "Let's go swimming."

All of the boys were keeping their voices low as they watched Mike, who was moving back and forth between the small room partitions at the far end of the basement. The remains of tumbled-down interior walls and broken doorways pretty much blocked their view of what he was doing. All they could tell was that he was busy doing . . . something. He kept appearing and disappearing as he carried granite blocks and pieces of broken timber out of sight into the farthest reaches of the basement. As he worked, he kept up a nearly steady stream of conversation with himself. His voice echoed dully from inside the basement. They all knew it was just nonsense, so nobody even tried to hear what he was saying. Mike might not be the "retard" Ray and the other kids said he was, but even Eddie had to admit — at least to himself — that his brother was odd. He couldn't help but wonder why Mikie was working so energetically. What the hell was he up to?

"I just want to get my magazine and get the hell out of here," Ray said. "I'll take my chances hiding it in the chicken coop."

"So go ahead and get it!" Charlie said.

"Yeah, what's stopping you?" Eddie added, hoping to capitalize on Ray's desire to get moving. "Let's get the damned thing and get the hell going. It's getting hotter every second, and I wouldn't mind getting out to Nickerson's *sometime* today."

"Well, I still wanna know what he's up to," Charlie said, craning his neck forward and watching Mike's activity with intense curiosity. "Maybe we could get a better view from the other side."

Shouldering Charlie aside, Ray peered into the basement. "Naw. There's too much shit in the way. 'Sides, all he's got is a little dinky candle." He snorted and spat. "Christ, the *retard's* even too damned stupid to bring a half-decent flashlight." He watched a moment longer, then sat back on his heels. "Looks to me like he's doing something in the space underneath the burned-out part out back." He was silent again for a moment; then, looking back and forth between Charlie and Eddie, he snapped his fingers as a wide grin spread across his face. "I've got an idea . . . What say we have ourselves a little *fun* with the *retard?*"

Chapter Two

"Smile for the Camera!"

Pushing aside his doubts and fears, Mikie ran down the stone stairway and into the mill basement. Sunlight poured through the windows, angling across the dirt floor. He made his way through the maze of tumbled walls and debris to the back of the cellar where a low, doorless entrance led into a small, narrow room. From previous explorations, he knew that this room was beneath the burned-out office addition aboveground. The low ceiling consisted of fire-blackened floor joists that looked as though they could barely support their load of charred debris. Mikie wondered if his first job should be making a door for the room or resupporting the ceiling. Or maybe he should go outside and clear off all that junk, and then rebuild the floor as best he could and cover it all with several feet of dirt. He had to start somewhere, but he knew that job alone would take more than all day.

Mikie wasn't entirely sure why he had decided to make his shelter in this particular room. In some ways, he felt as though he had been directed, almost commanded by the voices that whispered inside his head to come out here. This room was the deepest part of the mill's cellar. The walls were well below ground level. That, of course, would be best for his purposes. No radiation from a Russian atomic bomb was going to penetrate *that* much earth. He had seen a film in history class about the United States dropping nuclear bombs on Hiroshima and Nagasaki, so he had some idea of the power they packed. He was hoping he could make his shelter strong enough to withstand a direct hit.

After he figured out the problem of the ceiling, his only other concern was the lack of a solid, safe door to close off his homemade bomb shelter. Once the room was ready and stocked with a bed and blankets, clothes, food, and water, there had to be some way to keep intruders out. He would either have to barricade the doorway, using the granite blocks that littered the cellar floor, or else fill dozens of burlap bags with sand and stack them in the doorway. Maybe he could get a bunch of chicken feed bags from out behind Saunders' chicken coop. Buying a new door with a lock, especially a door thick enough to stop radiation, was definitely out of the question. How would he even get it out here? But maybe there was a door or something else down here in the mill basement that he could use. If he had to, he could probably make one using some of the scrap lumber that was lying around.

He took the stub of a candle he had brought from home, wedged it at about eye level between two stones in the wall, and lit it, using a book of matches he had stolen from the cupboard this morning when his mother wasn't looking. Once his eyes had adjusted to the feeble glow of light, he set to work. He decided that his first task would be to move some of the smaller granite blocks in front of the doorway to help block the entrance. He also wanted to use them to shore up the walls. There was no telling how close a Russian bomb might fall, after all, and he didn't want the walls caving in on top of him.

After he'd been working for a few minutes, though, he suddenly stopped, freezing in midmotion when he heard a voice, whispering just at the edge of hearing. He tensed, his eyes widening with fear as he waited for the voice either to get louder or else go away. He honestly couldn't tell if it had been in the building or inside his head, as the voices sometimes were, but he could sense that *someone* was nearby; he could *feel* the shadows shifting all around him, rippling like dark sheets in the wind. He tried to ignore them, knowing that if he turned to look, they would just flutter out of sight anyway.

"I . . . I know you're in here . . . somewhere," he said.

The sudden sound of his own voice startled him. He cringed as his words echoed from the stone walls with a curious ringing sound. As the echo faded away, he was positive he heard the faint chuffing of laughter.

"Y-Y-You don't scare me, you know!"

He turned around slowly and started walking backwards until he was standing with his back pressed against the cold stone wall. The teardrop-shaped candle flame shattered into a watery circle of light and seemed for a moment to burn with a weird bluish glow. Sweat broke out on Mikie's brow when the voice grew louder, whispering and sniffing words that sounded almost like another language.

"D-D-Don't try to f-f-fool me, talking like that!" he shouted. "I-I know you know English! If you h-h-have something to say, why don't you j-j-just come out and — and say it?"

His attention was drawn to the window nearest him where he saw a long, pale arm thrust into the cellar. Curled fingers raked the air with a wild, clawing motion. Dirt fell to the cellar floor with a rushing hiss as a voice rang out, sliding slowly up the scale until it was a piercing shriek.

"I'll . . . *get* . . . you . . . *yet!*"

Mikie's hands tightened around the shovel handle as he raised it protectively in front of his chest. Blood whooshed in his ears as his mind echoed with a loud peal of twisting laughter that was magnified in the darkness as it rolled like distant thunder.

"How *da-a-a-re* you come into *my-y-y* mill?" the voice wailed.

This time, it seemed to come from the far end of the cellar. Mikie turned and, for a fleeting, bowel-chilling instant, saw a face, glaring at him through one of the window openings. Then it disappeared, and a chorus of mean-sounding laughter rang inside the basement. Every dark corner of the mill reverberated with the high, keening sound.

"No! . . . *No, please,*" Mikie stammered, nearly passing

out from fear. His hands clawed at the solid stone wall behind him. "I — I didn't mean any harm by — by coming down here! I was just — was just — "

"How *dare-e-e-e* you?"

"I . . . I th-th-thought you t-t-told me to d-d-do this!"

Mikie's eyes darted frantically back and forth. His mind went blank with terror when he saw another arm reach through a different window. It pointed its middle finger at him and shook it wildly.

"For *sham-e-e-e,* Michael! . . . For *sham-m-m-m-e-e-e!*"

"No — no, I . . . I just was trying t-t-to . . . to do s-s-something . . . to h-h-help my . . . my family," Mikie whispered. There was a raw, frantic edge in his voice. "I was — was even g-g-gonna let Eddie in."

He wasn't sure if his legs could even support him as he edged over toward the pile of rocks below the small opening in the ceiling. It was the exit nearest to him. His eyes felt like they were going to burst out of his head as he stared up at the dimly lit interior of the mill. High overhead, shadows shifted in the rafters like bats fluttering lazily in the night sky. For a frozen moment, he thought he was looking through the distorting lens of his beloved Polaroid camera. The roof rafters seemed to twist inward into a distorted spiral that threatened to collapse down on him. His breath came in shallow, fitful gasps, but he couldn't get enough air into his lungs — not near enough to scream. Black, crashing waves of dizziness threatened to throw him over.

"You *mus-s-st* get *out-t-t-t!*" a voice wailed, this time sounding as if it were directly behind him, speaking through the stone foundation. *"Now!"*

"Y-Y-Yes . . . yes, I — I'll — "

"You must leave . . . *n-o-o-o-w-w-w!*"

Mikie dropped the shovel. It clattered to the dirt floor as he turned and bolted, leaping up onto the pile of rocks and reaching up for the edge of the trap door. His heart was throbbing, a cold, hard pressure in his throat as he grabbed the edge of the opening and clawed desperately at the floor to pull himself through.

"He's *running!*" a voice shrilled, breaking out with wild laughter. "Come on! Let's *get* him!"

Mikie was nearly blind with panic as he swung his legs up and rolled across the floor, unmindful of any splinters he might get. Shrill laughter and stomping feet filled the air all around him. He was frantic with fear as he looked toward the front doorway. He knew it meant safety but was afraid that his body wouldn't respond to his mental command to run. He screamed — a long, warbling hoot — as he leaped to his feet, doubled over with his fists clenched tightly, and rushed toward the door. The clear, bright light of day seemed hopelessly, impossibly distant, but he was just beginning to think he could make it out of here alive when a shadow as dark as ink, its arms high above its head, suddenly filled the doorway.

"*I've got him!*" shouted a shrill voice.

Wheeling around in terror, Mikie staggered and stumbled, regained his feet, then ran away from the doorway for all he was worth, hoping against hope that he could make it to the door at the far end of the building and avoid . . . whoever was after him. As he ran, sunlight flickered like a blinding strobe light through gaps in the siding. In every corner, inky shadows twisted and writhed.

They're everywhere . . . they've been waiting . . . all around me . . . just waiting to get me!

Glancing to his left, Mikie saw another shadow fill the doorway at the front of the building. He knew — he could *sense* — that there were more — dozens, maybe hundreds of shadows closing in on him from all sides. Voices howled and laughed as dim figures climbed through broken windows and reached up through cracks in the floor to get at him.

They're mad at me . . . for what I was doing!

Mikie ran for all he was worth as footsteps thumped heavily behind him. The floorboards shook as whoever — *what*ever it was — closed the gap. Tears blurred his vision, and chills danced up the back of his neck. He held his breath as he ran, waiting to feel the cold, dead hands snag him from behind.

Straight ahead, past the remnants of the sawing frame, was

47

the only other exit — his last chance to escape. Beyond the thin stand of trees, sunlight sparkled on the river with a distant, dreamy unreality. Mikie knew there was a long drop to the rocky ground outside that opening, but it was his only hope. The dark, awful presence behind him was closing the gap, getting closer . . . closer. He could hear heavy breathing as hands reached out for him.

"*Stop* or else I'll *kill* you!" the voice shouted, seemingly inches from his ear.

Terror exploded in Mikie's mind like a sheet of lightning. He heard but didn't understand the words as they reverberated all around him. All he knew was that he was close to freedom; he had to get out into the daylight where — *hopefully!* — he would be safe. He only heard the voices outside of the mill late at night, so he knew he would be safe once he was out there.

Brightness suddenly exploded across his vision when he reached the opening. Bracing both hands against the rough wood frame, he coiled himself up, preparing to jump, when from behind him, he heard a sharp *crack* followed by a wild scream that quickly diminished and then cut off. It echoed in his ears with an odd distortion that made it sound far away . . . as if it had come from across the river.

Nearly fainting with fear, Mikie turned around to see what had happened. There was no one there!

For a tense moment, an uncanny silence filled the abandoned mill, broken only by the distant thumping of footsteps outside. Mikie ran one hand over his sweat-slick face. Sucking in a deep breath, he took a few cautious steps forward. Dust glittered in the slanting rays of the sun like gold as it rose up from the opening of the cutting bed. Mikie could see a thin spray of blood along the edge of the toothed blade. His panic spiked even higher when he became aware of a high-pitched squeaking sound that crazily reminded him of his mother's whistling teapot. His pulse pounded heavily against the sides of his head as he approached the edge of the opening and looked down.

"Oh, Jesus! Oh, no!" he whispered when he saw the boy lying face down in the pile of rotting sawdust. It was dark down there, and he was still weak and numb with terror, so it took him the space of several heartbeats to recognize Ray Saunders. When he finally did, he couldn't help but snicker with laughter. While most of Eddie's friends teased him on occasion, Ray was the meanest of the lot and was responsible for some of the cruelest torments Mikie had suffered over the years.

"Serves you right," Mikie whispered with a snorting laugh as he stared down at the motionless form. Then he stood up straight and, shaking his fists, shouted, *"It goddamn serves you right!"*

He suddenly tensed and, looking around the deserted mill, whispered to himself, "So it wasn't *you* after all, huh? Here I was, thinking it was *you,* and all along it was just Sandy—" He snorted with laughter again as his fear gradually began to subside. "—Just Sandy and his idiotic friends."

But Ray was silent now, motionless as the dust slowly settled like snow around him. His left leg was cocked back so that his heel almost touched the small of his back. His hips were twisted around so far it looked as if he had put his jeans on backwards this morning.

No wonder he tripped and fell, Mikie thought, trying to contain a burst of laughter. *No one can run when they have their pants on backwards!*

A deep, red gash cut across the right side of Sandy's face. Fresh, dark blood was running like spilled ink onto the sawdust. Mikie watched with a mixed sense of horror and amusement as several rats, which had scattered as they fled their burrow, now approached the motionless boy and began sniffing at him and licking at his wound.

"Boy-oh-*boy,* but they're gonna be angry *now!*" Mikie said, cringing as he scanned the mill, coiled and waiting for the voices to start in again, shouting at him to leave. His gaze was drawn up to the darkened rafters where he expected to see the deepest shadows take on form and substance. Suddenly a chorus of faint voices hissed inside his head, but they spoke so softly and all at once that Mikie couldn't understand a single

49

word. Then, in a flash, he knew what he had to do. Unsnapping his trusty camera from his belt, he opened the case and focused on the motionless body below.

"Come on, now, Sandy," he whispered. "Smile for the camera."

His hands were trembling as he steadily applied pressure on the button until the shutter clicked. With a winding sound, the exposed sheet of film slid out of the camera's side. Just as he was tearing it off, a shrill voice behind him filled the mill, startling Mikie as if a firecracker had gone off next to his head.

"He pushed him! I saw him do it! The retard pushed Sandy down into the cellar!"

A solitary figure—nothing more than a hazy blur against the bright opening of the doorway—appeared at the far end of the building and started moving toward him. Footsteps sounded heavily on the floor.

"No, no, I didn't," Mikie cried out. "It wasn't like that! Not at all!"

He clutched his camera in one hand, the picture in the other as he moved away from the cutting bed. He backed up until he was at the edge of the opening. The hissing river sounded behind him like tearing paper as it frothed over the rocks. "I was just . . . was just—"

A vagrant breeze blew over his back, sending a wave of shivers racing through him. He watched with rising apprehension as Fish-eyes Costello cautiously approached him, his thin fists clenched and raised, ready to fight if he had to.

"Don't you be lying to us!" Charlie shouted, his voice wound up so high it almost broke. "I *saw* you! I saw you *do* it!"

Charlie was shaking as he knelt at the opening and looked down at the crumpled form below. From this high up, Ray's body looked twisted and pitifully small, like a broken, castaway doll. Charlie cupped his hands to his mouth, tilted his head back, and shouted, "Eddie! Hey, Eddie! Com'ere! *Com'ere!* Your retard brother just killed Sandy!"

He looked back at Mikie, his lower lip trembling as he said,

"Someone's gotta go down there and check on him." Then he tilted his head back and shouted again. *"Com'on, Eddie! Get your ass in here!"*

"I s-s-swear I didn't d-d-do it!" Mikie stammered. The sun was hot on his back as he glanced behind him at the foaming water and the rocks below.

"Ahh, Jesus! Ahh, *shit! Look!"* Charlie said, pointing down. "His head's bleeding!"

Mikie's eyes bulged from their sockets and his throat closed off as he shook his head in furious denial. While Charlie was staring down at his injured friend, obviously trying to work up enough courage to jump down there, Eddie appeared out of the shadows from the side of the building.

"What the hell happened," he asked, his voice flat and emotionless as he slowly approached them.

"Your friggin' retard brother pushed Sandy down into the cellar!" Charlie wailed. "I think he's *dead!"*

"Sandy was chasing him, right?"

Mikie grunted and nodded vigorous, silent agreement.

"So maybe Sandy just tripped and fell," Eddie said. He locked eyes with his brother and stared at him as he moved slowly toward the opening and glanced down. The widening puddle of blood beneath Sandy's face looked like a quart or two of spilled oil on the rotting sawdust.

"Jesus, I think he's dead," Charlie repeated in a high, trembling voice that caught with a repressed sob. "Shit, man, he — he ain't moving!"

"See? There's blood there on the saw blade and here," Eddie said, fighting for calm as he pointed to the wide, red splotch on the side of the cutting bed. "He must've cut his head on the blade when he fell."

"When he was *pushed!"* Charlie shouted. "I was back there, and I saw the whole thing! I *saw* it! He *pushed* him, Eddie!"

"Cut it out. You don't know *what* you saw!" Eddie snapped, glaring at Charlie.

"His whole face is ripped wide open! I bet his brains are all over the floor!"

51

"Seriously, I'll bet you ten bucks Sandy just tripped and fell," Eddie said. His voice was soft yet demanding. He still didn't dare to look down into the cellar for very long because he was having trouble processing the thought that Sandy — his best friend — might really be dead down there.

"No way!" Charlie said. "I saw Mikie push him! He was hiding over there on the side —" He hiked his thumb to a dark corner of the building. "When Sandy's back was turned, he rushed out at him and pushed him down."

"I did not!" Mikie said heatedly. "It couldn't have been me! I was — was way over here, by the door. I was just gonna jump! I didn't know *who* it was! I was just trying to get away from him!" He cut himself off suddenly and looked up at the dark ceiling again. "You know, I — I'll bet it was — it might have been one of *them!*"

"One of *who?*" Charlie cried.

"*Them!* I . . . I think they're angry . . . you know, about us being out here."

"Who's angry?" Charlie shouted. "What the fuck are you talking about?" He seemed not to care as fat teardrops rolled down his cheeks.

Mikie shrugged helplessly, aware of the burning wash of sunshine on his back. Suddenly he remembered his camera and the developing photo still clutched in his hand.

It must have been more than a minute by now, he thought in a sudden rush of panic. *Too long! I've probably ruined it!*

He ignored the other boys as he clutched his camera under his arm and quickly peeled away the photograph's protective covering to see the picture he'd taken. The lighting in the cellar had been poor to begin with, and the grainy black and white photograph was indeed overexposed, but it clearly revealed Ray's twisted body, lying in the pile of rotting sawdust as well as several rats, which had long since scurried away to safety. As Mikie studied the picture more closely, though, he saw something else . . . something that sent a white bolt of panic racing through him. In the surrounding darkness along the edges of the pictures were three — no, four — maybe more faces. Pale and thin, indistinct, they glared upwards, staring

52

into the camera lens with dazed eyes that were totally devoid of expression.

Mikie's breath caught in his throat. His first panicked thought was that the sawdust pile had been hiding several dead bodies, and the impact of Sandy's fall had uncovered them. Then he realized that he could see the rippled texture of the sawdust right *through* the faces . . . as if they had some-how been superimposed over the image of Sandy's body.

"Oh, Jesus! — Look! — oh, *Jesus!*" he said, his voice noth-ing more than a strangled whimper.

"Yeah, you better start praying!" Charlie said, looking at him with an angry glare. Fat teardrops rolled out from under his thick glasses, staining his cheek like glycerin. "If he's dead, you're gonna pay for it! You're gonna *fry* in the electric chair!"

"No, I didn't do it! . . . Honest, I didn't! It was *them!* It *must* have been *them!* They pushed him because they were scared or . . . or *mad* at him! See? Right here!"

Charlie watched Mikie as he backed away. Eddie remained to one side, his eyes dancing back and forth between his brother, Charlie, and the gaping hole in the floor.

"I couldn't do something like that," Mikie said. "Even for all the times Sandy's been mean to me. I just couldn't!"

"Oh, yeah — ?" Charlie asked archly. "You expect me to be-lieve that? I *saw* you do it!"

"I did *not!*"

Without another word, Charlie jumped down into the cel-lar. To Mikie's view, it looked as if the opening was a cavern-ous mouth that had swallowed him whole. He heard Charlie grunt softly when he hit the ground; then his voice boomed from down below, "He's still breathing, but — Jesus! he's bleeding real bad. We gotta get help, fast! Eddie! Your house is closest! Go get help!"

Eddie remained where he was, silent as he frowned and stared earnestly at his younger brother. All the while, Mikie stood in the doorway, shaking his head slowly from side to side in earnest denial and muttering senselessly to himself.

53

"Eddie! Hurry up, for Christ's sake! He'll *die* if we don't get help!"

"Yeah," Eddie said, but still he didn't move; he just stood there, staring at his brother as though waiting for him to say or do something.

"You gotta believe me, Eddie," Mikie said, his voice broken as tears poured from his eyes. "I wouldn't do anything like that — even to Sandy. I was just trying to get away from him! Honest!"

Eddie opened his mouth to say something, but no words came out — only a long, low groan.

"Don't you believe me?" Mikie asked. His eyes shifted back and forth between his brother and the grainy photograph in his hand. "I was over here . . . ready to jump out the door. I *couldn't* have pushed him from behind if I was over here, now, could I?"

With that, he spun around on one heel and, without looking down, propelled himself out of the doorway. For an instant he hung suspended in the air, his arms and legs flapping wildly, like an ostrich trying to fly. Then the rocky ground rushed up to meet him. First his feet, then his knees slammed hard against the rocks. Screaming out loud, he pitched forward. He twisted to his left side, and his shoulder slammed against the rocks. A hot bolt of pain shot through him. The impact sent his treasured camera flying out of his grip. It smashed into a dozen pieces on the rocks at the water's edge.

Mikie barely registered either his pain or his loss as he staggered to his feet. Nearly blind with terror and tears, he looked up at the mill. His brother was framed in the doorway, a huge, looming figure that threatened to come crashing down on him.

"They did it!" Mikie wailed, raising his hand holding the photograph up high and shaking it wildly. *"Not me! I didn't do it! They did!"* Hot tears flooded from his eyes, blurring his vision.

From inside the mill came a rising cacophony of voices — faint mutterings, low groaning sounds, and distant but piercing screams. Mikie glanced one last time at the photograph of the fallen boy and the four or more faces, staring up at the camera — staring at *him!*

"It was *you!* I know it was *you!*" he screamed.

His hands trembled wildly as he tore the picture to pieces and flung it into the river. The pieces were swept away and disappeared almost instantly in the raging white foam.

"I *swear* to God I didn't do it!" Mikie shouted one last time; then he started running . . . running for home as fast as he could because he knew the voices inside the mill would only get louder if he stayed here any longer; and he knew that he *wouldn't* be safe, even out here in the bright light of day.

They might even follow him all the way home!

"Mikie . . . Oh, Mikie . . . Where *are* you?"

"No! Not here! Not in here!" Mikie whispered as he crouched, trembling in the dusty heat of his narrow bedroom closet. He had lost track of the time, but the lessening of light that leaked underneath the closed door told him it must be approaching evening.

"Come on out, Mikie," the voice called, resonating in the darkness like a deep-throated bell. "Come on out, honey. No one's gonna hurt you."

Go away! Please! Just go away! he thought, squeezing his eyes so tightly shut the darkness behind his eyelids vibrated with flashing, spiraling colors. He pushed his back hard against the plaster wall, wishing to heaven he could fall through the closet wall into another world, like those kids in that story about a big lion his mother had read to him so many years ago.

"Everything's fine now. . . . You can come out now, honey."

Please, just go away!

Through the wall, he heard the soft *scuff-scuff* of footsteps coming up the stairs. They sounded like the heavy rasp of a saw blade cutting through wood.

"You must be getting hungry by now. Aren't you?"

Hot tears flowed down Mikie's cheeks, burning like a wash

of acid. The stale, dry air of the closet choked him, and for a paralyzing instant, he imagined that he was already dead — that he was lying in his coffin, buried six feet underground. That voice — trying so hard to sound just like his mother — was calling to him, trying to tempt him out of the safe darkness of his coffin into the eternal pain of hell.

But I didn't do it! he thought as he pounded his fists frantically against his ears, trying to block out the sound of approaching footsteps. *I didn't do it! Or . . . or if I did, I didn't mean to!*

"Mikie . . . Please answer me . . . I've made your favorite meal . . . a tuna fish sandwich and potato chips . . . Come on, honey. Answer me . . . You can even have a Pepsi if you'd like."

The voice was louder, and the footsteps were coming closer. Now they sounded like someone hammering on the floor right underneath him.

Or else they're nailing my coffin shut!

"I have news for you, too."

Please . . . just leave me alone!

"About that boy . . . about Ray Saunders."

I know, Mikie thought. *He's dead! You think I killed him, and you're coming for me now! But I won't be fooled!*

The floorboards creaked as someone walked down the hallway toward his bedroom.

It's not my mother! It's them! The people from the mill! They're the ones who hurt Sandy! Not me! But they know I'm in here! They're coming for me! I should have locked the bedroom door!

The doorknob clicked. The sound of squeaking hinges grated his teeth as his bedroom door swung slowly open. It vibrated like a drum when it banged against the wall. A heavy sigh filled the darkness, sounding as close to him as his own skin.

"You don't have to hide from me . . . not from your own mother."

You're not my mother! You're someone else! You're them, trying to trick me into coming out!

The floor shook as the footsteps came straight toward his hiding place. The doorknob on the closet jiggled, then turned. Mikie took a quick sip of air and held it, knowing this might be his last breath.

This is the end!

A light as bright and painful as an atom bomb blast shot across his vision. He remembered the film from history class and thought for a moment that maybe the Russians had launched an atomic bomb from Cuba. He cringed, waiting for the thundering rumble of the explosion before everything around him dissolved. Images of people melting and whole buildings getting squashed flat filled his mind. He was only dimly aware of the shadowy form that stood in the doorway and leaned down toward him.

"That boy who fell . . . out at the mill . . . Ray Saunders . . . he's hurt — he's hurt real bad, honey, but he didn't die . . . You can come out from hiding now . . . I — I want to take you somewhere . . . I want to take you to see a . . . a doctor."

His mother's kind and gentle words were lost beneath the rising wail of terror that ripped like a torrent of flame from Mikie's throat. He wasn't even aware that he was screaming as he waited for the burning flash that would dissolve his body. The sound of his screaming wound upward until it was lost when his throat closed off.

And then, once he had lost the ability to make any sound at all, the insane scream continued to spiral higher and higher inside his mind.

Part Two

The 'Old Witch Lady'

June and July, 1994

"A person often meets his destiny on the road he took to avoid it."

— Jean de La Fontaine

Chapter Three
Knife Edge

Only one person heard Dianne Fraser scream.

At the time, even Dianne wasn't aware that she had screamed. In the hospital several days later, with her jaw wired shut, her face swollen and wrapped in bandages, she acknowledged that she *must* have screamed, but all she remembered was losing her footing and then falling, pinwheeling her arms wildly for balance as she slid and rolled down the sheer, angled rock face of the cliff. She was unconscious by the time she hit the bottom of the thirty foot drop, so she never felt her impact on the rocks or heard her fading scream as it echoed from the surrounding mountains.

For the space of a single heartbeat, as the shrill cry rang behind him, Edward Fraser, Dianne's husband, thought she was playing a practical joke on him. He was leading the way along a narrow ledge on Mount Chocorua which the *A. M. C. Guide to the White Mountains* referred to as the "Knife Edge." The warbling scream rose to a piercing shriek and then faded in an instant, sounding almost fake, like the volume of a radio being turned down to nothing too quickly. But then the sudden, horrifying sensation of being utterly alone on the cliff edge filled Edward with a cold stirring of dread. Flattening himself against the rock wall, he turned around carefully, a smile twitching the corners of his mouth. He was prepared to laugh at Dianne's warped sense of humor, but already in his heart, he dreaded that the cry had been all too real.

"Jesus! No! *Dianne!*" he shouted when he looked down and saw her at the base of the cliff. The hot June sun illuminated the scene with a harsh, surreal glow. His wife's crumpled form lay sprawled face-down, motionless on the rocks. Her widespread arms and legs lifelessly conformed to the rough contours of the rocks, making her look like a casually tossed-aside rag doll. Her long, brown hair was like a tangle of seaweed cast up onto a rocky shore.

Edward's mouth hung open in amazement; his breath froze in his chest as his gaze focused on the quietly spreading pool of blood beneath Dianne's head.

Oh, my God! No! Please, no! Please don't let her be . . .

The next stretch of time was lost to him, nothing more than a whirling blur as he frantically sought a way down to her. He considered backtracking and looking for a way down, but finally in desperation he crouched at the edge of the cliff, braced himself with his hands and feet, and slid down the angled rock face in a controlled fall. The friction made his hands and feet burn, but he barely noticed that or the pain of the slices he got in the palms of his hands from the gritty rock. All he could think was how he and Dianne had met and married in a matter of just a few months, and how terrible it would be if it all ended like this.

Please, God! Please don't let her be . . . dead!

He knelt at Dianne's side and leaned close to her face, hoping—praying that he would feel a faint stirring of breath. Thick streams of blood were pouring from both of her nostrils. At first Edward could detect nothing, but then he noticed a warm, trembling breath—shallow, almost gone, bubbling through the blood that flowed from her nose.

"Oh, Dianne . . . *Dianne,*" he said softly as his hands fluttered helplessly above her. He didn't know whether to pick her up and comfort her or leave her where she was, in case moving her would make her injuries worse.

What should I do? Jesus Christ, what do I do?

He knew he couldn't just sit here and watch her bleed to

death. Should he make her as comfortable as possible and leave to get help? What if she went into shock and died—all alone—while he was gone? What if she regained consciousness and saw that she was alone? Would she know that he had gone for help? How far was it to the nearest phone or radio? How long would it take to get a medical team out here?

These and other questions filled his mind like a whirling storm as he stared down at his wife's motionless form. At last, knowing that, no matter what else, he had to make her as comfortable as possible, he eased his arms underneath her and lifted. A rushing gasp of air came from her lungs as her weight pressed her into his arms.

Was that her last breath? Edward wondered as he dragged her away from the rocks over to a small patch of tufted grass under some scrub pines. After clumsily removing her backpack, he eased her flat onto her back, careful to tilt her head to one side so the flow of blood wouldn't fill her throat and choke her. He was sobbing uncontrollably as he stared at the distorted, flattened side of her face. Thick, red blood mixed with the black clots, stone grit, and bone fragments that smeared the torn flesh of her cheek and jaw.

"Oh, Christ! Oh Jesus!" Edward whispered.

He was convinced that the bleeding was too severe, that she was going to die right there in his arms. He knew that any significant loss of blood could mean possible shock. That was the immediate danger; but he also knew that the trauma to her head as well as possible skull fracture and brain damage were the real dangers. Gently, carefully, he lifted first one eyelid, then the other, studying for a moment her glazed, vacant stare. Even in the bright sunshine, her pupils were dilated and her eyes were rolled up inside her head as though she were staring at the sky.

Edward drew his hunting knife from his backpack, cut a piece of cloth from his shirt, and pressed it gently against the side of Dianne's face. Even through the padding of the cloth, the jellied, pulpy texture of her face made his stomach do a sour little kick. It felt as if there were no bones underneath the skin; they were gone—pulverized.

Once he was sure the worst of the bleeding had stopped, he took his sleeping bag from his backpack and spread it over her to keep her warm.

"Damnit!" he said, his voice tight and high, struggling for control as tears poured from his eyes. "How could I let something like this happen?"

But he knew he couldn't lose control now. This was not the time for guilt or recriminations. He had to think . . . think clearly and act decisively so he could get help out here as fast as possible. It was a beautiful June morning, and the Piper Trail was one of the most popular trails up Mount Chocorua. Someone was bound to be out hiking. If he stayed with Dianne, making sure she was still breathing, still alive, a group of hikers would have to pass by. He could ask them to go down the mountain to phone for help so he could stay with his wife. If she was going to die, he didn't want her to die alone.

But the minutes stretched into what seemed like long, agonizing hours. Dianne's shallow breathing remained the same for a while, but then Edward noticed the muscles in her arms and legs were beginning to spasm. Her fingers clutched feebly at the sleeping bag covering her. Soft, fitful moans escaped her mouth, and her breath wheezed in her chest.

What if she's having some kind of fit or seizure or something because of the pressure on her brain? Edward wondered as the intensity of the tremors increased. With tears in his eyes and sobs wracking his chest, he stood up, looked around helplessly and then, cupping his hands to his mouth, shouted, "Help!"

—Help-p-p!

The echo rebounded from the sheer granite walls above him.

"Can anybody hear me?"

—hear me-e-e?

He looked down at Dianne. Framed by the sleeping bag, her blood-streaked face looked pitifully small, pale and lifeless. Edward fought the impression that she was already dead and that her muscle spasms were merely her dying nerves firing off one last time.

"Please!" he yelled, trying desperately to fight back his panic.

— Please-e-e!

"We need help!"

— need help-p-p!

The echoes of his cries faded, and he heard nothing in response except for the thin, high hiss of the wind on the cliff and the distant chatter of bird song far down in the valley. Fluffy white clouds drifted silently across the brilliant blue of the sky, casting gray washes of shadows over the trees and rocks below. Edward shivered, but then, reminding himself that this was the time to act decisively, he checked Dianne once again — dreading that this would be the last time he would see his wife alive — and then started off through the woods, backtracking until he hit the trail down the mountainside. As much as he wanted to break into a run, he knew it was at least a couple of miles back to the base of the Piper Trail. The worst possible thing for Dianne, now, would be for him to get injured or lost. Even if she *was* still alive, he knew he didn't have very long to get help . . . and conscious or unconscious, he knew she would never survive the night alone out here.

After no more than thirty minutes on the trail, however, he met up with a group of campers with their counselors from Camp Calumet who were on a day trip, hiking the mountain. After Edward blurted out what had happened and that his injured wife was unconscious back at the foot of the "Knife Edge," one of the counselors started down the mountain to get help. The incident obviously soured the day's outing and worried the remaining counselors, who seemed inclined to head in another direction with their young charges.

Edward immediately went back up the trail to be with Dianne.

***

Unless he had damaged his watch when he slid down the cliff, time was playing tricks on him.

It had been a little more than two hours since the accident, but to Edward it seemed as though he had waited at the bottom of the cliff for most of the day before he heard the distant *thump-thump-thump* of a helicopter's rotor blades. By the time the Air-vac rescue team had gotten Dianne loaded onto a stretcher and into the helicopter, her left eye was swollen shut. The blood on her face had dried to a thick, brick-red crust. Two wide streaks of blood ran from her nose, down into her jacket collar. Feeling drained and nauseated, Edward stared silently at the shreds of dark, mangled flesh hanging down over his wife's blood-caked cheek and mouth. Another death image — from when he was five years old, and his father had been crushed to death beneath a truck while changing a flat tire — filled his mind with a numbing sense of dread and finality.

This is how it will end!

The thought rang out clearly in his head, drowning out the softer, fainter voice that whispered a faint, fragile hope.

This is how it will all end!

The two person rescue team worked fast and efficiently, with little conversation above the thumping of rotors and the whine of the helicopter's turbine engine. They checked Dianne's blood pressure, made sure the bleeding from her nose had stopped, and then worked a plastic tube down into her windpipe so she wouldn't choke on her own blood and mucous. As the helicopter sped to the hospital in North Conway, the pilot used the radio to report their initial assessment of Dianne's condition and what steps had been taken so far. Edward caught only small snatches of the conversation, but none of it made sense.

Throughout all of this, Dianne was semiconscious — at times fitful and agitated; at other times quiet, nearly comatose. Her eyes were glazed with pain and confusion, terrifyingly vacant as she looked around the interior of the helicopter. Several times she twisted her head from side to side, as though trying to get away from these men — her tor-

66

mentors, but her arms and legs were securely strapped to the stretcher. When her gaze fixed on Edward, he had the distinct impression that she didn't even recognize him.

Once they landed at the hospital, the medics quickly loaded Dianne onto a gurney and rushed her into the emergency room. Covered with blood and feeling completely distraught, Edward was asked to remain in an office near the waiting room. The on-duty nurse — her name tag read Kate — explained what steps the doctors would take, but Edward barely heard her as he sat there, his gaze riveted to the double doors at the end of the corridor that led to the operating room.

"Would you like some coffee?" Kate asked.

Edward looked up at her as if he hadn't understood her question, so she repeated herself.

"Some coffee . . . would you like some?"

"Uh . . . no. No thank you," he said, biting his lower lip and shaking his head.

"There's a sink in the next room, if you'd like to wash up a bit."

"No, I — I'd just as soon wait here, if you don't mind."

"Not at all," Kate said, smiling sympathetically. "You know, this could take quite some time."

Edward remained silent, his eyes barely blinking as he watched the double doors. His mind was filled with tortured, horrifying imaginings of what might be going on behind those closed doors, and that damned voice in the back of his mind wouldn't stop repeating —

This is how it will end! . . . This is how it will all end! . . .

Edward sat beside the desk, his body rigid with tension as Dr. Miller, the neurosurgeon at the Conway General Hospital, explained to him the extent of Dianne's injuries. Most of the terms he used — Hemi-Leforte II midface fracture, communited displaced left zygoma and left periorbital fracture — didn't make any sense to him, but they all translated to one

67

thing: Dianne wasn't dead—not yet, at least, and the left side of her face had been smashed to shit!

"She's transferring to Maine Medical Center in Portland where Doctor Collett will be working on her," Dr. Miller said after finishing a thorough review of Dianne's injuries.

Christ!, Edward thought, *he makes it sound like she's a fucking car that needs an overhaul!*

"Hands down, Collett's the best maxillo-facial surgeon in the state. Believe me, after reviewing the CAT-scan, I'm positive your wife is going to pull through this thing just fine. It's not going to be easy, I won't deny that, but there's no indication of intracranial hemorrhage, which would cause pressure on her brain and some possibly very serious problems. Of course, now that she's calmed down, we'll observe her overnight, and then in the morning—"

"But her eye!" Edward said, his voice almost breaking. "Her left eye had no white—it was all bright red. Doesn't that indicate internal bleeding?"

"That's entirely normal in a situation like this. That's called an eccymotic eye. The condition is temporary. Her eye will look relatively normal in a few days and be just fine in a few weeks."

"Relatively normal," Edward echoed. "But what about the rest of her face? How will you—I mean, *can* you rebuild her entire face? You told me yourself that some of the bones weren't just broken, they were pulverized and that the surgeon wouldn't be able to get her face put back right the first time!"

"The most important thing for you to remember, Mr. Fraser, is how much I stressed to you that this isn't going to be easy, for you or your wife. She's facing several months, possibly up to a year of healing and reconstructive surgery. Doctor Collett will operate on her right away to begin reconstructing her face by supporting and replacing the broken bones with metal plates and wires. After a month or so of healing, she'll need a second operation to remove the temporary metal appliances and insert interpositional and onlay bone grafts. Even then, she won't look like herself because of the soft tis-

68

sue damage, so six months or more after that, she'll undergo the final plastic surgery to restore her face completely."

Edward tried to speak, but his mind was a roaring, white blank. He slouched back in the chair, feeling as though the air pressure in the room had suddenly doubled. He was dimly aware of his pulse, pounding like a jackhammer in his neck, and that the voice in his mind was back, whispering softly to him:

This is how it will end!
This is how it will all end!

Chapter Four
Scritch — scritch — scre-e-e-ch

Moonlight cast a silvery-blue glow on the windowsill and bedroom floor. Unable to sleep, Brian Fraser lay in bed. His throat was as dry as sand, his breath panting high and quick. The ghostly green illuminated numerals of the alarm clock on the bed stand told him that it was nearly eleven o'clock, but sleep wouldn't come. His gaze was transfixed by the thin branch that was tapping on the windowpane with every fitful gust of wind.

Scritch — scritch — scre-e-e-ch.

The sound reminded Brian of fingernails raking down a chalkboard, but it also gave him other, more unsettling thoughts. He imagined long, thin hands reaching up out of the darkness outside, prying at the window edge, pulling away cracked putty and jagged chunks of wood. Clutching his blankets close to his chin, Brian barely dared blink his eyes as he watched the gray shadows jiggle and dance across the glass. He tried not to think about how, out of sight on the floor, those bony shadows might be stretching out, rippling over the old floorboards and throw rug, reaching up toward him from the foot of the bed.

Scritch — scritch — scree-e-e-ch.

He tried to fill his mind with brave and reassuring thoughts. This was, after all, his grandmother's house, the house in which his father had been born and raised. He was in the same bedroom that had been his father's until he grew up and went off to college. This was the very same bed — even the same bedspread — his father had used when he was Brian's age.

So why was he so afraid? Why was he letting himself get so scared? Surely a windblown branch tapping against the window shouldn't be enough to frighten him. Good Lord! He was eleven years old, going on twelve in November. He was being a total *wuss* to let himself get worked up like this!

Scritch — scritch — scre-e-e-ch.

But it wasn't just the wind and the branches; it was the house and the person who lived in it that was making him feel so nervous. A subtle tension had filled him since the moment he had arrived on Thursday afternoon. Brian knew Grammy Evelyn was trying her best to make him feel comfortable, but something about her — he hated even to think it — but *something* bothered him. Maybe it was the way she moved so slowly about the house; or how she spoke so seldom; and even when she did speak, it was always with a leathery, whispering voice, so low Brian could barely make out what she said. And the way she looked — so thin and weak; it was frightening.

But whatever it was, there was something definitely creepy about her or her old house . . . maybe both. And whatever that something was, Brian didn't dare think about it. He couldn't stop the flood of scary images — especially at night.

He had to remind himself — continually — that his grandmother was an old woman, almost eighty years old. Didn't people usually die before that? Soon after his father and mother had gotten divorced, back when he was four years old, his mother had moved with him to Arizona. Other than one or two weeks a year, he had never spent much time with his father, much less his grandmother. He couldn't expect her to know or understand him any better than he could know and understand her.

But she scared the living crap out of him! He knew that much.

The only glimmer of hope in this entire situation was that he was only here for the weekend while his father and his new wife, Dianne, were off to New Hampshire for their honeymoon. They'd be back on Monday, so from then on, for the rest of the summer, he'd be staying at his father's house. He wasn't completely sold on the idea of spending the whole summer in Maine, away from all his friends in Arizona, but this weekend was the worse.

Of course, relating to Dianne, his new stepmother, was a whole 'nother story. He hardly knew his father, so he had no idea what to make of his new stepmother. It wasn't like she was ugly or mean to him. If anything, she seemed to be trying *too* hard to get to know him, almost as if she was just as nervous about having him around as he was to *be* around. As soon as he had arrived in Maine, she started in, asking if he wanted anything or if she could do anything for him. It reminded him of the way his mother had gone overboard, spoiling him after he'd had his tonsils out three years ago, and it made him apprehensive about the coming summer.

But for right now . . .

Scritch — scritch — scre-e-e-ch.

. . . Right now, he just wanted to forget all about his aging grandmother, this creaky old house, the branch scratching against his window, and the faint whisperings in the dark which he knew *had* to be his grandmother, muttering to herself in her bedroom. He was nervous without his father here, and all he wanted to do now was sleep and forget — at least for a while — all about how nervous this house made him feel. But still, there was . . .

Scritch — scritch — scre-e-e-ch.

The telephone rang with a sudden, loud jangle that split the night.

Brian was instantly ripped out of his thin sleep. Sweat broke out on his forehead as he raised himself onto his elbows and listened while staring blankly into the surrounding darkness.

After the second ring, he was fully awake and sitting up on the edge of the bed. His wide eyes were focused on the clock beside his bed. It was almost one o'clock. Calls this late could mean only one thing.

Trouble!

His gaze shifted over to the window where darkness stained the glass like a thin wash of ink.

"Who'd be calling at this hour?" he whispered.

A numbing ripple of cold radiating from his stomach ran down his arms and legs.

Please let it be a wrong number! But what if something's happened to Dad?

He struggled to push aside the thought and the tears it brought.

What if they were driving late at night, and he . . . and he—he. . .

Brian couldn't finish the thought. He shifted uneasily, resisting the impulse to bolt out of bed and start running or screaming or doing *something* to release the tension inside him. He waited to hear the sound of his grandmother's voice as she answered the phone, but the phone rang a third time, seeming longer and louder.

Why doesn't she answer it? What if she can't hear it? . . . Or what if she's—

Again, he wouldn't let himself complete the thought.

His ears tingled as he waited . . . waited for the phone to ring a fourth time. He wondered if he should get up and answer it himself, but he knew the only phone upstairs was in his grandmother's room. What if he went in there? What if she was lying in bed, staring sightlessly up at the ceiling . . . stone cold dead?

At last, on the fifth ring, the sound cut off mid-ring. Either his grandmother had answered it, or else whoever was calling had finally given up. He strained to hear, and then, through the walls that separated their bedrooms, he heard the sleepy buzz of his grandmother's voice. The sound made him think of a fly, trapped between two windows. He let his breath out in a long, slow whistle and eased his head back onto his pillow. His ears prickled as he tried to make out what she was saying. At first he couldn't, but then in a loud voice she said,

"Oh, my Lord, no! . . . My word, no! That—that's *terrible!*"

Brian's stomach twisted with a cold, sour tightness. Tears filled his eyes, and his breath felt like a hard knot in his chest.

Oh, no! Something's happened to Dad . . . something really bad!

"Are you sure that's what you want to do?" his grandmother said. Her voice was softer now but still audible—a dull, vibrating presence in the dark. "Yes—if you'd like, I can wait until you get home."

Get home! Brian thought. *She said 'get home' as if— Please, God!—as if she's talking to . . . Dad!*

"All right then. Certainly. I—I'll see if he's awake now. Yes, I'll tell him right now. No, no, I can do it. But are you—are you sure you're all right?"

Her voice dropped low again, too low for Brian to hear. The conversation in the other room ended shortly thereafter.

Brian considered faking sleep when he heard the creaking springs of his grandmother's bed as she shifted out of bed. Then came the soft *scuff-scuff* of her slippers in the hall as she approached his closed door. Brian's eyes were riveted to the window, where the slanting rays of moonlight still cast long, gnarled shadows across the glass. A corner of the moonlight now reached to the foot of his bed. A single, black shadow line cut across his bedspread like a jagged scar. A tightening sense of dread, of impending doom wound up inside him until he thought he was going to scream before his grandmother opened his door.

What if Dad's been hurt or . . . or is . . . dead?

A light, rapid knocking sounded on his door. Licking his lips, he swung his feet back onto the bed, pulled the covers over him, and called out, "Uhh . . . yeah?"

"Brian . . . ?"

His grandmother's voice was like the soft touch of a feather in the dark as she opened the door a crack. A sliver of light from the hallway angled like a razor blade across the floor. Brian's eyes darted to the window, where the thin, gray shadows still jiggled like bony hands against the window pane. The light from the hall made them fainter, but they were still there.

"Uhh, yeah—" His voice was tight with tension. "I'm—umm, awake."

His grandmother entered the room and eased the door shut behind her, then came over to the bed and sat down on the edge. She fumbled in the dark to find his hand and give it a gentle squeeze. Her grip was dry and soft; her hand trembled with hardly any strength at all.

"I just got a—"

"I heard the phone ring," Brian said in a voice at least an octave higher than normal. "Is—is everything okay?"

His grandmother took a trembling breath and, squeezing his hand harder, said, "No—everything *isn't* okay. That was your father on the phone. Dianne's been in an accident . . . a terrible accident—"

Her voice caught in her throat with a loud click, and for a moment she couldn't continue as she took a deep, wheezing breath. Brian saw her other hand—nothing more than a gray blur in the darkness—move up to her chest, grasping at the collar of her bathrobe.

"But my dad—! Is my dad okay?" Brian said, more demand than question.

"Yes, yes. He's fine, and—and he says that, although Dianne's injuries are quite serious, the doctors are extremely optimistic that she'll be just fine. She—she fell off a cliff and, from what he told me, has a quite serious head injury, but there's—there's every reason to—"

Again, her voice cut off. It sounded almost as if someone had wrapped their hands tightly around her throat and started squeezing. Brian waited expectantly, caught between the immense relief of knowing that his father wasn't dead and an enclosing sensation that—still—*something* was seriously wrong.

"We'll have to . . . to wait and see how she is, but there's something else I . . . I want to tell you." His grandmother spoke haltingly, with increasing effort. Her breathing shuddered in broken snatches. Brian could hear the short, high grasps she made as she tried to catch her breath.

"Grammy, are you—?"

"There's something—I—I have to tell you . . . well, actually, I was going to tell Dianne, now that she and your father are married. But there's something she should know, and I—I . . ."

Strong, hot currents of fear swelled inside Brian as he listened to his grandmother's halting voice.

What's wrong with her? he thought. *She's acting like she's really sick or crazy or something!*

"You know, over the years I've tried. Honestly, I've tried to do it myself, but—but the past few years have been so—have been so difficult for me. I didn't get out there as often as I should have. I know that, and I feel . . . feel really bad about it . . . responsible."

"No, Grammy, I—I don't understand. What are you—" Brian couldn't even finish his question as the black fear twisting inside him rose steadily higher. *She's crazy! She's freaking out about that phone call, and she's losing her mind!*

"I just figured that Dianne would eventually take over for me," his grandmother said. "She—because she's a woman, she has a gentler touch, a kinder understanding, and I think she's open to these kinds of things. I'd hoped to tell her . . . thought that she would understand. She's not in the direct bloodline, but now that she's married to your father, I'd hoped that she would—would—"

A raw gasp made her double over. Her free hand pressed hard against her chest.

"Now if she—if Dianne's been injured . . . If she might die—"

"But you told me the doctors said she was going to be all right," Brian said. His hand was getting sweaty in her tightening grip, so he tried to pull it away.

"You can never tell for sure," his grandmother went on, struggling to speak but clutching his hand all the harder. "You *never* know, but because I haven't been out there for so long, I—I've—" She made a high, funny-sounding noise in the back of her throat.

"Out where—?" Brian asked, shaking his head. "What

76

are you talking about?"

She finally let go of his hand. Inhaling deeply, she leaned forward and pressed both hands against her chest. Brian wanted to get out of bed and turn on the light as fast as he could, but his knee joints were locked. The dark room filled with the sounds of her labored breathing.

"Out . . . there," she said, little more than a gasp as she twitched her head in the direction of the moonlit bedroom window. Brian didn't dare look that way. He knew those branches that looked like skeleton hands were still out there.

Scritch—scritch—scre-e-e-ch.

"I know they're getting . . . restless," she said. "I can *feel* it, as if they're gaining strength and they're . . . they're not satisfied . . . angry again."

"Please, Grandma. Stop it! . . . You're scaring me!"

"I don't mean to, dear. Honestly, I don't."

Again, for just a moment, her hand touched him in the dark. It felt as light as a butterfly settling on his hand.

"Bad things, *bad* things have happened out there, and I— and *someone* has to—has to know about them. You should—find out—and—"

Before she could say more, she grunted loudly and almost fell onto the floor as she doubled up with both arms crossed over her chest.

"Grandma! Please, tell me! What's the matter?" Brian felt like crying as he watched her rock back and forth as though in a great deal of pain. "Is there something I can do for you?"

Choking back his fear, he wheeled out of bed, ran to the light switch, and slapped it on. The sudden blast of light stung his eyes like salt water, but he barely noticed the pain as he ran back to the bed where his grandmother—a seventy-nine-year-old woman he hardly even knew—was hunched over in pain. Her thin gray hair hung in a loose tangle over her eyes as she looked up at him and gasped, "It's my—my heart."

"Can I—"

"There's a little brown—a brown bottle on the night-stand—next to my bed. Bring it to me. Quick!"

Brian didn't think his legs would support him as he ran

down the hallway to her bedroom. He was nearly blind with panic, wondering what he should do — who he should call if she was really sick or if she died? He had no idea where his father was or what hospital he had called from.

"Nine-One-One — That's it, I can always call Nine-One-One if I have to."

He snatched the brown bottle off the bed stand and hurried back to his room where his grandmother was still doubled over, clutching her chest. In the glaring light, her skin looked papery thin and as gray as her hair. Her pale, veiny hands shook wildly as she reached for the bottle when he held it out to her.

"Is this the right one?"

She nodded. "This will — this is all I need," she said as she fumbled to open the safety cap. Brian expected her to spill the entire contents onto the floor, but she shook one small, beige colored pill into the cup of her hand. Still trembling wildly, she slipped the pill under her tongue.

"Should I call for an ambulance or something?" he asked, feeling a slight stirring of pride that his voice didn't break as much as he thought it might.

His grandmother looked at him, her eyes glistening with repressed pain, but she shook her head. "No . . . no, just — just help me get back to my bed. Sleep is all I need right now. Just sleep."

Cringing inwardly at her touch, Brian slipped one arm around her side and eased her onto her feet, shocked at how feathery light she felt — as if there was nothing more than fragile bones inside her bathrobe. Step by careful step, he guided her down the hallway back to her bedroom. Once there, he eased her onto her bed and pulled the covers up over her. Before she settled down, she made a single, strangled moan in the back of her throat; then, gradually, as the pill dissolved and started to take effect, her body relaxed. She slipped into light sleep, still muttering things that Brian couldn't quite catch. Her breathing was reedy and high, but Brian assured himself that it was steady and deep enough before saying good night, turning off the light, and backing out of the room.

But he didn't dare go back to his own room just yet. His heart was pounding fast and hard in his chest. His entire body was slick with sweat. The muscles in the back of his legs were trembling, threatening to fold up on him. After a trip to the bathroom, where he got a drink and splashed his face with cold water, he did a quick check to make sure the old woman was still breathing, then went back to his own room, turned out the light, and snuggled under his covers.

He tried his damndest to shut off his mind but wasn't able to. He couldn't ignore the questions that churned inside him like an angry sea.

Dad's all right, but what's happened to Dianne? How bad off is she really? Is she going to die?

And what the hell's wrong with Grammy? How sick is she? Is she going to die tonight once I fall asleep?

Like steel to a magnet, his gaze slid back to the moonlit window.

And why—? he wondered. *Why am I letting something as stupid as a little branch tapping against the window bother me so much?*

He closed his eyes so tightly that he saw swirling explosions of light as he begged for sleep to carry him away. And he would have slept except for the faint, hollow sound tapping like a bony finger on his windowpane . . .

Scritch—scritch—scre-e-e-ch.

"Grammy . . . ?"

It was early Saturday morning, just after dawn. Brian had hardly slept all night. He was standing outside his grandmother's bedroom, his hands clutching the edge of the wooden door frame as he leaned into the room. A thin wash of sunlight lit up the room with a dull lemon glow that did nothing to dispel the sickly, cloying smell in the room. His grandmother lay motionless in the double bed, her body nothing more than a pitifully small bulge beneath the heavy quilt.

79

"Grammy!" Brian said again, a bit more forcefully as he eased into the room.

His nostrils widened as he inhaled deeply, trying to identify the smell. He had noticed it the moment he had entered the house the day before yesterday, when his father had dropped him off. It was an odd mixture that reminded him of old soap, rotting leaves, and a wet cat that pervaded the house, but it definitely seemed to be centered here in her bedroom. As he glanced around, he more than half-expected to see a thick carpet of gray mold covering the walls and floor.

His fists were clenched tightly at his sides as he tiptoed over toward the bed. His grandmother was lying on her back with her eyes closed. Her mouth was hanging open, a distorted, black oval. A thin line of drool ran across her cheek from the corner of her mouth. Her thinning gray hair was spread across her pillow like a smeared spiderweb.

Brian stared at his grandmother's face, watching — praying for some slight indication that she wasn't dead. The subtle current of tension inside him was getting steadily stronger as he studied her motionless face, convinced that it did indeed look bloodless . . . *lifeless.*

"Oh, no," he murmured as he started inching his way closer to the bed, his feet scuffing over the hardwood floor. Aware only of the sound of his pulse, hammering like heavy footsteps in his ears, he was unable to tear his terrified gaze away from the slack expression on the old woman's face.

Oh my God! She died in her sleep! She's dead! She's dead, and I don't even know where my father is. I can't even call him!

When he was almost within reach of the bed, he stretched out one trembling hand toward her, choking back a scream as he moved closer inch by inch. A faint tingle went up his arm when his fingertips touched the edge of the bed.

Please don't be dead, Grammy! Please don't be dead!

"Hey, Grammy . . . you awake yet?" he said, forcing strength into his voice.

Her face remained passive without the faintest stirring of breath. Brian imagined that she was a statue carved out of pure, white marble. He wanted to touch her face — he knew he *had* to touch her face, to see if she truly was dead, but he couldn't quite bring himself to do it.

You can't be dead, Grammy!

The throb of his pulse sounded louder and faster in his ears, but as he stared at her, wondering what the devil he should do next, he became aware of another sound — a low, watery gurgle.

His vision was swimming as he lowered his face close to hers, trying desperately to detect a faint stirring of breath, the tiniest indication of life. When her eyes suddenly snapped open, he jumped back and would have let fly a wild scream if his throat hadn't closed off. His grandmother's cloudy blue eyes stared unblinkingly up at him, registering absolutely no surprise.

"I — you see, I thought — when you didn't — " Brian stammered as he slapped his hands helplessly on his thighs before taking a deep breath.

Without a word, his grandmother raised a hand and pointed at him. Her mouth widened, and the tendons in her neck moved, but no sound came from her throat. An intense pressure started to build in Brian's bladder as he tried to figure out what she was trying to say.

"You're not feeling okay," he said with a desperate edge in his voice. "Can I do something for you?"

His grandmother's lips trembled uncontrollably; her eyes remained fixed on him, pinning him like an insect specimen to a corkboard.

"Do you need another one of those pills?" he asked, glancing at the brown bottle on her nightstand.

Still, in spite of her efforts, his grandmother could make no sound.

Finally, Brian couldn't stand it any longer. He took a deep breath and said, "I don't know what to do, Grammy. I have to call someone . . . the hospital or the ambulance or someone!"

Without waiting for her response, he moved quickly over to the other side of the bed, and picked up the phone. His hands were trembling as he dialed nine-one-one. After two rings, a pleasant-sounding woman answered. He quickly told her what the problem was — that his grandmother was really sick and he was alone and afraid that she was dying. After answering a few questions about his grandmother's condition, he calmed down enough to give the woman directions to the house. Before hanging up, she assured him that an ambulance was on its way.

Just knowing help was coming gave Brian some slight measure of relief. He looked down at the old woman, who had settled back onto her bed. Her eyes and mouth were closed. The quilt covering her barely rose and fell with her faint breathing.

Brian wished earnestly that his father had been here to take care of everything. Kids his age weren't supposed to have to deal with stuff like this.

Please don't die, Grammy, he thought over and over as he stood stiffly by the bedside and watched her. While he was waiting to hear the sound of the approaching ambulance, her breathing seemed to weaken steadily. What little color there was in her face seemed to drain away until she was ghostly-white.

Grammy, please don't die!

"You live here?"

"Uh, no," Brian said, shaking his head quickly as he glanced at the boy who had walked across the front lawn to stand beside him. "I — I'm staying with my father . . . he lives on Pond Road." He hooked his thumb in the general direction of the road.

The boy, who was obviously a year or two older than Brian, nodded sagely. He was a solidly-built kid who looked like he would make a good lineman for the high school football team in a few years. He already had a "jock-style" crewcut with lightning bolts shaved on the sides of his head. His deep brown eyes shined in the bright morning sunshine, reflecting the flashing red lights of the ambulance that was parked at the foot of the driveway.

Brian wanted to say something more, at least introduce himself, but the boy seemed too intent on watching the medical attendants as they carried the stretcher bearing the old woman out of the house.

"Good thing," the older boy whispered. "Serves her right, you know, after all these years."

The boy crossed his arms over his chest and let a smug smile of satisfaction spread across his face as he straightened his back. "I just wish to hell the other guys were here to *see* this! I can't wait to tell them!"

"Wha—what do you mean?" Brian asked. He felt like a traitor for letting himself feel even a fraction of relief, knowing that his grandmother was strapped down and on her way to the hospital.

"That old lady—" the boy said, letting his gaze track the stretcher's slow progress down the rutted walkway to the waiting ambulance. "You know what we call her around here? She's the 'Old Witch Lady'."

Brian wanted to ask him why, but the hard lump that was lodged in his throat almost strangled him. The memory of how badly his grandmother had scared him last night and then again early this morning was still too strong, too immediate. When she had lifted her hand and pointed a finger at him, struggling to say something, she had looked like she was out of her mind. Her curled fingers had seemed as thin and as gnarled as the tree branch that had kept him awake all night, tapping against his windowpane.

No, he didn't have to wonder too hard why the kids around town might suspect that his grandmother was a witch. Although he tried to deny it, he'd had the same thought a few times himself.

"You know," the boy continued. He leaned closer to Brian and adopted a low, conspiratorial voice, as if the helpless old woman on the stretcher might be able to hear him . . . and do something about it. "People 'round town say that she's at *least* a hundred years old."

"You don't believe that, do you?" Brian said. He cut himself off before saying anything else, not wanting the boy to know that the Old Witch Lady was his grandmother. It was going to be a long summer, living with his father in a town where he knew absolutely no one. More than anything else, Brian was hoping to meet a few of the local kids so he'd have someone to hang around with.

"Absolutely," the boy replied, "and from what I heard, she supposedly drinks human blood." He looked at Brian with an intense stare. "That's what's kept her alive for more than a hundred years."

Brian, of course, didn't believe any of this, but he nodded as if in agreement as he and the boy watched the workers slide the stretcher up into the ambulance. A loud clang of metal — one of the stretcher's side arms banging against the door — made both of them jump. They glanced at each other, then chuckled nervously.

Brian was still trying to get up the courage to introduce himself when a policeman glanced over at him, caught his attention and, waving his hand, started across the lawn toward him. The other boy cast a suspicious glance at Brian and, muttering something under his breath that Brian couldn't quite hear, took a few cautious steps away from him.

"You must be Brian, right?" the policeman said as he approached.

Brian nodded with a quick, sideways glance at the other boy.

"Figured as much. You're the spitting image of your dad," the policeman said. "Well, you don't have to worry any. Your grandmother's going to be just fine now."

"Your *grandmother?*" the other boy whispered. He looked incredulously at Brian, who could think of nothing better to do but shrug. "The Old Witch Lady's your *grandmother?* I thought you said you didn't live in the Witch House!"

"I don't . . . Honest," Brian said as he shuffled nervously from one foot to the other. "My father lives — " He cut himself off when the doors slammed shut on the ambulance. With its red lights flickering, it started moving slowly down the driveway.

The policeman glanced back and forth between the boys, waited a beat or two, then said, "Well, from what you told the dispatcher this morning, we finally located your father at the hospital in North Conway, New Hampshire. He said to tell you that Dianne's doing much better, and that he'll be back home just as fast as he can make it."

Brian said nothing as he watched the ambulance disappear around the curve of the driveway.

"If you want, I can wait here with you till your dad shows up."

"No," Brian said, shaking his head. "I — I think I'll be all right."

The excitement was obviously all over, so, without another word, the other boy started away, crossing the lawn toward the road. He shot a last, suspicious glance over his shoulder at Brian, who watched him out of the corner of his eye. All Brian could think was, no matter what else he tried to say or do from now on, that kid — and all of his friends — were going to know that he *was* living in this house and that the Old Witch Lady was his grandmother! Any chance he might have had of making friends with this kid were obviously blown clear out of the water.

By the looks of things, it was going to be one long and lonely summer.

Chapter Five
Flatline

Edward was pale and visibly shaken when he entered his mother's hospital room and sat down in the chair beside her bed. The hissing of the respirator masked every other sound and filled his mind with a static, white noise that made him feel woozy, disoriented. An array of monitors registered various digital readings which he didn't even try to understand. After spending most of the past twenty-four hours watching and fretting over Dianne in a similar condition, he couldn't fully comprehend that this gaunt, thin shadow of a person lying on the bed was his mother. As he stared silently at her, he felt a curious dissociation due, no doubt, to stress and fatigue. But that didn't stop the dizzying rush of emotions that churned like dark tidewater inside him.

A crisp, white sheet and pale blue blanket were tucked up under his mother's armpits. Her arms were outside the covers, lying lifelessly at her sides. An IV was stuck into the back of her left hand and held in place with several strips of white adhesive tape. Her skin was almost as white as the tape except for the thin tracings of blue veins just below the surface. A transparent breathing tube had been inserted into her nose and was also held in place with adhesive tape. It looked as if his mother had tried unsuccessfully to inhale a long straw. Her eyes were closed. The deep hollow indentations of her eye sockets were two perfectly round wells of darkness. Her wrinkled skin hung loosely, draped like a thin cloth covering over the hard edges of her skull.

Edward shuddered, trying not to think that his mother was already more than halfway to being a skeleton. He sighed heavily, grateful—at least—that he had asked Brian to wait for him downstairs. After everything he'd had to deal with last night and this morning, there was no reason for him to see his grandmother looking like this.

The cold, dull ache of loss filled Edward as he tried to comprehend how dramatically his life had changed in the last twenty-four hours. The two most important women in his life had both been hospitalized and were in critical condition. It seemed, at times, almost as if Dianne's fall and his mother's heart attack had been timed by some malevolent force.

He had to believe what the doctors had told him in North Conway, that Dianne's injuries, while certainly horrible, were not life-threatening as long as her condition remained stabilized. Dianne would have to endure months, possibly years of reconstructive surgery; but thankfully at this early stage, there were no indications of any serious brain damage.

And Edward had vowed that he would be right there beside her, helping her in every way he could for as long as it took.

His mother's situation, on the other hand, was anybody's guess. Earlier this afternoon, the doctor—he had been so upset, he couldn't even recall the woman's name—had told him that his mother's heart attack had been quite serious. It *seemed*—and she stressed the word seemed—not to have done much permanent damage, but she had frankly admitted that how his mother responded to the medication and how strong her will to live was would determine how well she did over the next several days. As an ominous aside, the doctor had added, "Of course, you can't expect *too* much at her age."

But she sure as hell looks like death-warmed-over!

The phrase popped unbidden into Edward's mind as he stared vacantly at his mother's reposed, death-mask face. Tears welled up in his eyes and ran freely down his cheeks. He was unable to stop himself from wondering who looked closer to death—his mother or Dianne.

He suddenly realized with a jolt that his mother's eyes were open, and she was looking up at him with a cloudy glaze covering her eyes like a gauze curtain. Momentarily flustered and surprised that she had caught him with his guard down, he quickly wiped his eyes with his sleeve and smiled down at her.

"Hey, Mom . . . how you feeling?"

His voice warbled noticeably, but his mother's blank expression remained fixed on him, looking straight at—or *through*—him.

"I—I came as soon as I heard you'd had some trouble."

The glow in his mother's eyes brightened for just an instant, then it faded again just as quickly. Her lips moved, and her tongue darted like a snake's between her teeth. She looked as if she was trying to speak, but the hissing of the respirator masked any sounds she might have made.

Edward leaned closer to her and smiled reassuringly. "Do you know where you are?" he asked, and then, before she could respond, he added, "You're in the hospital . . . in the coronary care unit. I guess you—your heart decided to do a little kick flip for you last night, huh?"

His smile felt thin and phony, plastered on his face like a painted grin.

"The doctor says you're doing just fine—that all you need now is a lot of rest and—"

"Will she . . . will Dianne be all right, too? . . . She will, won't she?"

His mother's voice was barely audible above the sound of the respirator. For a frozen moment, Edward wasn't even sure he had seen her lips move. The words had just . . . *been* there, like an auditory hallucination that echoed in his ears, a product of his stress, worry, and fatigue.

"Mom, I . . . I—"

"Her face . . . will it heal?"

Edward was stunned into silence. He had no idea what to say as he leaned closer to her, his eyes darting frantically back and forth. He was unable to focus on her vacant eyes for very long. He remembered late last night, when he had called to

88

tell his mother about Dianne's accident, he absolutely had not mentioned the nature or extent of Dianne's injuries.

"Dianne—" his mother said, her voice sounding raw and fragile, as if her throat were lined with sandpaper. "I have to . . . tell her . . . Will she . . . be . . . all right?"

"Well, I don't know for sure," Edward replied, swallowing with difficulty. "Nobody does at this point, but the doctors assure me that she'll get better . . . with time. And you will, too, Mom, if you just—"

"I'm scared, Eddie . . . I'm *real* scared for her!"

Edward bit his lower lip and took a deep, steadying breath. He knew he had to be strong for her now, that that's the way life went—while you're growing up, with luck and love, your parents were there for you. His father had died when he was young, but his mother, as much of a struggle as it had been, had done a good job of raising him and his brother, Michael. Now that he was older and she needed him, he hoped he would find the strength to help her.

"I—I'm scared, too, Mom," Edward said softly. He was unashamed as his eyes filled with tears again. "But we have to have faith that she—"

"If she dies . . . if she dies . . ."

"Don't you talk about *anyone* dying, all right?"

Evelyn's eyes suddenly brightened with intensity as she looked up at her son. Her hand, the one with the IV sticking into it, reached up and grabbed hold of his shirt sleeve. He slid one hand over hers and squeezed gently. The softness of her skin, the fragility of her bones beneath his touch nearly broke his heart.

"If Dianne dies," Evelyn said, "I . . . I don't know what I can do . . . about it."

And if you die, I don't know what I'll do, Edward thought, although he wasn't able to say it out loud.

He had been only five years old when his father had died. That was too young to remember much about the funeral other than him, his brother, and his mother crying a lot. The thought of losing his mother now left him feeling cold and weak and alone. After the events of the weekend, he knew he could be on the brink of a physical and mental collapse. The best he could do right now was shake his head in confusion and watch his mother struggle to speak. Her lips were thin and drawn, making her mouth look like an oval, bloodless wound.

"There'll be no one left . . . if she dies . . . no one left for me to tell — " his mother rasped.

Edward found it extremely unsettling, the way his mother's eyes kept shifting back and forth, as though she couldn't see him and she was desperately searching for something to anchor her gaze. He wondered if the heart attack had done something else to her, perhaps sent a blood clot to her brain and given her a stroke or affected her in some other way that was making her talk and act half-crazy. Maybe the medication she was on was screwing up her thinking.

"Look at her picture . . . her portrait," Evelyn said, no more than a gasp. Her hand trembled like a small, frightened animal in Edward's grasp. "You know where it is . . . She looks so much like . . . her . . ."

"You need to rest, Mom. Maybe I'd better be going now," Edward said, fighting to keep the desperate edge out of his voice. "I don't want to tire you out."

"Tell her to be careful . . . to watch out . . . until I can tell her . . . tell her about all of it," Evelyn said a bit more forcefully.

"Don't worry. I'll tell her," Edward said. He nodded even though he had no idea what his mother was talking about.

"It's too bad she's not in the bloodline . . . but perhaps . . . perhaps she will do," Evelyn whispered. "If only you had had a daughter . . . I had hoped that your sister . . . your sister would have been the one . . . or that you would have had a daughter, but . . . but it wasn't meant to be, I guess, and now . . . now I'm afraid of what will happen next!"

Edward stared at his mother, stunned into silence. He never knew he had a sister; there had always been just him and his brother Michael . . . poor, retarded Michael. What was this talk about a sister? Either his mother was completely out of her mind, or else she was confusing him with someone else.

"I probably should have told you about her . . . long before this," Evelyn went on. She was obviously trying to focus on her son, but her eyes kept twitching wildly back and forth as if she had no control over them.

"Told me —? Told me what?" Edward asked, his voice sounding like metal scraping against stone.

"About Rachel . . . your sister . . . She was named for an ancestor of mine . . . from long ago. She was to have been the next one . . . the one I told, but when she died . . . of scarlet fever . . . she was only two years old . . . you were just a baby . . . Oh, my sweet, sweet Rachel! I feared so much for you, too, Eddie . . . The Lord knows we've all had our share of misery . . . more than our share . . . but I'm afraid it will only get worse now . . . if I don't tell someone."

"I — I had no idea," Edward said, shaking his head and feeling both foolish and perplexed. Could it be true, that he'd had an older sister who had died shortly after he was born, or was his mother simply babbling out of her mind.

"I had wished . . . I'd *prayed* for another daughter or that you'd provide me with a granddaughter . . . And Michael? . . . No, Michael never could have, but if you had, I could have shown her . . . I could have told her about the—" Her throat closed off with a loud click. After licking her lips, she spoke again, her voice fainter now, faltering with the effort. "I tried to tell Sally, your first wife . . . but she wouldn't listen . . . she wasn't receptive . . . I had hoped that Dianne would — would be the one . . . but I need time . . . time to teach her, to show her that the—"

This time her voice cut off with a high, tight strangling sound. Her body tensed and began to tremble as though she was struggling against a powerful force. After a few seconds, her body gave up the effort and relaxed. With a loud gasp, she dropped her head back onto the pillow and stared up at the ceiling, her eyes wide open and unblinking. What little color there had been in her face quickly drained away.

Still clutching his mother's limp hand, Edward looked frantically at her, then glanced over his shoulder at the monitors. He didn't know for sure, but it seemed as though the digital numbers were dropping lower. A cold sweat broke out on his forehead.

"Hey, Mom —? *Mom!*"

He jiggled her hand, trying to rouse her, but he was convinced her hand was growing cold in his grip. He leaned close to her face, praying to feel the soft flutter of her breath, but he was so wound up with panic that he couldn't tell whether or not he was feeling anything. Suddenly, one of the monitors let out a loud beep. The sound stabbed like an ice pick into his ears as he released his mother's hand and moved slowly away from the bed, his gaze riveted to the slack expression on her face.

Oh, God—no! Please! No!

She still hadn't blinked. The cloudy glaze in her eyes seemed to thicken. Her focus seemed fixed on something far, far away. No motion stirred the thin blanket covering her chest. Her hand lay where he had dropped it, palm up, the thin fingers curled in upon themselves like a dead, white spider.

Uttering a soft moan, Edward wheeled around and raced for the door. He was telling himself that he had to remain calm, that there were medical people nearby who could help, but a stronger, deeper voice inside his head was whispering that it was already too late.

She's gone! . . . She's gone!

Flinging the door open, he ran out into the corridor and collided head-on into a nurse who was rushing to the room. She pushed past him and hurried over to the bedside. A second or two later, a doctor, three more nurses, and two medical technicians wheeling a cart loaded with equipment burst into the room.

Numb with shock, Edward stepped back and leaned against the far wall, telling himself he'd only be in the way as the medical team made a frantic attempt to resuscitate his mother. They called out orders and vital signs readings to each other; then all of them stood back when one of the medical technicians shouted, "Clear" and zapped her with the defibrillator. Out of the corner of his eye, Edward saw his mother's body jump with the electrical jolt that was supposed to jump-start her heart. They tried this three times; then one of the nurses monitoring Evelyn's blood pressure shouted, "We're losing her! Fast!" The doctor called for something, but the nurse looked at him, shook her head and said, "Flatline."

That single word cut through the swirling confusion that raged inside Edward's brain. He knew damned right well what *flatline* meant.

Chapter Six
Summer Shadows

"Kinda hot for this early in June, don't you think?" Edward said.

Dianne was sucking lukewarm coffee through a straw as she sat with her husband at the picnic table under the trees out behind Edward's house. After living here less than two months, she was still painfully aware that this was Edward's home, not her's. Not yet. It was going to take a long time of living in this house before she felt like she belonged here. And now, following her accident and the death of Edward's mother, she was beginning to think that she would *never* feel comfortable again—here or anywhere. In some ways—in a *lot* of ways, Brian belonged in this house more than she did.

She glanced over at Edward and nodded. She could still talk, even though her face was wrapped with elastic bandages and her jaw had been wired shut, but over the past two weeks, she had learned quite a bit about communicating with guttural sounds and simple gestures. At times, she thought about how language must have evolved this way and that maybe that's what was wrong with the whole world today: words complicated everything.

"I have to meet with Frank this afternoon to go over the plans for the house I'm going to be building for him," Edward said. "Maybe we should take this morning to go over and start cleaning up around my mother's house." He took a deep breath, as though it was too difficult to continue. "We probably should clean it right out so we can sell it or whatever."

Dianne looked at him again, regarding him for a moment, then nodded stiffly.

"I suppose so," she said. Her voice was muffled and distorted. "But I told you, I'm still not feeling up to it. Maybe we should hold off on that for a while longer."

Edward, she noticed, had developed the irritating habit of leaning forward whenever she spoke to him so he would catch everything she said. She didn't like the way it made her feel handicapped. She *wasn't* handicapped! She was just recovering from a serious accident. This *wasn't* permanent!

"It's not exactly something I'm crazy about doing, either, but we have to get it done eventually. I think we've put it off long enough."

Dianne looked away from him, wishing to God she didn't feel so annoyed at him—at *everything* this morning. It had been a long and painful two weeks since her accident, and she damned-sure wasn't looking forward to spending the rest of the summer with her face bandaged up, her jaw wired shut, and her body and mind numbed by the narcotics the doctor had prescribed. Sure, the medication dulled the pain, but that might be what was making her feel so cranky and depressed all the time. There was another operation scheduled in two weeks, to take out the metal plates that were holding the broken bones in her face in place, and she was dreading it. This summer looked like it was going to be one long, agonizing ordeal.

She didn't feel like getting up for another cup of iced coffee, much less going through her dead mother-in-law's possessions to decide what to save, what to get rid of, and what to donate to Goodwill.

"You know," she said after a long pause, "I still can't accept the fact that you didn't even tell me that your mother had died until after the funeral. It—it boggles my mind."

Edward took a deep breath and remained silent as he looked out at the line of trees bordering the backyard. The forest was lush with the bright greens of maple trees and the darker greens of pine. A sultry breeze was blowing from the south, making the trees sway gently. His gaze automatically went to the darkened path that sliced into the woods. One branch of that path wound more than half a mile through the woods before ending in the side yard at his mother's house. Over the years, the path had been worn smooth from him tracking over it to go visit her.

"This hasn't exactly been very easy on me either, you know," he said, his voice barely above a whisper. "You were in the hospital, and I didn't want you thinking or worrying about anything else except getting better."

Dianne tensed and almost asked him what worried and hurt him more — her accident or his mother's death — but she let it drop. Far too many times over that past two weeks she had told him, and sometimes screamed at him, that he had no idea what she had to deal with. She realized that their relationship had suffered enough strain since her accident; there was no sense in adding to it . . . not on such a nice summer morning.

"I mean," Edward said, slapping his fist into his open hand, "Christ! Up until two weeks ago, I never even knew I'd ever had a sister!"

Dianne sighed and shook her head, wanting to ask him — truthfully — how much difference something like that would make in his life; his sister had been dead for over forty years. Instead, she said, "Do you think Brian would want to come along with us?"

As soon as the words were out of her mouth, she regretted them. Brian — now he was a problem. Even before her accident, her stepson had treated her at best with ill-disguised dislike bordering on outright contempt. Now that her face was mottled like rotten fruit and wrapped in elastic bandages, and her eyes still blackened and swollen, he was treating her as if she were some hideous monster, something to be feared and hated instead of pitied. She instantly found herself hoping Brian would want to stay at home.

Edward glanced up at the house and said simply, "I suppose I ought to ask him."

"Oh, he doesn't have to come if he doesn't want to," Dianne said, but she knew it was already too late as Edward got up and walked back to the house.

Edward pulled the car to a stop at the top of the dirt driveway and switched off the ignition, but he didn't get out of the car immediately. For several seconds he just sat there, gripping the steering wheel with both hands as he stared up at his mother's deserted house. A deep cold gripped his innards as his eyes darted back and forth, taking in the hard angles of the old structure. The house was well over two hundred years old and had been in the family since before the American Revolution. The sun was behind the house, casting the front door in shadows that made the peeling, brown paint look all the darker. The front windows looked as though they were covered by a mantle of deep, dark ice that reflected back only a small amount of the bright morning sky. There was a sense of loneliness, of disuse and abandonment about the house that wrung Edward's heart as an avalanche of childhood memories filled his mind.

"Well, what are we waiting for?" Dianne asked, looking back and forth between the house and Edward.

Brian sat silently in the back seat, slouched down with his arms folded almost defiantly across his chest. He hadn't said a word since getting into the car, but throughout the short drive to the house, Dianne had felt his cold, intense gaze linger on the back of her head.

Edward took a steadying breath and let it out slowly. "I don't know—you know? I—sometimes I just can't accept the fact that she—that my mother's not here anymore," he said, his voice trembling slightly. "I mean—ever since I can remember, she's *always* lived here . . . her entire life! I keep thinking that as soon as we walk in through the front door, she'll call out to us from the kitchen. It just makes me—I dunno." He sighed deeply and shivered. "I mean, all the time I was growing up, I never really liked this house. There was something about it . . ."

"Then why, once you were old enough, didn't you move out of Summerfield?" Dianne asked.

Edward shrugged. "I know, I know. I just never got the chance to leave, I guess, and I — well, I always felt like I ought to stay around and help my mother out, especially once she started getting along in years. There was no other family around who could do that. I —" He sighed again and shook his head. "But now, it just doesn't seem like the same place, knowing that she's . . ." His voice trailed away to nothing.

Dianne reached out and covered his hand with hers. She wanted to say something reassuring, something comforting, but her husband's dark mood was unsettling her, too; he looked so . . . so *haunted* was the first word that popped into her mind.

Like he expects to see his mother's ghost up there in one of the windows or something.

"We can wait until later, if you want to," she said softly. She squeezed his hand, surprised at how cold it felt in her grip.

Edward glanced quickly at her, but then his gaze was drawn back to the house as if it were a magnet and his eyes were iron. His lower lip began to tremble; the color had drained from his face.

"No," he said, taking a deep breath and squaring his shoulders. "We can't possibly get it all done today, anyway, but we have to at least get a start on it." He slid the keys out of the ignition, opened his door, and eased out of the car. The whole time he kept his gaze fastened on the house.

Dianne remained in the car, watching him for a moment before she got out on her side. She glanced back at Brian, who had made no move whatsoever, but didn't say anything to him. His mistrust of her cut to the heart, but she didn't want to — she *couldn't* let show how much it bothered her. Right now, she and Edward had enough problems of their own.

They met at the front of the car and, hand in hand, started up toward the house. Dianne kept watching the way Edward's eyes darted back and forth, as though he was looking for something or else trying to encompass the entire house in a single glance. The haunted look didn't leave his eyes; if anything, it intensified as they approached the back porch and mounted the steps. Edward's hand was trembling as he fit the key into the lock, turned the doorknob and then, stepping back, swung the door inward. He gestured for Dianne to enter first, but before she did, she turned to him, gripped both of his arms at the elbows, and said, "Edward? Honey? What is it? Tell me what's *really* the matter?"

His expression remained darkly expectant as he peered into the open doorway. His nostrils widened as he sniffed the stale air that wafted out of the house. He cringed back and tensed as if he expected something horrible to come rushing out at him.

"You have to talk about it, you know," Dianne said. The smell of stale air and mold made her feel slightly dizzy, but she forced herself not to let it show. "You have to tell me what it is. What do you think you'll find here?"

Edward shrugged and shivered slightly. "I dunno," he said. His voice was flat, barely above a whisper. "I just don't know. Maybe . . . maybe just the ghost of the child I used to be."

Brian waited until his father and stepmother had gone inside the house before getting out of the car. Just seeing the house again and thinking about how scared he had been that night two weeks ago, the night before his grandmother died, made his legs feel all weak and wobbly. Over the past two weeks, he had actually half-convinced himself that he had been so nervous that night because, at least subconsciously, he had *known* the old lady—the Old Witch Lady—was going to die. Maybe the surprise of the phone, ringing as late as it did, had started it all by frightening the old woman . . . or maybe, even though she had appeared to handle it quite well, the shock of the news his father had given her had started the heart attack . . . or maybe . . . just maybe—in spite of what that local kid had said about her keeping herself alive for over a hundred years by drinking the blood of children from around town—it was simply that his grandmother's number had come up, that it had been her time to croak.

Whatever the answer, all Brian knew was that the old house scared the bejesus out of him, plain and simple. There was no *way* he was going back in there!

He hung around at the car for a while, looking for something to do but couldn't think of anything. He was irritated that he had left his Walkman and tapes back at his father's house; and he knew from the boring though blessedly short drive over here that there was nothing interesting to do in the car.

Maybe I can just sit here in the car and play "Cujo," he thought, laughing morosely.

Shadowed by tall maple trees, the old garage and adjoining toolshed with its door partway open looked like they might be at least moderately interesting to explore. Brian started across the driveway toward them, but when he was halfway there, the sight of the dense shadows inside the shed made him suddenly draw up short. A bar of lemon sunlight angled across the front of the building, making the interior look all the darker. It didn't take much for Brian to imagine all sorts of creepy, terrible things lurking there in the dusty, cobwebbed shadows. A shiver ran up his back like teasing fingertips. As he stared at the open doorway, his breath caught in his chest when he saw *something* shift inside the shed — a dark blur moved against the shadowy interior. It might have been simply a trick of his eyes, but Brian couldn't stop wondering if it could be a ghost — the ghost of his dead grandmother, the Old Witch Lady!

Turning quickly on his heel, he walked back to the car, where he shoved his hands deep into his jeans pockets, leaned back against the hot side of the car, and — keeping a wary eye on the shed — tried to convince himself that he hadn't seen anything inside the darkened doorway . . . *certainly* nothing that had looked like it might be a person's shadow!

Before long, though, he was feeling bored again and more than a little bit irritated, so after casting a wary glance over his shoulder, he walked out into the backyard. Once upon a time, the large expanse of lawn might have been beautiful, but it obviously hadn't been cared for since last summer. It was a tangle of tall grass and weeds—daisies, pale blue flowering chicory, and white puffs of dandelion gone to seed. In the far corner of the yard, a rusted swing set, the swing and chains long gone, caught Brian's attention. Whistling softly to himself, he made his way over to it, wading through the thigh-high grass like a swimmer churning through heavy surf.

Could this really have been my dad's swing set, back when he was a kid?

Brian gripped one of the metal support legs and ran his hand over the gritty surface, watching the rust crumble and fall to the ground. Looking back at the old house, he tried to imagine what it must have been like back when his father was a kid. The house might have been in good repair then, the lawn freshly cut, and his father and younger brother would have been out here, playing on their brand-new swing set. He squinted for a moment and could almost hear the squeak-squeak of the shiny-new swing chain, a chorus of laughing voices, the heavy chirring of grasshoppers and crickets. A moist breeze carried to him the rich, pleasant smells of green growing things in the forest. It made him feel almost dizzy with pleasure.

With a sudden start, Brian opened his eyes. Dropping into a protective crouch, he spun around and stared at the thick woods that bordered the yard. He didn't know why he had reacted like this, but something—some primitive warning bell had sounded in his brain.

I'm being watched!

A ripple of goose bumps broke out on his arms. He looked up at the house, expecting to see his father and Dianne out on the back porch, watching him, but the porch was empty, and as far as he could tell, no one was watching him from any of the windows.

Still shivering, his gaze swung back over the surrounding forest. He tried to pierce the tangled green darkness, but the wall of foliage blocked his view; he couldn't see more than ten or twenty feet into the woods. Deep blue shadows shifted back and forth as heavy branches waved in the warm wind.

The woods were quiet — seemingly *too* quiet, Brian thought. Every bush, every spray of pine needles seemed to be alive with obscure shapes and unblinking eyes that glared right back at him, confident in the protection the woods afforded them. The heavy scent of pine filled Brian's nostrils, but beneath that, he thought he detected something else — the raw, nauseating stench of decay and death.

It's all in my imagination. I'm still all worked up thinking about that branch that was tapping against the window . . . and what happened after that.

His fists clenched at his sides as he scanned the woods, trying to see if any of the shifting shadows resembled a human shape — or something worse! Off to his left he saw a narrow path that disappeared behind the trees. The hard-packed brown earth danced with shimmering sunlight and shadow that dazzled Brian's eyes. As he was gazing up the path, wondering where it might lead, he saw from the corner of his eye something move from one tree to another. It wasn't much — just a shifting darkness, but he knew it wasn't just a shadow; it had looked like someone who was stooped over as he ran deeper into the woods, trying to stay out of sight behind the trees.

Brian opened his mouth, about to yell something, but then fell silent. He realized he had been holding his breath and let it out in a long, loud whoosh. A sharp pain jabbed up under his ribcage, feeling as if he had run a mile right after drinking a gallon of water. He stared so long and hard at the place where the shadow had disappeared that his vision began to blur.

"It wasn't anyone," he whispered to himself, although he sensed that he was trying to convince himself. "It *couldn't* have been anyone!"

But the feeling of being watched hadn't gone away.

Eyes!

From *somewhere* nearby, eyes were riveted onto him, drilling into him like invisible laser beams. He could *feel* it! He turned again and looked up at the house, positive that his father and stepmother were watching him. He flushed with embarrassment that they might have seen him out here, acting like a fool as he stared off into the woods.

But no — the porch and backyard were still deserted. Only the faint hiss of the wind through the trees and the steady sound of insect song broke the quiet calm of the day. But the peacefulness did nothing to quell the winding tension inside him.

He *knew* someone had been out here — somewhere — hiding and watching him.

And maybe there really was someone outside the bedroom window that night, he thought as another wave of chills rippled through him. Slowly, feeling his way with his feet, he started backing away from the swing set toward the house. Tangles of weeds and grass swished at his legs, tugging at his feet and almost pulling him off balance. He wanted more than anything just to turn around and start running, but he was suddenly terrified that *something* — whoever was out there, hiding in the fringe of the woods — would give chase, catch up with him, and drag him down before he could reach the house or even scream.

Should I yell? Would my father even hear me? And even if he did, would he know I was really in danger? Could he get to me in time, before I was caught and killed?

"But there's nobody there," Brian said aloud, hoping the sound of his own voice would give him courage.

He kept backstepping, moving faster and faster away from the swing set, but then his foot caught on a divot or something, and he fell backward. He hit the ground hard enough to knock the wind out of him, but that pain was nothing compared to the sudden jolt of terror he felt when he caught a glimpse of something moving in the shadows. It was right near the tree where he had last seen that dark blur of motion.

Uttering a low, moaning cry, Brian scrambled to his feet, spun around, and raced for all he was worth toward the house. Saw-toothed blades of grass slashed at his legs and arms, but he didn't feel anything except the rushing wind in his face and the cold, gripping fear that had taken hold of his stomach.

"Dad!" he shouted.

His cry seemed no louder than a whisper above the roar of the wind in his ears. His clenched fists chugged like throbbing pistons, and his sneakers pounded the ground hard, but he seemed to be getting no closer to the house. All he could think was — *How close behind me is he? Will I make it?*

Several times he chanced a quick glance over his shoulder but didn't see anyone. Still, he was convinced that he was being chased and that his pursuer was racing toward him, running with his head bent down low to keep below the level of the tall grass. He tripped and almost fell every time he looked behind to see who was chasing him, but he wheeled his arms wildly and maintained his balance, knowing that another fall could spell the difference between making it to safety and not.

"Hey, Dad!" he shouted as he neared the relative safety of the back porch. He strained to hear the sound of his pursuer's footsteps closing the distance between them. He tripped and went sprawling onto the porch floor when he tried to leap all of the steps at once. A sharp pain lanced the palm of his left hand, but he paid no attention to it as he got up and shot forward, slamming into the closed door. His heart was pounding heavily in his throat as he grabbed the doorknob and jiggled it.

"Shit!" he shouted, realizing the door was locked. He started hammering on the door with both fists. The drumming impact rattled the glass, threatening to break it. Before he could turn to see if he was still being chased, he saw a shadowy motion in the hallway through the dirty door window. For a heart-clutching instant, he wondered who — or what — this was; then the figure moved closer, and Dianne's bandaged face resolved in front of him like a leering apparition from an old horror movie. Through his raging panic, he couldn't tell what — if anything — she said as she smiled at him while working to turn the rusty door lock.

After agonizing seconds, the lock clicked and the door

swung open. Dianne stepped aside as Brian burst into the hallway, took one deep, gasping breath, and then spun around and slammed the door shut.

"Hey, Brian—is everything okay?" Dianne asked.

The wires holding her jaw in place restricted the movement of her jaw, so her words came out muffled and garbled. Through Brian's white blaze of panic, what she said barely made any sense at all. He was trembling all over and sweating profusely as he looked back and forth between her and the square of sunlit backyard he could see through the window. The long stretch of uncut lawn was deserted and undisturbed except where it was trampled down where he had been. At the border of the woods, the rusted swing set stood motionless, like a lonely sentinel. Brian made a faint whimpering sound in the back of his throat as he grabbed the lock and snapped it shut.

"I saw—there was a—I think I—"

"Hey, take it easy, will you? You're hyperventilating," Dianne said. "Calm down and tell me what's got you so worked up?"

She reached out in an attempt to place a reassuring hand on his shoulder, but Brian dodged away from her as if her touch was more dangerous than whatever he had imagined was skulking around out there in the forest. He wiped the slick of sweat from his forehead with the back of his arm and swallowed noisily before trying to speak. He wanted to say that he was all right, but he still couldn't catch his breath. He just shook his head and looked down at the floor, feeling like a complete idiot.

"Well, your father's just about done upstairs," Dianne said, obviously not wanting to force him to talk about anything he didn't want to talk about. "We should be heading home soon."

"Good," Brian said. His voice croaked, sounding like someone had stepped on a frog.

"Your father has to work this afternoon, but maybe after lunch you and I should head out to the beach," Dianne said. "Lord knows, it's hot enough."

105

"Umm —" Brian said, nodding his head stupidly. "Yeah, maybe."

"Did . . . uh, did something happen out there?" Dianne asked, eying him suspiciously as she nodded at the locked door.

Brian feverishly licked his lips and backed away from her, wanting to get as much distance as possible between them. "I, uhh — no, no . . . nothing happened at all."

Dianne regarded him for a moment, then shrugged and said, "Well, why don't you wait down here. I'll go see what your father's up to."

Brian considered for a second, then in a high-pitched voice said, "No, I'll go get him."

Before Dianne could respond, he ran down the hallway toward the staircase, thankful that whatever might have been outside — at least, for now — was *still* outside!

Chapter Seven
The Witch Is Back

"So what are your plans for today?" Dianne asked. She was using a plastic straw to sip at the cup of coffee she'd just poured, but it was still too hot to drink.

Brian glanced up from his cereal bowl and looked fleetingly over at his stepmother. The sight of her bandaged face made his stomach do a quick flip, and all of a sudden he didn't feel all that hungry anymore. Even after more than a month of seeing her face wrapped up like this, he wasn't used to her. He pushed the bowl of Cracklin' Oats aside and shook his head, wishing he had slept in a bit longer this morning . . . at least until she went off and did some shopping or something.

"I dunno," he said softly. "No plans, really."

Just like every other damned day so far this summer, he thought bitterly.

"Well, your father is working with Fred Pierce this morning to go over their plans for the subdivision — again! — before the planning board meets tomorrow night. He'll probably be tied up all day. I was thinking of heading into town to do a bit of grocery shopping. I have to pick up . . . something at the pharmacy, too. Want to come along?"

Brian ran his lower lip under his teeth and considered for a moment. In fact, he'd been thinking about riding his bike downtown to see if he could find any kids his own age. So far, it had been a long, lonely summer, living here with his father and Dianne. Tense, too, what with Dianne's accident and his grandmother dying and all. For the hundredth time already this week, he wished he'd never agreed to spend the entire summer in Maine. Sure it was nice spending time with his father, but his dad had recently quit his carpentry job and was subdividing the family property to make some money. He was so involved with getting the project approved, as well as making plans to build a new home for himself, that he hardly had any time for Brian.

Back home in Arizona, Brian had plenty of friends and there were lots of things to do. By now, he would have been off swimming at the public pool, or playing baseball or Nintendo, or doing *something* interesting. His idea of fun certainly wasn't hanging around the house with a creepy stepmother who looked like an extra from the remake of *The Mummy* and who sounded like she was choking on her tongue every time she spoke.

"Or—" Dianne said, leaning forward and clasping her hands tightly together on the table, "maybe we could drive to Portland. Maybe catch a movie in town. Didn't you want to see that new Robin Hood movie? What was the name?"

Brian looked at her again, forcing himself to maintain steady eye contact with her for more than a few seconds.

"Outlaws," he said, "but I dunno—I don't feel all that up for a movie." Then, before he could stop himself, he added, "But maybe I'll go with you and just . . . just hang around downtown while you do some shopping."

"Sure," Dianne said, her face brightening as she pushed the chair back and stood up. "If you're ready to go, just let me dash upstairs and grab my purse, and we'll be off." She left the kitchen in a hurry, her footsteps echoing on the stairs in the hall.

Brian sat there at the table, staring glumly at his now soggy cereal and wondering why in the hell he ever agreed to go along. Wasn't it obvious how uncomfortable he felt around her? Couldn't she pick up on how much he didn't even like being in the same room with her? Oh, sure—she seemed to be trying really hard to get to know him better, but the circumstances were pretty peculiar; he wanted simply to ignore her and avoid her as much as possible, if only to make the remainder of his summer here more bearable.

Before his thoughts got much further, he heard the clicking of her shoes on the stairs. Standing up with an almost studied, slouching indifference, he placed his half-full cereal bowl and empty juice glass in the sink and followed her out to the car.

The drive downtown to the Shaw's Supermarket was mercifully short, and—thankfully—Dianne didn't try to make any more conversation. She dropped him off on Main Street in front of the post office with instructions to meet her in the Shaw's parking lot in one hour. As soon as he was out of the car, Brian heaved a huge sigh of relief. With no idea where to go or what to do, he started walking.

Dianne was frankly relieved when she pulled the car to a stop in the grocery store parking lot. Ever since her accident, she had been taking a painkiller and antibiotics, and after she'd taken her first pill this morning—hell, ever since she *started* the medication, she'd been feeling really spaced out. Her concentration just didn't seem to be what it used to be. She had a lot more trouble than usual falling asleep and getting up in the morning. Her major concern had been that it wasn't just the medication, that she had some as yet undetected brain damage from her fall; but her doctor reassured her that her X rays and CAT scan looked absolutely perfect, and that the medication she was taking couldn't have such a side-effect. She just hoped—with time—that she would get used to it. She was tired of feeling like she was viewing the world through a foot-thick plate glass window.

"I'm sick and tired of feeling sick and tired," she muttered as she pulled the keys from the ignition and dropped them into her purse.

As soon as she was out of the car, her self-consciousness about how she looked to people returned with an almost over-

109

powering surge. She had spent hours upon hours, staring at her face in the mirror, so she knew exactly what she looked like. And she knew, just as surely as she knew that the sun rose in the East and set in the West, that people couldn't help but stare at her and talk about her as soon as her back was turned. Many of the townsfolk knew she was Edward's new wife and had heard about what had happened to her; the rest were left to speculate.

Fighting back an impulse to hurry through her shopping just to finish her errands, Dianne grabbed a grocery cart and wheeled it into the store. Not more than halfway down the produce aisle, she heard a little boy in one of the carts in front of her say, "Look at that *lady*, Mommy! What *happened* to her *face?*"

Feeling a rush of spite, Dianne considered waiting until the kid's mother wasn't looking and giving him a fright he'd *really* remember, but instead she hurried ahead, pacing up and down the aisles and quickly checking off her shopping list as she loaded up the cart.

It might have been the fluorescent lights in combination with the medication; it might have been the cool, actually cold air-conditioning in the supermarket; or it might have been something she ate or drank for breakfast, but whatever it was, the spacey feeling Dianne had felt all morning got steadily stronger as she went through the store. Her legs felt loose and rubbery, and she had to maintain an iron-grip with both hands on the handle of the shopping cart to support herself. She thought she was going to drop when she went to the checkout counter and started unloading the items onto the sliding belt.

The light, feathery hammering in her ears grew steadily louder and faster as she listened to the *beep-beep-beep* of the cashier's electronic scanner. Beneath her bandages, her face felt flushed and itchy. She kept eying the beautiful sunlit morning outside the store's front window, telling herself that she'd be fine just as soon as she got outside and could take a breath of fresh air. Whenever she looked down and saw her hand placing item after item on the counter, she felt over-

110

whelmingly dissociated from herself. It was as if she was watching someone else's hands do what she wanted to have done.

"Ma'am—?"

Feeling dazed and dizzy, Dianne shook her head and looked up, suddenly aware that the cashier had asked her something that she hadn't heard.

"Beg your pardon?" Dianne said. The wires holding her jaw together made her voice sound muffled and distorted. Her eyes blinked wildly, strobing her vision as she raised one hand to her face and rubbed the sweat from her forehead.

"I need to see your Shaw's ID card before I can approve your check," the young girl at the register said. She squinted as she looked at Dianne and added, "Are you feeling all right, ma'am?"

Dianne tried to say something, but the sudden tightness gripping her throat wouldn't let go. She felt as though strong, steely hands or a tight rope had wound around her neck and was tightening . . . squeezing relentlessly . . . choking off her air. Through a rising flood of panic, Dianne saw the cashier's eyes widen as her concern spiked.

"I can take these out for you if you're not feeling well," the cashier said. "Why don't you take a seat over there by the window?"

Dianne could see the woman's lips move, but her voice seemed curiously disconnected, as though she were shouting to her from the far end of the store. She gestured in the direction of the long bench that was located beneath the plate glass window, but Dianne was suddenly fearful that she would lose her balance and fall, so she didn't dare turn and look. Groaning loudly, she slumped forward, supporting herself on the counter on her elbows. Her foot kicked the food cart, making it swing around and bang like cymbals into the side of the counter. The sound was like an explosion inside Dianne's ears, but she barely noticed it as wave after wave of swelling darkness surged inside her mind like an angry tide.

"Barb! Com'er! Quick! Get Mr. Reardon!" the cashier yelled, her voice cracking with fright as she stared at Dianne.

111

That was the last thing Dianne heard before the darkness filled her mind completely and dragged her all the way down. She spiraled down slowly, like a windup toy ice skater winding down, and collapsed in a heap on the linoleum floor. Her last thought was that it felt like she was lying on a sheet of ice . . .

"Yeah, I'd heard that the old witch was dead," the boy said, "but I didn't really believe it. She'll probably be back!"

The boy's name was Nathan Beck — or Nate, as he insisted on being called. He was short with a stocky build sandy hair, and a generous sprinkling of freckles across his face. He was the boy who had been out to Evelyn Fraser's house to watch the ambulance on the morning of the old woman's fatal heart attack. On this beautiful July morning, Nate, Jim Fowler, and Ross Parker — his two "best buds," as he called them — were sitting in the shade on the curb in front of the 7-Eleven, busily stuffing their mouths with Ring-Dings and washing it all down with greedy gulps of Pepsi. Three battered and chipped skateboards were lying on the small patch of grass behind them.

Brian was standing with one foot on the sidewalk, the other in the street as he talked with the three boys. He wanted to feel comfortable enough to sit down and join in with them, but he felt awkward, trying to get to know them. Still fresh in his mind was Nate's derisive laughter when he had realized Brian was staying in the Old Witch House and that the Old Witch Lady was his grandmother.

"Yeah," Brian said, his voice winding high, "she died that afternoon in the hospital,"

He knew he should feel at least a twinge of remorse for his grandmother, but in truth he hadn't known her all that well; in fact, all she had ever done was make him feel nervous and scared, even before she had gotten so sick. She and her house, everything about her had made him feel all tense and spooked. It wasn't any wonder why the local kids suspected all sorts of weird things about his dead grandmother.

"Did you get to see her body?" Ross asked, his pale eyes

112

bright behind the curtain of long, brown hair that hung over his face.

Brian nodded even as he tried to forget how wasted away his grandmother had looked, lying in the coffin at her funeral home. Her skin had been so white, he had easily imagined that she was a wax statue, not the remains of a living, breathing human being.

"Was she — like, all gnarly and wrinkled and stuff?"

"What do you expect?" Brian said, wishing Ross would stop pressing him for details and talk about something else.

"For a witch who was over a hundred years old," Nate added with a note of wonder and tremulous fear in his voice.

"Bullshit," Jim piped in, waving a beefy hand at them and shaking his head in disgust. He was the largest of the boys, several pounds overweight, and had been busy eating his junk food until now. "She was just an old lady and nothing more. 'Sides, you seem to be forgetting that this here's her grandson. I don't think you should be insulting his family like that."

The other two boys regarded Jim as if he had been standing out in the sun too long. Then Nate said, "No, if we wanted to insult families, I'd guess we have to mention your older sister."

"Eat shit and die!" Jim said. He straightened his shoulders and puffed up his chest so his T-shirt rode up, exposing the thick roll of fat hanging over his belt.

"Eat shit and *live!*" Nate snapped back.

"But hey," Brian said. "I was just staying there for the weekend, while my folks were away. I don't live there or anything." He shifted nervously from one foot to the other. "I'm staying with my father for the summer, out on Pond Road." He was wracking his brain for some way to change the subject, but so far he was drawing a blank. When he had first seen these boys, his first impulse had been to ask them if they felt like getting a bunch of kids together for a baseball game or something; but with their long hair, *Anthrax* and *Megadeth* T-shirts, and skateboards, they didn't strike him as the baseball-playing type.

113

"So—uh, what do you guys do for fun around here?" he asked lamely.

All three boys shrugged and shook their heads. "Just hang out," Nate said. "Not much ever happens in Summerfield."

"It's too hot to skate," Jim added. "Too hot to do anything. I dunno. Maybe we'll go swimming later, if it stays hot like this."

Brian smiled and waited for an invitation to join them, but when it wasn't forthcoming, he decided not to push it. Why, after all, should they even want to include him, having just met him only a few minutes ago? And he knew he had a lot to overcome, being the grandson of the Old Witch Lady. He wanted to do or say something so they'd accept him, at least enough to let him hang out with them for a while. Although they had been acting friendly enough so far, they obviously weren't going to let him into their tight little circle, not until he proved himself.

"You said you was from Arizona, huh?" Nate said.

Brightening, Brian nodded.

"I thought so, from your funny accent. You sound like a freaking cowboy or something. What do you do for fun out in Ari-*zone*-a?"

"Nothing much," Brian said, adopting their casual shrug. "You know, it's pretty much like around here—just hang around, go swimming, listen to music . . . maybe play a little baseball."

None of the boys seemed to pick up on Brian's hint, so he let it drop for good.

"Hey, have you heard the new tape from *Anthrax?*" Jim asked.

"Listen to it all the time," Brian replied, although, in truth, he didn't have any of their albums. He was about to ask if they wanted to come over to his house and listen to some music when a sudden loud blaring sound punched the air. Brian flinched and looked around. "What the hell—?" he said, shouting to be heard above the noise. Before the echo of one blast had faded, it was repeated.

114

" 'S'just the fire horn — the noon whistle," Nate said casually.

"It's twelve o'clock?" Brian said, looking at them in surprise. "Oh, shit! I gotta get going." He didn't really want to leave yet, but he took a tentative step away from the curb and glanced again down the road behind him. "I'm — I was supposed to meet my stepmother at the grocery store half an hour ago."

"Catch'cha later then," Nate said lazily, as if he hardly cared whether Brian stayed or left.

Brian was going to say something else, but before he could, another loud sound — a car horn, tooting rapidly — caught his attention. He turned around and saw Dianne's car pull to a stop in the 7-Eleven parking lot. The electric window on the passenger's side slid down smoothly; then her horrible, bandaged face appeared in the window, resolving out of the gloomy interior of the car like a spooky special effect.

"Hey! Brian! Where have you been? I've been looking all over for you," Dianne called out.

Embarrassed that these boys might see her, Brian hurried over to the car, trying his best to block their view of her with his body. Waving to them over his shoulder, he called out, "Well, maybe I'll see you guys around," and quickly got into the car. He pressed the button to raise the window, but before it was all the way up, he overheard the surprised exchange among the three boys.

"Jesus Christ! Did you see *that?*"

"Holy shit!"

"The Old Witch Lady's back!"

"Just like I told yah."

As they drove away, Brian wasn't sure if Dianne had heard them or not, but for some bitter, hostile reason, he found himself wishing that she had.

The drive home was pure agony for both Dianne and Brian, but they each had their own different reasons.

Brian was still stinging from the embarrassment of having

115

those three boys see him with Dianne. Now he was *positive* none of them would ever want to do anything with him. He might as well consign himself to spending all of his time alone this summer . . . unless he went someplace with the walking mummy while his father was at work!

Dianne, for her part, was worried and confused by what had happened to her at Shaw's supermarket. After fainting in the checkout line, she had been revived with a quick sniff of an ammonia capsule, which the store manager had in his first aid box. He had wanted to call the town rescue unit, but she had insisted that she was feeling better, that coming into the air-conditioned building out of the heat must have gotten to her.

In truth, she wasn't feeling at all fine . . . worse, in fact.

Even after sitting and resting for more than half an hour, her head felt like it was stuffed with cotton, and her body was all weak and trembly.

What the hell's wrong with me? she kept wondering as she drove down Main Street, turned left onto South Street, and headed for home. She didn't even trust herself driving, but she forced herself to concentrate on the road and take things nice and easy. Her stomach felt hollow. Every bump and curve in the road filled her with a sour nausea that she thought for sure was going to make her vomit before long. All she could think was, she had to get home and lie down . . . and call her doctor first thing tomorrow. For once, she was glad Brian didn't want to talk to her. The silence in the car was a relief.

As soon as she pulled into the garage, Brian opened his door, jumped out of the car, and made a beeline for his bedroom. Once again, Dianne was grateful that she didn't have to deal with him. He'd be out of sight for a couple of hours at least. That would give her time to pull herself together.

Her legs felt like brittle sticks, barely able to support her as she walked into the kitchen and went over to the table where she collapsed with a sigh. The groceries were still in the car, but they could wait a few minutes while she calmed down. The pressure in her head felt like it was building steadily. Her pulse hammered in her throat, throbbing behind her eyes and making her vision jump with every heartbeat.

It can't just be the medication, she thought as she ran her fingers through her hair, pulling back so hard on her scalp tears formed in her eyes. Dark, churning fear filled her.

It's gotta be something more than that. There has to be something wrong with my brain! Christ! What if I'm going to . . . going to — but she wouldn't allow herself to complete the thought. She didn't dare think about dying.

She and Edward had talked all about her fears of permanent brain damage with her doctors. They had reassured her that all of her tests — absolutely *all* of them — indicated that she was recovering just fine, considering the trauma she had been through. Still, that didn't remove the dark, numbing fear that they might all be wrong.

What if there is something still wrong with my brain. Maybe there's a bruise or a tumor or something they haven't detected with all their fancy X rays and CAT scans.

And what if it was worsening steadily, day by day, putting more and more pressure on her brain, making her feel worse and worse until one day it was going to pop and . . . kill her!

She shivered as she looked around the kitchen, shocked for an instant at how pale, how thin the real world seemed. In a flash, she realized how temporary everything was — even her own existence.

When she glanced over at the counter, she let out a small squeal of surprise when she saw what had happened while she was out. The coffee carafe lay in a pile of broken glass scattered around the hot plate. The warming unit was glowing with a baleful red that refracted through the jagged shards of glass. Dianne knew immediately what must have happened: after taking the last cup of coffee this morning, before hurrying out the door with Brian, she must have left the coffee maker turned on. The empty pot had overheated and shattered.

Her hands were shaking as she pulled the plug out of the wall socket, then wet a paper towel and gingerly brushed aside the still hot pieces of glass. The area of the countertop around the coffee maker was scorched like burned toast, but she thought it would clean up—most of it, anyway. She would have to wait until the broken glass cooled before handling it.

Leaning forward against the countertop, she took a deep breath and held it, trying her damndest to focus her mind. She was genuinely surprised that she felt such a swelling rush of anger building up inside her.

Why the hell am I feeling so angry?

She knew that breaking the coffee pot wasn't what was bothering her. No, it was the idea that she had left the pot on and forgotten all about it. What was wrong with her thinking? There must be a defect in the coffee maker, so it didn't shut off when it got too hot, but she was aware that it could easily have started a fire and burned the whole house down.

"But what if it's *more* than that?" she whispered as she frowned and stared at the cherry-red heating element. The raw rasp of her voice sounded as if someone else was whispering in the next room. Her body shook as she fought to gain control of herself.

What if my brain really isn't all right? she thought. *Or what if . . . what if subconsciously I meant to do it?*

The teasing touch of a chill danced up her spine to the base of her neck. Still leaning forward, she glanced to one side and saw her face reflected in the polished side of the toaster. The bandages wrapped around her head looked bad enough when she saw them in a mirror, but her reflection was distorted even more by the curved metal surface. It made her look like the failed experiment of some mad scientist.

"What if—" she whispered. Her breath burned in her chest. "What if—for some reason—I blame Edward for what happened to me?" She touched the bandages with both hands and winced. "For *this!*"

She took a deep, trembling breath, no longer caring that tears were spilling from her eyes, running freely down her cheeks.

"And what if I *meant* to do it? . . . What if I was *trying* to burn the house down just to get even with him?"

118

Chapter Eight
Night Cry

For everyone except Edward, July passed slowly, miserably into August.

In spite of the obvious tension between Dianne and Brian, Edward couldn't contain his growing excitement as work on his dream project — his own housing development — gradually took shape. After working most of his adult life as a carpenter for other people, he had recently quit his full-time job and gone into business with Fred Pierce, a high school friend of his who was now president of Summerfield Savings Bank. Their plan was to subdivide the family acreage into eight other large lots, keeping a generous portion for himself to build his own home after selling the lots. They had planned to build one house on spec, but after meeting with a prospective client for the past several weeks, they were close to wrapping up a package deal including the best of the eight lots and a new house, to be built by Edward. Because the land had been in Edward's family since Colonial days, the profits, even if he only sold half of the parcels, would easily finance construction of the new home he planned for himself and Dianne.

That was all if things fell into place, and just last week, the town planning board had given final approval for the entire project. They were waiting to hear if the clients could get financing, and if they did, Edward might be able to start clearing the land for the first house in a matter of weeks.

With the hurdle of getting town approval behind him, and the pressure of beginning actual construction still in the future, Edward took a few days off to do a few fun things with his family. The problem was, as she had since her accident, Dianne was feeling too miserable to travel very far. In fact, she hardly left the house at all, choosing instead to sit in the living room most of the day, either watching TV or reading. She still blamed the medication she was taking for messing her up, so she stayed home the day Edward took Brian to *Funtown U.S.A.*, in Saco.

Edward wondered why Brian still hadn't made friends around town with any of the kids his own age. Brian had told him he'd made a few attempts but had obviously backed down, complaining that he didn't find anyone he met interesting. They were just a bunch of "skate-rats," as he put it. This bothered Edward, who, other than a four-year stint in college, had lived his entire life in Summerfield and had plenty of friends and acquaintances around town. But most of his friends' children were older, many of them already in college. Besides, Edward was aware that he couldn't live his son's life for him, so he decided not to push him too hard.

"Boy, that Astrosphere was some fun, wasn't it?" Edward said on the drive home from *Funtown*.

Brian nodded and said, "Yeah," but his expression seemed to indicate otherwise.

"You know," Edward said, nudging Brian's arm, "your mother's going to be mad at me." When Brian didn't respond, he went on, "You've been here well over a month now, and you still haven't gotten a tan. She's going to think I kept you locked up in your room all summer."

"I got plenty of sun yesterday," Brian said, wincing as he raised his shirt sleeve to show the bright red burn on his shoulders he'd gotten after a day at Crescent Beach. He eased his sleeve back down and turned to face the window beside him, seemingly content as he watched the scenery slide silently past.

Edward wanted to confront Brian about what he was really feeling. He knew the boy had been miserable ever since coming to Maine, but as much as he wanted to do something about it, he wasn't sure what he could do. Dianne's accident and his own mother's death certainly had started the summer off horribly, and he wasn't at all confident that he would be able to pull the time they had left together out of its tailspin. He certainly was trying the best he could. His hope — which he knew was mostly selfish — was that things would be better now that he was going to start working on the new house. Maybe Brian could help him out at the construction site if he felt like it.

"So—" Edward said after they had ridden along in silence for a while. "Do you feel as though you're getting to know Dianne any better?"

Brian stiffened noticeably, his hands clenching into fists in his lap.

"I hope you understand," Edward continued, "that she's under a lot of pressure. I mean — she's not usually the way she's been . . . since the accident. She's a great person — a lot of fun. I wish you could see her under better circumstances."

"Uh-huh."

"She's still in a lot of pain, and I think the medication she's taking is messing her up quite a bit."

"I'll say," Brian said, his voice barely audible above the steady hum of the car.

"Well . . . I hope you realize that she genuinely likes you," Edward said, casting a quick glance over at his son. "She really does. I realize this has been a horribly tough situation — for both of you, and I hope you can — you know, get to like her better once you get to know her."

Brian took a deep breath but said nothing.

"I suppose you're aware that she has to go back into the hospital in a couple of days to have that second operation."

Brian nodded.

"The doctor explained everything to us yesterday. They're going to take the metal plates out of her face and do the first bit of facial reconstruction. You know, bone grafts and stuff like that to put her face back the way it was before the — the accident." Edward heaved a deep sigh. "You know, it's going to be tough . . . on *all* of us, so I just want you to know—"

He reached one hand out and gripped Brian's shoulder, giving it a gentle squeeze. Brian pulled away as he turned toward his father, but he kept his eyes focused downward.

"Your stepmother feels genuinely bad about how you and she don't seem to have hit it off so far."

"We don't *have* to hit it off," Brian said. His voice was trembling, and his lips pursed tight and nearly bloodless as he looked his father straight in the eye. "Besides, I already *have* a mother!"

Edward sucked in a breath to calm himself and held it for a second before speaking. "That's true," he said, pushing back the small stirring of anger and resentment just thinking about how their divorce made him feel. "But Dianne's my wife now, and while I would *never* expect her to take the place of your mother, I would hope—I really *want* you and her to get along better. When she comes home after this next operation, she's going to have more than enough to deal with without you getting on her nerves, all right?"

Brian stared straight ahead and said nothing.

"Do you understand me?"

"Don't worry," Brain said, hissing with frustration as he looked away, out his side window. "I'll do *everything* I *can* to avoid her!"

A soft wash of moonlight skimmed the windowsill like a dusting of blue powder. The night wind was warm, sighing gently as it wafted the bedroom curtains back and forth like translucent bellows. From outside, the soft, steady whirring song of crickets filled the night with a lulling buzz. The sound wasn't loud enough to mask the steady, deep sawing of Edward's slumber.

But sleep wouldn't come for Dianne.

She lay next to Edward, her eyes wide open as she stared up at the ceiling, which glowed eerily gray in the dim light. A sheen of sweat stood out on her forehead like cold dew. Her hands were clenched into tight fists at her sides, and she seldom blinked her eyes. She waited until her lungs actually hurt before taking another shallow breath. The sound of her pulse in her ears was like steady hammering, distantly heard through the bedroom walls.

Her mind was filled with turmoil as she struggled to sort out her thoughts and feelings about what was going to happen to her in the morning. Two days ago, Dr. Collett had reviewed the surgical procedure with her and Edward to help reassure her; but since then, all she could think was, *It's going to hurt! Hurt like hell! Maybe not during the surgery, while they're removing the screws and plates that are holding my jaw and cheek in place . . . but afterward, once the medication starts to wear off, it's going to hurt like hell!*

She rolled over onto one side and stared at the glowing red numbers of the digital clock.

11:57.

Almost midnight.

Shit!

She was scheduled to be admitted to the hospital before seven o'clock the next morning, so even if she fell asleep right now, she wouldn't get a full eight hours of sleep. Would they still operate, even if she wasn't well rested? She couldn't postpone the operation—she didn't *want* to—but it was something she dreaded and would just as soon not have to face. She wished there was some way she could simply avoid it.

"But there's no way out," she whispered out loud. She cringed at the thin, papery rattle of her voice in the still night. Tension roiled like acid in her stomach, sending cold, rippling waves through her arms and legs. Her body trembled as though wracked with fever. The heat underneath the elastic bandages that were wrapped around her face grew intense, almost intolerable. It was like a steady blast of flame from a blast furnace, searing her flesh. She imagined that some horrible, multi-legged creature, like the monster in *Alien,* had wrapped itself around her face and was squeezing . . . *squeezing* ever tighter, crushing her face, caving it in on itself. She could feel her skull collapsing inward, could hear the bones breaking, crackling like a snapping campfire. She wanted to scream out loud, but the wires held her jaw firmly shut. Anxiety and fear twined through her body like cold snakes. She was filled with the impulse to leap out of bed and rip the bandages from her face just so she could breathe.

To hell with it! So what if she spent the rest of her life looking like a twisted, scarred monster? That's what she was, wasn't she? That's what her face and her life had become! Nothing more than a horrible, mangled ruin! And she was losing her mind, too! Why not just say to hell with it all?

Her breathing came faster, roaring and hissing into her throat through the metal grill that held her jaw in place. Her vision became blurred as she stared up at the ceiling, swirling and pulsating in time to the heavy throb of her pulse.

I can't stand it! I can't stand it! I can't stand it!

Strong rushes of panic swept through her like a churning, ocean tide. Her body felt like it was no more substantial than a feather, being tossed back and forth over towering, black waves . . . rising and falling . . . rising and falling . . . and tomorrow morning, it would crash below onto the dark, rocky shore.

She tensed as the pure white sting of terror gripped her. Her mind replayed brief, brightly underlit fragments of her fall down that cliff. Once again, she felt her foot slip away from underneath her, almost as if the narrow ledge had been greased. Lying in bed, she experienced again that terrifying instant when she was falling backward, her arms whirling wildly as she tried to grab onto something — *anything* substantial, but she found nothing but air. She imagined hearing her scream echo off the distant mountains as she rolled down the slanting rock face and then, in an explosion of bright light against a black velvet background, slammed hard against the sharp rock at the base of the cliff.

Help me! Please! Help me!

A voice cried in her mind, wailing in the close darkness that held her. She couldn't move. Lying in bed — at the foot of the cliff — her body felt like an inert lump of clay, nothing more. She could feel nothing now . . . not even the pain.

Ashes to ashes . . . dust to dust . . .

She was vaguely aware of Edward as he moaned in his sleep and rolled over onto his back. His hand flopped to one side and brushed against her hip. The touch, although light, spiked through her like an electrical jolt, making her body spasm.

Wake up! she thought, struggling futilely to make some sound—any sound to alert her husband to her rising panic. *Please, Edward! For God's sake, wake up! Help me!*

But Edward snorted once and slept on undisturbed, unaware of his wife's raging torment.

Dianne's breathing was a rapid, ragged hissing as she sucked air through the metal mesh that filled her mouth. Her pulse raced jackrabbit fast. The room was nothing more than an indistinct, watery blur of pulsating shadows that deepened to pitch-black and, at the edges, took on vague, hand-like shapes that reached out and grabbed her, tugging at her, pulling her further down in a trailing, dark, backward tumble.

"No!" she shouted.

Twisted and muffled by the wires in her mouth, her voice thudded like a body punch in the darkness. She bolted up out of bed, feeling every muscle, every bone in her body cry out in agony. She whimpered softly because she was unable to scream aloud as she swung her feet to the floor. Completely disoriented, she felt as though the motion continued, tumbling her over and over as she spiraled forward into darkness. With a sharp intake of breath, she straightened up and grabbed at the mattress. She looked, terrified, at the moonlit windowsill, wishing it looked more substantial, more stable. Her pulse raced high and fast in her neck.

Just a dream, she thought. *I drifted off to sleep, and it was just a dream!*

The sound of the crickets outside in the darkness started to lull her. She forced herself to take several steady, even breaths as she took an edge of the bed sheet and wiped her face. Her gaze was fastened onto the billowing curtains as they shifted back and forth.

"Just a dream," she murmured, mildly surprised at the

sound of her own voice.

But as she leaned forward on the edge of the bed, commanding herself to calm down, she became aware of something else — a sound that was dancing just at the edge of hearing. Once she was consciously aware of it, she wondered how long it had been there. Her first thought was that Edward was moaning softly in his sleep, but then she realized that the sound — a faint, hitching cry — was coming from outside.

Could it have been there all along? she wondered. Was this what had disturbed her sleep and initiated her panic in the first place?

Someone was crying!

Again Dianne tensed, but she was vaguely grateful that at least now the threat seemed to be external. The sound curled in the darkness like a fluttering ribbon of smoke. It was there; then it was gone; then it was back again, teasing and weaving through the night.

Is that Brian, crying in bed? Dianne wondered.

Weak and trembling, she stood up. Her legs felt unable to support her as she took a few quick steps away from the bed, then turned to look back at her sleeping husband. She held her breath and listened to determine if it might have been him, but he slept on, his breath sipping in long, steady draws. She strained to listen but realized that the sound was gone. It had vanished as though it had been swallowed by the night. Dianne was almost convinced that she had imagined it along with everything else when it came again, rising and falling in the night, this time sounding like the distant, lonely howl of a wolf.

No . . . That sounds like a baby crying!

A light shiver raced up her back.

Moving carefully through the darkened bedroom, she reached blindly for the doorknob, turned it, swung the door open, and stepped out into the hall. Blackness as deep as sin filled the hallway. It fairly vibrated as she looked down toward Brian's bedroom. His door, like the rest of the hall, was lost in darkness, but she knew that it was closed, just as he

126

kept it every night. With one hand on the wall for guidance, she felt her way down toward her stepson's room, moving haltingly, shuffling forward a few steps, then stopping and craning her head forward to listen for the sound to be repeated. When it came again, it rippled teasingly in and out of hearing, sounding both fainter and closer at the same time.

Is it in my head?

As soon as she reached Brian's door, the sound stopped. Dianne held her breath and listened, but all she could hear was the muffled beat of her own pulse in her ears. She found the doorknob in the darkness and twisted it slowly, careful not to make a sound that might wake him up. The door angled open, and she peeked into the room, her gaze gravitating toward the indistinct lump on the bed.

"Brian . . . ?" she whispered.

She touched the wall switch, wanting desperately to turn on the light, but she was afraid the sudden brightness might startle Brian too much if he was asleep.

"Psst! . . . Hey, Brian . . . You awake?"

She waited for a response — or to hear the low crying sound again — but the room was as silent as a tomb. She knew Brian might indeed be awake and simply not wanting to answer her, so she waited a second or two, then whispered, "Are you okay?"

Still, there came no reply.

Her throat was dry with tension as she stepped back and eased the door shut, cringing when the latch clicked loudly into place. Then she made her way slowly back to her own bedroom. Sighing deeply, she eased herself gently onto the edge of the bed, then swung her legs up off the floor.

Maybe I dreamed that sound, too, she thought as she settled her head onto the pillow, momentarily enjoying the feeling of cool cotton.

She closed her eyes, forcing herself to put all thoughts of that mysterious crying as well as her upcoming operation out of her mind. She told herself she could handle the anxiety and agony of the next few days simply because she *had* to.

As she courted sleep, though, her memory spiraled back

again to the day of the accident on Mt. Chocorua. And other memories stirred—flashes and fragments of pain and surprise, as she snuggled her head down into the cool well of her pillow. When the soft sound of someone crying in the darkness came to her again like the lightest of touches, Dianne stirred but didn't rouse to wakefulness. Instead, she let the sound lull her off to sleep, carrying her deeper and deeper. The crying seemed to grow louder, and she felt herself rocking gently back and forth in time with it. At first she didn't know what was happening; then she realized that her arms and legs were confined; she was strapped onto a stretcher, and the stretcher was swaying gently back and forth as it was hoisted into the grasshopper-shaped belly of the helicopter that hovered overhead. The helicopter's rotor blades made mushy, thumping sounds as they beat the dark air. Below those sounds, the faint crying grew steadily louder.

At last, Dianne realized what it was.

From somewhere in the darkness around—outside the house? on the mountainside? from inside the helicopter?—a baby was crying. Its breath caught in sharp hitches between long, keening wails that rose louder and louder, filling the night.

Dianne's body swung back and forth with a steadily increasing rocking motion. When she looked up again, the dark underside of the helicopter had stretched out into something else—a thick, gray line that bisected the dark sky above her. A cold ripple of panic filled her when she saw that it was a gnarled tree limb.

The tightening grip clamped Dianne's arms to her sides, pinning her tightly. She rolled her head back and looked up at inch-thick rope that was looped several times around the tree branch. The sky overhead was a mass of roiling, tumbling, gray clouds veined with jagged white lines of lightning.

Pure, numbing terror filled Dianne. She tried to cry out, but the other end of the rope was wrapped around her neck, strangling her, squeezing ever tighter. Her tongue felt swollen, too large for her mouth; it pressed outward against her teeth, trapped behind the metal wires that kept her mouth shut and prevented her from screaming. Brilliant flowers of light popped like Fourth-of-July fireworks across her vision as she struggled to move her arms and legs. The pressure around her throat increased, stopping off all hope she had of making even the tiniest sound. Hammering white flashes — either lightning or some defect of vision — filled her eyes, searing her with pain. A muffled silence embraced her, broken only by the agonized wail of the baby, growing fainter with distance.

Someone! Help me! I can't breathe!

Dianne's mind was paralyzed with panic. The crying of the baby was drowned out by the steadily rising beat of her pulse as it throbbed in her head. Every nerve in her body was on fire. She imagined that, out of the darkness around her, dozens — no, hundreds of thin, black hands reached out for her, trying to pull her down into the darkness where she knew they would rip her to pieces.

"— I curse this man! May the Lord smite him and all the liars who have brought me to this untimely end! — "

The words filled Dianne's mind as though someone was standing right beside her, shouting them into her ear. Her body trembled as she strained to move an arm or a leg so she could turn and see who was speaking to her. The baby's crying continued, unabated.

"— None of ye shall escape the cleansing fire of the Lord's judgment! Do ye hear me? — "

The voice rang in the raging darkness like metal striking metal. The fire-edged night closed down around Dianne like smothering smoke as she looked frantically to both sides, trying to discover who was speaking. A heavy, gray cloak flapped behind her, sounding like the flutter of unseen wings in the dark.

"— I beseech the Lord in heaven to smite with just retribution whomever is living in my house! Let them and all their kin burn in the agony of hellfire! — "

". . . No-o-o-o-o! ! !"

The single word rose up inside of her mind like the shriek of a jet engine. Higher and higher it whined, louder and louder until it passed beyond hearing. With a nearly superhuman burst of effort, Dianne forced her arms to move. It felt as though every muscle up to her neck and shoulders ripped from the strain. Her stomach muscles contracted, and with a sudden roaring exhalation through her mouth, she jerked forward into a sitting position. Her vision pulsated with bright flashes as she looked around the darkened bedroom.

"Hey! Hey, honey! What's the matter?"

Edward's voice came to her from far away. Cringing and trembling with fright, Dianne listened for the crying baby but could hear nothing. When Edward's hand touched her from out of the darkness, she squealed and pulled away from him, mistrusting everything. She feared that his hand might suddenly grab her and drag her back down into the pure, freezing darkness that had almost claimed her.

She swallowed and tried to speak, but the muscles and tendons in her throat were ruined. Each gulp of breath felt like she was swallowing liquid fire.

"Hey, it was just a dream—just a dream," Edward whispered as his hands sought her in the dark and pulled her to him. Dianne's mind went blank with terror as his embrace pinned her arms down to her sides.

"No!—I—"

"There, there," he cooed as he stroked her hair back from her sweaty forehead. He cupped her chin in his hand, turned her to face him in the darkness, then kissed her forehead. "You just had a bad dream, that's all . . . Nothing more."

Hot tears welled up from deep inside her until they exploded in a shuddering gasp. She pressed her face hard against his shoulder and tried to shut out the rush of horrifying images that filled her mind.

"It was . . . it was *horrible!*" she said.

Her shattered voice, distorted by the wires in her mouth, still sounded like someone else was speaking. Maybe, she thought, it was that person who had spoken to her in her dream, saying words that, try as she might, she could no longer remember.

"There was a—a helicopter, and I was . . . was hanging

130

from it. I—" She touched her neck with one hand, surprised not to feel angry welts around her throat where the rope had chafed her. "I was . . . *hanging!*"

"Okay, okay . . . Just calm down, now. It's all over. It was only a nightmare."

"But it was so *real!*"

"Just relax. It's all over."

"But I . . . I hope you realize that I don't blame you," she said, sobbing as Edward hugged her close and massaged the muscles knotting up in the back of her neck. Her warm tears made the skin beneath her bandages feel unbearably hot.

"Honest—honey!" she said, forcing out each word as if it were her last. "I don't blame you . . . for what happened . . . to me!"

Chapter Nine
Red Ball

A thin blade of morning sun sliced around the edges of the drawn bedroom window shade. A flat laser angled across the floor and clipped one corner of Brian's bed. Gentle puffs of breeze shifted the shade back and forth like a limp sail; then it snapped loudly once when a door opened downstairs. Brian heard his father's footsteps click like a turning gun cylinder as he walked out to the garage. He heard him open the garage door, start up the car, then back out to the back door steps before killing the engine.

Brian lay on his bed with his hands clasped behind his head as he stared at the glowing line of white fire around the window edge. He kept his mind focused on the activity downstairs and outside. When his father came back into the house, the window shade snapped again. Brian heard his father and Dianne talking in hushed tones, but he wasn't able to tell what they were saying. He guessed they were eating breakfast before heading out to the hospital. Brian figured that, as always, Dianne was complaining about how miserable she felt . . . as if she could make things better by making his father — and him — just as miserable as she was.

Brian knew the drive to the Maine Medical Center in Portland would take at least an hour. He had no idea how long his dad planned to stay around there with Dianne, but he knew his father would spend some time getting her settled in her hospital room before the surgery tomorrow morning. Brian figured he'd have pretty much most of the day to himself, the whole morning, at least. Last night before bed, his dad had asked him if he wanted to come along with them for the day, but he had declined, saying he'd just as soon hang out at home. Thankfully, his father hadn't called up to him this morning, asking again if he'd like to come with them.

Of course, there was nothing to do at home, but it sure beat spending any more time than was absolutely necessary with Dianne.

As soon as his father shouted "We're leaving," and he heard the car start up again and pull away, Brian leaped out of bed. He quickly dressed in his standard jeans and dark green T-shirt, and went downstairs for breakfast. The silence of the house seemed oddly both relaxed and tense as he poured himself a glass of orange juice, fixed a bowl of Rice Krispies, and sat down at the kitchen table to eat.

With the sound of crunching cereal loud in his ears, he stared at the sunlight pouring through the kitchen window, unable to stop thinking about what he'd have planned for today if he were back home with his *real* friends. It frustrated him that he still hadn't connected with Nate Beck and his "good buds." He'd talked to them a few more times downtown, but it now seemed to Brian as though those boys were purposely snubbing him. His ears burned whenever he remembered them shouting out, *"Did you see that? Holy shit! The Old Witch Lady's back!"*

Indeed, she was!

Over the past several weeks, at least in Brian's mind, Dianne *had* turned into a horrible, deformed witch. What little he could see of her face beneath her bandages was deathly pale and scarred, like some freakish creation of Dr. Frankenstein's or, in fact, a witch who drank the blood of little children to stay alive. But, he told himself, it wasn't just Dianne's looks that made him dislike her—it was a lot more than that. It was her attitude, her entire personality that bothered Brian. With each passing day, he found himself wishing more and more that his father had never married

133

Dianne. Once or twice, he had actually wished that she had died in that fall from the cliff.

"That would have solved *everything*," he whispered.

His hand holding the spoon curled into a fist, and he slammed it down hard next to his cereal bowl, making Rice Krispies and milk slop out onto the table.

"And if she had, that sure as *hell* would have made *my* summer a whole lot better!"

The day grew steadily hotter, but it was cool in the shaded backyard, so Brian dragged the spiderweb-encrusted croquet set out of the garage, intending to play a game against himself. After pounding in the posts and setting up the wickets, though, his frustration about being by himself all the time crested. Simmering with anger, he lined up all of the colored balls side by side and then fired them, one by one, across the lawn. With each hit, he muttered, "Fuck *you!* Fuck *you!*" He knew exactly whose face he was picturing on every single wooden ball.

Hissing through clenched teeth, he stalked around the yard, slamming a croquet ball whenever he found one. It didn't matter which direction they went or if they even came close to the wickets, just as long as he pounded the crap out of them. When one went sailing off into the fringe of woods that bordered the yard, though, a chill raced up his back when he considered plunging into the dense brush after it.

Hey, what's the big deal? he wondered as he stood on the edge of the woods, crouching as he peered into the tangle of green. The ball — he thought it might be the red one — was out of sight. Lost. So what?

But then he thought, what if his dad noticed the ball was missing? What if he got into trouble for it?

"God*damn* it!" Brian whispered as his frustration rose even higher.

He pounded the ground with his mallet, making a rounded divot in the sod, then swung the mallet viciously at the brush. The rustling sound startled a bird, who flew up, squawking, from nearby in the woods. The sudden noise made Brian squeal and jump, but then he took heart. Determined to find the ball even if it took him all day, he plunged into the woods. What the hell did it matter, anyway? He didn't have anything better to do!

But after fifteen minutes of searching, he still hadn't found the ball. He thrashed through the underbrush, and several times went back out onto the lawn and tried to reenact the hit, but he couldn't get a line on where the ball might have gone. Had it rolled down into a woodchuck's hole or something? He considered getting the lawn mower out of the garage and plowing through the underbrush but decided against it. It was too hot for that kind of work, anyway.

But he didn't want to give up. He *had* to find that damned ball. It had become a matter of pride.

Brian wasn't sure when the feeling first hit him, but at some point while he was swatting the brush with his mallet, he realized that he was feeling odd . . . as if someone hidden nearby was watching him. The hairs at the nape of his neck prickled, and a light chill that had nothing to do with being in the shadows raced up his back. He paused and looked around but saw and heard nothing unusual. When the feeling that he was being watched spiked into certainty, he had to force himself to continue doing what he had been doing while he glanced furtively around, trying to see who it was.

"Damned ball!" he muttered, hoping to convince whoever might be listening that he didn't suspect anything, that all he cared about was finding his croquet ball.

He wanted to believe that he was imagining things, that he had simply gotten spooked — for whatever reason — and was letting his imagination get carried away; but as much as he tried to deny it, the woods seemed suddenly alive with menace. The dappled blue shadows deepened like spreading ink stains. The sluggish breeze in the pines made a faint whistling sound just at the edge of hearing. It sounded almost like someone nearby, breathing heavily. A rippling chill sprinkled Brian's arms with goose bumps. His eye tracked the distance back to the house as he mentally calculated how fast he could get back there. And then, like a bolt of lightning striking from a clear, summer sky, a memory hit him.

He'd had this feeling before!

That afternoon out at his grandmother's house!

Icy tension knotted in his stomach as he recalled that morning more than a month ago. While his father and Dianne had been going through the house, collecting the dead woman's things to give to Goodwill, he had gone into the backyard. Over by the rusted swing set, he had the feeling that he was being watched.

Could there really be someone out there in the woods? Was someone lurking around and keeping an eye on him, for whatever reason? Could it have been the same person then as now?

He squinted and stared into the woods but saw nothing except a riot of green light and dark shadows. Sure, someone could easily be hiding *anywhere* in there. Brian's breath came in shallow gulps. His throat felt raw and dry, and he squeezed the mallet handle so tightly he lost all feeling in his hands as he started moving slowly back toward the house. The impulse to start running was strong in him, but he maintained the facade of searching for the missing ball as he retraced his steps.

To hell with the croquet ball! he thought when his apprehension suddenly jolted into needle-sharp panic. Uttering a low cry, he doubled over and started running toward the house as fast as he could. He crossed the small yard in a flash, almost losing his balance when he leaped up onto the top porch step. Flinging the mallet aside, he fumbled to turn the doorknob. He was fearful that the door was locked, but — thankfully! — it turned, and the door swung wide open. He stumbled on the doormat and practically fell into the house. As soon as he was inside, he spun around, slammed the door shut, and bolted the lock with a wild swipe of his hand. Then, without pausing to catch his breath, he ran down the hallway to the front door and made sure that was locked. As soon as that was done, he checked the bolt on the cellar door, then raced all through the house, making sure the latches on all the windows were secured.

"Okay . . . okay! . . . Just calm down! . . . No one's out there! . . . Nothing's gonna happen!" he gasped, clutching his knees as he leaned forward and tried to catch his breath. A trickle of cold sweat made him shiver as it dripped down the back of his neck.

"You're safe now . . . Just take it easy!"

His voice sounded thin and tinny, and as much as he tried to convince himself otherwise, he *didn't* feel at all safe. He still felt exposed, still in danger, as if whoever might have been watching him from the woods was still hidden somewhere nearby and was still able to see him. From *somewhere,* unseen eyes were watching everything he did, every move he made.

"Jesus! Jesus! *Jesus!*" Brian muttered. He wished he still had the croquet mallet, but that was outside on the porch, and there was no way he was going back out there to get it—not until his father came back home. If he needed something to protect himself, he could find something else in the house—a kitchen knife or something.

"But this is *ridiculous!*" he said. He straightened up, squared his shoulders, and looked around the silent house. "I've got to get a grip!"

His sneakers made mouselike squeaks on the floor as he walked into the kitchen. His empty juice glass and cereal bowl were right there on the table where he had left them, but he looked past them to the counter, where the handle of the large carving knife stuck up out of the cutlery block. His hand was trembling as he grabbed the knife and pulled it out. Light glinted wickedly off the blade as he twisted it back and forth and whispered, "All right! So just try and scare me *now!*"

He glanced at the clock and saw that it was almost one o'clock—past time for lunch. He knew he should just act like nothing was wrong. The thing to do was make himself a sandwich, sit down and relax, and enjoy the rest of the afternoon. But his stomach was so twisted with alarm that he didn't feel at all hungry. He didn't think he'd be able to eat for a week!

When's Dad gonna be home? was the question topmost in

his mind. It'd be no problem to stay inside all afternoon if he had to. He could watch TV, play Nintendo, listen to music, or read—whatever!

But what if Dad doesn't show up until after dark?

The thought gnawed at his stomach like a hungry worm.

What if he calls and says he's going to spend the night in Portland so he can be with Dianne before her surgery tomorrow morning?

Still clutching the handle of the carving knife, Brian moved from the kitchen into the living room. He paused at the big picture window, crouching low and pushing the edge of the curtain aside with the knife blade so he could peek out at the heat-hazed afternoon. Everything looked peaceful, completely normal. There were no threatening shadows shifting in the fringe of woods across the road. No skulking figure darting quickly out of sight.

Was there really someone out there? he wondered over and over. *Or am I just making it up?*

Back home in Arizona, he had never been afraid to be left alone for a few hours. Lots of times his mother had to work late at the real estate office, and he had to get supper for himself and sometimes even go to bed before she got home. He'd never had a problem with that before, so why now?

Was it just the unfamiliarity of this house? This town? This whole damned state of Maine? What was it about this place that was getting to him so badly?

It couldn't simply be his father's house. He'd felt just as threatened, just as vulnerable that other day out at his grandmother's house. So what was it? Was it only a fabrication of his loneliness? . . . Or was there *really* someone out there, hanging around the area and spying on him?

But why would anyone do that?

He knew he couldn't settle down and get involved in anything to distract himself, so he started going through the house again, pausing at each window and looking out to see if he caught sight of anyone out there, crouching in the woods or hiding out behind the garage. There wasn't a hint of trouble, but just to be sure, he decided to check the locks on each door one more time. First he checked the front door, then the cellar door, and finally the back door. At each one, he stopped and looked outside, gripped by the cold fear that some horribly mutilated face — maybe something even worse than Dianne's face — would suddenly slam up against the glass, slobbering and snarling as it glared in at him. He tried to keep such thoughts at bay, but they became increasingly vivid and real in his mind. Even so, he wasn't prepared for what he saw when he went to the back door window and peeked out into the backyard. His heart literally skipped a beat, and his mind got dizzy for a moment. There, balanced like a fragile egg on the newel post of the porch, was a round, red, wooden croquet ball. Leaning against the post just below the ball was the mallet he had flung aside before opening the door.

"Oh, God! Oh, Jesus — God!"

He backed away from the door until he bumped into the opposite wall. Then his legs gave out from under him. His nerveless hand let go of the knife as he slid slowly to the floor. Every muscle in his body was trembling as he brought his hands up to his face, covered his eyes, and released his pent-up anxiety in a single, long, anguished wail.

Chapter Ten
Removal

Around one o'clock that next afternoon, Dianne was starting to regain consciousness in the recovery room.

As her mind drifted slowly out of the anesthesia-induced fog, her first clear thought was how she had never been more frightened in her life than when they had wheeled her into the operating room before the second operation. Other than Dr. Collett, who had greeted her with a friendly smile before donning his surgical mask, the nameless, surgically-masked, green-clad mass huddling around her had made her extremely nervous. The anesthesiologist had smiled as she administered "just a little squirt" of sodium pentathol, but Dianne thought she had detected a leering, almost wolfish quality in the woman's eyes.

As she faded away, Dianne had tried to hold on to the thought that everything was going to be all right after this, but in the throes of a drug-induced nightmare, the medical assistants and physicians were transformed into a dangerous, threatening force — a circle of demons with eyes glowing like angry red coals above their masks as they cackled with laughter before sending her spiraling down into the depths of hell. Then there had been simply . . . nothing. She had plummeted down, deeper and deeper . . . forever into a bottomless, black hole.

But now, waking up groggily with blurred vision and a distant, pulsating memory of pain, Dianne knew that — no matter what else — her face still wasn't back to normal, and it wouldn't be for at least six more months, possibly a year.

Intellectually, she knew and could accept what had happened to her. Before the operation, Dr. Collett had described in graphic, at times gruesome detail the hemicoronal incision they would make from the bridge of her nose up around her hairline and down in front of her ear so he could peel back her facial skin and restore her left cheekbone, using a piece of cancellous bone taken from her hip. An incision underneath the edge of her jaw would allow him to reconstruct the shattered portion of her upper and lower jaw. Using a computer imaging system and what he called a "cephalometric X ray," he had explained how they would remove the screws, wires, and metal plates that were holding her jaw and cheek in place, and then apply two types of bone grafts — interpositional and onlays — to rebuild the bony structure of her face. Of course, after this her jaw would be wired shut for another six weeks while it all healed.

Dianne's biggest concern was that even after all of this was done, she still would not look like herself, that when the operation was over and she was healed and the wires were removed from her teeth, she would look into the mirror and see a person she wouldn't even recognize. Dr. Collett acknowledged that there obviously was a chance of this happening; he couldn't guarantee that she would look *exactly* as she had before her accident, but he reassured her that, by using photographs of her and the intact structure of the right side of her face as guides, he didn't expect there would be much of a problem in her case. He had warned her, though, that even after this operation, once the swelling went down, her face still would not be back to normal. There would be "some slight soft tissue deficiencies," he had called them, as well as scarring that would require one more plastic surgery operation before she truly looked like herself again.

If I'm ever going to look like myself again, she thought bitterly. *Why did this have to happen to me? It could have happened to anyone, but why me?*

The heavy clouds in her mind swirled and parted but didn't disperse entirely.

How can anyone go through something like this and not be changed? Even if the doctor gets every single detail of my face exactly right, I'll never be the same person I was . . . I'll never be "me" again!

The thought reverberated in her mind like someone banging with a hammer on an oil drum. She struggled hard to get away from it, and once or twice thought she heard a soothing voice, telling her simply to relax, that she was doing just fine; but she couldn't let go of that single thought as it tugged her once again down . . . down into the swirling darkness.

I'll never be me again . . . . I'll never be me again!

"I — I don't know who it was! If I knew, then I wouldn't be so — so — "

Brian cut himself off, but his father finished the sentence for him: " — So nervous about staying home alone . . . right?"

Brian smirked and shrugged as he stared blankly out the side window of the car. They had driven north on Route One and were now moving slowly down Congress Street in Portland, heading to the Maine Medical Center to visit Dianne. On the car seat between them was a bundle of roses, a "Get Well" card they had both signed, and a handful of paperback romance novels his dad had picked up at the Waldenbooks in the mall. All during the drive, Brian had been conscious of the irritating, hypnotic drone of the car's engine, but that sound had been preferable to conversation — at least to *this* conversation. He bit his lower lip and wished to hell he had never mentioned to his father what had happened yesterday. He was relieved that — at least — he hadn't told him *everything*.

"You know," his father continued, "a lot of people go fishing out there to the river. There's a couple of real nice coves I used to fish in as a kid. Actually, we should take an afternoon off sometime soon and do a bit of fishing ourselves." He

142

sighed and shook his head with frustration. "It's just that now I'm so damned busy with these house plans and all. You know . . . I'll just bet it was someone from town passing by. Maybe it was those kids you told me about."

"Yeah . . . probably," Brian replied, wishing his voice didn't sound quite so shaky.

They drove along in silence for a while, but then, as he was turning into the hospital parking lot, his father cleared his throat and continued as if there hadn't been any lapse in their conversation, "If you think it's a problem, I could talk to Jake Crockett down at the police station about it. He could ask around some and keep an eye open for anything suspicious."

"Naw!" Brian said. "I don't think it was anything. I probably imagined the whole thing, anyway."

But even before he was finished speaking, a wave of chills slithered up his back. There was no way he could have imagined all of it! He certainly hadn't imagined that red croquet ball out of the brush and up onto the porch post. And he knew damned well that he had thrown his mallet, not leaned it up against the porch railing. No matter *what* he or his father thought or said, *someone* had been out there in the backyard watching him at least long enough to see him blast that croquet ball off into the woods. And that *someone* had retrieved the lost ball and come right up to the house and purposely placed it on the post. The only thing that gnawed at Brian was, if whoever had done that meant any trouble, if they had wanted to hurt or kill him, they probably wouldn't have made their presence known in such a subtle, inoffensive way.

Subtle — yes, but scary, too . . . unnerving. Ever since yesterday afternoon, Brian couldn't stop wondering: *who would have done something like that?*

Like his dad said, it had probably been someone just passing by — someone out for a hike in the woods out behind the house or heading down to the river to go fishing or swimming. Someone who certainly hadn't meant him any harm . . . who had, in fact, helped him out by returning the lost croquet ball.

But who the hell could it have been?

If they were friendly, then why didn't they reveal themselves? Why play a sneaky little trick like that and then leave?

"Well, I just might mention it to Jake tomorrow, anyway," his father said, and that seemed to be the end of it. He flipped his turn signal and turned left into the hospital parking lot. He drove past the parking lot attendant's booth, took a ticket from the automatic machine, then pulled to a stop in an open parking space and shut off the engine. Before getting out of the car, he turned to Brian, placed a hand gently on his shoulder, and said, "Now look here, son. I'm gonna say this for the last time. I don't expect you to be all that excited about seeing Dianne, but I'm asking you — as a favor to me — to at least be nice to her, all right? Show her a little bit of concern, all right?"

"Sure," Brian said, feeling his expression tighten. Again, he found that he couldn't maintain eye contact with his father for very long.

"She's probably experiencing a lot of pain and worry right now. I shouldn't have to remind you how — how tough this has all been on her. You've got to try and see things from her point of view."

"Yeah, yeah! I know!"

"I'm just saying, you don't have to act like you — well, like you really like her, okay? I know you and she haven't exactly hit it off yet, but just be civil. I'm sure if it was you who'd had such a bad accident, she'd be as concerned about you as your mother would."

"Don't worry, all right?" Brian said tightly, but he was thinking, *Yeah, I doubt it!*

He pulled away from his father's touch, snapped open the car door, and stepped out into the hot afternoon sun. Heat waves rippled like water up from the baking asphalt. He locked the car door and slammed it shut behind him, shivering in spite of the heat as he looked up at the foreboding building. The old part of the hospital with its brooding, Victorian-era architecture etched in black against the heat-hazed sky towered above him like something straight out of a horror movie. As he and his father crossed the street to the hospital's main entrance, he couldn't stop thinking about how truly terrible he expected his stepmother to look.

He tried to push aside the thought, but he couldn't stop imagining what he *might* have seen there at the back door yesterday . . . his stepmother's mutilated face, pressed flat against the glass, drooling like a rabid dog as she stared in at him, her lips peeled back in a sick mockery of a smile that exposed the network of wires holding her jaw in place. Jagged scars like white bolts of lightning zigzagged across her face, and in her curled, gnarled hand, she held out to him a battered, red croquet ball and hissed, *"Wanna play?"*

"Hey, how you feeling?" Edward asked as he eased open the heavy door and tiptoed into Dianne's hospital room with Brian shuffling in a few paces behind him.

Dianne rolled her head to one side and looked up at him, forcing a smile which exposed her wired, discolored teeth.

"I've been . . . better," she rasped.

Edward's first sight of her sent a jolt of shock and fear racing through him. Her face—at least what little he could see of it beneath the bandages—was as pale as a corpse's except for around her eyes, where prune-purple bruises as dark as a football player's greasy eye smudges gave the impression that her eyes were sinking back into her head. A brick-red crust of dried blood streaked from both nostrils to her upper lip. Because of the swelling, her neck looked almost twice as thick as usual. Even her hair, which normally was so full and beautiful, was nothing more than a limp mass of dark brown snarls sticking out from underneath the elastic bandage.

"Well, I hope you're gonna be feeling a whole *lot* better real soon," Edward said. He approached the bed, leaned forward, and kissed her lightly on the forehead. Taking a deep breath and trying his damndest not to let his reaction show, he sat down on the edge of the bed, forgetting for a moment all about the card, roses, and books he was holding. He cast a quick glance over his shoulder at Brian but didn't say anything to him as his son shifted over to a corner of the room and leaned against the wall, his arms folded tightly across his chest as if he were standing outside in the winter cold.

Turning back to his wife, Edward said, "Oh. Here—these are for you." He displayed the roses, bringing them up close to her face so she could take a feeble sniff of their fragrance.

"Umm . . . They're . . . beautiful," Dianne whispered. "Thanks."

"Got some books for you, too," Edward said. " 'Course, I don't expect you'll be feeling up to reading for a few days."

He held the paperbacks up to show her the covers, wishing all the while that he didn't feel so goddamned awkward in front of her. At least for this first time, he thought, maybe it would have been better if Brian had waited outside in the car. Brian certainly wouldn't have given him any argument, but it was too late to change that now.

"If you've—ahh, already read any of these, they said at the store that I can exchange them."

Dianne nodded but said nothing, obviously wanting to save her voice if she could. Edward put the books and card on the table beside her, then got up and gently laid the roses on the windowsill. "I'll have to ask the nurses about getting a vase or something to put these in, huh?"

As soon as his back was turned to her, a cold, clinging tightness filled his chest. In the back of his mind, he was hoping that it had just been the initial shock of seeing Dianne that had made her look so bad; but when he turned around and looked at her again, he couldn't deny—even with the most optimistic outlook that he could muster—that she looked like hell. Dr. Collett had warned him about the bleeding, the swelling, and the discoloration, but—*Christ on a cross!*—she looked as bad, maybe even worse than the day she fell off the cliff!

He sat back down on the edge of the bed and took her hand into his, giving it a gentle but bracing squeeze. His stomach did a sour little flip when he thought about how cold and lifeless her returning grip was—as if in the operation the doctors had removed the bones from her hands.

"Hey, Brian. Why don't you come on over here and say

hi — " Edward said, turning and waving him to the bed.

Brian took a few tentative steps forward as if he were walking through a field of armed bear traps, then stopped halfway between the bed and the wall. He nodded curtly and said, "I . . . umm, I hope you're feeling better soon."

"Right now . . . I feel like . . . a piece of . . . homemade . . . shit," Dianne said, her voice barely above a whisper. The corners of her mouth twitched into what was supposed to be a smile, but even to Edward it looked like a silent shriek of pain.

Brian looked as though he was about to say something more, but then he shrugged, backed away, and resumed his position with his back against the wall. Edward didn't know whether to be shocked at Dianne's crassness or happy at her attempt at some humor. Finally, he attributed her loose language to the effects of the pain medication she was on and tried to put it out of his mind.

"Oh, by the way," he said, "I've got some dynamite news for you."

A warm current of excitement filled him, but it was tempered as Dianne stared up at him with hooded eyes; it obviously took a great deal of effort for her to keep her gaze focused on him.

"You know how hard we were working with the Cliffords, for that new house."

Dianne made a slight grunting noise as she nodded.

"Well, they got approved by the bank and we've agreed on a price for the whole deal. They've got the lot right there on the corner of Pond Road and Stackpole — the farthest one from our house, actually. We'll be closing the deal in a day or two and can start work on it any time after that."

Dianne's eyes flickered as she looked up at him. Her lips moved, but no sound came out. Edward honestly couldn't tell if she was trying to respond or if the motion was involuntary.

"God, sometimes I had the feeling it would *never* happen, but — well, it looks like we're in business. Isn't that great? They want to meet with us tonight to finalize some of the last details on the house plan, so I figure after we sign those contracts, I can start clearing the land in a couple of days. Pretty exciting, huh?"

He still had hold of her hand and, in his excitement, gave it a tight squeeze.

"What do you think?"

Dianne moved her lips, apparently trying to say something; but before she could, her throat made a strange clicking sound as if she were gagging. She grabbed the plastic bowl from her bed stand and lurched forward just as her stomach convulsed. A bright wash of bloody vomit came squirting out between the wires in her mouth and splashed into the pan.

Surprise and panic slammed through Edward. He watched, immobilized for a moment as Dianne vomited into the bowl. The only sounds in the room were the strangled, bubbly noises issuing from her throat and the splattering blood. Once Edward was sure she wasn't choking, he dashed into the bathroom, wet a washcloth with cold water, and returned, handing it to her. Dianne wiped her face as best she could and, as soon as the convulsions were past, eased her head back onto the pillow. Edward flushed the contents of the pan down the toilet.

"Jeeze, honey," he said, as he came back to the bed and took the pink-stained cloth from her. "Do you think I should call the nurse?"

Dianne shook her head. "No . . . That's the . . . third time . . . today," she whispered. "Doctor says it's . . . normal."

"To be puking that much blood?" Edward said, dabbing gingerly around her mouth. He didn't want to hurt any part of her swollen face.

"Don't worry . . . they said this . . . might happen . . . but anyway . . . I — I'm . . . real happy . . . about your news . . . honey."

Her eyes rolled back in her head, exposing the whites, which had turned a sour yellow color. Her hospital johnny and the bed sheet were sprinkled with blood, but she looked as though she was comfortable, so Edward decided not to call the nurse.

"I — I'm real happy . . . for you."

"For *us*," Edward said, his voice trembling with intensity. "I know you're probably feeling too beat to talk about it right now, but you know — I think this is really it! This is the turning point . . . for *both* of us."

Again, he squeezed her hand, wishing to God he could feel some response, but her hand was as limp as a dishrag in his grip. He couldn't look away from the tangles of blood dripping from the wire grill inside her mouth.

"I — I think, after all the . . . you know, after all the misery and shit we've been through so far this spring and summer, what with what happened to you and my — " His voice caught in his throat for a moment. "With my mother dying and all, I think this is it. You've had the second operation now, and I've got a done deal to build at least one house. I think — I *hope* we're finally turning the corner."

Dianne's head bobbed up and down, but Edward couldn't tell if it was in response to what he was saying or if she was exhausted from throwing up. The medication obviously was dragging her back under, but undaunted, he continued, "At last, we're going to make some *real* money, and you know what I've been thinking?"

Dianne's only response was a faint brightening in her eyes as her head rolled gently to one side. Her hand slipped from his grasp, but he quickly picked it up again.

"I've been thinking about this a lot, you see, and well, we both agreed that the house we're living in now is too small for us and we want to build something new — especially if we're thinking of having a baby sometime. I think, maybe as soon as this fall, we should tear down the old homestead, my mother's house, and build that house we wanted right there, using the old foundation. What do you think?"

Dianne made no reply. The glow in her eyes faded as her gaze drifted past him to the flat, blue square of sky outside the hospital window. A thin line of bloody drool ran from the corner of her wired mouth and down her neck. Edward wiped it away with the stained washcloth.

"Hell, that old relic is better than two hundred and fifty years old, and now that my mother's gone, we should just be rid of it. God, there isn't a single ninety degree angle in the whole house! And I—I want to do something special for you."

He began to say something about how there were too many painful memories bound up inside that old house, but he happened to glance over his shoulder at Brian. Sickened by the sight of blood, he was looking down at the floor. He seemed not to be paying the slightest bit of attention to what his father was saying, but Edward felt a twist of guilt, recalling that he had just mentioned the possibility of him and Dianne having a baby together. He thought guiltily that he should have said something about wanting Brian to live with them, maybe even for the whole school year, and go out to Arizona to stay with his mother during summer vacations, but the opportunity seemed to have passed.

"But—well." He looked back at Dianne. "No matter what we think about the house, it has a *beautiful* yard, and—especially if we sell all eight lots—we should have more than enough money to build whatever we want out there. Won't that be great, honey?"

He watched as her eyelids gently slid shut and her breathing slowed, bubbling softly in her throat. He placed her hand on her chest and patted it; then brushed his hands together and got up from the bed.

"Well, you just rest up for now, honey, and get your strength back," he whispered. He wondered if she could even hear him; her breathing was a steady, deep hissing that sounded like she was sleeping. "We've got a lot to talk and think about, but we've got plenty of time, too." He glanced over at Brian, who apparently hadn't moved a muscle since entering the room. "I—I'll come back tomorrow. Maybe you'll feel more up to talking then."

He leaned forward and kissed her again, then turned and left the room. All during the drive back home, he felt too emotionally drained to mention to Brian how upset he was that he hadn't shown Dianne the slightest bit of attention or concern. Even when she had been vomiting blood, he had just stood there, as if he was grossed out by the whole thing . . . as if he didn't even care about her.

But Edward consoled himself with the thought that summer wasn't over yet. In four or five days, once Dianne was home from the hospital, Brian would have plenty of opportunities to get to know her better . . . and maybe he'd even get to like her.

The entire time Edward was visiting with her, Dianne never saw his face clearly. He appeared to her only as a looming, black silhouette harshly outlined against the blue sky behind him. Whether he was standing beside her or sitting on the bed, holding her hand, it had looked as though he was swaying gently back and forth, from side to side, like a ponderous pendulum suspended from the ceiling. The image reminded her of her own dream about hanging from the bottom of the helicopter. It filled her with a cold, dark dread.

As soon as he left the room, she drifted back deeper into herself, but she didn't fall asleep. She was hovering somewhere between sleep and wakefulness, between life and death. Her mind played back snippets of their conversation. She tried to focus on what he had said, but after a while, it all blurred together, mixing with other words, other voices that echoed from deep inside her memory . . .

"I think this is it . . . I think—I hope we're finally turning the corner . . ."

"This is my land! . . ."

"She should be coming around soon, but she's going to be pretty groggy for a while . . ."

"Hell, that old relic is better than two hundred and fifty years old . . ."

"This oak tree, which soon will bear my lifeless body like some unrighteous fruit, is on my property! . . ."

"It took longer than I thought it would . . ."

"All the misery and pain we've been through so far this spring and summer . . ."

"And I tell ye all this. I curse this man! May the Lord smite him and all the liars who have brought me to this

151

untimely end! . . ."

"A Hemi-Leforte II midface fracture and a communited displaced left zygoma fracture . . ."

"My soul is as pure as I know thine is black . . ."

"It looks a lot worse than it really is, but she's going to be in quite a bit of pain for quite some time . . ."

"None of ye shall escape the cleansing fire of the Lord's judgment! Do ye hear me?"

"Do ye hear me?"

Chapter Eleven
Escapee

After a full five days in the hospital, Dianne was released early Sunday afternoon. The medication she was on was helping cut the edge of her pain, but still, usually about an hour or so before her next dosage was due, the nerves in her face and neck began to feel like they were on fire. After a few days, the swelling had started to go down. The nearly constant bleeding from her nose had finally slowed but not entirely stopped. Thankfully, after that first day, she was no longer vomiting blood.

The day was sunny and warm, with a tumble of purple thunderheads off to the west. Dianne rode a wheelchair down to the front door, said her goodbyes to the nurses, and walked with Edward out the front door. As soon as she was outside, she leaned her head back and took a deep breath, wishing to God she felt well enough to enjoy her first day out of the hospital. But after having been cut off from "real life" for nearly a week, all she felt was weak and disoriented. The sunlight dazzled her as Edward, supporting her with his arm around her waist, walked her down the walkway to his car, which was parked at the curb.

"God, I feel like an escapee, making a prison break," she said, glancing nervously over her shoulder up at the tall hospital building.

"Then let's make a clean getaway before they catch us and

bring us back," Edward replied, laughing perhaps a bit too heartily as he reached for the car door and opened it for her.

"Com'on! Let's go!"

In spite of their joking, Dianne cringed at the sound of her own voice. It was still distorted by the wires in her mouth. It had been almost two months since her accident, now, and she was beginning to think that she was never going to be able to eat or talk normally again. Just thinking about the possibility of having to go back into the hospital made her shiver. And deeper, darker doubts and fears slithered around inside her like blind worms.

Edward held the car door open for her as she eased onto the front seat. The cushion was warm from sitting in the sun, but she hardly noticed it. Right now, all she wanted to do was get home, take a dose of medicine, and go straight to bed. Before saying goodbye, the attending doctor had told her there were only three things she had to do for the next few weeks — rest, rest, and rest.

"So, Brian didn't feel like coming in with you to pick me up, huh?" Dianne asked. Moving in slow motion, she pulled the seat belt around her and snapped it shut.

Edward shook his head. "No, he — uh, he said he had some things he wanted to do around the house." He shrugged. "Kids . . . you know?"

He closed her door and came around to the driver's side. After tossing her suitcases onto the back seat, he slid in behind the steering wheel and started up the car. But before he pulled away, he looked over at her with genuine concern wrinkling his brow.

"I just hope you're not too upset . . . about tonight, I mean."

Dianne regarded him in silence for a moment, she took a deep breath and shook her head.

"Of course I'm not upset," she said. "If you think it's absolutely crucial to meet with your clients tonight, then you have to be there." She sniffed and winced, tasting the coppery sting of blood on the back of her tongue. "I don't expect I'll be much company for you, anyway."

154

Edward took her hand and gave it a gentle squeeze. "You'll *always* be good company for me, you got that?" He smiled at her, trying to convince himself that the horrible rictus that split her mouth was, in fact, a smile. "But we've already sited the foundation, and I'm going to start clearing the land first thing tomorrow morning. Because they've been so wishy-washy about a few points, I want to meet with the Cliffords one last time and make *sure* they're satisfied with the location and all. It's just that I — I feel a little bit guilty, you know, leaving you like this on your first night home."

"Don't worry about it. I'll be all right," Dianne said. "Besides, Brian will be there if I need anything."

Edward nodded, shifted the car into gear, and drove away.

They spoke very little during the drive home. Dianne leaned her head against the headrest and dozed off now and again. She woke up with a start every time Edward took a sharp turn or slowed down for a stoplight. Not wanting to disturb her, he let her sleep and tried his best to drive without too many sudden moves.

They stopped at the LaVerdier's Drugstore in downtown Summerfield so Edward could run in and fill her prescriptions for pain killers and antibiotics while she waited in the car. Dianne felt horribly self-conscious when a mother and her five-year-old son walked by, and the little boy glanced in and saw her, leaning her forehead against the glass. His face registered such genuine shock and fear, Dianne was stung. The boy wrinkled his nose with disgust and said something which, thankfully, Dianne couldn't make out. The boy's mother glanced at her, then jerked the boy's arm, pulling him roughly along behind her. Tears welled up in Dianne's eyes as she watched them go, but she wiped them away before Edward came back out of the pharmacy.

When they got home, Brian didn't even bother to come out of his room to say hello to her. The thumping sound of heavy metal music shook the walls until Edward knocked on the door and told him to turn it down or else use headphones. When he still didn't come out to see Dianne, she made excuses for him which Edward begrudgingly seconded. Then, while

155

Edward went back out to the car to get her suitcases, she took a dose of her medication and went upstairs. She changed into a comfortable nightie, pulled the curtains, and crawled into bed, grateful — at last — to be home.

Within seconds she was asleep, and for the first time in more than a week, she slept a deep, dreamless sleep . . . that is, until the telephone rang.

"The beast is back," Brian whispered.

Late afternoon was quickly fading into evening. He was sitting on his bed, his back propped against the wall as he listened to music through headphones. He was desperately trying to lose himself in the music, but he couldn't stop staring at the cassette tape case in his hands.

The band was called Necrophobia. Pictured on the cover of the aptly titled *Caged Fury* was a distorted face in close-up. The rotting skin was hanging in gray shreds from the skull which was riddled with gaping holes. Maggots and worms were crawling out of the holes, and thin rays of green laser light were shooting out. A thick glob of blood, glowing slickly black and red, dripped like a tear from one eye, but it was the eyes and mouth that held Brian's attention. The lips were skinned back, exposing a grimace of rotting teeth and black gums; the eyes were wide open, exposing glistening orbs veined with red. The mouth and both eyes were wired open with strands of metal tied off in knots like barbed wire that pierced through the upper and lower lips and eyelids.

A few days ago while at the Maine Mall, when his father had gone down to the bookstore to get Dianne some books, Brian had drifted down to Tape World. The cover art on the album had immediately grabbed his attention, and he had bought it even though he had never heard of the band before. The music was loud and aggressive, particularly the song titled "Let's Kill Her." Brian played the tape several times a day and couldn't stop thinking about how much the cover art reminded him of his stepmother.

But now, thinking about her sleeping in the room right next

156

to his, he was filled with a hot current of rage. As the song wailed on in a deafening crash of guitars and drums, he cocked his arm back and threw the case as hard as he could against the bedroom wall. With his headphones on, he didn't hear the sound of the impact, but he smiled with satisfaction to see the plastic case explode into dozens of pieces. Ripping off the headphones, he slammed them onto the bed and, clenching his fists tightly, shook them at the ceiling and said in a low, vibrating growl, "Yeah! The *beast* is back all right!"

Edward was surprised to see a light on upstairs in the bedroom window when he pulled into the driveway a little after eleven o'clock that night. He had been hoping Dianne would be sleeping peacefully, so any elation he might have felt about starting work in the morning instantly evaporated. Twisting with guilt and thinking that she might have been awake for hours, wracked with pain, he hurriedly parked the car, pulled down the garage door, and ran inside. Taking the steps two at a time, he went upstairs to find her sitting up in bed. She was propped against the headboard with two pillows, leaning forward and hugging her legs. Her body was hunched up either with tension or pain. Her face was pinched with anger.

"Hey, I thought you'd be—"

"Why didn't you tell me?" she shouted. Through the metal wire, her voice fairly hissed with anger as her fingers wove together, twisting like a knot of earthworms.

Edward stopped in the doorway and leaned on the doorjamb, trying to catch his breath. After glancing down the hallway at Brian's closed door, he turned to her, shrugged, and said, "Tell you what?"

"About your fucking brother!"

"My . . . brother?"

That was the most he could manage before the walls seemed to come crashing down on top of him. His ears throbbed with the sound of her voice, and his whole body went cold. The air in the room seemed suddenly stale.

"Yes! Your *brother!*" Dianne snarled.

157

She punched the bed, then swung her legs to the floor. She looked as if she was about to stand up, but then discovered that she didn't have the strength, so she slumped back down onto the pillows.

"You got a call—*another* call from Reed Park Hospital in Massachusetts tonight. From a Dr. Timothy Samuels. Does the name ring a bell?"

Edward considered saying it didn't but knew that lying wasn't going to work, so he nodded slightly.

"Dr. Samuels said he wanted to let you know—he wanted to 'bring you up to date,' he said—that they still hadn't *located* your *brother.*" Her voice twisted up high until it broke. She slouched back and sucked in a deep breath that hissed through the wires in her mouth. Clenching her fists, she pressed them against her forehead as if trying to stop her head from exploding.

"*Still* hadn't found him! Where *is* he? What's he *talking* about? Tell me, what the *hell* is going *on?*"

"I—uh, well, you see . . ."

Edward rolled his eyes ceilingward, fighting back the wave of dizziness that gripped him.

"Don't even *try* to bullshit me, all right?" Dianne yelled. "That phone call scared the living *shit* out of me! That doctor, whoever the hell he is, acted like this was something I should have known about!"

Edward took a deep, steadying breath, held it, then let it out slowly before walking over and sitting down on the edge of the bed. He placed his head in his hands and shook his head as a deep tremor ran through his arms and legs. He started to reach for her, but she shied away from him as if he had a contagious disease. A hard lump formed in his throat and wouldn't go down no matter how hard he tried to swallow.

"I mean, I—I can't *believe* the things I'm thinking right now," Dianne said in a low, measured voice.

Beneath her bandages, her face was flushed bright red. Her panting breath whistled between her teeth. Edward knew it wasn't good for her to be this upset, but flashing through

158

his mind was the panicked thought: *How much can I tell her? How much do I dare to tell her?*

"Well," he said, "I told you I had a brother. That was no secret." His voice sounded weak and trembling.

"Oh, sure — you *told* me about him! You told me that he lives 'somewhere' in California, and that you never see him — never even write or call! So what's with this call from Reed Park Hospital? Remember, I used to live in Massachusetts. I know damned right well what Reed Park Hospital is! It's a mental hospital. A nuthouse!"

"A psychiatric care facility," Edward said softly. "And — yeah, okay, maybe I didn't tell you the whole truth about Michael —"

"His name really is Michael? So I can at least believe *that* much of what you told me, huh?"

Edward nodded. He tried to look her squarely in the eye but found that he couldn't. Waves of guilt and worse feelings swelled up inside him.

How much can I tell her? How much do I dare to tell her?

"Yes. His name's Michael — Mikie, we all called him growing up. And yes — he *is* in a mental hospital . . . has been for the past —" He took a deep breath and, eyelids fluttering, blinking back the tears, looked up at the ceiling. "For the past thirty years. He — he's been diagnosed as severely schizophrenic. Really bad off. It's true that I don't contact him very much — only once or twice a year at most."

Dianne nodded, but she was still trembling as she leaned forward, her body tensed.

"He was committed . . . back when we were kids," Edward said. He slouched forward with his hands folded down between his knees, staring intently at the floor. A cascade of frightening memories filled his mind. The throbbing sound of his pulse in his ears grew steadily louder until it sounded like an overworked engine.

"You see, back when I was twelve, Mikie was ten, we were out playing in the — in an old building. A couple of my friends were kind of teasing Mikie. You know how kids can be when there's someone who's a little bit . . . different, you know?

Anyway, the best everyone can piece it together, they started chasing Mikie through this old building, and Mikie — well, I guess he jumped out from where he was hiding and knocked this kid — Ray Saunders — through a trap door in the floor. The other kid insisted that Mikie pushed him, but I — "

For an instant, his voice caught in his throat and he couldn't continue. Dianne almost softened toward him, but then she sat back until he could go on.

"Well, he fell and broke his neck. The kid, Ray Saunders, I mean, not Mikie."

"Did he . . . die?" Dianne asked, her voice fluttering in her chest.

Edward shook his head dejectedly. "No, he — "

"He . . . his face got smashed up real bad on the frame of the trapdoor, and when he hit the ground, his back got broken. He was paralyzed from the waist down."

For the first time since he had sat down on the bed, Edward found the courage to look his wife straight in the eyes. Her face, wired and bandaged as it was, seemed horribly alien to him — a Halloween mask with absolutely no emotion behind it. In some ways she looked a bit like how he remembered Ray looking that day. The memory of his face, with the entire left side peeled back and bleeding into the pile of rotting sawdust, filled him with an icy terror.

"So you see, Ray — well, people around here still call him Sandy — has been in a wheelchair ever since," Edward continued. "He lives in town here. I stop by to see him once in a while, but I — it's uncomfortable to see him because of . . . well, because of all the memories it stirs up and all."

"Umm, I can imagine," Dianne said, shaking her head slowly up and down.

"So — you know, everyone blamed Mikie for it, said that he'd done it on purpose and that he was insane and was too — too dangerous to be out loose, that he might try to kill someone else. I remember how, after the accident, Mikie really freaked out. It was like something suddenly snapped in his brain. He was — God! It was horrible! He was kicking and screaming when my mother found him and pulled him out of his hiding place in his bedroom closet. I'll never forget the way he was crying — howling, like a wounded animal or something. You've got to remember, I was only twelve years old at the time, and I was scared out of my mind, thinking that my brother was really insane. He wouldn't stop shouting and screaming, going on and on about how *they* were angry and that *'they'* did it, and now *they* were going to get even — with Ray, with him, with our mother, with *everyone!*"

"Good Lord," Dianne said, and finally she did relent and shifted forward to slide her arms around Edward, hugging him to her as he buried his face into the crook of her shoulder. Deep, wrenching sobs shook his body as he struggled to speak.

"So you see . . . probably the most horrible thing about all of this is . . . is all these years, while my brother's been locked up in the — in the mental hospital, I've lived with the fear that I—"

He suddenly jerked away from her and gasped for breath. Tears spilled from his eyes, glistening like quicksilver on his cheeks.

"I've been scared that I might have the same thing wrong with me, you know? That *I* might suddenly just — just snap, like Mikie did, and lose it — lose it completely!"

"No, no, it isn't like that," Her breath was warm on his neck as she whispered soothingly in his ear. "It isn't like that at all."

"Yeah, I know, I know, but I—"

Again his voice caught, and for a fleeting instant, he felt as though someone was holding him from behind, squeezing the breath out of him. "But for Mikie it's been . . . it's been thirty years that he's been locked up — thirty years that he's had to pay for something he never . . . for what happened to Ray Saunders."

Dianne was speechless as she nodded and hugged him all the closer. Her voice trembled when she said, "But now he's gone, right? And they don't know where he is."

Edward stiffened as if an electric jolt had passed through him. He sat up straight and looked at her, shaking his head.

"Yeah. He disappeared about three or four weeks ago."

161

Dianne took a quick sip of breath. "Well, that's why that phone call frightened me so much. I mean, it came like a bolt out of nowhere. I'm still a little pissed off, too."

"I'm sorry," Edward said softly. "I know I should have told you, but I didn't want you to worry."

"But they *still* have no idea where Michael is?"

Edward regarded her with a steady gaze as he ran his teeth over his lower lip. Then he said, "No . . . I'm afraid they don't."

"So why are they calling here? Just to keep you posted?"

Edward scratched the side of his face, and again the thought filled his mind: *How much can I tell her? How much do I dare to tell her?* Taking her hand in both of his and gripping it tightly, he forced himself to continue.

"Well, you see, after my mother died, I made the mistake of calling Michael to tell him. I'd talked with his doctor about it first, and he thought it was probably a good thing for Mike to know what had happened. Where Mikie's staying isn't like maximum security or anything. Then, a few days after I talked to him, Dr. Samuels called, telling me that Mikie had left the facility without notice."

"So where do they think he is?" Diane asked. "Do they think he might have come back home? Here?"

Edward shrugged. "He probably tried to. That was my first thought, of course. Dr. Samuels suggested that maybe Mikie wasn't able to handle the idea that his mother was dead, and that he might feel like he had to come back home if only to — I don't know, to see her grave so he can prove to himself that she's really dead."

"But how could he make it all the way back here? He didn't have any money or clothes or anything, did he?"

Edward shook his head and shrugged. "Not as far as anyone knows. He just took off, but — I dunno . . . I notified the local police, of course, and the hospital has filed a missing persons report on him, but — at least so far — nothing's turned up."

"I don't see how he could just walk out of there like that and disappear. That's quite a distance to travel, from south of

162

Boston to here—especially for someone who's—well, who's not mentally well."

"It sure is," Edward replied, his voice sounding hollow and flat. "But you know the state police in Maine, New Hampshire, and Massachusetts aren't going to make it a priority. It's not like he's committed a federal crime or anything, so there hasn't been any widespread search for him."

"But the local police—they haven't gotten anything."

Edward shook his head. "I've kept in touch with Jake Crockett, but he's overworked, too, so he doesn't have a whole lot of time to go around looking for him, either. He tells me he keeps asking around for anyone answering a description of Michael, but he hasn't come up with anything yet."

"My God!" Dianne said. "Then do you think he—"

Edward knew she was going to ask if he thought Michael was dead. He looked at her, then shifted his gaze to the dark rectangle of night outside the bedroom window. She followed his gaze. They both watched in fascinated silence as the window sheers shifted back and forth with the gentle night breeze. And suddenly—for some unfathomable reason—the night seemed to be alive with menace . . . for both of them.

Chapter Twelve
The Old Mill

The pleasant sounds of morning birds and insects filled the air, but suddenly the peace of the forest was shattered by the crackling burr of a chain saw. A haze of blue smoke rose up, catching angled shafts of the morning sun as it wafted through the trees like cigarette smoke at a crowded party. Bright yellow sawdust spewed into the air, sprinkling the ground like snow. Then, with a ripping, splintering of wood, the first tree keeled over. Branches of the falling tree lashed at the limbs of the trees around it as if it were trying to catch itself in its fall.

"All *right!* First one down!" Edward shouted.

He stood back and wiped the sweat from his forehead. The ear protectors he was wearing gave him a funny, panda bear look as he glanced over at Brian, who was standing a safe distance away from the action.

Brian gave his father a halfhearted thumbs-up and watched silently as he stepped over the fallen tree and started cutting into the next one.

Boy, oh boy! Is this ever going to be a ton of fun! Brian thought, rolling his eyes back and forth as he surveyed the dense tangle of trees and brush. He could see three of the four corner posts, tied off with fluorescent pink surveyor's ribbon. By his estimate, it was going to take at least a couple of days just to cut down all the trees.

His father cupped his hands to his mouth and yelled to him, "Hey! If you came here to help, grab some work gloves out of the truck and give me a hand."

Resenting having to leave the cool, shady spot he had found underneath a tall maple tree, Brian slowly made his way over to the truck. The temperature was already approaching ninety degrees. He broke out in a sweat just from walking; he could imagine how ripe he was going to smell by lunchtime.

After a bit of a search, he found a battered pair of work gloves underneath the front seat. He also grabbed a pair of ear protectors and slipped them on, then trudged over to where his father was working. He stood to one side, feeling as though he had no idea where to begin.

His father held the chain saw loosely in his hand, letting it idle as he surveyed the work they had to do.

"I figure this is about the center of what we want cleared. You can start piling up the trees and brush over there so we can burn it tomorrow."

Brian nodded, wondering if his father really thought they could get that much done in one day. He was still feeling useless as his father revved the chain saw and got back to work. He directed each tree's fall so most of them landed pretty much in the pile he was building, like spokes pointing to the hub of the wheel. Brian pulled them closer together, knowing that once his father started working away from the middle, he'd be dragging trees and branches from further and further away.

"Why don't you just bulldoze them all?" Brian shouted.

At first his father didn't hear him above the sound of the chain saw, so he slowed it down again and raised his ear protectors so Brian could repeat his question.

"Why not just bulldoze them?"

"See these trees with the blue ribbons?" his father asked, sweeping the area with his pointed finger.

Brian looked around and for the first time noticed that several large hemlocks and pines had dark blue plastic tape tied around them.

"Well, the people who are building here want me to save all these trees that are marked . . . if I can."

Brian nodded his understanding.

His father sniffed with laughter and shook his head. "Gonna be a real pain in the ass trying to work around them, but I told them I'd try."

"What are you gonna do about the stumps?' " Brian asked.

"The backhoe will take care of them when they come to dig the foundation," his father replied, and then it was back to work in earnest.

Most of the trees his father felled were saplings. He had explained to Brian that this area of the property had been logged off about twenty years ago, so most of what was here was new growth, easy to cut down. It seemed to Brian as though a different tree was falling just about every minute. The work was hard, but after a while he got into the swing of it. Before long, they had a good-sized area cleared out except for the stumps, which stuck up out of the ground like rotting teeth. Sweat ran in torrents down Brian's face and back. It sprayed from his face like when a prizefighter catches a haymaker as he flung branches onto the tall, teepee-shaped brush pile. Brian wanted to make sure he was out here when his father touched it off.

They couldn't talk much as they worked, except for when his father refilled the chain saw with gasoline and bar oil. When the chain saw wasn't running, Brian was amazed by the deep, muffled silence of the forest. Birds and insects were hushed. He no longer thought about the sweat and grime of the job. He was actually enjoying the physical activity, and he realized that even busting his hump like this piling up brush was better than sitting home alone in his room, listening to music and thinking about how much he disliked . . . *her* — that wired, bandaged *monster* sleeping in the next room who had taken the place of his mother in his father's life.

Lunchtime came before he knew it, and side by side he and his dad settled down to eat the tuna fish sandwiches they had packed this morning. The gallon jug filled with lemonade, which had looked like so much this morning, now didn't seem to have near enough to quench their thirsts. They chatted small talk as they ate, but all the while Brian felt tensed, waiting for his father to start in on him again about how he should try to show some sympathy and concern for Dianne. Fortunately, he never did. By the time Brian finished off the last of his sandwich, he was feeling exhausted, more ready for a nap than another stint hauling brush.

"I don't know if I'm even going to be able to stand up," he said, smiling as he burped loudly and rubbed the bulge of his stomach.

"I know what you mean," his father said, leaning forward and wiping his forehead with the back of his arm. "But it's good to work hard like this, don't you think?"

Brian laughed. "Yeah," he said. "I'll probably sleep like a log tonight."

"You know, actually, if you want to take the afternoon off, I can handle the rest of this by myself."

Brian wondered if his father honestly wanted him to take a break or if he was trying to get him out of the way. Hadn't he been doing a good enough job? He cleared his throat, then said, "Yeah — well, I wouldn't mind heading home and taking a shower." Stifling a yawn, he stretched his arms over his head and flexed.

"Whatever," his father said. He drained his cup of lemonade, crumpled up his paper trash, and stood up. "We were working like the dickens there for a while, and I think I'll slow things down a bit. It's not like we *have* to have it all done today. Go ahead. Take the rest of the day off. It's not that much of a walk back home."

Brian considered for a moment, then nodded and stood up. "Well . . . if you're sure you won't need me this afternoon."

"You've been working like a dog. I mean it. Take the rest of the day for yourself. Thanks for the help, though. I really appreciate it."

"Hey, no sweat," Brian said; then he chuckled and, sniffing under his armpit, said, "Actually, quite a *bit* of sweat."

He took care of his trash, tossed his work gloves back

under the truck seat, then started for the road. Before he was very far, though, his father called out, "Hey! Wait a second."

Brian looked back at him.

"You know, there's a path right through the woods here that will take you straight to the house." He indicated with a wave of his hand the wall of trees on the far side of the area they had been clearing.

A cold knot suddenly twisted in Brian's stomach as he glanced at the woods. Without warning, the memory of what had happened that day when the red croquet ball had disappeared into the woods popped into his mind. These were the same woods. What if that person was still out there, still watching him and waiting to catch him alone?

What if he followed that path, and as soon as he was out of sight, he ran into that same person?

"It'll get you home in half the time," his father said, apparently not noticing his hesitation. "Plus, it's shady. It'll be hotter than hell out there on the road."

Brian almost said he would just as soon take the long way home, but he didn't want to appear scared or nervous in front of his father.

Yeah, nervous, he told himself. *Not scared — just nervous . . . cautious.*

"The path is easy to follow. You can't possibly lose it," his father added. Without waiting for a reply, he flipped the starter switch and pulled the cord. Brian stood there a moment, watching his father, unable to take a single step toward the woods. The saw sputtered on the first few pulls, then kicked into life with a crackling roar that filled the woods. Brian realized he was breathing too fast and consciously slowed himself.

What's there to worry about? he asked himself. *It will just be a short walk through the woods. No sweat!*

He sniffed with repressed laughter as he started slowly out across the clearing toward the trail. Beneath the loud sputtering of the chain saw, he knew his father couldn't hear him when he said, "Actually . . . quite a *bit* of sweat."

As he walked along the narrow trail, shivers raced up Brian's back. He wondered if the day was actually getting cooler, or if he had caught a chill from sweating so much as he worked. Overhead, the sky looked pale and impossibly distant through the thick tangle of branches. The shadows beneath the trees seemed to deepen with every step he took. As the sound of his father's chain saw faded away steadily, his tension rose. Several times he thought he saw something—a person or a crouching animal—lurking in the shade of the woods, but after a few cautious steps, his heart thumping heavily in his throat, the shadow would shift and reveal itself as . . . nothing but a shadow.

"Don't be stupid," he said aloud, hoping to find courage in the sound of his own voice. Although he had been born in Maine, he had been raised mostly in Arizona, so he told himself it was normal for him to feel claustrophobic in the woods. The woods were unnatural to him, threatening. He needed wide open sky and a long, flat expanse of land to feel comfortable . . . or better yet, the arrow-straight streets and sidewalks of his hometown.

The path wove through the green-shadowed woods like a thin, brown stitch of yarn. Brian followed it up a slight, wooded crest, but at the top of the crest, where the path angled off to the right, he noticed something off to his left. Although he couldn't be sure, it looked like a road. He stopped for a moment, confused, and looked back and forth between his two options. The road, his house was on, when and if he saw it, should be off to the right; he knew that.

So what was this? Another road? Or had he gotten disoriented by the twists and turns of the path and was now heading in the wrong direction.

His father hadn't said anything about a road; he'd said the path led straight to the house. Brian knew he should stay on the path, but he couldn't push aside the rush of curiosity about this road. Where did it lead? Was it a better and faster way home?

He held his breath and listened for the sound of his father's chain saw but could hear nothing except the whispered sighing of the pines overhead and a chorus of bird song. For just an instant, he had the overwhelming sense — just like that afternoon outside his grandmother's house . . . and then that day in his father's backyard — that he was being watched. His hands went sweaty as his gaze darted back and forth as he tried to pierce the dense foliage.

"No," he told himself. "I'm just imagining things . . . That's all!"

But it didn't make the feeling go away. Should he stay on the path like his father said, or try the road to see where it went?

He made his decision in an instant. He cut through a dense knot of scrub brush and then scrambled up a stony embankment and onto the single lane, dirt road. As soon as he was standing on it, he knew he'd made the wrong choice. Through the trees off to his left, he could see the silvery sparkle of water that had to be the Saco River. It was obvious this road, whatever it had once been, hadn't seen any traffic in a lot of years.

Brian was about to turn around and head back to the path again when he saw through a break in the trees up ahead the sagging roof line of a building. Its harsh, black line cut across the pale sky like the sharp edge of a knife.

"What the—" Brian muttered. He took a few cautious steps forward to get a better view. That was when, for the first time in his life — but not for the last — Brian Fraser saw the old mill.

Why didn't my father ever tell me about this place? Brian wondered as he cautiously approached the decrepit building. He moved slowly, continually glancing around as if he expected at any moment to see someone come screaming toward him from the woods or from behind the building.

The well-worn road ended in a wide, flat area in front of the building. Brian figured it must have been the loading area at one time for this mill or factory or whatever it used to be. The empty lot was choked with knee-high weeds — Queen Anne's lace, cornflower, and gold-tasseled grasses. Old wrappers and rusted beer and soda cans littered the roadside. The humid wind swayed the tall grass and kicked up a tornado swirl of yellow dust.

Through the trees off to his left, Brian could see a wider stretch of the Saco River. It sparkled in the sunlight like hammered metal. He thought for a moment about the great fishing spots his father had said were out here, but then his gaze was drawn back irresistibly to the building that towered above him. Black, glassless windows gaped like toothless mouths in the flat, gray wall. The roof on the river side of the building had collapsed inward, exposing rotting rafters that looked like decayed, broken ribs. What had once been a small addition on the other side of the building was now a flattened mass of charred timbers, worn to a dark, polished gray by time and weather.

Right away, Brian noted a few places where he would be able to enter the building, but something — a dull sense of danger or menace — told him to stay back. Once again, he was filled with the sensation that he was being watched, but this time it felt . . . different somehow, as if he realized that it might be okay for him to be here, that whoever might be watching him meant him no harm. He suddenly froze. He thought he saw, in the corner of his eye, someone moving under the shadow of the trees off to his right; but when he looked, there was no one there.

Why didn't my father ever tell me about this place? he wondered again.

He cupped his hands to his mouth, surprising himself when he suddenly shouted, "Hey! . . . Hello!"

His voice echoed back from inside the building with a dull reverberation. He waited a few seconds but got no response. Scanning both sides of the road, he picked up a baseball-sized rock, cocked his arm back, and threw it at the building. The rock sailed through one of the second story windows and landed on the upper floor with a clatter that sounded like a distant roll of thunder. Brian jumped and yelped with surprise when a dozen pigeons fluttered up from their roosts in the attic and started circling the building. They were tiny white dots against the hazy blue sky. Brian's hands clenched into fists as he tracked the birds for a moment; then he tensed and looked around again, fully expecting someone to reveal himself. But the building and surrounding woods remained silent . . . perhaps too silent, he thought.

He took a few shuffling steps forward. As soon as he was inside the shadow of the building, a wave of chills skittered up his back. Other than a couple of dumb pigeons, the place seemed totally deserted, but he still couldn't shake the feeling that someone—somewhere—was watching him.

He knew he should leave this place and head straight home. There had to be a good reason why his father had never mentioned this place to him, since it was so close to where they lived. It was probably a really dangerous place to play, or maybe the owner was a real nut case who didn't want any kids fooling around out here.

But the pull of the old building was steady and strong, and Brian was caught helplessly in its grip. He *had* to check it out at least a little to find out what—if anything—was inside there.

Moving quickly to the side of the building, he reached up to the edge of the door frame and hoisted himself up onto the first floor. His breath came fast and thin as he took a few steps inside, all the while looking around. Deep shadows closed down around him like a flow of cool water. The bright sunlight outside made the interior of the building seem all the darker as his eyes tried to adjust to the gloom. The walls had been stripped bare, and the floors were littered with rocks, dead leaves, and other debris. The corners up near the ceiling were clogged with thick clots of spiderwebs and bird nests. The air was stale and carried a curious blend of age and rot. Brian shivered when he imagined hundreds of fat-bodied bats, hanging upside down in the darkest corners of the rafters overhead.

But in spite of the subtle currents of caution and fear that he felt, Brian was also intrigued by the building and felt

172

drawn farther into it. There was a vague, almost dizzying sense of familiarity to this place, and he couldn't shake the feeling that he had been here before. He took a few more steps into the cavernous building, cringing at the hollow echo made by his footsteps. Through jagged holes in the ceiling, he could see all the way up to the roof which was riddled with fist-sized holes. Golden bars of sunlight shot through the dusty air, striking the floor around him like spotlight beams. As his eyes adjusted to the gloom, he could make out more details of the place and could see where there had once been interior walls and doors.

How long has this place been like this? And why is it even still standing? Why hasn't someone torn it down . . . or burned it flat by now?

He jumped when a floorboard creaked loudly underfoot, crackling like thin ice. Then, from down in the cellar, he heard a dull thumping sound. Freezing where he was, he looked down at the floor. It was old and rotting, and lined with inch-wide gaps between shrunken planks. He knew the boards might be brittle and could give out beneath his weight at any moment. Ever so cautiously, he started moving back toward the door; but before he was halfway there, he heard the sound repeated from down below. It was a dull, heavy thud that sounded a little like someone dragging something across the floor.

Pressure built up in his bladder, and he had to struggle hard to resist the impulse to turn and run. In an odd way, though, he felt as though he was the one who belonged here, and that the *real* intruder was whoever — or *what*ever — was making that noise down in the cellar.

Taking one slow, careful step at a time, he made his way back to the doorway, then turned and jumped down to the ground. He landed hard. His knees buckled beneath him, and he rolled once before standing up and quickly beating the dust off his pants. Crouching low, he ran to the front of the building where he remembered seeing some windows that opened into the cellar. He dropped onto his hands and knees, and eased his face around the window edge to peer inside.

The stale, rotten smell was much stronger down here; it almost gagged him. For a few seconds, it was too dark for him to see much of anything; but as his eyes adjusted to the light, he could make out a hard-packed earth floor and a series of tumbled down interior walls. Close to him, where a stray beam of sunlight illuminated the floor, he could see that the floor was scored and pitted with footprints and other scuff marks. Piles of broken, rotting lumber, stone blocks, and old barrels and wooden boxes were scattered about on the floor. At the far end of the cellar, there was a single low doorway, and for just a flickering instant, Brian thought he saw something dark melt back into the opening. He tried to dismiss it as a trick of the eye.

He watched for a while longer, trying to figure out what could have made the sounds. He knew he hadn't imagined them, but everything looked so quiet and undisturbed down there. He finally decided that it must have been a raccoon or squirrel or something, maybe a rat scurrying away to hide from him. Sighing deeply, he got up and turned to leave. Just as he did, he caught another blur of motion off to the side of the building. This time he was positive he had seen someone duck back out of sight behind the building.

Brian was filled with a stronger urge to start running, but he was determined to find out if someone was following him. He certainly didn't want to let whoever it was know he suspected or feared them. The palms of his hands were clammy as he slipped them into his jeans pockets. Straightening his shoulders, he started whistling an off-key tune as he walked away from the building, heading back to the road. As soon as he was out of the shadow of the building, the sunlight spread a glorious warmth across his back that started to relieve the knotted tension in his shoulders.

"Nothing in there but bats and cobwebs," he whispered to himself, but he only half-believed it. When he turned to take a final look at the building, his heart gave a heavy thump in his chest. Through one of the lower story windows, he saw a dark shape — black against black — suspended in the air, framed by the window. It hadn't been there before. He knew *that* much.

He'd just been inside. He swallowed hard, but his tongue felt like a swollen slug in his mouth, blocking his throat as he stared at the object, horrified. The dark bulk seemed to sway gently back and forth. Then it started to turn.

He had no idea where the thought came from, but Brian was suddenly — absolutely convinced that he was looking at a person, hanging from a rope. Uttering a low, trembling cry, he turned and started running down to the road. He wasn't exactly sure where he should strike out into the woods to find the path he had been following, but all of a sudden he didn't care.

All he knew was, he had to get as far away from this old building as he could . . . as *fast* as he could!

Chapter Thirteen
Spooked

The night suddenly ripped apart.

Old pinewood floorboards snapped like balsa wood.
Dagger-shaped chunks of wood exploded into the air in a
shower of splinters and swirling dust. Hands—twisted and
gnarled with decay, some stripped of all flesh—reached up
from inside the floor, flailing wildly for something to grab
onto and hold. Harsh beams of blazing red light shot up
like glowing iron bars through the holes in the floor, cutting
through the dark backdrop of coiling, black smoke. Bright
orange sparks corkscrewed into the air like crazy comets.
The room was filled with deep, rumbling groans and high,
keening shrieks.

Then heads and shoulders thrust into view, pushing up
through the smashed flooring. In the crazily flickering
light, faces appeared—mutilated wrecks with charred strips
of skin and scalp flapping like rotting flags. Eyes glowed
with dull, lambent fire as they shifted back and forth, scanning the darkness. Lips black with rot peeled back, exposing dirt-crusted teeth and pale, swollen tongues.

Huddled on his bed, his body frozen with fright, Brian
watched as the figures—he had no idea how many—struggled to their feet and then, fixing him with their burning,
unblinking gazes, began to shuffle and crawl toward him.
Skeletal fingers clicked on the floor and sliced like vicious

cutting shears as they reached out for him. Groans blended into deep chortles of laughter, and just at the edge of hearing, Brian caught the warbling sound of a baby, crying.

Brian's mind went blank with terror as one of the figures climbed up over the edge of the bed. The face loomed close to him and, beneath the grave mold and rot, he recognized the face—his mother's. She grinned at him as worms twisted inside the holes that pocked her face. When she opened her mouth to speak, a shower of maggots rained onto the bed and floor, splattering like heavy rain. When she spoke, her voice was low and sludgy, as though every syllable were an effort.

"Hell-o . . . Brian," she said. "I've . . . come . . . back . . . for . . . you!"

The scream that had been winding up inside of him suddenly burst forth so loud it felt as though it ripped the flesh of his throat. As the ghoulish figures closed in on him, chittering and snarling, he cowered back, pressing so hard against the headboard of his bed it creaked like a tree branch about to snap.

No . . . No! . . . NO!!!

The shrill cry gathered strength inside his mind like an onrushing tide. It lifted him up, carrying him forward in a blinding, head-over-heels spiral. He lost all sense of direction and had no idea if he was screaming out loud or if the long, piercing wail he heard was only in his mind. He tried to close his eyes, but even the darkness behind his eyelids was alive with flickering light and twisted, tormented figures that lunged at him.

"NO!—NO!—NO!—NO!—NO!"

Suddenly another light filled his vision—a brilliant but somehow soothing yellow burst. He heard more than saw the dark figure silhouetted against the light as it leaned over him, growing to an unimaginable size before strong, rough hands seized him and began to shake him.

"Hey! Brian! Come on! Wake up!"

The words seemed to come from far away. They had an

177

odd reverberation, as if the person were speaking down at the bottom of a deep, stone-lined well.

"Come on, Brian! Wake up! It's only a dream! It's just a dream!"

The hands clamped his shoulders hard, almost painfully. He felt his head roll loosely back and forth as if his neck was broken. With a sudden, roaring intake of breath, he opened his eyes and found himself staring up at his father. He sputtered, trying to say something, but the tightness in his chest made it all come out as a long, anguished groan.

"Hey, take it easy there, champ," his father said. One side of his mouth was twisted up into a half-smile. "Come on. You've got yourself all worked up."

Brian felt tears burning in his eyes, but he struggled not to let them fall as he sucked in a breath through gritted teeth. He nodded his head quickly, like a brave little boy trying not to cry after he'd skinned his knee, but still his voice wouldn't work.

"Boy, it must've been a doozy, huh?" his father said.

He released his grip on Brian's shoulders, then sat down on the edge of the bed. The bedsprings squeaked under his weight. The sound set Brian's teeth on edge. Still wide-eyed with fear, he looked at his father and nodded again.

"Yeah," he said with a ragged gasp. He wiped the flats of his hands over his face and sighed. "It sure as heck *was!*"

Again, his father's hand touched him on the shoulder, lighter this time as he rubbed in small, gentle circles. Brian tried to ease the tension that was bunching up his neck and shoulder muscles, but his whole body still felt all wound up and ready to explode.

"Do you want to talk about it?" his father asked mildly. "You know, sometimes it helps if you talk about it."

Brian looked his father straight in the eyes but could only hold the gaze for a second or two before another dizzying wave of nervousness swept over him. He was suddenly filled with the vague panic that this wasn't *really* his father—that this was still part of his dream, and all of a

178

sudden, his father's face was going to start peeling away in raw, red chunks of flesh. His hand would suddenly transform into a bony, white skeleton that would grab his throat and squeeze, unrelentingly, until he was . . .

Dead!

"No, I, uhh—"

"Hey, you don't have to," his father said. His voice was calm, soothing, but still Brian couldn't shake the thought that reality was suddenly going to rip open right there in front of him and he'd catch a glimpse of the horror that was lurking behind it.

"Let me get you a glass of water," his father said, getting up from the bed. "Be back in a jiffy."

He glanced back at Brian for a second before leaving to go down the hall to the bathroom. As soon as he was out of sight, Brian had a powerful urge to shout for him not to leave, but his throat closed off as if there really was a bony hand wrapped around it, strangling him to silence.

When his father came back—mere seconds that had seemed like several minutes later—Brian nodded his thanks as he took the glass and drank most of the water down in three huge gulps. Some water dribbled down his chin, but what he did swallow didn't even come close to soothing the painful rawness in the back of his throat. Once the glass was empty, he smiled at his father and, smacking his lips, handed the glass back to him.

"Yeah—" Brian said. His voice sounded paper-thin. "That's—I feel a lot better now."

"So, are you all set now?" his father asked. He was smiling down at him, but Brian could still see a trace of concern clouding his eyes. "You know, if you want me to—"

"How come you never told me about it," Brian said. The words seemed to leap out of his mouth before he had even thought them.

"Told you—? About what?"

"That big, old building . . . out by the river."

His father's eyebrows contracted. His lips tightened, and

179

the light in his eyes seemed to dim momentarily. He took a step away from the bed, his eyelids fluttering as he glanced up at the ceiling and cleared his throat.

"The old mill, you mean," he said.

Brian tried his best to convince himself that he hadn't detected a slight tremor in his father's voice. He slowly nodded and replied, "Yeah . . . that."

A thick silence filled the room for several seconds as Brian looked at his father, fighting back the surge of panic that rose up inside him again.

Was it his own fear he was seeing, projected onto his father? he wondered. Or was there really something wrong here—something his father didn't want to talk about? He found himself wishing he had kept his mouth shut about the whole thing.

"I—uh, you know, today, when I left you at the work site, I guess I kinda lost my way, and I found this road that goes out to an old building." He turned his gaze to his hands, which were folded tightly in his lap. "I—I didn't mention it at supper because I figured—you know, that you had never told me about it 'cause you . . . you didn't want me to know about it or something."

"Didn't *want* you to know about it—?" his father said, shaking his head and laughing. "Whatever gave you *that* idea?" His laugh was high and tight, and sounded completely forced.

Brian glanced up, about to speak, but the choking sensation around his throat suddenly increased, silencing him. He squeezed his folded hands together so tightly the knuckles began to hurt, and his mind filled with the shocking images of his dream of decomposing corpses crawling out of the darkness and reaching toward him.

"Did you see . . . was there anyone else out there today?"

The tone of his father's voice did nothing to allay his steadily rising fear. His pulse throbbed rapidly with a dull ache in his neck.

"I . . . well, no—not really." He took a deep breath, held

it a moment, then let it out in a slow whistle. "But I had this—this feeling, like I was—I dunno, like someone was—" Before he could say more, he recalled seeing what had looked like fresh traces of footprints on the dirt floor in the cellar, and for the first time it all came together in his mind. He shivered as he shook his head, realizing that the floor in his dream hadn't been his bedroom floor at all; it had been the mill floor, cracked and weakened with age; and the burned, disfigured people he had seen, including his real mother—not Dianne, his ugly, bandaged step-mother—had burst up out of the mill's cellar. Trembling wildly, he grabbed his head with both hands and closed his eyes, but he couldn't stop the horrifying rush of images.

"Look here, son," his father said, leaning close and forcing him to make steady eye contact. "The truth is, I never told you about that old place because—well, frankly because I just never thought to mention it to you. But now that you know where it is, I have to tell you that I'd really appreciate it if you stayed away from there."

"Why?" Brian said, his voice no more than a whisper.

"I just don't want you out there, that's all."

"Does anyone live out there or something?"

"No," his father said with a quick shake of his head. "It's on my property. It's an old lumber mill my grandfather used to run. Did you see someone out there today?"

Brian shrugged tightly and shook his head. "No, not really. I don't think so. I mean—I dunno." He shrugged and slapped his legs. "I kinda checked the place out—"

"You went inside?"

Brian bit his lower lip and nodded. "Just for a quick look around, but it looked like maybe someone's been out there recently."

"Probably some kids from around town. They still go out there now and then to hang around; but I told you, I don't want *you* going out there, got it?"

"Sure, but I don't see why not?"

"Because when I was a kid, *I* used to play out there with

181

my friends, and my mother used to tell me not to go out there. Then one day . . . something happened. One of my friends fell down into the cellar and broke his neck."

"Did he die?" Brian asked.

In a flash, Brian remembered seeing—or *thinking* he saw—a dark figure that sure as heck *looked* like a person standing—or *hanging!*—in one of the windows.

His father grunted and shook his head. "No, he didn't die, but he's paralyzed from the waist down, and he'll be like that for the rest of his life." He looked away and swallowed noisily. "And I—well, in some ways, I feel responsible for what happened. We never should have been out there, and I—just like I'm warning you—should have listened to my mother's warning. It's a dangerous place."

"Then why don't you just get rid of it? Why not tear it down or burn it or something?"

Brian watched his father's gaze shift from him to the black rectangle of the bedroom window and the night beyond. It might have been the light or just his imagination, but for just an instant, he thought his father's face paled. He swallowed again and took a deep breath before continuing.

"Good question," he said at last. "I don't know why. Lord knows I've thought about doing just that plenty of times, but I—" He shrugged helplessly. "I just never got around to doing it." He suddenly stiffened and turned back at Brian. He shook his forefinger at him and said, "But I'm telling you this: I don't want you going out there—ever! Understood?"

"Yeah," Brian said, in a sheepish voice. "Sure thing. Don't worry."

Goddamn it! Brian's starting to sound just like Mikie did, back when we were kids!

Edward couldn't get that thought out of his mind as he opened the back door and stepped out into the night. A

182

fingernail moon rode low in the western sky, illuminating the gauzy, blue mist that twined like smoke through the woods. Only the brightest stars shined through the overcast. The night was alive with the sounds of crickets, and from far off came the ruffling hoot of an owl. Absolutely no breeze stirred the hot air, but still, a ripple of goose bumps broke out on his arms.

Feeling his way in the dark, Edward entered the side door of the garage and walked to the back of his truck. He snapped open the lid of the large metal toolbox and rifled around blindly until he found what he was looking for—his high-powered flashlight. He snapped it on and, after giving the light a few quick shakes, a feeble beam shot out. The circle of light looked like a distorted, pale eye as it danced over the garage wall. Positive there were no fresh batteries in the toolbox, and not wanting to take the time to drive downtown to get some at the 7-Eleven—or chance disturbing Dianne's sleep—he decided to make do with what he had. He gently closed the toolbox lid and followed the circled beam back out into the night.

The hike out to the mill took longer than he had thought it would. Because of the darkness and disuse, the path wasn't quite as easy to follow as he remembered it. He stumbled through thick overgrowth, unsure, at times, if he was even on the right track. The further he went, the more everything seemed . . . different, somehow. The trees surrounding him seemed to close in on him, muffling the heavy sounds of his breathing. His sneakers scuffed the earth with a dull, plodding sound.

It had been at least twenty-five years since he had sneaked out of the house at night, and he realized that he was looking at this night-stained world through different eyes. Childhood memories were being filtered through an adult perspective. He encountered trees and rocks and brush that he didn't remember ever being there, and he had to fight back the steadily rising panic that he had gotten himself lost on his own property. But then the path led over a slight crest, and he recognized the stone-covered slope that led up to the old dirt road. Feeling a slight measure of relief, he followed the road for a short distance until the dark hulk of the old mill appeared, rearing up tall and solid against the misty night sky.

Edward sucked in his breath as he directed his steps through the knee-high weeds toward the building. The sound of crickets in the weed field was nearly deafening. Above the building, small black dots—bats out hunting—flitted in crazy spirals. It had been years, he realized, since he had been out here even during the daytime. Maybe it was just the altered perception of seeing things at night, but the building seemed to be much larger than he remembered it. He had expected it to seem shrunken down to fit his adult perspective, but its solid, black walls blocked off his view of the woods like a dimensionless hole in reality.

"Holy shit," Edward whispered, feeling a stirring of trepidation. His grip tightened on the flashlight handle as he swung the beam back and forth, trying to push back the darkness.

But the darkness wouldn't stay back.

As soon as he looked away, it closed back around him like a blanket, pressing closer, tighter.

He moved nearer to the building. The night seemed to swell and pulsate, vibrating with shadowy menace. The closer he got to the mill, the better he could make out the hard edge of the roof line and the darker rectangles where the windows and doors had been. The stone foundation glowed, an iridescent white line that followed the gentle curve of the land. A shiver raced up his back, and he almost cried out when, for just an instant, he thought he detected a fluttering of motion in one of the windows. He dropped to one knee and shined the flashlight at the window, but saw nothing except the gaping hole with its rotting wooden frame.

"Come on, man!" he whispered harshly. His throat felt as dry as sand. "Get a grip, will yah?"

He straightened up and brushed off his knee, but the tension coiling inside his stomach didn't ease up; it only got stronger as he ran his flashlight beam across the gray flank of the building and recalled the horrible events that had happened out here when he was a kid.

Thirty years ago! God, how can it have been that long?

He tried to shut out the chilling rush of memories, but then, like a stainless steel spike, a thought suddenly hit him:

What if that's Sandy in there? . . . Or Sandy's ghost?

The image of his friend, lying sprawled and bleeding on the rotting pile of sawdust in the cellar while curious rats sniffed at him, licking the blood from his face, grew sharper in his mind with every hammering beat of his heart. He sucked quick sips of air through his teeth, wishing to hell he could permanently blot from his memory the events of that day in 1963; but it was clearer in his memory than where he was when, a month later, he'd heard President Kennedy had been shot.

"But that *can't* be Sandy in there!" Edward hissed through tight, dry lips. "Sandy can't even walk. Besides, I didn't—he's not dead! Sandy didn't die!"

Edward's hands were sweating and shaking so badly the flashlight beam jiggled back and forth like a strobe light. The metal tube almost slipped from his grip. He suddenly had a strong impulse to run away, but something else urged him to move forward. He clicked off his flashlight and moved up to the side of the building on legs that felt as stiff as boards. He was close enough to reach out and touch the weathered siding, but he couldn't bring himself to do it. He was more than half-convinced that, the instant his hand touched the mill, a bolt of blue electricity would flash out and strike him dead, so he just stood there, listening to the rapid flutter of his pulse.

But then he heard—or *thought* he heard—something else.

From far off, blanketed by the steady chirring of

crickets, there came a low, hitching cry, like someone sobbing.

"What the hell?" Edward whispered.

His eyes widened and he held his breath as he strained forward, moving alongside the building until he came to one of the glassless cellar windows. The sound seemed to be coming from down in there, so he dropped onto his hands and knees, leaned forward, and listened.

The sound was maddening. It wavered in and out of hearing—teasing and taunting, like a radio signal fading with distance. First it was there . . . then it was gone . . . then—was that it again? . . . or was it merely his memory of the sound?

A warm, fetid breeze wafted up out of the cellar, carrying with it the heavy aroma of damp earth and rot as it stirred his hair and raised goose bumps on his arms. The smell had an instant familiarity that reminded him of all those times he had played out here with his friends. He wondered if Ray Saunders's copy of *Playboy* was still hidden somewhere down there, moldering away in the dark just like the young women pictured within its pages, now more than thirty years older and, no doubt, much the worse for wear. His body shivered with apprehension—and a deep, stinging sense of loss. He and all his childhood friends were grown-up now. What they'd had back then, and what they'd all shared was lost . . . forever.

Why? Goddamnit! he wondered. Why couldn't he and his friends and all those naked women he had lusted over all stay permanently fresh and young, like their photographs, frozen forever in time?

Although with the flashlight off he couldn't see much of anything down in the cellar, a feeble wash of moonlight shined through a hole in the wall, illuminating the slouched pile of rotting sawdust at the far end of the cellar. A trick of the moonlight and shadow made it look like a giant, lying sprawled facedown on the floor. But while Edward couldn't see it, he definitely sensed there was *something*

186

else down there . . . something that was hiding from him in the pitch darkness. He could *feel* it as much as hear it, shifting about like the sluggish flow of dark water deep underground.

Is it just my imagination getting carried away, or could there really be someone down there?

A thin current of panic rippled through him. He wanted more than anything to snap on the flashlight and sweep the inside of the basement with its beam, but he wasn't sure he wanted to—or dared—to because of what he might discover.

And if there is someone down there, who could it be? Sandy . . . or maybe Michael?

"No! No way," he whispered.

If he had heard anything down there, it probably had just been some kind of animal. What would anyone be doing out here this late at night? Sandy, obviously, could never have made it even in the daytime, not in his wheelchair . . . and Michael?

No!

Although he had run away from the hospital and was listed as missing, Edward didn't think it very likely that his brother could have made it all the way back here. And even if by some miracle he had, why would he be staying out here in the cold, damp mill instead of coming home? No, he hated to think it, but in all likelihood, Michael probably had died days or weeks ago, lost and lonely somewhere probably not very far from the hospital that had been his home for the past thirty years.

Edward's throat felt feverishly raw. He swallowed and licked his lips, preparing to call out; but before he could do that, the faint sound came again, drifting to him like a thin tendril of fog. He froze as he strained to catch it, warbling up and down the scale like a police siren heard far off in the distance. After a few seconds, he realized that it sounded like a baby . . . crying.

"He pushed him! I saw him do it! The retard pushed

Sandy down into the cellar!"

Edward's mind echoed with those angry words and the long, sniffling sobs of Charlie Costello as they crouched on the edge of the trapdoor and looked down at their motionless friend, absolutely convinced that he was dead.

Bullshit! That's not Sandy, lying down there on the floor! Edward thought, narrowing his eyes as he stared at the pile of old sawdust.

He pressed his thumb against the flashlight switch, but he still didn't dare flick it on. A cold rush of panic rose up from his stomach to his chest.

What the hell is down there? What could be making that sound?

His vision blurred as he focused on the rounded pile of sawdust. The sound disappeared before he consciously realized it, fading away as subtly as it had begun. Edward shook his head as though dazed, but as much as he strained to hear it again, the sound was definitely gone. The night seemed to explode with the swelling song of crickets.

"Ahh, fuck it!"

—fuckit!

Edward's voice sounded unnaturally loud as it echoed from inside the cavernous cellar.

"There's *nothing* down there!"

—downthere!

" 'Cept for maybe a couple of lousy rats!"

—lousyrats!

He straightened up and snapped on the flashlight. The sudden harsh glare stung his eyes, but as soon as there was even this single beam of artificial light, whatever spell had held him was broken. The eerie sense of foreboding that had spooked him so badly instantly evaporated. He shined his flashlight beam all around inside the cellar, pausing a moment to study the sawdust pile. And he saw it for what it was—just a pile of rotting sawdust, riddled with rat holes. He scanned the outside of the mill as well and saw it for exactly what it was, too—nothing more than an old, rotting, deserted hulk of a building surrounded by a rank tangle of weeds.

Nothing more.

Nothing less.

With a heavy sigh of relief, and feeling a tinge of disgust for allowing himself to get so worked up, he started back down the road toward home. With every step, he berated himself for letting something as innocent as a simple question about this place from his son bring him out here in the middle of the night to stir up memories . . . memories of things that were over and done with thirty years ago. Like regrets, they were gone, and he couldn't do a damned thing about it.

"And maybe that's all for the best," he whispered to himself because he was *damned* sure, if he had his way, that's just where he would keep all those memories — lost and buried and rotting down there in the darkness of the old mill's cellar.

Chapter Fourteen
A Bad Day

Brian didn't sleep late that next morning. In fact, he was up and out of bed long before his father and step-mother. His thoughts and dreams had been filled to over-flowing with questions as well as tantalizing fears about the old mill. He hadn't been able to stop wondering what treasures might be hidden out there, what secrets the mill might contain . . . and why it would be the source of such a vivid nightmare. He got dressed and came down-stairs as quietly as possible just as the sun was peeking in through the kitchen window, washing the countertop with a patina of gold.

As soon as he entered the kitchen, he saw the utility flashlight on the kitchen table where his father had left it last night. A long, angled beam of sunlight illuminated it like a spotlight, as if it had been purposely placed there just for him to see. Brian immediately thought of a use for the flashlight, so after scarfing down a bowl of cereal and a glass of juice, he grabbed the flashlight and pulled on his jacket against the early morning chill. He left the house and headed straight into the woods.

Warm morning sunlight was burning off the cool mists of night as Brian followed the twisting path through the woods. Plenty of doubts entered his mind about what he was doing, but after so many weeks of being bored just hanging around the house—especially with his witch of a stepmother home all the time!—he was glad finally to have something that actually intrigued him. He was intent on exploring the old mill . . . especially now that his father had told him so emphatically that he didn't want him coming out here. As he followed the twists and turns of the path, it seemed unnervingly familiar, as if he had trod it dozens or hundreds of times before.

A stirring of apprehension filled him when, through a break in the trees up ahead, he saw the stretch of dirt road. He again considered turning around, but he couldn't stop thinking how strange, how really weird he had felt yesterday as soon as he had entered the mill. He didn't deny that he was feeling cautious, now, if not outright fear, but he had experienced something else out there, too—a sensation almost of recognition about the place, of familiarity . . . as if, like this path, he had been out there many times before in his life.

He knew that was impossible. He had lived in Phoenix since he was four years old, and had visited with his father in Maine only a few times for very short stays over the past seven years. Unless his parents had taken him out here when he was a baby, he *knew* he had never seen this place before yesterday. Whatever the case, the old mill stirred deep feelings within him, reminding him of *something* that he found irresistibly intriguing.

The day was heating up quickly. By the time he broke out onto the road and the mill came into view, he was sweating. He shucked off his jacket and tied it around his waist like a loincloth. His grip on the flashlight handle was slippery with sweat as he approached the building. Sunlight angled across the front wall, illuminating every detail of the rotting wood and moss-covered stone foundation. Again, that surge of familiarity came over him, stronger this time. Every board, every granite block in the foundation, every empty window and door frame, even the punched-in roof and the building's placement on the land, backed by the wall of pine forest and the slick, blue Saco River — everything about this place seemed as clearly etched in his mind as if he had seen it every day of his life.

He drew to a halt and stared, long and hard at the empty window where, the day before, he had thought he had seen a person standing — *or hanging!* With a different angle of sunlight, he could see now how the contours of the ruined walls and the shadows inside might suggest such a shape. He trembled, as much from excitement and allure as from fear.

What the heck is it about this place?

Taking long, confident strides, he started toward the building once again. He was momentarily concerned that someone might be out here and see him, but he dismissed the thought, telling himself that the mill was, after all, on his father's property; he had as much right as anyone else to be here — maybe more.

He went straight to the side door he had entered yesterday and hiked himself up onto the first floor. He tensed when he heard a faint ruffling noise from overhead, but then he remembered that there were pigeons, roosting up on the second floor.

"Nothing to be afraid of," he whispered, trying to bolster his courage. "Nothing at all to sweat."

He walked carefully across the floor, pausing every time a floorboard creaked or buckled underfoot. In spite of its age, he thought the building seemed to be holding up quite well. He snapped on his flashlight and swung it around, but the beam was swallowed by the dusty gloom inside the building; it barely pierced the darker corners of the expansive room. He cautiously made his way across the floor to the large, square gap at the far end of the building. Through the open doorway, he could hear the hissing, hypnotic rush of the river. Holding his breath, he looked down through the trapdoor. Not much light entered the cellar from the windows. Looking at it from above, the pile of rotting sawdust looked like a gigantic splotch of gray oatmeal or vomit.

"This must be it!" he said in an excited whisper. "This has to be where that kid fell and broke his back!"

Sweat broke out on his forehead as he directed the flashlight beam straight down and studied the rat holes that honeycombed the sawdust pile. Dead leaves and other trash littered the dirt floor as well as the scuff marks of footprints. Again he was struck by how fresh some of the prints looked. He wanted to believe that, protected from wind and weather, even year-old footprints would *look* fresh, but he couldn't stop thinking that some of them looked as if they had been made within the past day or two.

Or maybe even today!

For a moment or two, he considered jumping down into the cellar through the trapdoor opening, but he decided against it, not wanting to risk breaking his neck, much less disturbing the rats who probably still lived in the sawdust pile below. Besides, if he got his courage up enough to go down into the cellar later to have a look around, there were plenty of other, easier ways to get down there. Keeping a wary eye on the opening, he started backing away from it toward the other side of the building, heading back to the doorway through which he had first entered.

He spent the next hour or two casually inspecting the downstairs, including the part of the mill out back that had burned flat. Outside he found more evidence that people had been poking around out here. Some of the burned timbers had been moved around, and there were more footprints in the loose dirt. He went around to the front of the building and looked down the stone stairway leading into the cellar, but still — even with his flashlight—he couldn't quite get up his nerve to go down there. Instead, he went back into the building through the side door and poked around some more on the first floor.

Convinced that, even after all these years, there might still be something of value that had been overlooked by everyone else, he rapped on the few remaining wall sections, hoping to discover a hidden compartment behind one of them. But he couldn't stop thinking about the cellar. That's where the neat stuff would be. He definitely wanted to go down there and have a look around, but he felt a certain caution because of what his father had told him about the mill . . . especially the story about that friend of his who had fallen through the trapdoor and was paralyzed from the waist down.

The floorboards creaked underfoot with every step he took, and grit sifted between the cracks in the floor. Other than the sound of his own footsteps, though, a strange, muffled silence filled the mill. Brian found being inside the abandoned building soothing but somewhat disconcerting. Whenever he glanced out one of the large, empty windows or doorways, the warm summer morning seemed curiously distant, almost like a flat, movie screen projection. The trees tossed back and forth in a fitful breeze, but there was no sound, even when a gust of wind carried yellow dust swirling up from the loading yard and sprinkled it like snow onto the windowsills and floor. The whole effect had an almost dreamlike dissociation.

After a while, the hollowness in his stomach told him it must be getting near to lunchtime. He was just about to leave by the side door when, down the road, he saw something shifting in the shadows under the trees. He tensed. It took him a moment to realize that someone was walking up the road, heading toward the mill. At first the person was hard to see, lost as he was in the splatter of shadows from the trees, but when he stepped out into the direct sunlight, Brian instantly recognized him.

"Oh, shit! It's dad!"

Brian dropped to his knees so he wouldn't be seen through the open window. He knew his father would be mad as hell at him for defying his order not to come out here, so he knew he had to hide.

But where?

There weren't any good places on the first floor. The cavernous room had been stripped bare. Most of the wall partitions were either gone or knocked down. The attic, with its bats clinging to the deepest shadows in the rafters, didn't seem like a very likely spot, either; then again, neither did the cellar.

Maybe he's finished lunch and is just out for a little walk, Brian thought frantically. *Maybe he doesn't realize I'm out here. But then again, maybe not. He should be out at the construction site.*

Nearly paralyzed with panic, Brian skittered across the floor over to a window. Gripping the sill, he peeked outside but had to duck back quickly out of sight when he saw that his father had left the road and was angling across the weed field, heading straight for the mill.

Oh, shit! How the heck did he know I was out here? Boy oh boy, am I ever going to catch it if he finds me!

Brian knew he didn't have many options left: he could either give himself up now and face the music, or else find a place to hide—fast!

Over by the side door, he knew there was a rectangular opening in the floor where a stairway had once led down into the cellar. Crawling like he was doing a cossack dance, he made his way over to it and shined his flashlight down onto the pyramid stack of granite blocks that were piled up below the opening. The pile was tall enough so he could at least get down there without breaking his neck, and he knew he *had* to get down there in a hurry if he didn't want to get caught.

Why not just give up and suffer the consequences? he thought, but he already knew the answer to that. Just yesterday his father had told him to stay out of here, and no doubt he had guessed that Brian might disobey him; that was why he was coming out here now.

Brian's grip on his father's flashlight tightened as he swung his legs into the opening and then dropped down. He almost lost his footing on the uneven pile of stones but quickly regained his balance and crawled halfway down the rock pile before jumping the rest of the way to the dirt floor. He made a loud grunt noise when he hit but hoped that it hadn't been loud enough for anyone outside to hear.

Crouching low, he snapped on his flashlight and quickly swept the area, looking for the best place to hide. There were lots of tumbled down walls and piles of rotting junk, but over by the far wall looked like the best place. There was a wooden door behind an uneven barrier of loosely piled granite blocks. The stones had been stacked about waist-high and looked like a giant's grin with several teeth missing.

As good a place as any, Brian thought.

His sneakers scuffed the dirt floor as he raced over to the doorway and snapped off the flashlight before flattening himself on the ground behind the rock wall. He fought back a rush of fear as the darkness of the cellar closed down on him, and he started imagining all sorts of things, lurking around him just out of sight. His throat felt raw and dry, and his lungs were aching, but he forced himself to take slow, even breaths.

Just be quiet and wait it out, he cautioned himself. *Just wait it out.*

His ears began to ring as he waited to hear the heavy clomp of his father's footsteps upstairs, but they didn't come, even after he knew his father had had more than enough time to get up into the building. Could his father move that silently, or had he walked past the building, maybe gone down to the river?

Consumed with curiosity, Brian finally chanced a peek up over the edge of the makeshift rock wall. He scanned the area, shifting his gaze from one narrow cellar window to another. A dusty gloom hung like smoke in the air which was dank and laced with the aromas of mold and decay. After his eyes had adjusted to the diffused glow of sunlight, he looked over at the sawdust pile at the far end of the cellar. He thought he saw a plump, dark shape scurry out of sight.

He was beginning to think that, rather than enter the building which he had said was dangerous, his father had walked on by. Maybe he was heading someplace else . . . or maybe he was circling around to the back of the building, hoping to catch him off guard. Brian tensed, waiting to hear footsteps or see his father's feet and legs shift by one of the windows he could see, but the glow of daylight was never interrupted, and he never heard the creaking of floorboards overhead. The mill was encased in silence as palpable as darkness.

What the heck is going on out there? Brian wondered. *Has he gone home or back to work? Or is he positive I'm hiding in here and is just waiting for me to show myself?*

The damp cellar air sent a chill through Brian as he sat hunched behind the stone wall. His leg and shoulder muscles began to cramp up. After what he thought was a safe enough wait, he silently shifted to his feet and crouched in the darkness. He still waited, listening, but the cellar was as quiet as a tomb. He could hear nothing from outside—not even the high hiss of the wind or the distant singing of birds.

He wasn't wearing his watch, but he figured he had been down here for at least ten, more like fifteen or twenty minutes. He was positive his father would have gone by now; but still, he didn't dare move.

What if it's just a trick? he thought.

No, he should stay right where he was.

Then again, he knew he couldn't very well stay down here all day. In all likelihood, his father was long gone. If he had known he was hiding in here, wouldn't he have come into the mill and called for him? Brian was positive he would have heard *something* by now. He started to think this whole thing was a silly waste of time, hiding and waiting to get caught. His legs were tingling with pins-'n-needles, and the damp chill was working deeper into his bones.

At last, heaving a deep sigh, he unfolded his body and stood up. Blood rushed from his head to his legs, making him dizzy for a moment as he flexed his arms over his head. He was just about to move out into the cellar when a loud bang sounded behind him. Brian screamed and turned around just in time to see the wooden door behind him slam against the stone foundation wall. A dark, impossibly large shadow filled the open doorway, and then powerful hands reached out and took hold of him, locking him in a tight grip as they turned him around. Strong arms hugged him from behind and began to squeeze tightly.

"—*Help!* . . ." Brian managed to say before the air was forced out of his lungs.

Bright lights exploded like comets inside his head. Faintly, from far away, he heard a thud and a tinkle of broken glass and knew that he had dropped and broken his father's flashlight. But he didn't care—he was past caring as the arms embracing him squeezed ever tighter, and he spiraled down . . . down . . . down into a deep, impenetrable darkness.

It was a little past ten o'clock in the morning, and already Dianne was having a bad day . . . a *very* bad day.

198

After the euphoria of being released from the hospital the day before yesterday, and the relief of having the second of three operations behind her, she was starting to sink into a deep depression. Dr. Collett had warned her about this and had given her the name of a therapist she could call if she needed someone to talk to, but she wasn't sure she needed a shrink; she was convinced that all she needed was a couple of good night sleep. That would get her back on track and allow her natural healing processes to take over.

But for the last two nights, she hadn't slept well at all. Maybe it was because she was taking so many naps throughout the day, or maybe it was the combination of medications that was screwing her up. Whatever the reasons, what little sleep she got at night was haunted by fearful nightmares. For two nights in a row, masked, green-clad figures leaned over her bed, cackling with laughter as they tugged at her bed covers. Other faces, leering and diseased-looking, appeared out of the darkness around her. Flaps of decaying skin were peeled away from their foreheads so their inside-out faces flapped like strips of wet meat against their lower jaws when they spoke to her, saying things she could never quite understand. Every time she started to drift off to sleep, a sudden, blinding panic would seize her, and she would startle awake with a scream . . . except it wasn't a scream because with her jaw wired shut, she couldn't open her mouth wide enough to scream.

She thought that part of the problem was that she still couldn't breathe properly, especially when she was lying down. The nosebleeds—which, according to Dr. Collett, were a normal occurrence after such an operation—weren't as frequent, but blood and mucus from the operation was still lodged in the back of her throat, sealing off her nasal passages. She could still taste the thick, coppery aftertaste. Breathing in through her nose was nearly impossible as every breath she took, sucking air viciously through the wire mesh that blocked her mouth, sounded like the watery rattle of a severe asthmatic. She had to prop herself up in bed with three pillows to keep herself from choking, but she always ended up sitting there wide awake more than half the night as she stared around the darkened room. The few times she would start to drift off, she would start breathing through her nose and startle awake with a soft, frantic cry.

But even now, as she sat on the back porch with the warm morning sunshine washing over her, she was unable to breathe in enough air. Her lungs felt like they were being compressed. Even in the bright light of day, she felt an undercurrent of panic building up inside her, just waiting to burst out.

By the time she had come downstairs, around nine o'clock that morning, Edward had already left for work. She realized he must have gotten up early without disturbing her, fixed his own breakfast, cleaned up the kitchen, and left. There was a note on the kitchen table, letting her know that he planned to be home for lunch. He offered to make lunch for them if she wasn't feeling quite up to it.

Some lunch, she thought bitterly, *liquefied goop— morning, noon, and night!*

And where was Brian?

She had no idea and could care less where Brian was. He might have gone off to help his father, or he might be upstairs, listening to music on headphones or still sound asleep in bed. She was so wound up with her own problems, she gave him zero consideration as she leaned back and looked up at the sky, wishing to God the warm sunshine would raise her spirits.

But it didn't help!

Nothing seemed to help!

Already, she was tired of hearing herself try to talk

200

through the restraint on her jaw, and she was longing for the taste and texture of *real* food in her mouth. The bandages squeezed against her face, pulling it inward with a prickly warmth, but—thankfully—they were coming off tomorrow. She wished to hell her face didn't feel so numbed out, all puffy and . . . and just plain *wrong*. She had to fight the feeling that, during the operation, the doctors had peeled off her entire face and replaced it with someone else's; that when the bandages were removed, she wouldn't even recognize herself. That thought struck too close to the core of her worries—the idea that she was no longer the same person she had been before she had fallen off that cliff. And there was a deeper worry that she would *never* be that person again!

Maybe I should give that therapist a call, she thought as she sipped pureed scrambled eggs through a straw and swallowed noisily. There was almost no taste except for the metallic sting of blood clinging to the back of her throat. She forced herself to finish the drink and then quickly washed it down with a few sips of orange juice.

She had no definite plans for the day ahead. All she knew was, for at least the next week or two, she had no intentions of going shopping or of even leaving the house. Maybe she'd *never* leave the house again. That incident in the pharmacy parking lot on her way home from the hospital, like so many others over the past several weeks, was the last time she wanted to see or even to think that people were staring at her and wondering— *What in the world ever happened to that woman's face?*

She finished her orange juice and, sucking in a deep breath, leaned back in her chair, letting the full strength of the sunlight hit her face. As soon as her skin underneath the bandages began to feel prickly from the heat, she took one of the lawn chairs and the book she was reading, and went out into the backyard under the shade of the trees. She settled down and tried to get involved

201

with her reading, but her eyes hurt so badly she closed them, leaned back, and tried to fall asleep. The early morning chatter of birds and insects began to soothe her, but she didn't stay relaxed for long. Behind her eyelids wove zigzags of light, bright reds and yellows that exploded like dandelion puffs and faded to black. After a while, through the twisting curtains of light, indistinct faces began to materialize, zooming straight at her from the center of darkness. With a quick intake of breath, she sat up in the chair and opened her eyes.

She heard rather than saw the motion off to her left. There was a hard pounding sound for only an instant, then the scratchy, rustling sound of shaken foliage. Grunting with surprise, Dianne sat up and looked. The brightness of the day stung her eyes, but she saw the branches of a large clump of bushes jiggle. She was no nature person, but she suspected that only a heavy body, not just a bird or squirrel, would account for that much motion.

"Oh, shit," she whispered.

She stood up, not daring to take her eyes off the spot for an instant. The woods were a riot of greens and browns. The longer she stared at the spot, the more everything around her seemed to vibrate with light and shadow until it became a carousel of color. A strong wave of dizziness swept up inside her, blurring her vision. Her gaze kept drifting away from the spot where she had seen the movement, and she had to struggle to keep pulling it back.

"Who . . . who's there?" She called out as loud as she could, but her voice sounded like a nervous whimper. Her fists clenched at her sides, and she took a few quick steps forward, thinking it was better to challenge than to retreat.

"I said, *who's there?* Don't try to hide on me! I saw you, so you might as well come out!"

202

The surrounding woods were hushed. Even the birds seemed to have stopped singing as Dianne took a few more steps closer. She peered into the woods, trying to see through the screen of foliage, and thought she could make out a dark shape, huddled on the ground behind the thick bush. It might be a person, but it very well could be only a shadow, too.

Dianne paused at the edge of the lawn, wondering what to do next.

That had to have been a person, but who in their right mind would be out here, spying on her like this? Probably it was a curious kid from town, come out to gawk at the "ugly woman." But what if it wasn't a kid? What if it was someone who might prove dangerous if trapped?

She wished she had something to use as a weapon, but she didn't dare look away from the spot to find a branch or something she could use as she took her first, few tentative steps into the woods. Cool shadows wrapped their arms around her. Dried leaves and twigs crackled like a blazing fire underfoot. With every step, the shadow huddled underneath the bush resolved itself more clearly into human form. Dianne became absolutely convinced there was a person cowering there on the forest floor. She was just about to call out again when her foot caught on a hidden root. Crying out with surprise, she stumbled and had to look down to regain her footing. As soon as her head was turned, she heard another, louder rustling of leaves. Looking up quickly, she just caught sight of some-one—a dark figure, crouching low as it dashed from the bush to a thick clump of trees deeper in the woods. She listened to the heavy sound of feet pounding the ground. The figure was gone before Dianne could even blink.

"Hey! Hold it right there!" she shouted, but the person—whoever it was—was masked behind the trees. She knew it would be futile to pursue, possibly dangerous; but anger and panic rose up within her as the thudding footsteps and thrashing of branches faded only to be replaced by the silent hush of the forest.

"I saw you, you know!" she shouted, horribly aware that her muffled voice wouldn't carry far enough for the person to hear. Whoever it had been, he was long gone by now. Seething with frustration, Dianne turned and made her way out of the woods, casting worried glances over her shoulder with every other step.

She didn't have to think too hard about who that might have been. She was sure word had spread all around town about her. She still stung when she thought about the intense horror she had seen on the face of that little boy in the LaVerdier's parking lot. And her face still burned with embarrassment whenever she recalled that afternoon she had picked Brian up downtown and heard the exchange between those three boys he'd been talking to:

"*—Jesus Christ! Did you see that? Holy shit! The Old Witch Lady's back! Just like I told yah.*"

No doubt she had become the talk of the town—the ugly, bandaged woman living out on Pond Road who had once been so pretty. No doubt this intruder had been some curious kid who thought he could sneak up on her and get a good view of her so he could brag to his friends that he had been out to the house, spying on the Old Witch Lady.

"Little bastards!" Dianne shouted, shaking her clenched fists one last time at the silent woods before going up the steps and into the house. She shut the door firmly behind her and locked it for good measure.

When Edward came home for lunch that afternoon, she told him about the incident and asked him if there was anything they could do to keep anyone from coming around and bothering her. Edward didn't offer much of a solution other than maybe to buy a dog that would bark if someone came around. He hugged her and told her simply not to worry, but that didn't satisfy Dianne. All it meant to her was, if sitting in the backyard made her feel uncomfortable, it was just one more place she would have to avoid until her face was back to normal.

If it ever will be! she thought.

"Hey . . . You're finally waking up."

The voice came to Brian from far away, but it was something real, something almost tangible enough to hang onto, like a life raft.

"You know, I didn't mean to hurt you there," the voice continued in a low, soothing tone. "Honest. I'm sorry. I was just trying to surprise you a little."

The voice was deep and masculine, but it teased and danced, flitting like a gentle breeze as it dragged Brian closer to consciousness. Rolling his head from side to side, he tried to peel open his eyelids, but a glaring white light stung his eyes, making him cry out in pain.

"Hey, hey—don't rush things. Take a little time to let your eyes adjust." There was a short snorting laugh. "That's what *I* have to do all the time."

Brian licked his lips and tried to say something, but the closer he came to consciousness, the stronger the cold, black fear growing inside him became. He tried to remember where he was and what had happened. When he reached out blindly with one hand and felt that he was lying on something cold and gritty and hard, something like a dirt floor, it all came back to him in a roaring rush—

The mill!

"The mill . . ." he gasped.

"Yeah, you're in the mill, all right," the voice said. It sounded deeper, almost threatening or defensive, but it also had a familiar ring to it . . . almost—but not quite—like his father's voice.

"What am I—? How did—?"

Brian shook his head and shifted forward, feeling that the ground was firm but slightly yielding beneath his weight as he pushed himself up onto his elbows. Again, he tried to open his eyes, and this time, in spite of the harsh white glare that made everything blurry, he could make out a figure standing a few feet in front of him. Looking up from the ground, Brian thought the person looked incredibly huge as he stood there looking down at him with his hands on his hips. Like the voice, the silhouette looked vaguely familiar, like his father, but there was something . . . something different, too. Brian hiked himself up into a sitting position, rubbed his eyes, and shook his head harder, trying to clear away the last few cobwebs clouding his mind.

"Welcome to my home, Brian," the man said as he indicated the room with a wide sweep of his arm.

"How did —? . . . How do you know my name?"

Brian glanced down and saw that he was sitting on a worn-out mattress on the dirt floor. As he leaned forward, still trying to see what else was around him, a cloying, moldy smell wafted up into his nostrils, almost choking him. His fingertips brushed against the coarse texture of an old woolen blanket.

The light in the room was too bright, but second by second, his eyesight was adjusting. He could make out the crude wooden door on one wall. Against the wall right in front of him was a hand-made table constructed out of two-by-fours and planks that had obviously been scavenged from upstairs. He guessed that's what the door was made out of, too. There were piles of stuff on the table, but from this angle, Brian couldn't make out what they were. He figured it must be the man's food and clothes.

Hanging from a nail on one of the rafters was a Coleman lantern. It made a loud hissing noise as its core sent out a strong, white light that pushed back the shadows of the rafters, exposing every wood grain pattern and knot hole in sharp detail. The ceiling overhead was made of blackened timbers and charred planks. All in all, the room was maybe ten feet long and six feet wide. Brian guessed that he was in the small room at the back of the mill, probably directly beneath the part of the mill that had burned down.

"Who the . . . hell are you?" Brian said, looking again at the figure that stood in front of him. With the light behind him, the man's face was lost in shadow, but Brian could sense that he was smiling—maybe laughing at him.

"Who the hell am I?" the man said in a voice that quickly spiraled up the scale. "Who the *hell* am I? Why, for crying out loud, Brian, I'm your uncle . . . your Uncle Mike.

"My—*what?*" Brian bolted forward, but the sudden motion sent a bolt of pain through his head.

"Oh, you probably don't know a thing about me, do you?" the man said, laughing in the back of his throat as he shook his head from side to side. "Oh, no, no, no, probably not. Eddie—your father—he's my brother. He probably never even mentioned me to you, did he? But I sure as heck know who *you* are. Oh, yes indeed-I-do, I know *plenty* of things about you."

"Is that a fact?" Brian said, forcing strength into his voice. He shifted forward, wondering if he was strong enough to fight or run if he had to. Deep inside his brain, a warning bell was sounding. He was still disoriented from passing out, and had no idea what was really going on here, but one thing was certain: this man, whether or not he was who he claimed to be, was without a doubt dangerously crazy!

"Oh, absolutely," the man said. "I know a lot about you 'cause I've been watching you."

He chortled and took one step to the side, letting the lantern light fall across his face. Brian couldn't help but gasp with surprise. His doubts vanished in an instant, but not his fears. The man was wearing faded jeans that had a hole in one knee and a wornout flannel shirt over a green T-shirt. His face, hands, clothes, and sneakers were smeared with dirt and twigs, but it was obvious he had the same build, the same hair color, the same color eyes, even the same tight, cockeyed smile as his father. The only major difference Brian could see was in the man's eyes. Even in the bright light, they remained wide open and staring, and seemed not to blink very often as they danced crazily with reflected lantern light.

"Was that . . . was that you I saw, coming up the road a while ago?" Brian asked.

Michael smirked and nodded. "Could've been . . . could very well have been. I have no idea when you got here. Nobody told me. I didn't even know you were down here until I heard you climbing around outside my door. 'Course, at the time, I didn't know it was *you*. Could have been anybody!" His eyes rolled upwards, scanning the ceiling as though he expected to see someone clinging up there. "I didn't mean for you to—you know, to get so scared that you'd faint."

"Umm," Brian said, feeling slightly embarrassed. All the while he was studying the man, waiting to see if he would make a threatening move toward him. Finally, he sucked in a deep breath and started to stand up. When Michael suddenly moved forward, Brian cowered back, thinking he was going to attack him; but Michael grabbed his arm and helped him roughly to his feet.

"Thanks," Brian said, bending over and brushing off the seat of his pants. He took another opportunity to look around the room but didn't see much more. His hunch had been right—the makeshift table was covered with an assortment of food and drinks and a few odds and ends of tools—a saw, hammer, and what looked like bags of nails. Other than the table, the old blanket on the

208

mattress, and a rolled up paper bag on the floor, the room was empty except for the four blank, stone walls.

"You said that you—uh, do you actually live down here?" Brian asked, unable to hide the incredulous tone in his voice.

"That's right," Michael said with a curious twist of glee in his voice. "I started fixing this place up a long time ago." His eyes suddenly went unfocused and he stared at the stone wall. Then he shook his head and continued as if he had never stopped talking. "It was gonna be my shelter—my bomb shelter, but I suppose, now that the Russians have left Cuba and the whole Soviet Union has collapsed, that's not much of a worry anymore, huh?"

"No, I—uh, I suppose not," Brian said, shaking his head as he cast his uncle a curious glance. How could this *really* be his uncle? He never even knew he had one, but then again, he had spent so little time with his father he hardly knew him at all.

"But you can't have—you haven't been living out here all your life, have you?"

Michael burst out in a spray of snot and laughter. "Of course not! I've been away, living someplace else, but I came back. I *had* to come back!"

His voice and facial expression suddenly shifted, lowering and deepening with menace. The lantern cast deep lines on his face, and the wild light left his eyes like candles that had been snuffed out. His mouth firmed up into a thin, bloodless line.

"I had to come back," he said in a whisper, "because she . . . she might need me."

Brian was about to ask who might need him, but then he thought that it might be better to direct Michael onto some other point of conversation, something that might not upset him as much.

"So . . . well, how long have you been here?" Brian asked.

Brian looked at the wooden door. As far as he could see, there was just this one entrance into the room. He took a single step toward it, wondering if he could get it open and get the hell out of here fast enough if he had to.

"Oh, not long . . . not long," Uncle Mike said, shrugging and slapping his thighs with his hands. "I came as soon as I heard what had happened, but I have to stay out of sight, you know. I can't let them see me."

"Can't let *who* see you?" Brian asked as he inched another step closer to the door. His muscles were tensed as he coiled up, getting ready to make a run for it.

"Well my brother, for one—your father!" Michael shouted. His voice suddenly flared up like a fire that had been doused with gasoline. His face went bright red, and his eyes bugged out of his head like someone in the grips of complete terror. "If *he* knew I was out here, why—he'd send me back to the hospital as quick as a wink. So I can't let him find me. No sir-ee-bobcat! And there are others. You must realize that! Haven't you seen or heard any of them?"

"Oh, yeah—absolutely," Brian said, realizing that he'd been right about another thing: his Uncle Mike, or whoever this man was, was very close to—if not already over—the edge of insanity.

"No, he wouldn't understand at all," Michael went on, shaking his head. "I wouldn't expect him to. When he called and told me about what had happened . . . to my mother, that she was . . . was—"

He wouldn't say the word, but Brian thought it for him: *Dead!*

"He sounded so . . . so detached from it all, like it hadn't affected him at *all!* But it got to me!" Michael slapped the flat of his hand against his forehead, making a wet, smacking sound. "Oh, yes-sir-ee! It got to me all right!"

As Brian watched the range of expressions shift across Michael's face, from humor to anger to sadness, he couldn't help but feel a stirring of sympathy for him. In some ways, he was almost envious that his obviously crazy uncle could let his emotions fly so freely. Ever since he was little, Brian was used to bottling up everything inside him until it finally exploded out, usually in anger. At the same time, he realized that Uncle Mike could easily turn his anger and remorse onto him, and that he wasn't going to be safe until he was far away from here.

"But what about my dad? If he knew you were out here, I'm sure he'd want to help you."

"Oh no, he *wouldn't!*" Michael said, waving his hands in front of Brian's face. "He'd put me away again, just like they did back then. But you see, now that she's gone, now that my mother's—"

Again, he couldn't bring himself to say the word *dead*.

"I just want to stay out here for a while," he said, his voice edged with pleading. "I won't cause anybody any trouble. Honest, I won't."

Tears filled his eyes, and he folded his hands to his chest as if he were praying. His whole body shook as he spoke.

"I wouldn't hurt anyone, no matter what *they* say. I couldn't! I gave you back your croquet ball, didn't I? Well—" His voice lowered threateningly. *"Didn't* I?"

Brian bit his lower lip and nodded slightly. He remembered the stark terror he had felt that day in the backyard, just knowing there was someone out there in the woods, watching him. Now he wished he had told his father everything that had happened that day. If he had, his father might have found his brother out here before now, and this wouldn't be happening. Watching his uncle carefully, he took another step closer to the door.

"Well, you know, I really ought to be getting back to the house," he said softly. He didn't want to say or do anything that might set Uncle Mike off, but he knew it was a little like tap dancing on a land mine; there were no ground rules. The slightest pressure in the wrong direction could set him off, and he had no idea what the right or wrong direction was. "I—I don't want my father to be worried about me."

"Worried, oh, he should be worried, all right, but not about you—about *me!* I'm the one who's had to live with it all my life, you know, and now she's . . . gone, and they're all telling me things aren't going to be the same anymore." He reached for Brian and grabbed him roughly by the shoulders. "You have to promise me one thing—okay?"

"Wha—what?" Brian said, cringing back, expecting to be hit in the face.

Michael let him go, took three steps backwards, and planted himself in front of the door, blocking it.

"I need your help out here," he said in a ragged gasp. He hunched his shoulders and craned his head around as though listening for something. "Not for long. I won't stay here much longer, now that I've seen where she . . . where she's—" His voice choked off sharply, and tears formed in his eyes. "But I've been looking around and asking for someone to help me, you see. You can keep a secret, can't you?"

Almost against his will, Brian nodded agreement. If he wanted to get out of this room alive, he knew he had to agree with *anything* Uncle Mike said right now; but he couldn't deny the surge of sympathy he felt for him, either.

"That's good, that's real good," Michael said, his voice softening a bit as his posture relaxed. "I need some more food and some warm clothes. And something to drink beside water. Some beer would be nice. Can you manage that? Maybe a sleeping bag or some more blankets, too. The nights have been pretty chilly out here, you know."

"Why don't you just—" Brian started to say but then stopped himself.

"I promise I won't stay here more than another week or two," Michael said, his voice whining like a kid who wanted something too expensive for Christmas. "A month at the most—honest! I just have to make sure that everything's . . . everything's all right around here, you understand? After that, I promise I'll go."

"Go where?" Brian asked.

Against his will, he felt his heart softening for this man. Even standing there in front of the door, looking like an immovable statue with his arms folded across his chest, he looked so lost and pitiful. The expression on his face was like a little boy's who had lost his mother and didn't quite understand how or why.

"I . . . don't know," Michael replied, shaking his head quickly. He looked at Brian with a distant glaze, like frost in his eyes. "I just know that I don't want to go back . . . there—back where I was before." His face and voice suddenly hardened. "I'm *not* crazy, you know."

Brian gave him a noncommittal shrug as he considered what to do next.

"Yeah," he said after a moment. "I suppose I could bring you some stuff."

Even as he said it, he wasn't quite sure if he truly meant it or if he was simply saying this to get out of here. Either way, it didn't matter. His fear was that Uncle Mike wasn't going to let him go unless or until he wanted to. He was obviously strong enough to do whatever he wanted to him.

"I don't need a whole lot," Michael said, his face brightening. "I've been walking into town, all the way to Biddeford to get stuff. No one recognizes me there, but still, I only go at night in case—you know, in case the police are looking for me."

Brian wanted to ask if there was any particular reason

213

the police might be looking for him but decided not to.

"Can I . . . go now?" he asked with a tremor in his voice.

Without a word, Michael backed away from the door. Brian walked up to it, flipped the homemade latch, and pushed the door open. The edge scraped like sandpaper across the dirt floor. A draft of cool air washed over him, making him shiver.

"You won't forget about me, now, will you?" Michael asked. Once again, his voice was edging up to a hysterical whine.

Brian looked at him and was struck again at how pitiful the man looked. He shook his head and said, "Don't worry. I won't."

"And you promise you won't tell your father that I'm out here, will you? You already promised me you wouldn't."

"I said don't worry." Brian said, making an X on his chest. "Cross my heart and hope to die—"

"Stick a needle in my eye," Michael finished for him, and they both laughed out loud.

"I'm not sure when I can get back out here," Brian said. "I've been helping my father work at the—"

"You think I don't know that?" Michael said simply.

Brian shrugged and said, "Look, I'll do the best I can, all right? But you have to trust me. I'll try to get out here tomorrow, but it'll be the next day at the latest." He started to leave, amazed that he was really going to be able to walk out of here this easily. At the door, he turned back and said, "I wish you'd come home with me, though."

"Uh-uh! No way," Michael said. His eyes glistened with tears in the lantern light. "Your father would pack me off back to the funny farm in a second."

Brian took a deep breath and wished he could ignore the tortured, lonely expression on his uncle's face. He

214

knew, no matter what else, that he would probably dream about him tonight.

"It's just that I just feel so—" He sighed and shook his head. "It's just that it must get awfully lonely for you out here."

"Oh, no. Don't worry," Michael replied, sniffing with laughter, "I have all the company I need." He leaned forward and tapped his head lightly with his forefinger as if he and Brian were sharing a deep secret. "And anyway— although I think everyone's a little bit angry with me right now, I'll be all right. Don't you worry about me."

Brian had no idea what he meant by that, so he let that comment slide like so much else his uncle had said. He said a quick goodbye, then hurried out into the cellar, scrambled up the pile of rubble to the stairway opening, and jumped to the ground from the side door. He wanted to run away from the mill as fast as he could, but he forced himself to keep his pace slow and casual, just in case Uncle Mike was watching him.

Once he was halfway down the road, he turned and looked back at the mill, his whole body feeling rubbery with relief. He didn't see Uncle Mike anywhere, but that was no guarantee that he wasn't hiding somewhere nearby. Even in the bright sunlight, the mill looked odd, almost like an illusion that wasn't really there. Brian couldn't repress the shiver that raced through him when he was struck by an unnerving thought:

What if he's not in there? What if he's not even real? What if I imagined everything that just happened?

He stared at the old mill for a long time, studying the way the sunlight glanced off the slick, gray siding. He found the difference between being inside the building and out here in the sunshine stunning, nearly staggering. He felt completely disoriented, as though he had just zapped between two entirely different worlds.

And then another thought struck him:

215

How did Uncle Mike get into that room so he was be-hind me?

Uncle Mike had all but admitted that Brian had seen him coming up the road. Brian had been so scared that he was going to be caught by his father, he surely would have seen or heard *something* if anyone had made any noise getting into that small room in the cellar. One thing was for sure, he hadn't used the door.

So how did he do it? How did Uncle Mike sneak in there without me knowing it?

He tried to laugh it off, but the sound was hollow and false. In a lot of ways, he thought Uncle Mike was like the old mill — full of mystery and secrets. And Brian found that he was curious to find out more about him. He started for home again, and long before he got there, he had made up his mind. Against his better judgment, he was going to keep Uncle Mike's secret, at least for a while longer . . . long enough to find out a few more things about him *and* the old mill.

Chapter Fifteen
Memory Lapse

Dianne's first meeting with Ruth Murray, the therapist Dr. Collett had recommended, was two days later, the day after she had the bandages removed from her face. The meeting went about as well as she could have expected, considering the circumstances. After fifteen minutes or so of casual conversation, in which she felt completely self-conscious about her red, swollen face, Dianne started to feel at least relaxed enough to begin to talk about some of the negative feelings she harbored concerning her accident and the operation. Several times, a sour, stomach-churning tension started to rise up inside her—especially when she told Dr. Murray how bad it got at night when she was terrified of falling asleep because she was afraid of vomiting and choking on blood or of not getting enough breath through the strands of wire that held her jaw in place. She didn't mention the nightmares, thinking she'd keep them in reserve for the next session—if there was a next session.

Intellectually, Dianne realized that she couldn't choke on her own vomit simply because she hadn't eaten any solid food in weeks, but just having her jaw immobilized made her *feel* like she was in serious danger. She had also mentioned to Dr. Murray her concern that the medication she was taking might be screwing up her perceptions, affecting her concentration, and making her absentminded.

Dr. Murray reassured her that all of her fears were, while certainly normal and entirely understandable, not rational, and that she simply had to believe that she was going to be all right. She couldn't allow her negative thoughts get so out of control. She taught Dianne a quick mental exercise of creative visualization which she could try the next time she felt a panic attack coming on. She also suggested speaking with her doctor about reducing the dosage of medication, just in case it was too strong for her.

Dianne left the office feeling a bit more upbeat, but that quickly faded when, an hour later, she was slowed almost to a stop on Route One in Saco, stuck behind a slow-moving U-Haul rental truck. Her car's air conditioner was barely functioning, so the air swirling inside the car felt sluggish and sticky. Her breathing came in shallow gulps, and before long, that same old cramp of apprehension turned into a cold rush of panic as it crept up from the pit of her stomach. She snapped on the radio, rolled down her window, and took several deep breaths to try and distract herself, but the prickly feeling quickly spread up her back, dancing like needles of ice between her shoulders to the back of her head.

Jesus Christ, not now! Not now! she thought, her lips moving as she mentally formed the words. Her tongue pressed up like a trapped animal against the metal cage in her mouth.

She started to think—now—that maybe visiting the therapist hadn't been such a good idea after all; if anything, it had only made her feel more threatened and vulnerable. She tried to focus clearly on a single thought—all she wanted to do was get home before lunchtime so she could put together a picnic lunch and surprise Edward out at the house site. But her anxiety rose steadily, spiking into pure, stainless steel terror with her frustrated desire for traffic to get moving.

"Come on . . . Come *on!*" she said tightly, resisting the urge to honk the horn. She tried several times to pull out around the van, but the steady flow of on-coming traffic forced her back, earning her nothing more than a blasting toot or an angry gesture from the other drivers.

Jesus! Jesus! JESUS! Stop it, please! Stop it now!

Tears welled up in her eyes. Her hands were slick with sweat, and her knuckles turned white as she squeezed hard on the steering wheel. The clammy chill skittered like dead fingers up over the top of her head and embraced her skull. The slow-moving truck loomed large in front of her, sunlight reflecting wick-edly off its shiny back door. Several times she had to jam on the brakes suddenly when the truck stopped and she spaced out for a split second and didn't notice until almost too late. She wanted like hell to lay down hard on the horn and hold it, but the choking sensa-tion tightening around her throat convinced her that she couldn't handle any more noise. Even the hissing *whoosh* of passing traffic made her nerves crackle like thin ice.

"Jesus, please . . . *please* get me out of this!" she begged in a low whisper. The muscles in her jaw were aching. A sour taste filled the back of her throat, warning her that she was about to throw up.

"Get the *fuck* off the road," she mumbled, deep in her throat.

But Jesus Christ, U-Haul, and she herself couldn't manage to get her car around the truck. They were so close together that she thought it must look like the truck was towing her as they lurched in the stop-and-start traffic down Route One. They never went faster than twenty-five miles an hour until they stopped for the traffic light at the corner of Main Street and Beech.

"Come on! . . . Come *on!* Move your *ass!*" Dianne whispered, her voice hissing between the wires in her mouth.

She remembered the mental exercise Ruth had taught her and wanted to give it a try, but towering wave after wave of cold nausea flooded through her, breaking her concentration. And anyway, she knew the panic attack had already progressed too far to stop now. Feeling faint and wanting more than anything else just to scream out loud, Dianne looked out at the heat-hazed town, unable to dispel the eerie sensation that none of it was real—that the scene around her was nothing more than a pale, thin shadow of what it used to be. Shoppers, businessmen, and women on lunch break moved along the sidewalks with a curious, silent glide. Litter and pigeons swirled almost soundlessly in the gutters, distantly rattling like bones on the pavement.

"Please, please, *please* just get *out* of my *way!*"

When she stuck her head out the window, trying to see around the van, the fluttering sound of voices, deadened by the blanket of humidity, drew her attention. She looked around and saw two people, a man and a woman, squared off against each other on the sidewalk in front of a shabby building. A neon Moosehead Beer sign flickered in the window behind the woman's head. Above it was a faded, painted sign that read THE FIREHOUSE.

Dianne's chest felt compressed; she couldn't even breathe as she watched the couple argue. The man had his back turned to her, so she couldn't see his face, but the angered expression on the woman's face struck Dianne with a sharp jab of recognition.

What the hell—? Dianne wondered. *What is it about her that's so familiar?*

The tight grip she had on the steering wheel made the heels of her palms ache. She knew she should focus her attention on her driving, be ready for the light to change, but she couldn't tear her gaze away from the couple. She made a frightened squeak in the back of her throat when she saw the man clench his fist, cock back his arm, and throw a roundhouse at the woman's face. The man was obviously drunk, and the woman dodged easily to one side as he spun around with the momentum of his swing. She came up beside him with her own clenched fist, jabbed with precision, and caught him on the right side of the jaw.

The wet smack of the woman's knuckles against the man's fleshy jowls cracked through the air like a gunshot.

But it wasn't the trading of punches that kept Dianne's attention; it was the expression on the woman's face just before she hit the man. It was there for an instant, flickering like summer lightning, but the gleam of absolute determination and delight when her fist connected was stunning. Her eyes flashed wickedly in the sunlight. The grim set of her jaw blended into a triumphant smile when she saw the man stagger backward with a goofy-legged stagger. He spun around on one heel, his hands clapped across his mouth as thin streamers of blood leaked between his fingers and ran down onto his chest.

"Don't you *ever* talk to me like that again!" the woman shrieked, her voice carrying clear and shrill in the humid air.

The man hunched over and said something, but Dianne couldn't quite catch it. Suddenly the driver behind her blasted his horn. Dianne jumped, glanced in her rearview mirror, then looked ahead. The van was only a few feet from her front bumper but moving forward slowly. She stepped down on the gas to start moving with the flow of traffic.

Dianne's mind swirled with confusion. Although she was sure she had never seen her before in her life, she was positive she recognized that woman. The mixed expression of stark fear and triumph flashing across that woman's face reawakened something deep inside Dianne . . . something that had been dormant a long time but was now stirring like a slimy creature that had slept too long in the muddy bottom of a pond.

The world outside the car withdrew, looking incredibly distant as rippling patches of darkness nibbled at the edge of her vision, threatening to sweep across her sight. She wasn't even conscious of her own breathing as the black bubble of a long-buried memory rose to the surface of her mind.

I've seen that look before! she thought, only distantly aware of the cold, clammy feeling that washed over her. Her mind was spinning out of control, shuffling through memories she hadn't had in years.

Where have I seen that look before?

She was feeling so overwhelmed she barely reacted at all when, at the next intersection, the moving van turned right onto the Old County Road, heading to Summerfield like she was. She couldn't stop the gnawing wonder and worry about what she had seen back there at the traffic light. She knew if she thought about it long enough, she could figure out exactly what that woman's situation was, and she should be concerned for the woman's eventual safety once her husband or boyfriend or whoever that was finally sobered up.

But that wasn't what filled her with such gut-twisting apprehension.

Waves of cold, clenching panic and deeper stirrings of dread wrung her out, making her feel numb. For a moment, she had the curious sensation of being outside herself, watching from the back seat as she drove along the winding country road behind the moving van. Her mind was so lost in thought that she was barely aware of the loose play of the steering wheel in her grip or the pressure she alternately applied to the accelerator and the brakes as the van finally gained a bit of speed and got up to a whopping thirty-five miles per hour.

Where have I seen that look before?

She no longer cared how fast or how slow the van was going; she had to figure this out—*right now!* It must have something to do with seeing a therapist for the first time in her life this morning. She had always held the opinion that only crazy people—real nut cases had to see shrinks. Was she so far gone that she had to talk to someone so she wouldn't lose her mind completely? Was the next step a straitjacket, a shot of Thorazine, and a rubber room?

At first she was almost convinced that maybe that look of pure, outraged delight on the woman's face had something to do with herself . . . that it was something she had felt or might have looked like at one time or another. But when had she ever been that angry at someone?

Damnit! Where have I seen that look before?

When had she ever wanted to *hurt* someone the way that woman had obviously wanted to hurt that drunken man? When had she ever—

The thought gave her a sudden twisting in the pit of her stomach.

When had she ever wanted to *kill* someone?

That's was it! That woman had truly wanted to *kill* that man!

And then it hit her . . . It hit her so hard she jammed on the brakes and skidded to a stop by the side of the road. Dust rose up behind her car in a funnel-shaped cloud. She sat, watching numbly as the van pulled away, stretching out the distance between them, dimly grateful that there hadn't been a car tail-gating her the way she had been tailgating the van. The dust swirled and then settled onto her car and the roadside weeds like pollen. The throbbing tightness in her chest and throat became unbearable. From behind the wires trapping her jaw, her throat warbled with a low, building howl that sounded like an animal in pain. Hot, plump tears ran down her face and dripped onto her hitching chest.

Oh, God! My mother!

The thought was like a blinding bolt of light spear-ing the darkness inside her mind. Shivers raced through her like electricity.

It wasn't me! . . . It was my mother!

The bright green field beside her disappeared in a watery blur. Her hands trembled, no matter how tightly she held onto the steering wheel as though for dear life. Her breath whistled through the wires as she took sharp, panting breaths.

I was—what? Only eight years old when I saw that same, exact expression on my mother's face.

The hitching in her chest felt like sharp knife blades, sliding up under her ribs.

It was just before dad left home for good . . . the time—like so many others—when he was drunk on his ass and they started arguing . . . only this time . . . this time they didn't just argue . . . she got mad . . . so mad at him that she—

"Oh, my God!" Dianne muttered, pressing her fists hard against her closed eyes as if she could somehow reach inside her brain and push the memory back

224

down into the darkness where it had remained—forgotten—for all these years.

So mad at him that she tried to kill him!

"Hey, Uncle Mike! You in there?"

As he walked boldly through the field of weeds up to the old mill, Brian tried to make his greeting sound hale and hearty, but his voice echoed back from inside the building with an odd flatness. The pigeons nesting in the attic cooed softly and ruffled their wings. Six or seven of them shot up into the air and started circling around as Brian walked over to the stone stairway that led down into the cellar.

"Hey, I've got some of that stuff you wanted," Brian shouted. He stopped at the top of the stone stairway and put the bag of food and the folded blanket down on the ground. Wiping the sweat from his head with the back of his arm, he leaned forward and peered down into the gloom below. A cold draft blew up from the cellar into his face, carrying with it that almost-but-not-quite nauseating smell of damp earth and decay. Brian chuckled at how the smell already seemed so familiar—almost welcoming.

"Yo! Uncle Mike! It's just me, Brian!" he shouted, cupping his hands to his mouth. "It's okay!"

No reply came from inside the mill, but Brian couldn't shake the sensation that Uncle Mike was hiding somewhere nearby, watching every move he made. Was this some kind of test, to see what he would do?

He straightened up slowly and glanced around. To his left, the river glistened in the morning light, sparkling with flashes of silver through the trees. A strong, hot breeze whisked through the weeds, flattening them as if invisible hands were pushing down on them.

"I got some food here for you!" Brian shouted. He

noticed this time that his voice carried a slight waver. He swallowed and licked his lips before adding, "If you want, I can just leave it downstairs."

Still, no answer came except for the wind, whistling as it gusted warmly at his back with a gentle shove. Taking a deep breath, Brian picked up the things he had been carrying and started down the steps. Cobwebs brushed against his face with a feathery touch, but his hands were full, so he couldn't brush them away.

He couldn't dispel the sensation that he was sinking down into cold, brackish water as the damp air and gloom of the cellar embraced him. He reached around to his back pocket and fished out the small flashlight he'd gotten from the kitchen cupboard. He clicked it on, but the beam, although strong, barely cut the darkness as he made his way across the cellar floor to the back room door. His sneakers scuffed in the dirt with a harsh, gritty sound that reminded him of someone munching on cereal. A current of tension ran through him, but he commanded himself not to let it get the better of him. If Uncle Mike was dangerous, he never would have let him leave here yesterday. Besides, wasn't it obvious that he was here to help him?

The rough wooden door was shut but not locked. Brian lifted up on the door as he pulled it open so the bottom wouldn't catch on the uneven floor. Inside, the room was dark, and a quick survey with the flashlight revealed that it was unoccupied. Brian swallowed hard as he entered the room, closing the door behind him. He found it difficult to believe that anyone could actually live down here. It was so confined, so, so dismal . . . like a jail cell.

But maybe that's what he got used to at the mental hospital, Brian thought with a shiver.

He walked over to the homemade table and deposited his load of goods. He considered writing a note but realized he didn't have a pen or pencil—besides, he wasn't even sure Mike knew how to read, so he contented himself with taking the boxes and cans of food out of the bag and spreading them across the table.

"There—" he muttered, brushing his hands in satisfaction.

He wondered if he should stick around until Uncle Mike showed up or just head back home. He certainly didn't have anything else important to do, but he wasn't so sure he wanted to wait down here. He was thinking he could at least go upstairs and poke around in the mill some more, but then a thought hit him—

Two days ago, the last time he was out here, how did Uncle Mike get down into this room without being seen or heard?

As far as he knew, there was only this one entrance into the room; but he had seen Uncle Mike coming up the road, heading toward the mill, and later, after they started talking, Uncle Mike had admitted it was him, so how did he do it? Somewhere, there had to be another entrance into this back room.

After glancing out into the main part of the cellar and calling out again to make sure Mike wasn't around, Brian began a systematic search of the small room. Scrambling around on his hands and knees, he checked underneath the table, behind the old mattress, everywhere, but the stone walls were just what they appeared to be—solid granite blocks that didn't move no matter how hard he pushed against them. Brian considered that there might be some hidden mechanism that could trigger a hidden doorway, but how likely was something like that in a building this old? It was a real stumper, but he knew there *had* to be a solution. After the better part of half an hour, he had scanned every square inch of the walls twice and still couldn't find anything. Sighing with frustration, he sat down leaned his head back against the wall. By chance, he happened to look up.

"The ceiling! That's gotta be it," he whispered.

He stood up and ran his flashlight beam up and down along the ceiling rafters. The charred timbers of the floor above him were supported by thick joists that were worm-eaten and blackened by fire. Several decade's worth of cobwebs draped down in thick, black tangles. Brian knew this room was underneath the pile of burned rubble at the back of the building. Maybe there was a trapdoor, like in the other part of the mill.

"That *has* to be it!" he said, punching his thigh with his fist.

All of the ceiling joists were evenly spaced a foot and a half apart, but as far as he could tell, there was nothing to indicate a hidden trapdoor. Uncle Mike might have a few of the boards up there loosened so he can move them aside whenever he wanted to drop down into the room; but Brian was positive that, as nerved up as he had been that other day, he would have heard him. Still, this seemed like the only possibility, so he crossed the room, standing up on tiptoes and pushing up against the floorboards to see if anything moved. Gritty soot fell down, sprinkling his face like pepper.

"Damn! It's *gotta* be here *somewhere*," he whispered as he probed every bay between the joists.

But twenty minutes and an aching neck later, he had tried every board in the ceiling, and nothing had moved. Okay, so Uncle Mike didn't gain entry from above. That only left . . .

"Of *course!*" Brian shouted, clapping his hands together. "The floor!"

His gaze went directly to the blanket-covered mattress, and before he could take another breath, he was on his hands and knees, lifting up one edge. The moldy smell of the rotting wool blanket gagged him, almost making him vomit, but underneath the mattress he found a flat piece of plywood. And it looked like *new* plywood, not something that had been rotting out here since the mill had been operating. Sitting back on his haunches, Brian pushed the board and mattress aside with the heels of his sneakers. The thing slid begrudgingly, but even before it was halfway over, Brian knew that he had found what he was looking for. Beneath the plywood was a dark hole with earth-lined walls. With a cautious glance over his shoulder, he scrambled forward and shined his flashlight down into it.

"All right!" he whispered.

Brian's guess was that the tunnel had been dug recently, probably since Mike had returned to the mill. It dropped straight down maybe five or six feet, and then angled sharply toward the stone wall. The hard-packed earth walls were festooned with hairy roots that hung down in tangled clumps. The rich smell of freshly dug dirt filled Brian's nostrils. He had no doubt that, once the tunnel passed under the outside wall of the building, it angled upwards. He hadn't found it outside because Uncle Mike had probably covered it with debris from the burned portion of the building.

"That's the ticket," he whispered, satisfied that he had finally figured out how Mike had gotten into the building and snuck up behind him. He was still glorying in his discovery when he became aware of a faint, whispering voice. He snapped off his flashlight and tensed, straining to listen, but the voice—if it had ever been there at all—was gone.

Am I hearing things, or was that—

Down inside the tunnel, he saw a soft glow of light appear from the other end. There was a gentle hissing sound, like light rain patting against a window as dirt sifted down into the hole. The diffuse glow got steadily brighter. Brian heard the sounds of heavy boards being moved aside.

Oh, shit! That's gotta be Mike, up there! He's back! Brian thought with a sudden flush of panic.

For a single heartbeat, he watched as the light shining down into the hole was suddenly blotted out; then he sprang into action. He knew he couldn't let his uncle catch him here, especially now that he'd found out about the secret entrance. He jumped over to the other side of the mattress and quickly shoved the plywood and mattress back into place. He hoped to hell Mike wasn't in the tunnel yet, and that he hadn't heard the noise he was making. Once the plywood was back in place, he got up, brushed off his pants, and ran to the door without looking back. Gritting his teeth, he carefully lifted up the edge of the door and, grateful that the hinges didn't squeak, wedged it open just enough so he could slip out. Just as he was easing the door shut behind him, he heard a loud scraping sound from inside the room as Uncle Mike shifted the plywood aside to open the secret entrance.

Panting lightly to control his breathing, Brian leaned against the door, pressing his ear against the rough wood so he could listen to the sounds coming from inside the room. First he heard a low grunting sound followed by a heavy thump. That must have been Uncle Mike, hiking himself up out of the tunnel opening. Then there came that scraping sound again—the plywood dragging against the dirt floor as Mike slid the mattress back into place.

So far so good, Brian thought, but he knew he

230

wasn't in the clear yet. The air in the cellar seemed to have gone suddenly bad. He tried to swallow down the lump that had formed in his throat, but it wouldn't budge.

He knew he had to get the hell out of here before Uncle Mike discovered him, so he turned and ran. He scrambled up the stone stairs, blinking in the bright sunlight, and then ran as fast as he could across the field. Weeds and grass whipped against his legs and arms, stinging. Brian wanted to be out of sight and down the road long before Uncle Mike even noticed the new supplies on his table. He thought to check his watch so, when he saw Uncle Mike again, he could lie about what time he had been out there.

As he ran, he kept glancing over his shoulder. As soon as the mill was out of sight, he slowed to catch his breath. Just as he was leaving the rutted dirt road and entering the woods, the sudden blast of a horn, far off in the distance, made him jerk to a stop. His pulse surged for a moment, but then he shook his head, embarrassed that he had let the sound surprise him. He knew exactly what it was—the town fire horn. He stood in the dancing shadows of the tree and patiently counted out the number of horn blasts.

"Two-two-four-four."

They meant nothing to him, so after one more glance over his shoulder to make sure Uncle Mike wasn't following him, he resumed his leisurely pace toward home.

"Hey, you seem kind of quiet today," Edward said. "Is everything all right?"

Edward had already eaten the tuna fish sandwich and drunk the thermos-full of coffee Dianne had brought out to him, and now they were sitting side by

231

side under one of the few large maple trees he'd left standing in the wide clearing. Off to their left, in the spot where the excavator would start digging the house's foundation on Monday, orange flames glowed inside the tangled pile of branches and stumps. Bright sunlight made the flames almost invisible. A thin, gray wash of smoke curled up and vanished like heat haze into the blue sky. Shadows of leaves dappled their faces as the wind gently stirred the trees overhead.

Leaning forward, Edward placed one hand gently on Dianne's leg and tried to nudge her closer to him. She resisted, twisting away from him and focusing intently on the tumbler she was gripping tightly with both hands. It contained the remains of a greenish concoction of pureed vegetables, the bulk of her lunch.

"Did you have another confrontation with Brian or something this morning?" Edward asked.

Dianne shook her head. "No," she said simply, and then fell silent, letting her gaze follow the drifting wisps of smoke up into the sky.

"Hey, com'on now, hon. Tell me what's bugging you?"

Dianne stared blankly at him for a moment, her eyes watering as she forced a smile. She was horribly aware that what constituted her smile these days was skinning back her upper lip and exposing the network of wires that was strung inside her mouth. She quickly looked away.

"Was it . . . Does it have anything to do with your visit with that doctor this morning?"

Dianne shrugged and cleared her throat, trying her best to ignore the hot rush of discomfort that rippled through her stomach. She couldn't get the right words to form in her brain, much less on her tongue.

"I know how tough—that is, I *suspect* I know how tough all of this is on you," Edward went on, "but one thing you've got to understand is that you can talk to me—about *anything!* You got that?"

Dianne grunted softly as she nodded. She wanted more than anything to tell him about what had happened on the drive home, but something made her choke back the words, as if speaking them would somehow bring harm both to her and to Edward.

"It's just . . . I dunno. Everything, I guess," she said at last, if only to break the uncomfortable silence that had settled between them. Her breath caught in her throat, and she struggled hard to keep herself from crying. God, it seemed like all she did these days was cry.

"I—we talked a lot about things but nothing—you know, nothing really deep," Dianne said in a soft, shattered voice. "I mentioned to her how I thought the medication I was on was messing me up."

"What did she say?"

"She thought I should mention it to Dr. Collett. Maybe he'd prescribe something not quite as strong."

Edward took a deep breath. "That's understandable," he said, "but after everything you've been through, don't you think it's also reasonable that your emotions would feel all—all tangled up?"

"I suppose so . . . Sure, but I—I just don't like what I've been thinking and feeling lately. I don't even feel like myself anymore, if that makes any sense. I'm so forgetful all the time, and I . . . I don't know . . . I feel so . . . so agitated, like I want to—to . . ."

Her voice trailed away before she could finish the sentence—*to slug somebody.* The memory of that woman, punching the drunken man in the face this morning rose up in her mind, leaving her feeling cold and hollow. A chill ran through her like electricity.

"That's quite understandable, too," Edward said softly, nudging her on the leg again. She thought he

233

was signaling that he wanted to go back to the house for some afternoon sex, but she banished any such thoughts, wondering—*How can he even stomach looking at me, much less wanting to kiss me?* They hadn't had sex since the night before her accident, and she didn't think they would until this whole thing was all over.

If it will ever be all over!

That thought finally broke through the last of her resistance, and she could no longer hold back her tears. Burying her face in her hands, she leaned forward and sobbed in long, wrenching groans. She was only distantly aware of Edward's arms twining around her and pulling her tightly against his chest.

"There . . . there," he said, his voice soft and soothing.

But rather than making her feel comforted, his embrace sent a jab of alarm racing through her. The confinement—like the confinement of her jaw by those goddamned wires!—filled her with a sparkling panic. Before she could stop it, the memory arose again of that woman's expression, her eyes gleaming with near ecstasy as she smashed her fist into the drunken man's face. In a sizzling flash, the woman's face became first her mother's face, then her own. Her whole body tensed, filled with a wild impulse to haul back and slug Edward.

"She tried to *kill* him!" she whispered, aware of the ragged, strangled sound of her voice as she struggled to move her jaw even a fraction of an inch. She pushed away from him and sat back, blinking rapidly, trying to focus clearly on something—*anything!* But at the edges of her vision, there was a vibrating blackness, and that blackness seemed to be swelling, closing inward like a hungry mouth about to swallow both of them.

"What—? Edward asked, his voice sounding far away. *"Who* tried to kill *who?"*

"My mother—" Dianne rasped. She couldn't resist the sickening sensation that someone else was speaking through her, controlling her throat and tongue and mind!

"Hey, come on, now. Come on! You're getting yourself all worked up over nothing."

"I never told you about it," Dianne said with a raw waver in her voice. Hot tears were streaming down her face. "I—I never even *remembered* it, not until . . . not until today. But after I saw that therapist this morning . . . I don't know, maybe it was something she said coupled with this . . . this couple I saw arguing in the street, but *whatever* it was, on the drive home today, I suddenly remembered it. For the first time in nearly thirty years, I remembered!"

This sudden burst of emotion had obviously caught Edward completely off guard. He looked at her blankly with his mouth hanging open. At last he cleared his throat and, in a trembling voice, whispered, "Why don't you try to calm down and tell me about it?"

Two opposing impulses warred inside Dianne as she looked at her husband. She wanted to collapse into his arms, dissolve in his embrace and forget all about everyone and everything except the two of them and, at the same time, she wanted to get up and run away from him as fast as she could, never see him again— ever! Frozen by indecision, she could only sit there, withering under his gaze and trembling as though in the midst of a mild epileptic seizure.

"Seriously," Edward said, his voice firmly in control. "Take a few deep breaths and relax, and then tell me all about it . . . That is, if you want to."

Although her chest felt like it was constrained by

tight, steel bands, she took a sip of air, let her shoulder drop, and closed her eyes.

"It was back when I was eight," she began, leaning back. She thought her voice still sounded as if someone else was speaking through her, but she forced herself to continue. "My dad was an alcoholic. I told you that much, and that he left home when I was little. But I didn't remember, not until today, how—how—"

The cold twisting in her guts made her want to open her eyes and scream, but she took another even breath and continued.

"He used to beat up on my mom—a lot, even when he wasn't drunk. This was—God!" She brought her fist up to her mouth and pressed it hard against her lips. "It was right around Christmastime. I remember there were Christmas decorations all around the kitchen. It was night—sometime at night. I think my mother and I were making Christmas cookies or something when my father came home, drunk as usual. I think I remember him saying something about a Christmas party at the office, but I have no idea what kind of work he did. Anyway, he and mom started arguing, like they always did, and he hit her. I—I remember her falling back against the kitchen counter and knocking something onto the floor that broke. It might have been a bowl of cookie batter. I—I was sitting on the floor, in the corner, screaming. I—I—"

Dianne opened her eyes and stared long and hard at Edward. He was looking back at her with the warmest, gentlest expression she had even seen. Before she knew it, she lunged forward and threw her arms around him, clinging desperately to him.

"You don't have to talk about it if you don't want to," he whispered in her ear as he stroked her hair.

But Dianne shook her head and said, "No, I think it's better if I do. If this is something I've been blocking all these years, it can only be good if I talk about it, right? If I work it out of my system?"

Edward nodded silently.

"So anyway, this night, when my father hit my mom, he knocked her back against the counter. I don't know how she got it, where it was or anything, but the next thing I remember was, she leaped at my father with a knife in her hand. God! The way I remember it now, it looked as big as a guillotine blade. She brought it up over her head and swung it at him. My father ducked to one side, but the only thing I can remember clearly is the look on my mother's face—how she looked thrilled, almost *happy* that, after years of suffering this man's abuse, she was finally *doing* something about it."

"Did she—you know, did she kill him?" Edward asked.

Dianne could feel him shudder as he held her.

"No. He turned away in time, and she just cut him on the arm. I don't think it was very bad." She shook her head, trying to force the memory to get clearer. "I don't remember any blood or anything."

She shuddered as she closed her eyes again and took a steadying breath.

"I . . . I seem to remember that the . . . the blade went right through his arm and was sticking out the other side, but that—" She shook her head as though in fevered denial. "—That could just be something I imagined, don't you think?"

"Umm . . . probably," Edward said with a shrug. "A lot of times, I think we exaggerate the violence we see—especially as kids."

"But do you know what stayed with me all these years, even though I didn't know it consciously until today? That look—that terrible look I saw in my mother's eyes. God!" She shivered again and hugged

237

herself. "It was . . . it was *scary* as hell seeing how much she wanted to kill him!"

"I'll bet it was," Edward said simply as he rubbed his hand gently up and down her back.

"And do you want to know the scariest thing of all—?"

Dianne spoke in a voice barely above a whisper. Her eyelids fluttered, and the tightness in her chest made it almost impossible for her to catch her breath. Edward looked at her reassuringly, but before she could continue, a thought rang in her head as clearly as if she—or he—or *someone* had spoken it aloud:

It makes me worry and wonder if someday I might try to kill you!

"I—I," she said but then faltered.

Edward drew her closer, squeezing her tightly, but much as she wanted to let herself dissolve in his embrace, she felt equally repelled by him—almost threatened by the way he clung to her. The churning tension inside her turned to sudden, violent anger. She was coiling up, preparing to scream and push herself away from him when a loud blast of sound suddenly filled the air. She sat up straight and looked at her husband, her eyes wide with shock.

Edward smiled and said, "Hey, it's nothing—just the town fire horn."

The blaring noise kept sounding its short, coded blasts. Dianne watched as Edward flicked up a different finger, counting each toot.

"Two . . . two," he said.

His smile froze, and a grim tightness squeezed his eyes.

"Four—"

He frowned as he held up four fingers. She could see that his hand was trembling as the horn started another series of blasts. With each one, Edward counted aloud, his expression dropping as the cold realization hit him.

"One . . . two . . . three . . . *four! Four!* Oh, *shit!*"

He gnawed the inside of his mouth as he waited for another blast to follow, but the echo faded after the fourth blast. Edward's face was lined with worry as he looked at her, then rose unsteadily to his feet.

"Twenty-two forty-four," he said in a tight, trembling voice. "That—that's the code for *our* house!"

Dianne looked up at him, feeling his panic. "What do you think—?"

"It's upper Pond Road!" he said, reaching out and helping her to her feet. His hand was clammy to the touch. He turned and looked in the general direction of the house, obviously debating whether it would be faster to get into the truck and drive home or take the path through the woods. Dianne's legs felt weak, as if they weren't going to support her much longer. Then the fire horn started its series of blasts again.

"Oh, my God! Look!" Edward suddenly shouted, pointing up at the sky above the trees to the north. A funnel-shaped column of black smoke tumbled like a flapping curtain against the hazy blue sky. Moving slowly, as though in a trace, he started toward the path in the woods. The fire horn continued to blast out its coded message.

"Come on! Follow me!" Edward shouted, turning back to Dianne and waving her on.

Dianne hesitated a moment, then she started after him. He waited only a second or two before he turned and ran down the narrow path. Fleeting, panicky thoughts filled Dianne's mind as she picked up her pace to catch up with him as they ran along the path toward home.

Edward and Dianne got to the house a few seconds

239

after the first two fire trucks showed up, pulling to a screaming halt and parking at an angle at the top of the driveway. Hand in hand, they stood back at a safe distance in the backyard, watching in shocked silence as several black-and-yellow-clad fire fighters unspooled the hoses, ran up to the back of the house, and kicked the door open. With oxygen masks in place, they entered through the back door, crouching low and lunging shoulder-first into the tangled ribbons of black smoke that poured over them like liquid. They were soon lost from sight. The hoses they were carrying stuck out of the heavy smoke like thick tree branches. More fire fighters stretched other hoses out from the second fire engine and entered the house through the front door.

Through the window, they could see flames flickering like wicked tongues inside the kitchen. A wide sheet of fire curled around the edge of the open window and slid up the outside of the house, scorching the siding all the way up to the bottom of the second story window. The air was filled with a loud crackle as wood was consumed. The paint on the side of the house blistered up. Overhead, the rolling column of smoke was as thick as night.

Brian's bedroom, Edward thought with a sick twisting in his stomach as he looked up at the second floor of the house. Then another thought hit him. *Where is Brian! Oh, shit!* A singing rush of panic went up his spine like a high-speed drill. *Where is he? Could he have caused the fire? Could he still be inside the house?*

"Jesus Christ! Jesus Christ!" Edward suddenly shouted, lunging toward the house. "Is Brian in there? Is my son in there?"

None of the fire fighters seemed to hear him, or if they did, they ignored him as they went about their business. Halfway to the house, someone intercepted him by snatching his arm and bringing him to an abrupt halt.

"Now hold on there, Ed," a gruff voice said. "You can't be going in there."

Edward turned and saw Andy Jones, the town's fire chief. His expression was grim, almost emotionless as he held Edward lightly by the forearm.

"My boy!—" Edward said, shouting to be heard above the hissing spray of water and the wailing siren as another fire truck approached the scene. "—I don't know if Brian's in there!"

Andy shook his head grimly. "I don't know either, but it looks to me as though the fire's just in the back of the house here. Likely as not, he'd a' been able to get out the front door pretty easily."

"Who called this in?" Edward shouted. His body felt all weak and tingly with shock.

"Someone passing by in a car called in on one of them car phones," Andy replied. He seemed to be forcing himself to keep his voice steady. "Didn't say who he was. Pretty nifty invention, them car phones. Probably saved you most of your house."

Another fire truck arrived along with a heavy rescue truck, and soon there was a tangle of hoses, swollen with water pressure, crisscrossing the lawn like bulging arteries. Several policemen stood down in the road to reroute any traffic.

"I have to find out if he's still in there," Edward said. He was only controlling his panic with effort; his mind was filled with the horrifying image of Brian, lying on the floor, writhing in agony as his clothes and flesh were consumed by flames.

"We got men in there now," Andy said patiently. "Trained men. No sense you risking your own life at this point."

"Edward! Hey, Edward!" a voice shouted from behind him. "Here he is!"

Edward was so pumped up with adrenaline he didn't recognize his wife's voice.

"Hey, Dad! What happened?"

Edward turned and in a staggering instant was swept with relief that almost unbuckled his legs when he saw Brian coming toward him from the fringe of woods behind the house. The boy's face was pale with shock and confusion as he slowed his pace and stared up at the burning house. The flashing red lights reflected like summer lightning in his eyes. He stumbled as he walked past Dianne, not even bothering to glance at her, and joined his father and Andy on the lawn. The heat from the blaze hammered their faces, making their skin prickle, but Edward hardly noticed it as he clasped his son in his arms.

"Christ-all-mighty, you had me worried!"

"What happened?" Brian repeated, still staring wide-eyed up at the burning house.

"I'd say we got to this one in plenty of time," Andy said, letting his guard down and smiling for the first time. "It ain't gonna be too bad, considering. We should have it under control in a couple of minutes."

Stunned speechless, Edward nodded and then, holding Brian by the arm, directed him back to where Dianne was waiting. He stood between Dianne and Brian, with one arm holding each of them tightly, as though he needed them for support. Tears rose in his eyes, but he choked back his emotions as he watched his house burn, unable to believe what he was seeing. He couldn't stop shaking his head in amazement and puffing out his breath every time he exhaled.

More firemen charged into the house, and more hoses were stretched out across the lawn and turned on. The ripping sound of spraying water filled the air, interspersed with curt commands shouted back and forth and the crackling sounds of cooling timbers as water saturated everything inside the house. A wide spray of water shot out into the yard through the kitchen window. Before long, the heavy, black smoke had turned into a thick, gray steam that hissed like a waterfall. A few men emerged from the house. Their faces were streaked with soot and grime, and their heavy rubber coats looked as slick as sealskin, dripping with water.

"Hey, Andy!" one of them shouted. "Looks to me like we got it pretty much under control."

Andy looked back at Edward and Dianne, and gave them a thumbs-up.

Edward sighed with relief, then glanced back and forth between Brian and Dianne. "Jesus Christ," he whispered, shaking his head in amazement.

"I wonder when they'll let us in to see what's left," Brian said in a low, wavering voice.

Part Three

The 'Old Witch Lady's' House

August 1994

"I had borne a great deal in this house."
— Henrik Ibsen
Ghosts

Chapter Sixteen
The Only Alternative

Half an hour later, Fire Chief Andy Jones declared that the fire at the Fraser house was officially out. Armed with plaster hooks, the cleanup crew entered the house and started pulling out the walls and ceiling, hosing down any hot spots they found. There was broken wallboard all over the kitchen floor, and timbers were still streaming with thin ribbons of smoke when Dianne, Edward, and Brian went through the house with Rick Anicetti, the town fire marshal.

"It's fairly obvious the fire started in here somehow," Rick said as they walked into the devastated kitchen.

The heavy smell of steam and burned wood mingled with other, more noxious fumes to produce a lingering ozonelike sting in the air. That, if not the impact of their loss, would have brought tears to their eyes. A glaze of soot and ash covered everything, making it look as if a volcano had erupted inside the house. Especially over by the counter, where the fire had been centered, the linoleum floor was curled up and bubbled where it had burned. The thin black crust crunched underfoot as they walked slowly around the room, staring in disbelief at the extent of the damage.

The kitchen wall had a jagged, teardrop-shaped hole to the outside that revealed charred two-by-fours and the tangled remains of melted wiring and burst water pipes. From the inside, it looked as though a gigantic cannon shell had slammed through the wall and exploded. On the sides that had been facing the flames, the kitchen table and chairs were burned to waffled charcoal. Anything plastic—especially the small appliances and containers on the countertop—had melted into unrecognizable, black lumps. The counter and cabinets were rippled with scorched wood and blackened laminate, and the wood paneling on the walls was flaking off in large, black chunks that looked like autumn leaves. The ceiling above the sink had burned through to the upstairs room, into Brian's bedroom. The refrigerator and stove were scorched with brown and black streaks that looked like splashes of paint. The wall phone was a formless green puddle of plastic and wires on the floor, almost lost beneath the jumble of burned and smashed wallboard. Even in the adjoining hallway and dining room, everything that hadn't been damaged by the flames and intense heat, was skim-coated with greasy soot.

"I'm still not sure yet if it first broke out inside or outside the house," Rick said, "but it definitely looks as though the flames traveled up the outside of the building first. It's possible the fire started inside the walls, from faulty wiring or whatever."

He scratched his chin in concentration as he looked at Edward as though studying him, gauging his reactions.

"But there are some mighty odd-looking scorch marks angling up the exterior of the house that look suspicious to me."

"Suspicious," Edward said. "What do you mean, suspicious?"

Rick shrugged. "Almost as though someone splashed

the side of the house with gasoline before touching it off. I dunno—" He shook his head. "Maybe the fire was purposely set."

Brian stiffened, and Edward regarded Rick with a numbed, nearly uncomprehending expression, but Dianne blurted out. "Set? Who would have done something like that?"

Rick didn't answer right away as he looked around with his hands on his hips. "Impossible to say. You don't mind if I take a day or two to investigate this a bit, do you, to determine if it was arson."

"Of course not," Edward said, vacantly nodding his agreement. Dianne had the impression that he had mentally taken a backseat to all of this and was watching things the way he would watch a movie.

Rick grimaced and said, "It's just a niggling little doubt I have. I don't think I have to get the state involved with any of this, though no doubt an adjuster and probably an investigator from your insurance company is gonna want to take a look at it in a few days, too. You probably ought to notify them."

Again, Edward nodded absently as if he was barely paying attention.

"I've got to post the property so no one will come in here, and as much as I don't want to, I'm gonna have to ask you to stay out of the house for a few days. You couldn't very well sleep here tonight, anyway."

"Where *are* we going to sleep?" Brian asked, but no one answered him.

"Can we get some things first—clothes and stuff?" Dianne asked. She was acutely aware of how frail and tight her voice sounded.

"Oh sure, sure," Rick said. "No sweat. Usually in a case like this, we gotta be pretty careful about—well, if either one of you tried to torch the house—you know, for the insurance money or whatever, we don't want to let you tamper with the evidence. But—hell, Ed, I've known you all my life. I'm willing to bet a few week's salary that you had nothing to do with it."

"Of course I didn't," Edward said in a voice that sounded raw and tired.

They all went back outside and waited until the last fire truck left after two hours of "cleanup" work. That, Dianne thought, was exactly the wrong term for what the firemen had done to the inside of their house, but she knew it was necessary to rip out the walls and ceiling to make sure all the smoldering embers had been extinguished. Once the fire trucks were gone, the last few straggling bystanders also left. Several people stopped by and offered their assistance in helping them get things squared around, but Edward gratefully declined, saying that he and his family could take care of things—at least for now. A few neighbors offered the family a place to spend the night if they needed it.

Rick Anicetti and a helper posted the house with NO TRESPASSING signs and strung the area with police line tape, pending the outcome of his investigation into the cause of the fire. He reassured Edward that he honestly didn't *think* the fire had been set, but he didn't want to rule anything out until he had a chance to go over the evidence carefully.

Feeling physically and emotionally drained, Dianne followed Edward and Brian back into the house to see again what was left of their kitchen and to gather any clothes or whatever else they needed that hadn't been damaged. All of them were silent as they stood in the kitchen, looking around and wondering what to do next . . . or even where to start.

Heeding Rick's warning to be careful because of the piles of debris and the weakened structure, they cautiously went upstairs. Except for the nauseating smell and the heavy coating of soot everywhere, they discovered that there—fortunately—wasn't very much damage. Not much, that is, except in Brian's bedroom, where the window had been broken open. Hundreds of gallons of water had been sprayed against the wall to control the fire's spread, so the blue shag rug was saturated with black water that squished underfoot as they picked their way carefully through the broken wallboard, checking to see if any of Brian's clothes and personal possessions had escaped a damaging soaking. The fire had burned through the floor, and they could look down into the kitchen. Luckily, the firemen had gotten to the blaze before it had done much damage up here. The ceiling and roof seemed to be intact.

Dianne cleared her throat, the first sound any of them made as they inspected the room.

"Do you really think someone could have . . . could have started the fire—I mean, deliberately?" she asked.

She half *wanted* to believe Rick Anicetti's suspicion that arson was involved because the thought was nagging at the back of her mind that *she* might have done something stupid or forgetful that had started the blaze.

Edward shrugged dejectedly, slapping his hands against his legs as he looked around the bedroom. He wrinkled his nose as he sniffed the caustic air. Brian was stooping over beside his desk, sifting through the wet jumble of music magazines, cassette tapes and cases, and other things that had fallen to the floor. Everything was coated with a greasy film of black soot. Brian's radio/tape player now was nothing but a bubbly, melted plastic mess. When the boy picked it up, water gushed out of the base onto his feet. Uttering a frustrated cry, he straightened up, raised the tape player

251

high over his head, and then dashed it angrily to the floor. The burned plastic housing shattered loudly.

"Goddamn it!" he wailed as he kicked wildly at the remains of his tape player. "Jesus Christ! Goddamn it!"

"Hey, hey! Come on, now! Take it easy," Edward snapped at him. "We can replace everything you lost — easily." But when he saw the pale look of despair on his son's face, his resolve weakened. He moved over to Brian, but he felt curiously reluctant to take the boy in his arms and hug him. They locked eyes, and for a moment neither one of them said anything.

Dianne cleared her throat again, but it did no good; the cloying, chemical taste on her tongue wouldn't go away. She stepped forward and said, "Well, at least we have *one* thing to be thankful for. No one was hurt." Coming from behind the wires in her mouth, her voice sounded strangled and high, paper-thin.

Edward looked at her and forced a smile, but his eyes held an odd, flat glow when he turned back to Brian. It struck her then that, as real and as tangible as this disaster was, he still hadn't allowed the full impact of it to hit him; it was almost as if he couldn't . . . not yet.

"It's true," she said a bit more forcefully as she stepped close to Edward and wound her arm around his waist. She wanted to reach out to Brian, too, but something held her back. "Okay, so we have a gigantic mess to clean up and a lot of repairs to do, but so what? What have we lost? I mean — *really!* Tell me. What have we lost?"

"I'll tell you what!" Brain shouted as he turned around and glared at her. *"I* lost *plenty!* Look at this! Almost everything I brought with me for the summer has been *destroyed!* I don't even have any clothes! And all my tapes are destroyed!"

252

"We can get you new ones," Edward said, but Brian seemed not to hear him as he bent over, scooped up a handful of melted cassette tapes and cases, and threw them violently against the wall. The plastic shattered and fell to the floor like broken glass. Before either Dianne or Edward could say anything, Brian lunged over to his sodden bed. The bedspread was singed on the edge that had faced the burning wall. He tore off the soot-coated covers and flung them hard against the wall. They hit with a loud squishy sound before plopping like a gigantic wad of Jell-O to the floor. A winding sob sounded deep inside his chest, and his face flushed bright red. Veins swelled in his neck, looking as thick as pencils. For a terrifying instant, Dianne had the impression that the house was still on fire, and that he was standing in the middle of the raging inferno.

Simultaneously, both she and Edward took a step toward him, but then they both shied away, each of them seeming to sense that Brian had to let out his pent-up emotions. The room was a disaster anyway, so why not let him trash it, get everything out of his system? But within seconds, his rage ebbed, and with tears and sweat glistening on his face and arms, he turned to his father, looking for all the world like a little boy who was lost, lonely, and frightened.

"What are we gonna do?" he cried, shaking his hands frantically in front of his face. "Where are we gonna stay? All of my stuff—everything I own—is *ruined!*" He took a deep breath that rattled loudly in his throat. *What are we gonna do?*

Edward stepped forward and took his son into his arms, pulling him so close his face was smothered in the crook of his shoulder. As soon as they embraced, Brian let out a long, warbling cry that cut to the core of Dianne's heart. The boy's shoulders shook violently

253

as he sobbed while his father continually stroked the back of his head and murmured comforting words. Over Brian's shoulder, he locked eyes with Dianne.

"There, there," he said. "Take it easy, Brian. Come on — just take it easy. We — we'll think of *something*. Don't worry. We still have each other."

Dianne watched them silently, wishing she dared to share their intimacy.

"Well," she said hollowly, sniffing the air and wrinkling her nose. "We can't very well stay *here* tonight." Her glance flickered toward the view outside the broken window. "I suppose — " Her voice caught for an instant. "We could sleep in your mother's house . . . for the time being, anyway." Her voice sounded so distant and strained, she had the uncanny feeling again that it wasn't her but someone else speaking in the room.

For just an instant, Edward's face registered a measure of dulled shock; then he nodded slowly and said, "I . . . suppose so." He gave Brian a bracing shake. "I — I think it's the only sensible alternative."

The numbing horror of what had happened was compounded for Dianne because she still couldn't get rid of the gnawing worry that — somehow — she was responsible for it all. As far as she knew, she had been the last one in the house before the fire had started. What had she done? How could she have caused it?

She turned away and looked out the shattered window at the late afternoon sun. Everything outside seemed so calm, so peaceful, as if the world had barely taken notice of their catastrophe. She was amazed at how fast things could change — how a gorgeous summer day could plummet so fast into such a pit of loss and despair. She closed her eyes and tried to mentally reconstruct everything she had done since coming home from the meeting with Dr. Murray. She had been upset about uncovering that horrible childhood memory that there didn't seem to have been anything else on her mind, but what else was there? What could she have done?

She remembered taking her medication and then making lunch for herself and Edward—a tuna fish sandwich, chips, and an apple for him; pureed vegetables and a diet Pepsi for her. And then—and then . . .

Oh, shit!

A thought went through her mind like a quick, white slice of lightning. Her face suddenly felt like it was on fire.

I made some coffee for Edward! she thought. *And when was it . . . sometime—days or weeks ago? Sometime recently I left the house with the coffeepot still on when it was empty, and it had gotten hot—red-hot. Was that it? Maybe the coffee maker was defective? Did I leave the pot on? Could that have started the fire?*

A cold, clutching sensation worked its way up from her stomach to her chest. Even without going back down to the kitchen to verify it, she knew that the worst of the flames had been to the right of the sink, under the cabinet where she kept the coffeepot. Rick Anicetti had even commented on how badly melted the coffee maker was, as if he suspected but hadn't wanted to say anything just yet.

Oh, Jesus! Oh, shit! That must have been it!

A wave of nausea swept through her. She took a staggering step toward the window, hoping to catch a breath of fresh air. Neither Edward nor Brian seemed to notice when she covered her mouth with both hands in an attempt to push back the scream that was building up inside her.

That was it! her mind shouted as the soft, whimpering sound vibrated in her throat. Waves of dizziness crashed over her, and she almost collapsed.

I did it!

The thought reverberated in her mind like an echo that steadily diminished but would never entirely fade away.

That was it! . . . I did it!

   That was it! . . . I did it!

      That was it! . . . I did it!

"I don't like this idea at *all*," Brian said as he rolled onto his side and pulled the bed covers up over his shoulder. Up until a few days ago, he had been confident that he would never have to think about this room again, much less sleep in it; but Jesus Christ! Here he was!

It was well past eleven o'clock at night—almost midnight. The three of them had spent the rest of the daylight hours sorting through their smoky, soot-covered clothes, gathering a few things to bring over to Edward's mother's house. After that, Edward and Brian went into town to pick up a few groceries and to replace Dianne's medicine, which had been destroyed in the kitchen. Dianne stayed at the house and ran their clothes through the old washing machine and dryer, hoping to get rid of the cloying, smoky smell. For a while there, she thought the old Maytag washer was going to give up the ghost, but it eventually got the job done.

Around nine o'clock, they had a quick supper of submarine sandwiches and pureed food for Dianne. Then they spent the rest of the evening trying to get the house into some kind of livable order. It smelled musty and old after being closed up for the two months following Evelyn Fraser's death. Edward mentioned a few times how grateful he was that he hadn't had the electricity and water shut off. Dianne opened all the windows to air the place out and did some dusting while Edward ran the old Hoover vacuum around, but it seemed as if all they succeeded in doing was stir up more dust.

Conversation throughout the evening was sparse. All of them were exhausted and depressed by the recent turn of events. It was almost as if each of them had to retreat into themselves to process what had happened before they could speak about it with each other. Finally, around ten o'clock, they decided to call it a day. Each of them took a quick shower to wash away the clinging smell of smoke from their skin. Around eleven-thirty, Edward went upstairs to settle Brian into bed.

Brian was trying his best to relax, but as sleepy as he was, he couldn't get it out of his mind that this was the same bed he had slept in the last time he stayed here — probably the same sheets, blankets, and pillow, too. That had been the night he first heard about Dianne's accident and the same night his grandmother — the Old Witch Lady! — had the heart attack that had finally killed her.

"You know," his father said, "this is the same bedroom I had when I was a —"

"I know — I know. You already told me a dozen times," Brian said, huffing with exasperation. "This is the same room you grew up in and shared with your brother Mike."

"My brother — ?" Edward said, jerking back in surprise. His eyes blinked rapidly, and for just an instant his glance shifted to one side as though he suspected someone was creeping up behind him. "When did I — ? I don't remember ever telling you about my brother."

257

Brian flushed, realizing that his reaction may have already given him away, but he stammered, "Sure—sure you di-did. I—I don't remember when it was, but sometime tonight . . . you mentioned him."

His father shook his head, looking completely confused. His mouth opened as if he was about to say something more, but he remained silent as his gaze shifted over to the bedroom window. Brian looked in that direction, too. Outside, the moonless night was as black as slate. The single overhead light reflected double in the windowpane, looking like two glowing eyes, staring in at them. And he couldn't stop thinking about that tree branch right outside the window, all set to start tap-tap-tapping on the glass as soon as a little night breeze came up.

Scritch—scritch—scre-e-e-ch.

Just the thought of that sound set Brian's teeth on edge. He wished he was young enough to ask his father if he could sleep in his room.

"Well," his father said, "just don't you worry about anything, all right? Everything's gonna be just fine." Brian detected a slight tremor in his voice, as if he didn't quite believe it himself, but all Brian could think was—*I already blew it! Scritch—scritch—scre-e-e-ch! I've given Uncle Mike away!*

His father leaned forward and ruffled his hair, but Brian pulled away, not wanting to be treated like a little kid. He realized that he had his own concerns and fears to deal with—plenty of them!—but wasn't it about time he started dealing with them on his own? He watched his father, feeling a pinprick of loneliness and loss when he got up from the bed and headed for the door without giving him a good-night hug.

"Hey, Dad—?" Brian said. His voice sounded tight in his throat.

His father snapped off the overhead light, then turned and said, "Yeah?"

The words were right there on the tip of his tongue, all set to come gushing out—the truth about how he had met Uncle Mike out at the mill. Why was his uncle living alone out there? Why had he come back home? What was he up to? Could he be trusted, or was he really as dangerous as he seemed at times? and the scariest thought of all: could Uncle Mike have started the fire at their house today?

The glow of the hall light haloed his father's head, making his features indistinct. Brian stared at the silhouette, feeling a faint stirring of mistrust and doubt. Twisting internally with guilt, he recalled his promise to Uncle Mike not to tell anyone—especially his father—that he knew he was out there.

And isn't that what growing up is all about? Brian thought. *Giving and keeping your word!*

"I, uh—I hope everything's gonna be okay, you know? . . . for all of us, I mean."

"Yeah, me too," his father replied as he backed out into the hallway. He eased the door shut in front of him, but paused and pointed his index finger like a gun back at Brian.

"Now do what I told you," he whispered. "Go to sleep . . . and stop *worrying* about everything, all right?"

Brian licked his lips, swallowed hard, and said, "Yeah—sure, Dad. Uh, could you keep the door open a crack?"

"Sure thing."

Then he was gone.

Brian listened to the light tread of his father's footsteps as he moved down the hall to the bedroom where they were staying.

They're sleeping in the same bedroom . . . the very same bed Grandma was sleeping in that night last June, the night before she died!

A cold prickly feeling raced up his back, making him hunch up his shoulders. The faint glow of light from the hallway seemed not nearly bright enough to push back the heavy shadows that lurked in the corners of the bedroom. Dull yellow light reflected off the flat, black windowpane, looking like a thin line of fire. Brian could still taste the acrid tang of burned wood and plastic on the back of his tongue. Sucking in a deep breath, he licked his lips again and swallowed, but the taste only sharpened. From outside, against the windowpane, he heard a low whistling sound as the wind began to pick up.

And then . . .

Scritch—scritch—scre-e-e-ch.

Dianne wasn't feeling any better than Brian about all of this, although at the time she didn't realize it. While Edward was talking to Brian in his bedroom, she was sitting on the edge of the bed in Evelyn's room, lost in thought as she towel-dried her hair. She couldn't stop fretting over whether or not she had caused the fire, but whether it was that or everyone's obvious discomfort at spending the next few nights in the house or something else—*something* was making her feel as jumpy as a cat.

Dianne thought the old house was creepy, there was no doubt about that! It was furnished throughout with old-fashioned items that looked as though they'd be better off heading to Goodwill. In every room and on the stairs, floorboards creaked underfoot. Old, rusted door hinges wailed like banshees whenever a door was opened or closed. The gauzy curtains, yellowed with age and heavy with dust, hung like funeral lace in the windows. The smell and feel of disuse filled the house like heavy incense.

But beneath the superficial atmosphere of creepiness, Dianne also sensed on a deeper level that there was something dreadfully wrong with the house. If it had been human, she thought, it would have been diagnosed as having a terminal illness gnawing away at its insides. It might be as simple as the fact that Evelyn Fraser had lived for so long in this house—her entire life, in fact—and even now that she was gone, the walls and floors—everything in the house was still imbued with her presence; but Dianne couldn't help but think it was more than that . . . that there was something essentially "wrong" or "evil" lurking either inside the house or nearby.

The instant they had entered the house, she had wanted to mention to Edward how she felt, but he seemed too shattered and preoccupied by the day's events to bother. Besides, there were too many things around the house to get into order, so she never had the opportunity to speak with him without Brian around. It was close to midnight now, and they were finally settling down for the night. Just as soon as Edward came back to the room, she knew she should tell him her concerns and fears, but she wasn't sure she wanted to burden him further. Didn't he already have enough to deal with without her laying another load of worry on him?

And what would I tell him, anyway? she wondered as a light tickle of chills traveled up her neck and shoulders. *What is it I'm so afraid of?*

The sound of Edward's footsteps coming down the hallway drew her attention. She dropped the towel to her lap, took a deep breath, and squared her shoulders as her husband eased the door open and entered the room. The door hinge squealed loudly.

"Is he all set now?" she asked. Her voice sounded off-key, but Edward seemed not to notice as he went over to the bureau where Dianne had stacked his pile of clean clothes. He took off his work shirt and slipped on a fresh T-shirt, shaking his head and masking a yawn behind his hand.

"Yeah," he said. "He's still a little bit wound up, though." He looked at her, but his gaze seemed to pass straight through her. His eyes had a haunted, hunted look that bothered her deeply.

"I think we're all due a good-night's sleep, don't you?" he said.

Dianne nodded, but a faint voice in the back of her mind whispered, *How are you ever going to sleep, knowing what you know?* The thought chilled her, and she watched silently as Edward took his toiletries bag and went down the hall to the bathroom.

And what—exactly—do I know? she wondered, hugging her arms tightly to her chest as strong shivers coursed up and down her back.

Do I know *that I started that fire? Do I* know *that I might have done it on purpose? And do I* know *that my mother once tried to kill my father, and that, ever since I dredged up that memory, I've been wondering if I had that same kind of rage bottled up inside me—the kind of rage that would make me want to* kill *someone? Should I—can I even talk to him about any of this?*

The current of panic inside her grew stronger. She covered her mouth with her hands, but a faint whimper escaped her. From down the hall, Edward called out, "Did you say something, honey?"

262

"Uh—no, no," Dianne called out in a voice barely above a squeak. She listened as he ran the water and brushed his teeth, and then started back to the bedroom. When she saw his face, the winding tension inside her spiked even higher.

Is that what I'm so afraid of—that I'm still angry at Edward? That I blame him for what happened to me, and I'm afraid that I might want to do something to hurt him? Like maybe burn his house down? Or that someday I might even try to kill him?

Edward didn't seem to pick up on her anxiety. Without a word, he went over to the other side of the bed, slipped off his jeans and dropped them on the floor, then turned down the bedspread and slid under the covers. After punching the pillow into shape, he let out a loud sigh and, folding his hands behind his head, eased himself down. Dianne could feel him staring at her back, but she didn't move. She didn't dare to. She was immobilized by the mind-numbing thought that *this* was the problem eating away at her: she had the same thing wrong with her that her mother had wrong—a black widow drive that forced her to bottle up the resentment she felt for her husband until it would suddenly boil over, and she tried to kill him!

"Aren't you tired, too?" Edward asked, sounding more dejected than sleepy.

"Yeah," Dianne replied, but she made no move to turn out the light or get under the covers. Her mind was filled with the need to talk to Edward, but still, she held back, knowing with a gut-twisting certainty that, no matter how upset she might be, and no matter how much he understood how she felt, he wouldn't—he *couldn't* even kiss her . . . not with her jaw wired shut.

Tears formed in her eyes, but before they could fall, she boosted herself off the bed and went over and slapped off the wall switch. The room was plunged into darkness. A stifled sob was lodged in her chest, aching as if her heart were about to burst as she felt her way blindly back to the bed and crawled under the covers.

"G'night, hon," Edward said.

His hand fumbled around in the darkness until it found hers and clasped tightly, but Dianne lay there with her back to him and said nothing. She couldn't. Fighting back her tears, she squeezed her eyes tightly shut.

And all she could think was, *That's okay . . . There are no words left to say, anyway!*

Chapter Seventeen
Hearing Voices

The next two days were busy ones. The family reluctantly decided to stay in the old homestead until Edward found time to repair the fire-damaged house, and they all worked hard to salvage what they could from the wreckage and make Evelyn's house—the Old Witch Lady's House, as Brian now thought of it—at least marginally livable. Most of the time, though, Brian thought that—just like the whole damned town of Summerfield, Maine—there wasn't much point in even trying; the rickety old place seemed damned near impossible to get used to. His mother had been upset the night he called her in Arizona and told her what had happened. More than once he had thought of asking his father to send him home earlier than originally planned, but he held back, not wanting to hurt his father's feelings. He at least had to give his dad credit for trying so hard to improve their relationship. Brian just wasn't sure it was all worth it.

For the past two days, though, his agitation had been steadily mounting, and not just because he was stuck in the house, usually with Dianne working somewhere nearby. Since the day of the fire, the distrust and hostility in his and Dianne's relationship had grown steadily stronger until it was at the point where neither one of them could communicate or even look at the other without bristling with defensiveness. But angry words seldom flew; they retreated, instead, into hostile silence. More than once, Brain's father talked to him about it and asked him—almost pleaded with him to cut Dianne some slack, and he was sure his father was also giving Dianne the same pitch, but it did no good. Throughout the day, whenever they met, they eyed each other like caged tigers who each wanted the choicest scraps of meat.

Was it his father they were competing for? His attention? Or was it the house and the sense that one of them belonged here more than the other?

Brian didn't know—or care. He just knew that he couldn't *stand* being around her, and he was anxiously looking forward to the end of the summer just so he could get away from her!

Another reason Brian was feeling so frustrated was because for the past two days he never found an opportunity to go back out to the old mill and talk some more with Uncle Mike. He felt some pride in the fact that he still hadn't told his father that his brother was living out there, but besides wanting to make good on his promise to deliver more food and supplies, he wanted to ask his uncle a single, simple question . . .

Did you do it?

Did you try to burn down my father's house?

The thought was utmost in Brian's mind most of the time, day or night, but it didn't seem to bother him as much as he thought it should have. Wasn't he, after all, living in danger if Uncle Mike *had* tried to burn down their house? If his uncle was truly, dangerously insane— and he had admitted that, until recently, he had been in a mental hospital—he might try something like that again on *this* house. And they might not all be so lucky next time. Someone might get hurt . . . or killed.

If only I could make sure it was Dianne who got hurt! Brian thought, feeling only the slightest twist of guilt.

On Monday morning, his father went out to the new

266

construction site to oversee the work while Henry Lessard and his son, Josh, started excavating for the foundation and septic system. Brian had wanted to go along with him, if only to get away from Dianne for a while, but he had promised to get the upstairs bathroom cleaned and was doing that now in hopes of getting out to the mill in the afternoon. He was doubly frustrated because, now that his tape player was plastic slag, the best he could do for music was a pop-rock station from Portland on his dead grandmother's AM radio. The mall-metal strains of Bon Jovi filled the house as he swirled the bristle brush around the inside of the toilet bowl.

He flushed the toilet, and as the water was whooshing away, he thought he heard something in the next room or downstairs. He cocked his head and listened, but could hear nothing over the cranked-up radio and the rush of water as it refilled the tank. This was far from the first time he thought he'd heard something in the house — a voice whispering or a faint, crying sound — and he shuddered, hating the creepy feeling this house gave him. But he pushed all of that aside and told himself he was just nerved up, imagining things because his grandmother — the Old Witch Lady — had frightened him so badly.

"But now she's dead," he whispered, not really liking the feeling *that* thought gave him.

The toilet finished filling, so he poured a dash of Lysol into the water, swirled it around with the brush, and flushed it again. He watched vacantly as the cloudy disinfectant water drained away with a deep-throated gurgle. He shivered in spite of himself when, as the water was filling the tank, he heard the sound again. He strained forward to hear it but could only make out a faint, wavering voice just at the edge of hearing.

"Brian . . . Brian . . ."

He glanced over his shoulder as goose bumps broke out over his arms. Through the bathroom door, the hallway seemed unusually dim. For a fleeting instant, he thought he saw a shadow shift against the wall. Then the voice came again, louder this time.

"Brian . . . Could you come down here and help me?"

It still sounded far away, but he finally realized what it was—the strangled sound of his stepmother, trying to call to him through that damned bird cage that filled her mouth!

After shaking the water from the toilet brush, he put it back into the closet and stepped out into the hallway.

"You call me?" he shouted. His voice bounced back oddly from the hallway walls as he looked back and forth, trying to get a fix on where she was.

"I need help . . . with this!"

She was downstairs. Her voice sounded tight with tension.

Good! Brian thought.

He started down the stairs, taking his time just to show her he wasn't going to jump at her beck and call. At the foot of the stairs, he almost laughed aloud when he looked into the living room and saw her in front of the picture window, balanced on the back of one of the cushioned chairs. Her arms were high above her head as she struggled to put the recently laundered curtains back onto their support brackets. She twisted her head around, her face flushed with effort, and nodded at him as he made his way over to her.

"If you could . . . just get that . . . other end for me," she gasped. The curtain rod was at least seven feet long. The unsupported end weaved and dipped dangerously.

"You know, it might be a little easier if you used a stepladder," Brian said.

"I couldn't . . . find it," Dianne said, struggling to keep the far end from dropping. "Could you hurry . . . just reach up and . . . and hook that end on?"

As she spoke, she let go with one hand and pointed. As soon as she did that, the end of the curtain rod started to drop. She made a grab for it and lost her balance. The curtain rod fell, rattling and banging against the windowsill, and with a stifled scream, Dianne lost her balance and started to pitch to one side. She twisted toward the window, her hands clawing furiously at the window frame for support, but she missed. Before he could think about what he was doing, Brian darted toward her. When she fell, he was there beside the chair with his arms up to catch her. She screamed and he grunted heavily as her weight bore him down. They both hit the floor hard, with Dianne landing on top of him.

"Oh, God!" she shouted as she rolled off him and then scrambled to her feet. "I'm so sorry. Are you all right?"

Brian stood up slowly, unfolding his body like a battered accordion. The wind had been knocked out of him, but he hunched over, took a deep breath, and nodded before gasping, "Yeah—yeah . . . I'm okay."

"God, I feel like such a klutz," Dianne said. From behind the wires holding her jaw, her voice sounded muffled and flat. "You could have been hurt bad. Are you sure you're all right?"

She started to reach for Brian, as though to comfort him, but he pulled away quickly and squared his shoulders as if his chest didn't hurt half as much as it did.

"Yeah, don't worry about it, okay?" he said, backing away from her even more. "Let's—let's just get the curtains up so I can get back to what I was doing." He almost said the *"fucking"* curtains.

"Sure . . . sure . . . okay," Dianne said. A frown creased her forehead as she looked at him darkly.

Brian could hear it there in her voice again—or *still,* that same, old defensive tone. So for—what, maybe fifteen seconds? she had seemed actually worried that she might have hurt him. But any traces of concern were already gone, replaced with her customary iciness. She nodded curtly, then bent down to pick up the fallen curtain rod. Without a word, Brian took the other end and steadied it. After flouncing out the curtains, Dianne

269

stepped up onto the back of the chair again, bracing her knees for balance, while Brian stood on tiptoes and reached up. After a moment of fumbling around, he got the hook onto the edge of the bracket and swung it down into position.

As soon as the job was done, Dianne muttered a quick thank you, then turned her back on him and went about her business straightening out the curtains. Simmering with anger and still smarting from having her land on him so hard, Brian backed slowly out of the living room. He stared at her back for a few seconds, thinking hateful thoughts, then turned and ran upstairs. As his feet pounded on the steps, all he could think was: *why'd I ever do that? Why'd I even try to help her? It would have been better for all of us if she had fallen down and broken her goddamned neck!*

It was already early evening, just after supper, when Brian finally got out of the house. He told his stepmother he was just going for a walk and didn't even try to explain the bag he was carrying, loaded with bread, potato chips, Skippy peanut butter and a half gallon of milk. The sound of crickets buzzing in the backyard gradually faded as he entered the woods. The damp shadows embraced him like cold arms. Through the trees to the west, he could see the sun already lowering, sending spikes of orange light like fire through the leaves. There was a raw, tangy smell in the air that made him almost dizzy.

As he walked along, he noticed the curious, muffled stillness in the forest and realized how much he had actually come to like it. Taking the path out to the abandoned mill was almost like moving backwards in time; he felt like he could come out here and seal himself off from the "real" world, forgetting all about it. Having been isolated and friendless all summer, he had come to relish this feel-

270

ing of having his own, private world into which he could escape. He understood now that *this* was why—even after the fire—he hadn't asked his father to send him home to Arizona ahead of schedule. He liked—no, he *loved* coming out here! And in spite of the weird, creepy feeling the old mill and Uncle Mike gave him, he felt almost like he was coming home when he went to the mill.

So what is it about this place—these woods and that old mill?, he wondered as a shiver of excitement coursed up his back. *What seems so special about them?*

But his private world and the delusion that he could somehow insulate himself from real life all came crashing down the instant he broke out onto the road and saw the roof line of the mill far off in the distance. At least today, he was out here with a purpose. He was determined to get an answer—no, a *lot* of answers from Uncle Mike.

His breathing came high and fast as he crossed the weed field, sending grasshoppers and crickets flying in wild trajectories. Moving quietly, he approached the steps leading down into the mill. At the top of the stone stairway, he hesitated a moment as the feeling that he was being watched gripped him with a near palpable pressure. Gnawing on his lower lip, he looked all around but saw no indication of anyone lurking nearby. The humid summer wind blew heavily through the opened windows and doorways of the mill, and for a split second, Brian thought it sounded almost like a person—like several people, heaving deep sighs . . . or groaning in agony. Remembering the human shape he had seen standing—*No, it was hanging!*—in the window, he nervously glanced up but saw nothing except the dusty shadows inside the mill.

Take it easy now, he cautioned himself. *No need to get all worked up!*

He placed one foot on the top step and leaned forward, peering into the darkness below as he cupped his hands to his mouth and called out, "Hello . . . ?"

Something—probably a rat—scurried out of sight over

271

by the pile of rotting sawdust. His voice echoed dully from the stony throat of the building. He took a deep breath and called out again.

"Hey! Uncle Mike! . . . You in there?"

An icy shiver danced up his back when, after one last glance over his shoulder, he started down the steps. His sneakers scuffed on the stones and echoed from inside the cellar. He looked up at the sky, tinged with the first purple traces of evening, and wished he had thought to bring a flashlight . . . or had decided not to come out here at all!

"Hello-o-o . . . It's just me—Brian! . . . I—I'm alone!"

The dank smell and clammy air almost gagged him as he picked his way across the cellar floor toward Uncle Mike's room at the back of the cellar. His shoulders were hunched up, and his fists were clenched tightly as he walked forward, waiting for some indication that his uncle was down here. Without a flashlight, he had to inch forward, being careful to avoid tripping over fallen stones or any of the other junk that littered the floor. He wished the feeling that at any second he was going to be jumped would go away, but it heightened with every shuffling step, tingling his nerves.

I probably should just forget all about him being out here, Brian thought as he wiped his sweaty forehead with the back of his arm. *Just leave him the hell alone—turn around and go and never come back!*

This wasn't the first time he'd had such thoughts. Especially since the fire, he had wondered how smart it was to deal with this man. But Brian didn't turn around and leave. Something drew him on. He was almost to the wooden door when he heard the faint sound of an opening latch, then the rough scraping of the door edge, dragging in the dirt. A slice of hard, white light from Mike's lantern shot out like a knife blade across the floor through the opening door, illuminating every detail of the rough dirt floor. Then an ink-black silhouette loomed

272

into sight, blocking the light.

"Well, well, well," said a deep, resonating voice. "It's about fucking time you came back. Where the hell have you been?"

Uncle Mike's voice sounded so different that for a panicky instant, Brian was convinced this wasn't really him; but as the door opened wider, he recognized the man's curiously stooped posture.

"I—umm, I never got a chance to get out of the house till now," Brian said. His throat felt as dry as sand. He licked his lips and swallowed furiously. "I've been real busy. We—uhh, we had a bit of a prob—"

"You don't have to tell *me* what happened!" Mike snapped. "I know all about the *problem* you had!"

And did you have anything to do with it? Brian wondered but didn't dare ask. Uncle Mike didn't sound at all like himself, but maybe that was part of his problem. Maybe Uncle Mike had ferocious mood swings or multiple personalities, like the crazy people in the movies or that woman his teacher talked about last year in science class.

"The—uh, well, I promised you I'd bring out some food and stuff," Brian said. "You got that stuff I left out here a few days ago, huh?"

Uncle Mike nodded and backed away from the door. Brian stepped into the harsh light of the room, his eyes stinging from the sudden brightness. He could barely see as he handed the bag of groceries over to the man who grunted his thanks as he took it.

Every muscle in Brian's body was tensed and ready either to fight or run. He was hoping to keep an open path between himself and the doorway, but after depositing the bag on the table, Uncle Mike went over to the door, shut it, and latched it.

"I hope you didn't think I was going to—you know, not do what I promised," Brian said. He hated the trembling edge he heard in his voice, but Uncle Mike seemed

273

not to notice or care.

"I don't give a rat's ass about what you promised!" Uncle Mike said. "I've got plenty of other friends who can help me out if I need them! All I gotta do is ask."

Brian noticed a winding tension, both in Uncle Mike's voice and in his posture that set off alarms in his head, but he took a deep breath and told himself to stay calm. If Uncle Mike was on a hair-trigger, there was no sense saying or doing anything that might set him off.

"I—you know, I should probably get going," he said. "It's gonna be dark soon, and I don't want to have to walk through—"

"What, you ain't gonna stay and talk with me a while?" Uncle Mike snapped. "Christ! You'd think the least you could do is visit with me for a while!"

"It's . . . it's getting dark already. I don't want my dad to be worried."

"Worried? He *should* be worried!" Mike shouted. His voice was suddenly much sharper and higher, sounding almost like someone else was speaking. "He should be *damned* worried!"

"And why's that?" Brian asked. He winced with anticipation but still didn't dare ask his question.

"Why? Because they're all so pissed off! That's why! They're all so *fucking* pissed off!"

Brian's breath felt like a hot lump of coal lodged in the center of his chest. He mentally calculated how far it was to the door and how long it would take him to get out of here. Once in the open, he didn't have any doubt that he could outrun Mike; but in the close quarters of the mill, he knew he didn't stand a chance.

Dreading the reaction it might get, he cleared his throat and, in a voice barely above a whisper, said, "Who? . . . Who's pissed?"

"I don't want you to use fucking profanity in my place, understand?" Uncle Mike shouted. He closed his eyes tightly, clenched his fists, and, arching his back, shook

274

his hands wildly above his head. "They're fucking angry enough as it is because they've all been forgotten . . . *All* of them! *Forgotten!* You see, I've been to my mother's grave, and she—" He closed his eyes, and tears squeezed out between his closed lids. "—and she told me about them! And she said she wants me to . . . to—"

His voice suddenly roared with a sharp intake of breath; then he started coughing so hard his face turned bright red, almost purple in the lantern light. While Uncle Mike was doubled over in his coughing fit, Brian took a few quick steps toward the door.

Every inch counts, he told himself.

"Honestly, I'd really like to stay and talk, but I've got some—"

He was about to say, *some questions to ask you,* but this time he caught himself, sensing that if he asked his uncle anything about the fire, no matter if he had started it or not, it would set him off even more. "I—I've got some work to do at home. You probably know we're living in the—"

"I *know* where the fuck you're living!" Mike shouted. "Do you think I'm *stupid?* You think I don't know?"

Brian shook his head violently. Cold sweat was running down his neck, making him shiver. "No . . . no," he stammered. "I don't think you're stupid."

Just insane, he added mentally.

Uncle Mike looked up at him, his eyes glistening with a wild, crazy gleam. His face twitched and contorted as if it were the battleground for raging, conflicting thoughts.

"I know what you're thinking! They told me *exactly* what you're thinking," he said in a tight, strangled whisper. "You think I started that fire, don't you? *Don't you?*" Thick spittle sprayed from his lips, glistening like diamonds in the lantern light.

Brian shook his head in vigorous denial.

"Oh yes you do!" Uncle Mike shouted, punctuating his words with a deep, sinister laugh. "You sure as shit do.

Well, maybe I did, and maybe I didn't. And so what if [I] did? So what if I tried to burn down the house and ki[ll] all of you? Who gives a flying fuck? That wouldn't mak[e] them feel any better, would it? Do you think it would? I'[ll] have to ask them!"

"I . . . I have no idea," Brian said. His body was ho[t] and trembling. His ears throbbed with the heavy hammer[r]ing of his heart.

"Well maybe it would, and maybe it wouldn't! I can'[t] say one way or another! *They'd* have to tell *me*, and the[y] haven't yet! Not yet!"

The tight ache in Brian's chest blossomed as h[e] watched his uncle, writhing in misery. He was ready t[o] fight back if he had to, but again, he couldn't resist th[e] wave of pity he felt for the tormented man.

This isn't the same person I met a few days ago! Bria[n] thought. *Crazy or not, something's happened to him . . . something bad has happened!*

The room felt like it was closing in on Brian. The gath[h]ering pressure made his tension spike even higher. Feelin[g] dizzy and weak-kneed, he turned and fumbled with th[e] door latch, all the while expecting Uncle Mike to com[e] charging up behind him and slam the door shut on him[.] Miraculously, though, he didn't make a move to stop hi[m] as he swung the door open wide and stepped out into th[e] cellar. The clammy air was almost a relief after the sti[[]fling heat inside the small room. When he turned to clos[e] the door, he saw that Mike was still doubled over, clutch[]ing his stomach and shaking as though he had a stomach[]ache after eating a bag of sour apples.

Brian's step faltered. He almost went back inside th[e] room to make sure the man was all right before he left[,] but then he lifted the door edge and swung the doo[r] closed, cutting off the harsh glare of light.

"Look," he said softly, not knowing if Uncle Mik[e] could hear him through the door or even if he *wanted* t[o] hear him. "I'll come back tomorrow, once you're feeling better. I promise I will!"

He pressed his ear to the wood and listened, but the only sound coming from the room was a high-pitched whimper. He told himself to get moving, to run home before night closed down, but he didn't move. Flattening himself against the stone wall beside the door, he listened as the heavy hammering sound of his heart gradually slowed. Then, from inside the room, he heard a voice, talking in a harsh, grating whisper.

"I never—never wanted him to find out! Him—or—or *anyone*—else! No one needs to know that I was—I was—out here, you know."

The voice was tight and crackling with tension, but it sounded very close to the way Brian remembered Uncle Mike's voice sounding the first time he'd met him.

After a short pause, when another, deeper voice spoke, a flood of panic rushed through Brian.

"I believe you," the other voice said, "but the fact of the matter is, he *does* know."

The extreme difference in tone and inflection shocked Brian, hitting him like a solidly placed punch out of the darkness. He tensed, wondering if this, also, could be Uncle Mike talking, or if—somehow—there was someone else in the room with him. How had this person gotten in there so fast? Had he been hiding in there all along, or had he used Uncle Mike's secret entrance? Was he one of the "friends" Uncle Mike had said would help him?

Brian's hands went clammy with sweat as he strained forward to hear, but then another person spoke, this time with a broad Maine accent.

"You know, you should'a stayed hidden when he first came out here. That would have been best all the way 'round."

"Well, we can't very well do anything about that now, can we?" said a still different voice. This one sounded

277

like a prim and proper woman with a thick Scandinavian accent that was flat and emotionless.

"He hasn't seen us, but I think he suspects we're here." said another voice. "He's sensitive. He might be able to see or hear us." This voice also sounded feminine, but she spoke with a bit more earthy tone.

"If we want him to."

"He's no problem, though," someone else said—a man with a Scandinavian accent. "None of them will be once we—"

"—Once we're strong enough," finished a still different voice that sounded like a young boy.

Brian couldn't believe what he was hearing. Each voice had a distinct personality and spoke separately, without intruding on any of the others. He had the distinct impression that Uncle Mike's room was filled with people, but he knew that was impossible. He had just left there, and there was no way, even by using the secret entrance, that this many people could have gotten into the room so fast and so quietly.

"So what do you think we can do about it?"

Again, this was the voice that Brian thought sounded most like Uncle Mike's, but now he wasn't so sure until he added, "I just wanted to come back and visit my mother's grave!" Then his voice rose high and almost broke with a pained sob. *Does anyone know where my mother is?*

"We already told you, we don't know where she is," said the strong, masculine voice. "We haven't seen her in so long. Has she forgotten all about us?"

"We also told you what you have to do!"

"But I don't . . . I don't know if I want to do that," Mike said, followed by a tight, dry whimper. Brian could picture Uncle Mike, sitting on the floor and rocking back and forth as he knuckled his head with his fists. "I don't know if I *can.*"

"Now that she's gone, there may be no other choice.

You know that," the masculine voice said evenly.

"*Someone* has to know what happened," said the gentle feminine voice. "Someone has to know . . . and remember . . . *everything* that happened out here . . . or *else* . . ."

The last word was whispered like a slow hiss of steam.

"Fuck you!" another voice suddenly shouted. "Fuck you *all!*" No one has to know *shit*, and I say we can't fucking *make* him do any—"

"Please, please watch your language in my place," said the woman with the Scandinavian accent. Brian wasn't sure, but he thought whenever she spoke, he could also hear the distant sound of a baby, crying. It was faint, just at the edge of hearing, winding up and down, reminding him of something . . . something he had heard before.

When? Where?

"Fuck you!" the man's voice shouted. "This is *my* fucking place as much as it's *yours*. Maybe more!"

"If it's a question of whose place it is, we should ask Rachel."

"Well, Rachel . . . what do you think?"

"Rachel?"

There followed nothing but a prolonged silence that stretched out like a long, dark road. As it lengthened, a chill rippled like a spider's touch up Brian's back. He glanced nervously over his shoulder and saw that the sun had already set. Dark evening shadows spilled from the corners of the cellar and spread like ink stains across the dirt floor. The darkness pressed in close around him, and he had the sudden overpowering sensation that he was no longer alone in the dark.

No!

Not at all!

There were several people, maybe dozens of them, standing nearby, lurking in the shadows just out of sight, watching him. As the cellar steadily darkened and Brian's panic rose to new heights, these unseen presences shifted closer to Brian. He could feel them reaching out for him with hands that he could just barely see—or imagine—in the thickening gloom.

Terror choked him. A small corner of his rational mind whispered that he had to be imagining all of this. He was scared and all worked up, and his imagination was running wild because he'd heard his crazy Uncle Mike's wild ramblings. That *had* to be it! Uncle Mike was doing all of those voices, carrying on a seven- or eight-way conversation with himself.

Was something like that even possible? Could people be *that* crazy?

Goddamned right they could! Brian thought. He wanted to run, screaming from the mill, but was immobilized with fear. *Uncle Mike had been stuck in the mental hospital for a goddamned reason!*

As the silence continued unbroken, Brian started worrying, wondering if Uncle Mike was okay. He wanted to slide the door open—just a crack—and have a peek inside the room, but the fear raging inside him held him back. Instead, he turned and, on trembling legs, started walking toward the stairway, stumbling as he went.

He felt only a slight measure of relief when he made it out into the open air and started for home. As soon as he was on the dirt road, he looked back over his shoulder, convinced that Uncle Mike or someone else—someone quite possibly more dangerous than his uncle—was following him. Wave after wave of fear crested inside him until he broke into a run, dashing full speed into the woods along the dark, uneven path.

In the dense shadows under the trees, everything seemed threatening. Branches lashed out at him like angry, slapping hands. Roots tripped him up and grabbed at his feet. The night air roaring into his lungs was as thick as hot honey. He was dimly aware that he was whimpering as he swatted branches away from his face and bounced off unseen trees. If he could have taken a deep enough breath, he might have screamed.

He was afraid he'd taken the wrong path, but at last, he saw the Old Witch Lady's house up ahead. With a final burst of speed, he crossed the back lawn and made it up the stairs and onto the back porch. His body was slick with sweat and trembling when he threw open the door and went inside. Fortunately, his father, who had gone out to a town planning board meeting, wasn't home yet, and Dianne wasn't downstairs. She was probably upstairs in her bedroom with the door closed and—hopefully—hadn't heard him come in. Trembling with fright, Brian locked the door and went straight up to his room. He resisted the temptation to wedge his door locked with the back of a chair or his bureau.

Later that night, alone in his room long after his father had peeked in to say good night, Brian lay wide awake, staring at the ceiling until well past midnight. He was trying like hell to figure out what must have *really* happened out there at the mill, but he wasn't at all sure what he *wanted* to—or *dared* to—believe.

Chapter Eighteen
Shadow Show

"Who was that?" Dianne asked after Edward hung up the phone in the hallway and walked back into the kitchen. A perplexed look played across his face as he sat down at the table, picked up a fork, and began twirling it around in his hand like a magician, trying to make it disappear.

"That was Andy Jones, from the fire station," Edward said, heaving a deep sigh. "He finally got an answer on how the fire got started in the kitchen."

"And—?"

And now you know, Edward! Dianne thought with a tingling rush. *You know I started it by leaving the coffeepot on, right?*

"—And . . . it looks like it started between the walls somehow—something wrong with the wiring." Edward shrugged casually. "Who knows? Maybe a mouse or chipmunk or something got in there and chewed on them. Or else they were just old enough and frayed enough to cause a spark to jump and then—*poof!*"

I don't believe you! You know, and you're hiding it from me!

That was Dianne's first thought, but she didn't say it out loud. Smiling weakly, she turned back to the eggs she was frying for her husband. She looked longingly at the food—*real* food. As usual, all she was having for breakfast was a Carnation Instant Breakfast—the only *complete* breakfast you can drink through a straw!

"So it—it wasn't arson, then . . . like Andy first suspected?" she said. Her voice trembled and was barely audible above the snap and sizzle of frying eggs. She glanced at the square of morning sunshine shining on the floor through the opened screen door. Warm air wafted into the room, but that didn't stop her from shuddering.

"I guess not," Edward said. He took a deep breath and added, "Umm, that smells good."

Dianne's grip on the spatula was white-knuckled as she turned back to her job and looked down at the food, practically swimming in a brown-skimmed pool of melted butter in the old, blackened frying pan.

Evelyn Fraser's frying pan! she thought bitterly. The room seemed to darken as if a cloud had passed in front of the sun. *And Evelyn Fraser's old gas stove in Evelyn Fraser's kitchen because everything I had to cook with was destroyed in the fire!*

She flipped the eggs over and stared down at the two round, yellow egg yolks as if they were a hypnotist's eyes. A surge of . . . of *what,* she wondered—resentment? relief? fear?—rippled through her. A sudden tightening caught her chest as emotions welled up inside her. She found herself speaking before she could hold back the flood of words.

"Are you sure *you* didn't start it?"

She was horribly aware of her distant, hollow tone of her voice. She didn't turn and look at Edward, but she could sense him stiffen and stare at her back. She withered beneath his look, frozen like a fox caught in the sudden glare of headlights.

"What did you say . . . ?"

She knew this was her chance to take it back, to unsay it, but she spoke again, feeling almost as if someone else was controlling her mouth.

283

"I said, are you sure *you* didn't start it? The fire in our house, I mean."

Edward gave a quick, snorting laugh as if he couldn't possibly take her seriously, then said, "Now why would I do something like that?"

"Why?" Dianne said.

Her face flushed with a hot rush of blood. Her vision went all blurry as she turned around slowly and regarded her husband with a steady, hostile stare.

"Why?" she repeated, her voice sounding strained and muffled by the wires holding her jaw in place. "Why, so you could make us all move back here, into your *mother's* house! *That's* why!"

She made an angry sweep with the spatula that flung hot grease in an arc. Edward cowed back, although the grease didn't come close to hitting him. Behind her, the sound of sizzling food grew so loud in her ears it sounded like the pulling rush of the tide. Her anger—hot, red, and irrational—grew stronger with each hammering pulsebeat in her ears.

"We've been married—how long? Less than a year, and in all that time, it seems to me when*ever* you even *thought* about this place, much less visited it, you'd get all . . . all weird or whatever . . . as if you—" She raised her fists and shook them with pent-up frustration. "I don't *know* what! It's like you—you wished you somehow had never grown up or something—like you're still a little kid, and I'm—I—"

"Come on, Dianne. Cut it out," Edward said. He made a quick move to get up from the table and go to her, but then reconsidered and sat back down. "You're sounding like—"

He cut himself off before he said it, but Dianne finished for him. "—Like I'm crazy, right? *That's* what you were going to say, isn't it? That I'm sounding *crazy?*"

She swung the spatula several times, cutting the air with a sharp *whisk-whisk* sound.

"Well maybe I am! Maybe after everything that's happened to me, I'm crazy as *shit!* Fucking loony tunes crazy! All right? Does that make you feel better?"

"No," Edward said, keeping his voice level.

"Or maybe I'm just fed the Christ up with you and the way you . . . you cling to this old house like it's some kind of . . . some kind of relic or something! Christ, I don't know!"

She took a hissing breath through the wires in her mouth as she glared at her husband.

"All I know is, I'm sick and fucking tired of you holding onto this house like it's the last piece of your childhood, and you can never let go! *Never!*"

Edward hooked his hands into the tops of his pockets, leaned back in his chair, and took a deep, steadying breath. Dianne could tell just by the way he was looking at her, with a faint twist of a smile at the corners of his mouth, that he wasn't taking any of this seriously. That drove her anger even higher. She slapped the spatula against the side of the stove, snapping the handle in half. The eggs in the frying pan sent up a thin haze of blue smoke, but she ignored it as she threw the broken handle into the sink, then clenched her fists and pounded them against the counter.

"I can't stand it! I just can't stand it anymore!" she wailed as hot tears ran from her eyes. *"I just can't stand what this is doing to us! To you and me!"*

"What? What's doing what to us?" Edward asked, looking genuinely confused as he kicked back his chair and stood up. But he stopped himself from going over to her and regarded her with deep worry. Dianne could see the genuine concern in his eyes, but it was too late. The floodgates were open, and she couldn't possibly stop the rush of anger and rage that was directed at him.

"I don't *know* what!" she shrieked so loud her voice cracked. "I just—just *feel* it! This house! You! Me! Brian! Everything that's happened! I feel like I'm losing my mind! Look at what's happening to you and me? When I look at you, sometimes all I feel is anger, like I—

I *hate* you so much for what you let happen to me!"

"What *I* let hap—?" His voice dropped off sharply as if his throat had been cut.

Dianne reached up to her face with both hands, wishing she could reach into her mouth and pull the wires out. Bright bolts of pain shot like lightning through her head. Her vision swirled with tears, turning the old kitchen into a wild kaleidoscope of smeared colors. The smoke rising from the frying pan behind her was thicker, now, but the hammering of her pulse in her ears was so loud it drowned out the crackle of the burning food.

"Hey! Watch it! The eggs are burning!" Edward suddenly shouted. He darted forward and reached past her for the pan.

"So what?" Dianne wailed. "Let them burn! Why not?" She dodged to one side, convinced that Edward was going to take the frying pan and nail her on the side of the head with it. "Why not let the kitchen burn? Let the whole goddamned house burn down . . . just like you did to *our* house! Who'd give a shit! *Then* what would you do, huh? *What would you do?*"

Edward snagged a hot mitt from the counter and wrapped it around the pan handle. He moved quickly to the sink, dropped the pan, and ran cold water over it. A billowing cloud of steam rose in a hissing rush as a gray haze wafted like fog up to the ceiling.

Whimpering like a hurt dog, Dianne turned and raced down the hallway without looking back. She shouldered open the bathroom door, slammed it shut behind her, flipped the lock, and leaned her full weight back against it. Through the heavy door, she could hear a loud clattering from the kitchen as Edward went about cleaning up the mess, but the raging confusion in her mind blocked out everything else.

What's happening to me?

Jesus—God, what's happening to me?

She pressed her hands tightly against her head as though it was about to explode. Her whole body trembled, shivering as if she was outside in a raging snow storm. A hot, sour churning rose from her stomach and filled her throat, gagging her and cutting her breathing into short, painful gasps. She was suddenly afraid she was going to throw up, and the memory of the first few days after the operation when she had vomited blood only made things worse. A hot, rancid taste flooded the back of her throat.

"Oh, my God . . . my *God!*" she whispered as she gazed into the bathroom mirror, unable to believe it was really her she saw reflected there. She wiped her hands viciously across her fevered face.

She was shaking all over as she bent over the sink and ran the water until it was ice cold, then splashed her face. A slight measure of calm swept over her, and after a while—she couldn't tell how long—her frenzied nerves began to unwind. Deep muscle tremors rattled her like an earthquake. The muscles in her legs felt hopelessly weak, as if they were about to collapse and spill her onto the floor. She gripped the edge of the sink with both hands and stared long and hard into the reflection of her own eyes.

And then—at last—she realized what that churning sensation in the pit of her stomach was.

It was guilt.

Upstairs in his bedroom, Brian could hear the argument that was going on down in the kitchen. He'd been lying in bed half-awake when it had started, not really even aware of the buzzing of voices downstairs until they suddenly rose in anger. A faint stirring of pleasure went through him when he heard his stepmother yell, "Like I'm crazy, right? *That's* what you were going to say, isn't it? That I'm sounding *crazy?*"

Yes, you're absolutely right! Brian thought as he sat up in bed and wrapped his arms around his legs, positioning himself so he could hear better. *I think you're crazy as all hell, and I think my dad is even crazier for ever marrying you!*

As the argument flared higher, he smiled grimly to himself, taking surreptitious pleasure in hearing Dianne react—or *over*react—like this. This wasn't the first argument he'd ever heard them have, but it sounded like the worst. He had been too young to remember what it had been like when his *real* parents had been going through their divorce, but he found himself hoping that *this* was how people sounded when their marriage was heading for the rocks. Another thought registered dimly in the back of his mind, but he knew it was too much for him even to begin to hope . . . that—eventually—his mother and father might get back together again.

He breathed in shallow sips of air and listened as the voices got increasingly loud. He jumped when he heard a sudden, loud snap followed by a clattering noise.

What, are they throwing stuff at each other now? he wondered as he strained forward and tried to picture what was going on down there. *She's been complaining about how her medication was messing her up. Maybe she's really lost her marbles and is trashing the place.*

He quickly spun out of the bed and tiptoed to the door, opening it just enough so he could stick his head out into the hallway and hear better. He wished he dared to sneak down the stairs, but he was sure he'd get nailed—bad—if either one of them caught him spying on them.

"I can't stand it! I just can't stand it anymore!" Dianne shouted.

Brian smiled, knowing by the crack in her voice just how close to tears she must be.

"I just can't stand what this is doing to us! To you and me!"

"Yeah, and *me,* too, you lousy . . ." he whispered.

His grip on the edge of the door tightened almost painfully. He itched to go downstairs and see exactly what was happening. Maybe he could pretend that he was innocently coming downstairs for breakfast and hadn't realized they were arguing. But he dismissed that thought, knowing they would no doubt stop fighting as soon as he entered the room. He wanted them to really go at it. He listened as the voices alternated between his stepmother's rising, angry wail and his father's lower, steadied tones. Then his father shouted in a voice so loud and sudden that it sent a cold jolt of fear racing through Brian.

"Hey! Watch it! The eggs are burning!"

Using the noise as a cover, Brian took a few quick steps out into the hallway. He was prepared to run the instant he thought they might discover him there. His stomach tingled with tension as he crouched at the top of the stairs. He sniffed the air and caught the first faint traces of smoke. The immediate shock was still reverberating along his nerves when Dianne yelled, "So what? Let them burn! Why not? Why not let the kitchen burn? Let the whole goddamned house burn down . . . just like you did to *our* house! Who'd give a shit! *Then* what would you do, huh? *What would you do?*"

Then came the sound of heavy footsteps, followed by more crashing and banging noises. Brian saw someone's shadow—Dianne's—as she ran into the downstairs bathroom and slammed the door shut. A loud hissing sound and the sound of running water filled the house. When Brian leaned out over the railing, he saw a faint wisp of gray steam wafting from the kitchen into the hallway and chimneying up the stairwell. The burning smell was getting steadily stronger, but still Brian stayed where he was, not wanting to reveal that he could hear what was going on unless he had to. Besides, his father knew he was still upstairs in bed; if there truly was an emergency, he'd yell to him.

The sizzling sound coming from the kitchen gradually subsided. Wrinkling his nose from the stink of burned food, Brian took a deep breath and got ready to go downstairs. Before he could, he heard his father slam open the screen door and go outside, his footsteps clumping heavily on the back porch. Then the truck engine roared to life. With a crunching of gears, it started to back down the driveway. Brian heard his father rev the engine as he drove away, but even after the sound had faded, he stayed where he was, listening for some indication that Dianne was still down there. As far as he knew, she was still locked in the bathroom. His nostrils flared as he tested the smoke-tinged air.

"Why not let the kitchen burn? Let the whole god-damned house burn down . . . just like you did to our house!"

His stepmother's shrill voice still echoed in his ears like metal scraping against metal, and her words filled him with fear. What did she mean by that? *Just like you did to our house!* Did she honestly think his father had started the fire at his own house?

That was crazy! Why would his father want to do something like that? What would be the purpose? Just so they would all have to come and live *here?*

No doubt about it, Dianne *was* crazy as a coot if she was thinking like that. But now Brian remembered hearing the telephone ring while he was still half asleep. That must have been just before they started arguing. Could that have been the insurance company investigator or the town fire chief, calling to tell his father that *someone* had, indeed, tried to burn down his house?

The ball of fear in the pit of Brian's stomach got bigger and colder. "And I have a pretty good idea who," he whispered to himself. "Shit!" He shook his fists in frustration. "I should have confronted him yesterday out at the mill."

As soon as the words were out of his mouth, he shivered and glanced nervously over his shoulder, filled with the sudden, overpowering feeling that Dianne—or *some-one*—was standing behind him, watching and listening to everything he said.

He shuddered when he saw that no one was there, but he didn't allow himself to think about it for very long.

Dashing back to his bedroom, he slipped on a clean T-shirt, jeans, socks and sneakers, then ran downstairs. He thumped his feet heavily on the steps so Dianne would know he was coming down.

He searched through the kitchen cabinets until he found a flashlight. After making sure that it worked, he froze and, cocking his head to one side, listened again. His ears felt hot as he waited to hear Dianne call out to him, asking him what he was up to in there, but he heard nothing. Finally satisfied, but feeling a sharp edge of uneasiness, he started for the back door. His hand trembled as he turned the screen door latch. The feeling that he was being watched was back again—stronger this time!

His eyes widened as he looked back into the house, feeling a sudden wave of nervousness.

Was Dianne still at home, or had she taken off with his father? Maybe they realized he was home and wanted to argue in private.

Or maybe Uncle Mike was hiding nearby. What if he had plans to burn *this* house down?

Brian actually caught himself wishing Dianne was still home. If she was, maybe he would let his guard down, at least enough to confide in her and tell her what he suspected about Uncle Mike.

And maybe it wasn't such a good idea to go out to the mill without telling *someone*—even Dianne! What if something happened to him? What if Uncle Mike got crazy and dangerous and tried to hurt him?

"Dianne . . . ?" he called out, his voice warbling up and down.

He held his breath and waited in the doorway for several seconds. The house remained perfectly silent except for a faint humming sound coming from behind the refrigerator. Suddenly Brian felt so alone, so utterly abandoned by his father, by his mother, by *everyone*—even Dianne—that his eyes began to sting.

"Don't be such a wimp about it!" he whispered harshly as he wiped his eyes with the backs of his hands. That only made the stinging worse. "Maybe this is just . . . just something I have to face on my own!"

He swung open the door and went outside, not caring if the door slammed shut behind him as he started out across the back lawn and into the woods. Jogging at a leisurely but strong pace, he followed the trail out to the dirt road. When the old mill came into view, he forced himself not to stop and look at it or even *think* about how uneasy it made him feel. With his head down and his fists clenched tightly, one hand gripping the flashlight, he crossed the field to the cellar steps and went down into the cellar.

"Hey! Come on, open up! Open the door!" he shouted as both of his fists pounded a thumping drumroll on the rough wooden door. "Come on, Uncle Mike! It's me, Brian!"

He paused for a moment, shining the flashlight all around as he stood back to listen. He could hear nothing except his own heavy breathing. The cool air inside the cellar chilled his sweaty body. Goose bumps sprinkled his arms and the back of his neck as he directed the flashlight beam at the door.

"Come on!" he shouted. He started banging on the door with both hands again, even louder this time. The flashlight jiggled, sending the beam of light shooting off wildly all over the place. It caught him in the eye and momentarily blinded him, but he kept up a steady hammering as he yelled, "I know you're in there, Uncle Mike, and I know what you did!"

For just an instant, he thought he heard something—a low, chuffing sound of laughter. It stopped the instant he glanced over his shoulder, so he forced himself to forget about it as he drew back and then, grunting like a bull, slammed his shoulder hard against the door. The dry wood crackled like a string of firecrackers as it splintered; the top hinge gave way beneath the impact, and the door sagged inward. Brian ricocheted off the door and almost fell down, but he quickly regained his balance, pulled back, and rammed into the door again. This time, the wood snapped like an exploding gunshot when the other hinge let go and the door fell forward. It slammed onto the dirt floor like a huge, swatting hand.

Brian pinwheeled his arms for balance as his momentum carried him forward into the pitch black room. His foot caught on the edge of the fallen door, and he fell face-first onto the floor. The flashlight flew from his grip and skittered across the floor. Fortunately, it didn't go out. He got onto his hands and knees, but before he could stand up, he was doubled over by a coughing fit as dust swirled up into his face. The dust sparkled like flakes of diamond in the narrow beam of light.

"Uncle Mike!" Brian called out, coughing and waving his hands in front of his face. A razor-thin edge of terror cut through him when, again, he heard a faint ruffle of laughter behind him. It stopped when he snatched up the flashlight and directed the beam back out the empty doorway. His lungs felt clogged with dust. Sweat ran freely down his neck and back as he slowly straightened up, frowning as he surveyed the small room.

"Jesus Christ," he said, followed by a low, reverential whistle. The yellow eye of his flashlight darted back and forth like a dragonfly, but try as he might, Brian found it almost impossible to absorb what he was seeing.

The room was empty! The mattress, the moldering blankets, and the makeshift table were still there, but everything else—the food, clothes, and tools—was gone.

"Well I'll be damned!" Brian said, a bit more forcefully.

"Maybe you will," a soft voice whispered from somewhere in the darkness. It was followed by another light ripple of laughter that instantly faded.

Brian tried to convince himself that he had imagined the voice and the laughter, but that didn't stop the strong rush of shivers that zipped up his back. He continued to swing the flashlight beam back and forth, feeling as though he was simply missing seeing these things and that a more careful inspection would reveal them. But they were gone—as if they had never been there.

"Uncle Mike?" Brian called out. His voice was broken by tension, but this time he didn't expect a reply. Uncle Mike and every trace of him had disappeared. Except for the footprints and scuff marks he had just made during his rather clumsy entrance, the dirt floor looked smooth and untracked, as if someone had smoothed it over with a broom or something.

Maybe he was never even here, Brian thought. A cold, tingling tension filled his stomach. *Could I have imagined him?*

He knew that was impossible. He had touched Uncle Mike; he was solid flesh and blood.

Or maybe—Brian thought as a deeper dread gripped him—*just maybe he started the fire; and now that he did what he came here to do, he took off for good.*

"Did you hear that?"

". . . huh?"

There was a rustling of sheets as Edward rolled over in bed.

". . . hear what?"

"That sound. There's something outside," Dianne said. Her voice was a tight whisper in the dark bedroom. The night was hot, so the windows were wide open, but there wasn't even the slightest bit of breeze to stir the humid air. "I—I thought I heard something . . . in the backyard."

". . . uh-huh."

Edward groaned as he rubbed his eyes. His lips made wet smacking noises as if he were eating. He groaned again, then raised himself onto one elbow and looked at her. His face was an indistinct blob that hovered in front of her in the darkness.

"Wha . . . what time is it?"

"Almost midnight," Dianne replied after glancing at the glowing alarm clock dial.

"You think you heard something? What?" His voice was thin, sleepy-sounding.

"I don't know," Dianne said. "It sounded sort of like a—"

—*A baby, crying,* she almost said, but she held herself back. She knew damned right well there were no families with babies within earshot of the house; besides, who would be out at this time of night with a baby?

"—Like some kind of animal or something . . . sounded like it was in pain."

Edward swung his legs over the edge of the bed and sat up. He inhaled deeply, his breath sounding like he was wearing a deep sea diver's helmet as he cupped his hands over his face and rubbed his eyes some more. Dianne stayed where she was, too afraid to move as she watched Edward get up and walk over to the window. Kneeling down and resting his hands on the windowsill, he looked out at the night. Dianne could see his profile, sharply etched by the glow of moonlight.

"See anything?" she whispered.

Edward was silent for a moment as he cocked his head back and forth; then he shook his head and turned to her. "Nope," he said. "Don't hear anything, either. Probably just a raccoon or skunk or something."

"But it sounded like a—like it was in a lot of pain. It was squealing like it was really hurt."

That didn't come close to describing what she had heard, but after the scene she had pulled this morning, accusing Edward of deliberately trying to burn down his own house, she didn't want to say *anything* that would make him think she was any crazier than he already did. The truth was, the sound that had come wavering to her in the night, tugging her out of her thin sleep had sounded *exactly* like a human baby, crying its little eyes out.

"Might have been a fox or coyote," Edward offered.

"They make some pretty strange noises."

"No . . . I don't think so," Dianne said softly.

She pulled the sheet up to her chin and gripped it tightly. Edward came back to his side of the bed and sighed heavily as he lay back down on top of the sheet.

He reached for her hand in the dark and gave it a light pat, then rolled over and kissed her on the cheek before flipping his pillow over and settling his head back down.

"Isn't it hot as holy-ole hell?" he said, his voice already thick with sleepiness. "Maybe you were just dreaming."

"No, I—I don't think so," Dianne said.

Her lips were still wet from his kiss. She was surprised that he had shown even that much affection to her. They had both apologized for the argument this morning, each saying it was their fault, but Dianne thought he seemed a bit tense, distant toward her, as though he hadn't—or couldn't—fully forgive her yet for her irrational outburst.

"Go to sleep now . . . Don't worry about it," he said.

Before long, the room was filled with the heavy sawing of his breathing, but Dianne knew she wasn't going to get back to sleep that easily. She lay there in the dark, her eyes wide open as she stared up at the ceiling. She tried to command her body and mind to relax, but she was still tensed as she waited for the sound to come again.

She knew it would.

Relax! Maybe it was just a dream!

But then the sound drifted to her from the open window, sending a cold tingling though her.

The sound started out low, just at the edge of hearing. It drifted through the night like a gauzy sheet, flapping lazily in the wind. It was, in fact, so faint at first that she wasn't exactly sure when it had started. In some ways, it seemed as though it was always there, floating through the night, and it was just a question of when she became aware of it. It rose and fell with an eerie warble, but the longer she listened to it, the more she became convinced that it was no animal: this was a human baby, crying . . . crying in pain!

"Oh, Jesus!" Dianne said.

She pushed the bed sheet down and sat up in bed. Her breath hissed through the wires in her mouth; her pulse throbbed like a wild drumbeat in her ears as her eyes fixed on the window. The screen and sill glowed with a powdery blue light. The sound rose and fell, curling like tangled streamers of smoke. Then, below that sound, Dianne became aware of something else, other sounds—voices, some shouting, some crying out in the darkness, and dogs, barking and howling like bloodhounds hot on the trail. These sounds also danced teasingly at the brink of hearing, so she couldn't make out anything anyone was saying, but it sounded as though a crowd of people, at least ten or twenty, was out there in the woods behind the house.

Tingling with fear and expectation, she eased herself off the bed so she wouldn't disturb Edward and went over to the window. Kneeling down, she stared out at the moonlit backyard. It was empty. The humid night air hung in moist curtains of mist that seemed to deaden all sound. She turned one ear toward the window and strained to hear the baby crying and those voices again, but there was nothing except the steady buzz of crickets.

I can't be imagining all of this, can I? she thought.

Dr. Collett had reduced the strength of her medication; but maybe she was still taking too many drugs that were inducing hallucinations.

The woods were silent again, but just as she was about to give up and go back to bed, it came again—that same distant, tantalizing, warbling wail of a baby in pain. And then, through the thick stand of trees bordering the backyard, she saw something—a faint flickering of light that winked and danced like a cold, distant star.

"What the—?" Dianne muttered.

Even as she watched it, the light shattered and multiplied into two, then three, then four and more pieces until there were more than a dozen slivers of pale yellow light piercing through the black canopy of leaves and branches. They looked like flaming torches, seen at a distance. Dianne also detected a vague sense of motion, several black shapes winding among the trees as though the people she had heard were walking about in the woods, intent on some midnight mission.

She flashed on a memory of a Frankenstein movie in which the enraged citizens of the town, armed with torches and pitchforks, converged on Dr. Frankenstein's castle, intent on destroying both the mad doctor and his horribly disfigured creation.

Is it me they're after? Dianne thought crazily.

A thick, sour taste filled the back of her throat. She wished she could open her mouth to scream as tears started forming in her eyes.

Could that be it? There's a whole crowd of people from town out there—people who have come out here to burn our house down?

A chill raced up her spine as she straightened up and clutched her nightgown collar to her neck. With barely a look back at Edward, she went downstairs and into the kitchen. She didn't turn any lights on because—if there really was someone prowling around out there, she didn't want to alert them. She almost choked on her fear, wondering who these people were and why they were converging on her house at midnight.

Moonlight glowed on the kitchen floor and lit the screen door handle with a pale, blue light as she pressed the button and gently swung the door open. In spite of the warm night air, she shivered as she stepped out onto the back porch and looked at the woods. She had thought—had *hoped*—that once she came outside, the dim lights and the voices would be gone, but as she leaned over the porch railing and watched, they got clearer and louder. Flickering tongues of flame and thick, dark shadows edged with fire wove between the night-drenched trees.

Thank God at least they're not coming here! Dianne thought when she saw that their general direction was taking them away from the house. Their voices were clearer, now, but she still couldn't make out anything that was said. They spoke in loud, excited tones, a cacophony of voices that sounded almost like a babble of foreign languages. Dianne had an inkling that, like in a dream, it all made sense, somehow, she just couldn't quite grasp it. Some of the voices were shouting as though issuing commands. The baying of hounds rose and fell as though carried on fitful gusts of wind. Then from off in the distance, there came a chugging *putt-putt* and backfiring of what sounded like an old automobile. The shadowy figures, now appearing to number more than twenty or thirty, blended into the darkness.

At first Dianne was only distantly bothered by the irrationality of the situation; but as she watched the people move away, she was frustrated that she hadn't understood anything they were saying. Other questions formed in her mind.

Who are they? And what are they doing, marching through the woods in my backyard at this hour? What are they up to? Where are they going?

Before she consciously thought about it, she acted. Unmindful that she was barefoot and wearing only a thin nightgown, she went quickly down the steps and across the moonlit yard into the woods. She was lured on by the swelling voices and the still visible glimmer of torchlight through the trees up ahead. The air was tinged with the sooty smell of burned kerosene.

This is crazy! This is insane!

A tremor of fear went through her when she considered that it all might be just a dream, and she was somehow aware that she was dreaming. Her throat closed off with an audible *click,* and her breath felt like bottled fire in her lungs.

"No . . . no," she whispered as she stopped in her tracks. Holding up both hands, she stared at them in the eerie blue glow of moonlight and flexed her fingers. When she pinched the back of her hand, the pain was as sharp as a mosquito bite.

"No, damnit! I'm awake!"

In the short time she had taken to do this, the crowd of people had moved away from her, shifting and dissolving into the woods like soft currents of wind. Their torchlights had faded until there were no more than three or four, glimmering like faint stars through the dark tangle of the trees. Dianne had no idea where she was going or what she intended to find out or accomplish, but she forged ahead, following a narrow path that seemed to unscroll before her like a silver ribbon, shimmering in the moonlight. The voices were too distant for her to make out now, but still, hovering just at the edge of hearing, was the keening wail of a baby—a baby who was in great pain.

"What the hell is going *on?*" she whispered as she followed along the path at a brisk walk. When the way opened up, brightly illuminated by the soft wash of moonlight through the treetops, she broke into a run. The crowd seemed to be moving away from her no matter how fast she went. The night wind whispered softly in her ears, and she had a vague, uneasy sense of other unseen presences lurking in the woods all around her, watching and reaching out to her.

The path suddenly veered up a steep, rocky embankment. Without slowing her pace, she ran up it and found herself on a wide dirt road. The heavy foliage of pine and oak trees hung over the road like curtains. Along the center strip of the road was a Mohawk strip of long grass. Off to her left, she could hear a loud, tearing rush of noise and realized it must be the Saco River.

After checking up and down the road, Dianne started in the direction of the flickering torchlight. Before she had taken more than a dozen steps, she jumped into the brush along the roadside when an old-fashioned Model-A came chugging up behind her. It wound back and forth as its wheels tracked along the ruts in the road. Ducking behind a tree, she watched as a sputtering antique car rattled past. A faint glow of light from the dashboard lit up the two grim-faced men who were sitting in the front seat. Both of them were staring vacantly straight ahead, almost as if they weren't really watching the road. The driver had a smoldering cigar that glowed like an oversized firefly stuck into one corner of his mouth; the man in the passenger's seat had a shotgun resting across his lap. The dashboard light reflected off the five pointed silver stars they had pinned to their shirts.

This is absolutely impossible! Dianne thought, but as soon as the car was past her, she stepped back out onto the road and followed in its wake, choking on exhaust fumes that hung in the air. Up ahead, she could see a large building. A tremendous throng of people was gathered all around it, many of whom were waving torches overhead as they all talked excitedly, hooting and yelling like madmen. Sparks and sooty coils of smoke spewed up into the night sky. The chorus of voices rose and fell as though tangled in the eddies of a fitful wind.

Dianne drew to a halt about a hundred yards or so from the building, at the edge of a wide field. Standing stiffly, she watched in rapt fascination as the crowd faced the old building. She strained to hear what they were saying but still could make no sense of anything. The voices weaved and blended together into one long, incoherent babble. She thought it might just be a trick of her eyes, but it seemed as though the torches burned with a dull, smothered light, as if the air between her and them was too dense to permit the light to pass freely. As people shifted back and forth, she had the distinct impression at times that she could see the torches and the rough, black outlines of the building right through the milling figures.

Above all else, the sound of the crying baby rose so sharply in the night it was like a slender, hot needle, piercing her eardrums.

The Model-A pressed slowly through the crowd, which parted like the Red Sea to let it by. After pulling to a stop, both men got out and moved slowly toward the building. The driver walked with a confident strut while the passenger, looking more cautious, held the shotgun up to his shoulder and trained it on one of the windows in the small addition at the back of the building. The driver cupped his hands to his mouth and shouted something, but the sound was lost beneath the confused murmur of the crowd.

What is going on? Dianne wondered. *What the hell is this place?*

Fear sliced through her like a cold, stainless steel razor blade. Her body was trembling wildly. Sweat covered her face and arms, and made her nightgown cling to her body as if she had just been dunked in the river. She was torn between a frantic urge to run back to her house or move closer to the building so she could find out what was going on, but her body was frozen into immobility. She could do nothing except cover her mouth with both hands to keep from screaming when she saw what happened next.

With a swelling roar that sounded like a deep-throated belch, fire exploded like a gigantic orange flower from the windows and door of the small addition on the back of the building. Glass shattered, tingling like madcap sleigh bells to the ground. Weirdly flickering flames underlit heavy smoke as it rolled up into the sky, looking like a tornado of fire that blotted out the stars. With a single, collective gasp, the crowd fell back, their bodies seemingly made transparent by the raging flames. Firelight etched the lines of everyone's faces, but all of them looked curiously cold and lifeless. The air was filled with the snap and crackle of burning timbers that exploded like gunfire in the night, but still, above that rose the shrill, agonized wailing of the baby. Before long, other voices joined in the warbling chorus of pained shrieks.

Terrified and entranced, Dianne watched as the fiery jaws opened wide and, like a hungry mouth, consumed the far end of the building. Through the sheet of flame, she thought she saw movement. Several people were moving about inside the building. She shielded her eyes with her hand as the heat pounded against her face with a hammering, prickly sting.

It's real! I can feel the heat!

In spite of the heat, the two men from the Model-A stood their ground at the front of the crowd. Then there came the clean, sharp snap of gunfire. The man holding the shotgun grasped his chest with one hand and doubled over, falling to his knees. The shotgun dropped from his nerveless hand before he pitched face-first onto the ground. The other man dodged to one side, quickly bent down and snatched up his fallen companion's shotgun, and then, going down on one knee, aimed at the burning building and blasted off two quick shots. A wild scream of pain sounded from behind the wall of flame. As the echoing thunder of the double shotgun blasts faded away like thunder, the fire suddenly died down as if it was being controlled by a dimmer switch. With a nearly audible *whoosh,* the thick, black night closed down around the scene like a curtain at the end of a play.

"Oh, my sweet Jesus," Dianne muttered, staring in utter amazement at the building. Her legs suddenly gave out on her, and she sank slowly to her knees.

Everything was gone!

The crowd, the torches, the flames, the smoke, even the screeching cry of the baby. All of it. Gone.

The only thing that remained was the looming, dark hulk of the building, which stood out like a huge, black cutout against the star-sprinkled sky. A moist breeze wafted across Dianne's sweat-streaked face, chilling her. From far off in the woods, an owl hooted. Overhead, a dozen or more bats darted back and forth, slicing the sky above the building like boomerangs.

What in the name of God is going on? Dianne wondered as she knelt there on the ground. How could something that had seemed so real simply vanish in an instant? She had seen and heard the people; she had smelled the smoke from their kerosene-soaked torches and the exhaust from the Model-A; and she had felt the hammering heat of the blaze. How could it all be gone just like that?

She was drained and exhausted, no longer able to sustain the high level of fear raging inside her. Feeling wrung out and numb, she got slowly to her feet and took a few steps toward the building. It loomed like a mountain against the night sky.

The building, she thought—at least *that* is real enough.

But what in the name of Jesus *is* it?

It looked like an old factory or mill or something. Edward had lived nearby all his life, in the house not more than a mile from here through the woods. He certainly had to know about it. Why had he never even mentioned it to her?

And who—or *what*—were those people whose actions had lured her out here in the middle of the night?

They were gone now, and Dianne was left with the uncanny feeling that they had never really been here. Were they something she had imagined or hallucinated? Was her mind *that* messed up from her medication? If—somehow—they really had been here, how could they disappear so fast? Did she pass out or something after the fire had broken out and the gunshots had started? But it couldn't have been for long. What the hell was going on?

She stared up at the building, its angled roof glowing eerily blue in the moonlight. Her glance darted back and forth between the vacant windows as she started walking slowly toward it through the knee-high grass and weeds. She stumbled now and again, but she held her course. Her gaze was focused on the far end of the building where she could clearly see the ruins of fallen timbers. No smoke trailed from it up into the sky, but she could easily imagine that the pile of rubble was charred black and still smoldering with glowing embers. She intended to go up to it and find out. Had this place burned flat tonight?

But once she crossed the weed field and entered the moon-cast shadow of the building, her attention was drawn to one of the large open windows directly in front of her. She stopped in her tracks and stared intently up at the black void that looked as solid, as dimensionless as polished marble.

A wave of vertigo swept through her as she stared up at the window, trying hard to focus on it. Everything in her field of vision went blurry and wiggly. She felt herself being pulled toward the window, and had to fight the vivid impression that she was falling down into a black void that had slid open underneath her.

Her breath hitched painfully in her throat when she caught a flicker of motion, black against black, inside the window. Unable to move or react, she watched as the blackness took shape. It folded outward, rippling like thick tar until the features of a sleek, black face resolved. Cold light highlighted the features that leered at her like a horribly underlit Halloween mask.

"Jesus . . . *No!*"

It was an old woman's face. Her expression was frozen into a horrible grimace as she stared at Dianne with a wide, unblinking gaze. A deep furrow under her left eye gave her a horribly distorted look, as though one half of her face was made of black wax that had started to melt. Her frozen expression was one of astonishment . . . pure shock, as if death had caught her by surprise. Age lines crosshatched her features with dark, crooked gashes. Her thin lips were cracked, and her mouth was opened as if she was about to speak. As Dianne watched, horrified, the woman's head suddenly snapped back violently. There was a loud *crack* sound that Dianne knew was a bone, breaking. With a faint, strangled scream, the apparition's mouth sagged open like melting wax. Her eyes rolled up into her head, and from far away, Dianne heard a hoarse gagging sound as the woman's tongue wiggled out from between her broken teeth like a bloated, black slug.

Dianne started to scream—a low, warbling sound that gradually gathered strength deep inside her chest, but it was muffled, trapped behind the wires that clamped her jaw shut. Her vision pulsated with flickering light that kept time with her racing pulse. The woman's face, frozen like a mask carved out of black marble, glowed so brightly out of the darkness that it hurt Dianne's eyes. Then, with a loud dull concussion, the face disappeared, swallowed by the deeper blackness inside the window.

Feeling completely dissociated from her body, Dianne somehow found the strength to start running. She was aware of nothing but her blinding need to get away from this building. Like a disembodied spirit, she dashed through the field, down the dirt road, and into the woods. She wasn't even certain if this was the way back to the house, but for now it didn't matter.

Nothing mattered except getting away from that building and whatever horror was inside it.

Her arms and legs pumped furiously, and her breath roared into her lungs as she ran; but no matter how fast she ran, she was filled with the hollow, terrifying fear that the face of the old woman was following close behind her, staring at her, drilling the back of her head with vacant, death-filled eyes. And through the turmoil inside her mind, the only clear thought Dianne had was to get away . . . get away . . .

If she possibly could!

Chapter Nineteen
Unraveling

Early that next morning, Edward was surprised when he walked into the kitchen and found Dianne sitting at the breakfast table. She looked peculiarly slouchy, supporting her head with both hands with her elbows on the table. Her hair looked damp and disheveled, as though she had just stepped out of the shower and had not bothered to dry or comb it.

"Hey—" he said, taking a surprised step backward. "How long've you been up?"

"A while," Dianne replied, her voice a raspy whisper as she shook her head and looked right through him out the window. Her eyes shimmered with a distant glow as though she had been staring for a long time at something far away.

Edward felt a tightening nervousness as he watched her. Obviously something was seriously wrong, but it was too early for him to think clearly. She looked so wound up and ready to explode that he didn't want—or dare—try to pry out of her what the problem was. He said nothing as he shuffled over to the sink and got the automatic coffee maker ready to go. He flipped the switch, then leaned back against the counter, thinking it was more than a little bit strange that Dianne hadn't even bothered to look at him. Even if, because of the wires holding her jaw, a morning kiss was out of the question, she could at least give him a token smile and hug like every other morning. But she just sat there, staring out the window at the gradually brightening sky. A thin, gray mist was slowly peeling away to reveal a powder blue sky. Through the open window came the distant song of a robin.

"Is it . . . Do you want to talk . . . about anything?" Edward asked, horribly aware of the low tremor in his voice.

Dianne sighed and shifted in her seat, but still didn't look at him. Shaking her head, she grunted but said nothing. Edward was about to press her further when a thought hit him. Glancing at the wall calendar by the phone, he saw that she had an appointment with Dr. Collett today at one o'clock to have the wires removed from her jaw. She looked like she'd been up all night sitting here, worrying, and no wonder! She must be scared as hell about the appointment. Although she had never said as much, he knew she was self-conscious about going out in public. He wanted to say something comforting and reassuring, but — again — he didn't know how or where to start.

The awkward silence was suddenly broken by the sizzling hiss of coffee dripping into the carafe. Uttering a low groan, Dianne's eyes, wide with fear, suddenly snapped into focus. She glared at the counter as though expecting it to burst into flames. Before Edward could stammer an explanation, she saw what was making the sound and eased back into her chair. Still, her body looked rigid with tension as she shifted her gaze back out the window.

"Why didn't you tell me about it?" she said after a long silence. The rasp in her voice was louder, harsher, but the tone sounded drained, completely defeated.

"Tell you about what?" Edward said.

A cold, tickling sensation filled his belly.

"About that old building out in the woods behind the house," she said. Her voice was louder as she jerked her thumb toward the kitchen window.

"What—? The old mill, you mean—?"

"I don't know what it is," she said. This time her voice had the sharp crack of a whip as she glared at him. "Why didn't you ever tell me about it?"

The cold prickling feeling in his stomach got stronger, but Edward forced himself to smile and say, "Tell you about it? Why, because it—it's—" He shrugged and slapped his hands together. "It's always been there, ever since I was a kid . . . I never really thought it was all that important enough to mention, I guess."

"Oh, really?"

The wild gleam in Dianne's eye sent off warning signals. She looked like a drug-addled nut case, even worse than when they'd had that argument about how the fire had started in their house. Edward was convinced it had more to do with her fears and anxieties about having the wires removed from her jaw today, but whatever it was, *something* was pushing her right up to the brink of sanity. Edward saw how close she was to breaking and wanted like hell to prevent it, but had no idea how.

"Look, it's just an old sawmill that my grandfather ran back in the eighteen-hundreds, all right? It's no big deal! It's been abandoned for years—ever since I was a kid, anyway."

"Abandoned, huh? Is that a fact?" Dianne said. She pushed the chair back and stood up to face him over the table. "There's no one living out there that you know of?"

The crazy gleam in her eyes was brightening, as though the fear or panic or whatever it was inside her was surging out of control, and there was no way she could bottle it up or stop it. Edward shrugged again, but now that she was standing, he noticed for the first

309

time that the bottom of her nightgown from the knees down was wet. It clung to her, outlining the smooth curve of her leg muscles. The hem was smeared with streaks of dirt, and leaves and twigs were stuck to the lacy trim. Her bare feet were caked with dried mud as though she had been engaged in a little predawn mud puddle wading.

"What the—? Where have you—?"

He stopped and gritted his teeth as a thought struck him.

"Do you mean to tell me you've been out there, to the mill this morning?"

Dianne's upper lip curled back into a sneer that was made all the more horrible by the tangle of wires that covered her teeth. For the first time since her accident, Edward saw how horrible, how truly repulsive she looked. A cold wave of guilt and pity cut through him when he considered that *this* must be how Brian sees her.

"I—I just don't see what you're upset about. I mean, so there's an old building out behind the house. What's the big deal?"

"There's someone out there," Dianne said, her voice crackling with intensity. "There's someone living out there!"

"Don't be ridiculous," Edward said. He wanted to sound confident but couldn't stop the shudder that raced through him.

"And you're right," Dianne went on, glaring at him with wide-open eyes. "I *was* out there late last night and early this morning. I don't know *what* the hell was going on, but I saw . . . I saw *somebody* out there!"

Edward was staggered. The mere mention of the mill instantly brought to mind a single, clear image of Ray Saunders, sprawled on the pile of rotting sawdust with his back and legs bent around at an impossible angle. For some crazy reason, even though he knew that Ray

Saunders was still alive and living in town, confined to a wheelchair, all he could think was that if Dianne had seen *anything* out there, it must have been Ray Saunders's ghost . . . or at least the spirit of the person Sandy would have been had he not been crippled for life in that accidental fall through the trapdoor.

No! It wasn't an accident!

Edward had to grind his teeth together hard to keep from crying out.

You know damned right well it wasn't an accident, and you know damned right well whose fault it really was!

"It — it's nothing . . . really," he said. To his own ears his voice trembled horribly, but he hoped Dianne wouldn't notice. "I — I don't know why you'd even be going out there in the first place — especially at night, but — hey, if the place bothers you, just don't go out there. Forget it's even there."

"Forget about it!" Dianne screamed as she clenched her fists and shook them. "That may be easy for *you* to say, but I saw something out there. Something that . . . scared the shit out of me!"

"Do you want to tell me about it?"

"As if you'd *give* a shit!" she shouted. With that, she turned on her heel and strode out of the room, her sodden nightgown swishing like sandpaper as she stomped upstairs and slammed the bedroom door shut — hard — behind her.

For a tense, silent moment, Edward just stood there, staring at the empty kitchen doorway. His legs felt rubbery, and he had to lean back against the counter for support. The coffee maker had long since stopped sputtering and hissing, but the thought of drinking a cup of coffee — of anything — made his stomach do a sour flip.

He knew that right now, without even thinking, he should go upstairs and talk to her, try to get her to talk about what was *really* bothering her. Now more than

311

ever, she needed his support, but looking deep inside himself, he knew that he didn't have that kind of strength . . . not right now. Talking about the old mill had filled him with a dark, nameless dread.

No . . . not nameless.

He knew *exactly* what was bothering him. He had already been out there recently, after Brian mentioned being out there, but he thought maybe after breakfast he should go out and have another look around.

Then again, maybe the best thing would be to forget it even existed — let the place rot away into ruins . . . just like the horrible memories he had of the place!

Edward went through the mechanical motions of preparing himself breakfast, sitting down and eating it. Then, without another word to Dianne, he got into his truck and drove out to the construction site. Somewhere along the way, he convinced himself that going out to the abandoned mill would only stir up more painful memories. He had already checked it out and had decided that the best thing to do was forget about the whole thing. If nothing else, he could immerse himself in his work, and maybe when he went home for lunch, Dianne would be feeling better and they could talk about everything that was bothering her. He convinced himself the way she was acting had nothing to do with him or the mill — it had everything to do with the trauma and surgery she was going through and the prospect of having her jaw free after so many months of being wired shut. But if she was starting to unravel, he had to let her know that, above everything else, he was going to be strong for her, whenever she needed him and for as long as she needed him . . . no matter *what* was gnawing at *him!*

Dianne had the bedroom window shades drawn and was lying on the bed with her hands pressed hard against her eyes, watching as bright spirals of light trailed across her retina. At some point — she didn't even bother to look at the clock — she heard Brian's bedroom door open and shut. She listened tensely as he went downstairs, but as soon as he was out of hearing, she pushed aside any more thoughts about him.

She had enough problems of her own.

This afternoon, Dr. Collett would be taking the wires from her jaw and checking on how well her face had healed. As much as she wanted to be done with this ordeal, she was terrified, wondering what it would feel like to have the use of her jaw back. And beyond that, she couldn't stop fretting about what she would look like once this was all over. Dr. Collett had assured her time and again that he could remove most of the disfiguring scar tissue with plastic surgery, something he called "Z-plasty," but day after day, what echoed in her thoughts was the word — *most!* . . .

"*Most* of the disfiguring scar tissue!"

When this was all over, how much damage would remain?

She'd have the use of her jaw, but for the rest of her life, how disfigured would she be? When — if ever — would she recognize herself when she looked into the mirror?

She kept reminding herself that such thoughts were normal; her therapist had assured her of that. But *knowing* and *feeling* were two different things. The stark fear that she was no longer and never would be the same person she had once been — both inside as well as outside — had burrowed deeply into her mind and wouldn't let go. Being able to eat and talk normally wasn't going to be near enough to make her feel like herself again.

And besides all of that, right now she was angry . . . angry as hell!

She didn't know or even *want* to know the source of

her anger, but it, too, wound around inside her like a violent rage she was afraid would sometime, without warning, suddenly burst out of her against her will. Deep down in her soul, she knew that this wasn't like her—not the *real* her. She couldn't stop wondering if the person she used to be had indeed died in that accident up on Mt. Chocorua.

New face and all, like it or not, she *was* somebody else now.

Christ . . . who? Who the hell am I?

Whimpering softly, she heaved herself up off the bed and walked over to the bureau . . . the bureau that had once been Evelyn Fraser's. Her hands trembled as she opened a drawer and took out some clean underwear. She cursed again as she slid the drawer shut because every time she used the dresser, she was painfully aware that this was not *her* dresser, just as the mirror hanging above it was not *her* mirror, and this was not *her* bed or her bedroom or her house. They had *all* belonged to Evelyn Fraser, and in many ways, they *still* belonged to Edward's mother . . . certainly more to Evelyn than to her.

Sighing deeply, she rubbed her red, swollen face as she stared into the mirror. The skin looked like ripply, red leather—completely fake. She probed the wires inside her mouth, feeling an overwhelming impulse to rip them out with her bare hands.

But it was her eyes—her *eyes* that held her, fascinated.

A cold grip tightened inside her, and she almost screamed out loud when she had the uncanny sensation that she was looking at someone else. Her eyes were someone else's eyes—someone who blinked when she blinked, and shifted her eyes when she shifted hers.

"Oh, *Jesus,* you're losing it, girl! . . . You're *losing* it bad!" she whispered.

A deep chord of terror thrummed in her heart when

314

she saw her lips move as she spoke. The hard, grating whisper of her voice set her nerves even more on edge.

And then it hit her!

—*That face I saw in the mill window last night! What if . . . when the doctor's all through with me . . . what if once the wires are gone and I look into the mirror for the first time . . . what if all I see is that same, horrible, expressionless, lifeless face I saw in the mill window?*

She watched, curiously detached as tears formed in her eyes and spilled over, streaking her cheeks like glycerin. Her vision went blurry, and a wave of dizziness almost unbuckled her legs, but she gripped the top of the dresser and stared long and hard at herself, praying desperately to see even a faint spark of familiarity in the eyes that were staring back at her. She blinked her eyes slowly, wishing to hell the dissociated feeling would go away, but with every hammering beat of her heart, it got worse.

What's the hell's wrong with me? . . . What's the hell's wrong with me?

And then, in a whisper as faint as an evening breeze, another voice spoke inside her head.

It's all because of him, you know!

She tensed, knowing exactly who *"him"* was—

"*Edward!*" she whispered.

She continued to stare at her reflection and watched as her lips peeled back, exposing discolored teeth and a gummy network of wires. Every ragged breath she took hissed through the wires, making saliva bubble up like foam on a rabid animal's mouth. She realized with an aching pain just how horrible she must be to look at. Why would Edward even want to be *near* her, much less want to *kiss* her? She could easily imagine that, behind the wires, her mouth was filled with the convoluted, backward pointing teeth of a lamprey eel.

"*And this is all because of Edward!*"

315

She couldn't distinguish if it was a thought or a voice.

A low, rumbling sound started deep within her chest. A small portion of her mind wondered why she would let herself get so worked up. Why did just thinking about make her feel such hostility, such hatred? Sure, she had been scared by what she had seen last night, but all of that *must* have been in her imagination . . . or she had been sleepwalking and had dreamed the whole thing, mistaking a nightmare for reality.

But she pushed such thoughts aside as the anger welled up inside her like a raging, black tide.

My whole life's become a waking nightmare, and it's all because of Edward!

She glanced down at her hands as if they belonged to someone else and saw that they were clenched into tight, white-knuckled fists. The veins stood out like blue pencils beneath the skin. Deep muscle tremors shook her body as a flood of heat rushed to her face. When she looked back at the mirror, she saw that her complexion—*No! That's not really my face!*—had turned a mottled scarlet.

None of this would have ever happened if it hadn't been for him!

She wanted to scream, but no matter how hard she struggled, the wires held her jaw shut, her teeth clamped firmly together. She thrashed like a person whose arms and legs were secured by loop upon loop of thick rope. The pressure was steadily building up inside her until—at last—it exploded. Nearly blind with rage, she twisted to one side and then, spinning on her foot, brought her clenched fist around in a wide arc. There was a heavy thump followed by a dull, splintering sound as a white cobweb exploded across the mirror.

Dianne was mildly surprised that the noise wasn't

louder. She had been expecting—had *wanted*—to hear an ear-shattering, shotgun blast of glass and wood as the mirror and its frame were pulverized by her single blow. She took a deep breath that sounded like the wild roar of a racing engine, then collapsed forward onto the bureau and stared at her reflection, now broken into dozens—hundreds of jagged triangles. She counted at least ten reflections of her eyes—eyes that she was now positive were no longer hers.

"Damn you!" she whispered in a raw, shattered voice. "God*damn* you all to *hell,* Edward!"

"Hey, man, it's been a while. Too goddamned long! What the hell've you been up to?"

"Not a whole helluva lot," Edward said.

He forced himself to smile as he stood in the doorway of the living room. The shades were drawn to block out the bright morning sunlight. The room was cast with a pressing, pervasive gloom. The air smelled old and stale, like a house where someone had recently died. In the far corner, the blue glow of a TV flickered, but the sound was turned down too low to hear.

There came a high dentist-drill whining as Ray Saunders worked the controls of his wheelchair and swung around so he could face his visitor. The sight of his crippled friend sent a jolt of sadness mingled with anxiousness racing through Edward. He took a few hesitant steps forward, then abruptly stopped when Ray started moving his wheelchair forward.

"Hey, don't worry. I won't run you over," he said with a forced, hearty laugh. "And even if I do, I have collision insurance."

"Uh—your brother was just leaving when I got here," Edward said, shrugging with a smile that inside felt completely phony and forced. "He told me it was okay to come right in."

"Sure, no problem. Come on in and have a seat," Ray said, twitching his head in the direction of the couch.

Edward rubbed his hands together as he went over to the couch and sat down. He perched on the edge of the cushion as though ready to bolt out of there in a flash. There were more mechanical sounds as Ray jockeyed the wheelchair around into position in front of the couch. Before the wheelchair turned, Edward noticed the bumper stickers plastered on the back of the leather seat: *CAUTION I BRAKE JUST FOR THE HELL OF IT!* and *GAS, GRASS, OR ASS—NOBODY RIDES FOR FREE!* The grim humor made him chuckle . . . at least a little.

"Something the matter?" Ray asked once the two friends were seated and facing each other. "I mean, no one we know has died or anything, have they?"

It never failed to surprise Edward how clear and precise Ray's voice sounded. For some reason, he always expected a person who was confined to a wheelchair to have slurred speech; but he didn't need to remind himself that Ray's condition wasn't the result of any mental deficiency.

"Ah—no, no. Nothing's the matter," Edward said softly. His knuckles crackled as he twined and twisted his fingers together. "It's just that it's—" He shrugged. "I hadn't stopped by for a visit in quite a while, you know, and I thought—"

"In a while! Christ, man, it's probably been something like five or six fucking years," Ray said. "I think the last time I saw you was at Charlie Costello's funeral." There was no trace of bitterness or anger in his voice, and his face seemed not to betray any hidden thoughts or emotions, but Edward cringed under his friend's words as if he had been given a lashing with a whip.

"Umm, that's right."

"Good ole' Fish-eyes," Ray said, taking a deep breath and shaking his head. "Who'd've thought he'd ever end up like that, huh? Getting into a barroom brawl and getting knocked into a coma he never came out of. Key-rist! You know, it's crazy how we all ended up over the years, isn't it?"

All Edward could do was grunt and nod as he stared down at his fingers, which were melded together like a knot of earthworms in a bait bucket.

"So if nobody's died, why'd you stop by?" Ray asked. His tone of voice was a little sharper, and he looked at Edward with his head cocked to one side as though he was studying him.

Edward's eyes had finally adjusted to the gloomy room. As he looked back at his friend, it seemed as though Ray was staring at him intently with eyes that had taken on a dull, lambent glow. Deep in his gut, Edward felt a strong stirring of nervousness. Ray's voice, so quiet but strong in the darkened room, had a curious, almost frightening presence . . . as if he were whispering close to his ear through a megaphone.

"No—like I said, nothing's wrong. I just felt like stopping by."

Edward resisted the impulse to wipe away the sheen of sweat that had broken out over his forehead.

"I realized, you know, how long it's been since I'd seen you. I bump into your brother around town now and then, and he keeps me posted on how you're doing, but I was wondering—" He ended lamely with a shrug, letting his voice trail away with a faint, "You know . . ."

"Well, I still haven't learned how to do the rumba, if *that's* what you were wondering," Ray said, and this time Edward did detect a trace of bitterness in his friend's voice. "I'm still strapped into this goddamned, fucking wheelchair . . . like I've *always* been. Ever since that retard—"

Ray caught himself before he said any more, then sawed his teeth back and forth over his lower lip, the muscles of his face twitching as he looked at Edward. The silence lengthened uncomfortably between them; then Ray took a deep breath and said, "Look, I'm sorry I said that. I—I shouldn't have." His eyes looked huge and moist, filled with deep sadness. They no longer shined with even a trace of the light Edward had noticed before. They had that flat, black marblelike reflectiveness of a dead person's eyes. Edward's body tensed when—again, just like this morning when he'd had that argument with Dianne—he was struck by the thought that maybe what had really happened was Ray Saunders *had* died in that accident out at the mill back when they were kids.

No! It was no accident!

Most of Ray's body and spirit had died that day, and now just a small piece of him was left hanging on to life as if—as if . . . somehow . . . miraculously—he could eventually get it all back!

The heat inside the room pressed in on Edward. He was dimly aware that his mouth had dropped open as though he were about to speak; air from his lungs pressed up into his throat, and he could feel the gathering strain on his vocal cords, but any sound he might have made was blocked, trapped inside him as firmly as if cold hands had wrapped around his throat and were squeezing, grinding, and crushing inward. The words he wanted to say were words he had wanted to say, had *needed* to say ever since he was, twelve years old. They echoed like a long, hollow roll of thunder inside his brain.

Don't you know what really happened, Ray? Don't you realize, even after all these years, that Mikie never did it? That he wasn't the one who pushed you through the trapdoor?

"Are you sure there's nothing the matter?" Ray asked.

320

His voice seemed to come from far away, echoing with a rippling distortion that further heightened Edward's rising panic. "I dunno, man. You're looking kinda pale."

"No, I—" Edward replied in a voice that sounded extraordinarily thin and strangled. Those cold hands hadn't eased up their ever-tightening grip on his throat. He tried to laugh, but in the dimly lit room, even his own breathing was frightfully magnified, sounding like the hiss of heavy raindrops, bouncing off a metal roof.

Don't you know that I did it? That I was the one who pushed you!

The words reverberated so clearly in Edward's mind that he was absolutely convinced, if Ray was listening hard enough, he would have been able to hear them in the muffled silence of his living room.

Don't you realize that I'm the one who tackled you from behind! That I knocked you down into the cellar! I'm the one who broke your back and put you into that fucking wheelchair for the rest of your miserable, goddamned life!

"—I really just started thinking about how it'd been too damned long since I'd seen you. You must've heard about the fire we had out at our house."

"Oh, yeah—sure," Ray said, nodding. The motion made something on his wheelchair squeak. "And you're staying out at your mother's house until you rebuild. Don't worry—I may not get out of the house much, but I've got my antenna out. I know just about everything that's going on in this town." He snorted as if about to spit, then added, "For all the fucking good it does me!"

A florid rush filled Edward's face. He realized that, no matter what topic of conversation he tried to bring up, he or Ray seemed inevitably to bring it back around to the uncomfortable subject of Ray's confinement to a wheelchair. Like a jagged gap left by a broken tooth, no matter how hard you try, you just can't stop yourself from probing it with the tip of your tongue. Was this because, at least subconsciously, Ray *did* know the truth of what had happened out at the abandoned mill that day?

For the next half hour or so, Edward never relaxed as he remained seated on the couch, talking with Ray. They covered a wide scope of topics, but their conversation always steered clear of anything of any depth or anything that might raise the specter of Ray's injury. They discussed recent events around town — the new hardware store that had opened and closed within the span of a year, the residents of a local housing development who were suing the developer for absconding with the funds; and they reminisced a bit, talking about "old times," but Edward could tell that this kind of talk made Ray just about as uncomfortable as it made him. At one point, Ray casually mentioned the hiking accident last spring and asked how Dianne was doing. Edward immediately sprang to his feet and clapped his hands.

"Oh, shit! Oh, *shit!*"

He glanced at his wristwatch and saw that it was almost twelve-thirty. He had been so preoccupied that he had forgotten all about meeting Dianne back at the house for lunch and then driving her to Portland for the appointment with her doctor.

"Hey, can I use your phone?"

"Sure," Ray replied as a look of consternation crossed his face. "It's in the—"

"I know where it is," Edward snapped as he raced out to the front hallway, picked up the receiver, and hurriedly dialed his home number. Ray's phone was an old-fashioned rotary type, and Edward's impatience bubbled over as he waited for the slow-turning dial to spin back.

"Come on . . . come *on!*" he muttered, tapping his

322

foot impatiently on the floor. After the dial had stopped turning after the last number, he gritted his teeth, still tapping his foot, as he waited for the connection to be made and for the phone to start ringing on the other end. Once . . . twice . . . three times the receiver buzzed in his ear, but nobody picked up at the other end.

"Is everything all right?" Ray called from the living room.

"Yeah! Yeah!" Edward paused and listened to the fourth ring. "It's just that I forgot to . . . do something."

Edward's frustration rose like a black cloud as the steady ringing continued at the other end.

"Come on! At least *Brian* should be home!" he whispered, his voice rasping in his ear through the receiver. Another ring blasted. "Where the hell *is* everybody?"

But he knew the answer, at least a part of it. Wherever they were, they certainly weren't at home. Anxious and impatient, Dianne had probably driven out to the house site looking for him; but by now, probably pissed as all hell, she was no doubt on her way to Portland—if not already there, sitting in Dr. Collett's waiting room and nervous as hell about what was going to happen within the next half hour.

And where was Brian?

Well, who knew where the hell he was. A slight tingling raced through Edward when he considered the possibility that—against his wishes and orders—Brian might have gone back out to the mill, but there was nothing he could do about that right now, either.

"God*damn*it!" Edward muttered.

A cold wave of guilt swept through him. He had been so wound up in his own concerns and guilt that he had entirely forgotten about Dianne and how she must be feeling. He listened to the unanswered phone ring a few more times before finally giving up. Resisting the impulse to slam the receiver down, he instead gently depressed the button, cutting off the phone in midring.

"Hey, Ray," he called out, painfully aware of the low tremor in his voice. "I have to head on home. There's something I have to do."

A voice as irritating as the raw scratch of sandpaper whispered in his mind: *But there's something you have to do here, too, Eddie! . . . You have to admit it! Admit what you did! Didn't you come over here today to tell Ray—finally, after all these years—what you did to him? Didn't you want to confess it all and—at last— take the guilt and blame that Mikie has been carrying all these years?*

Edward closed his eyes, fighting hard to hold back the tears that welled up inside him. His hand was slick with sweat as he put the receiver back into the cradle.

But I can't! another, nearly frantic voice whispered, sounding like a child inside his head. *I can't do it! After all this time, what good would it do? I've paid for what I've done. Every day of my life since that day, I've paid!*

From behind him, he heard the soft whirring of Ray's wheelchair as he negotiated the turn from the living room into the hallway. The sound was like a red hot spike that slid up along the core of his spine, raking the nerves in each vertebrae like a xylophone.

But you HAVEN'T paid enough! the first voice whispered, harsh and slithery like a snake. *And you can NEVER pay back enough because of what you made your brother and Ray live through their whole lives! How can you EVER give ANY of that back to either one of them?*

Edward's pulse was banging heavy drumbeats in his ears, almost drowning out the sounds of the wheelchair as he turned to face Ray. Knowing how bad he must look, he kept his head titled to one side. He opened his mouth and licked his lips, desperately wanting the words of confession to be there, but he knew they wouldn't come.

They would *never* come!

Not after being buried inside him for so long, down in the core of his soul where they had rotted and turned to a sour, black, eternal agony.

"I . . . I have to . . . to drive Dianne to Portland," he said in a voice that sounded completely shattered. "For a . . . for a doctor's appointment. I completely spaced it off until you mentioned her."

Before Ray could say anything, Edward turned and started for the door, not wanting or daring to look his old friend straight in the eyes. He knew, sure as hell, that his guilt would be written all over his face. He fumbled with the doorknob but was unable to turn it. An icy chill stabbed through him, almost making him cry out when Ray said, "Well thanks for dropping by. It's good to see you after all this time."

"Yeah," Edward said through his clenched teeth.

The doorknob finally yielded, and the door swung open with a chattering shriek of rusty hinges. The sound set Edward's teeth on edge, but he tried to ignore his reaction as he stepped out onto the front steps. A warm blast of summer heat washed over him like a torrent of hot, putrid water.

"Drop by again," Ray said, his voice sounding muffled from inside the cool gloom of his house.

From behind, Edward could hear the mechanical whir of the wheelchair as he came up behind him. He knew he was going to have to turn and say goodbye, but he was terrified that just seeing Ray's face—his housebound, pale skin and the wounded accusation in his eyes—would completely unravel him. Without another word or even a backward glance, he started down the walkway to the curb to his parked truck. He could still feel Ray's gaze boring into his back, and he couldn't stop the voice that was screaming wildly in his mind:

He knows the truth! the voice said with a razor-sharp edge bordering on hysterical laughter.

You can pretend he doesn't know, but he does! After all these years, this has been the secret you two have been sharing—the secret that you have an unspoken pact never to reveal! And the reason he doesn't say anything about it, to you or anyone else, is simple. He knows it's killing you, eating at you from the insides like a vulture, tearing raw flesh from your still barely beating heart.

And he's enjoying the hell out of it all . . . every damned second of it!

Confined to his wheelchair, it's the height of pure entertainment and revenge for him! He's absolutely loving being able to watch . . . or even just think about the gut-squeezing guilt and misery you've had to live with every day of your life since that day.

This is Ray Saunders's ultimate act of revenge . . . watching you unravel like this!

Chapter Twenty
Unwrapping

Dianne was feeling no better—even worse, actually, once she was seated in Dr. Collett's waiting room. She crossed her legs at the knees and couldn't stop shaking her foot rapidly back and forth as she ran her fingernail along the cloth seam of the couch arm. After waiting at the house until it was almost too late, she had scrawled a note and left it on the kitchen table:

"WHERE THE HELL WERE YOU??? THANKS A LOT!"

She had stormed out of the house, slamming the door behind her so hard the window rattled and almost broke. Throughout the drive to Portland, she had worked over and over in her mind what she would say to Edward when she saw him back at the house later this afternoon.

Why you lousy, rotten son of a bitch! You tell me you love me, but when it comes right down to it, you leave me stranded high and dry! Everything's that happened to me has all been your fault, and you don't even have the common decency to come in here with me! What the hell's the matter with you? You probably don't even dare come and see what I look like now.

Is that it? Are you afraid to see me and face the reality of what you did to me?

She didn't care if he had genuinely forgotten about the appointment or if he had gotten delayed for some reason, legitimate or otherwise. The *least* he could have done was call; and the bottom line was, no matter what else he said about being supportive and loving and caring and all that, it was bullshit of him not to show up when he said he would! He'd let her down on the one day she genuinely *needed* him. And the truth was, he was *never* really there for her!

Ever!

Shades of things to come, perhaps? Dianne thought bitterly.

Gathering tears stung her eyes. She was fuming with anger as she slid her fingernails up underneath the couch edge and sawed at the loose stitching. Her tongue pushed furiously against the metal prison of wires as she mentally formed the words she wished she had the physical freedom to scream out loud. Her heart went cold with the thought that soon, within the hour, those restraining wires would be gone, and she *would* be able to speak—and shout—if she wanted to.

"The doctor will see you now."

The sudden voice broke into her reverie like a gunshot. Startled, Dianne looked up at the nurse who was standing in the doorway. She rose shakily to her feet, feeling as though she had to say something, but the only sound to come from her throat was a muffled groan.

Oh, shit! This is it!, she thought nervously.

The nurse held the heavy oak door open for her, then turned and beckoned for her to follow her down the narrow corridor to a small operating room. She paused in front of a half-open door, slipped a manila folder into the plastic holder on the wall beside the door, and then signaled for Dianne to go into the room.

"Have a seat and make yourself comfortable," the nurse said cheerily. With a sweep of her hand, she indicated the padded dentist's chair. "The doctor will be with you in a moment."

With that, she was gone, closing the door softly behind her. Cold dread filled Dianne as she listened to the soft tread on the nurse's footsteps going down the hallway.

"Hey, com'on now," Dianne whispered as she looked around the room. "There's nothing to get nervous about. It's going to be a relief to get this frigging bird cage out of my mouth."

The overhead fluorescent light reflected off the pure white cabinets and stainless steel equipment so brightly it stung her eyes. She quickly scanned the medical diagrams and charts on the wall, then took a deep breath and eased herself into the chair. The cushion made a loud *whoosh* sound, and she almost giggled aloud, thinking it sounded like a soft fart. She took another deep breath and tried to settle herself. She gripped the armrests and placed her feet onto the padded footrest, but the tension kept winding up inside of her. When she glanced down at her legs, she had a momentarily dizzying sensation that she was suspended high above the floor. Like a wash of cold water, a prickly chill quickly spread upward through her body. In an instant, her legs, her stomach, her entire body felt numb, completely lifeless. A tightness gripped her throat, and her heart pounded heavily in her chest. A cold sweat broke out on her forehead.

Hey, com'on! Get a grip!

She realized she hadn't been breathing deeply and tried to take a long, steady breath, but the flood of panic was too strong now; it swept her up like the blast of a hurricane wind. Her breath came in short, whistling hitches through the wires in her mouth. The back of her throat was clogged with thick mucus and felt like it was on fire.

Com'on! Jesus Christ! Get a grip on this! You should be excited, relieved to be getting rid of this stuff . . . finally!

She started wiggling her feet, but the senseless feeling wouldn't go away. No matter what she tried to think about, she couldn't stop the powerful surges of anxiety that were gushing inside of her. She knew that behind it all were her worries and concerns about how she was going to look after the wires were gone, but all of those were swept aside by the surging charge of anger that churned in her stomach like sour acid. No matter what she tried to think about — Edward, or Brian, or their home, or the house they planned to build together, or anything that she had enjoyed doing, at least before the accident — everything filled her with a dizzying nausea.

And then, when the memory of what she had seen that night out at the mill popped into her mind, she felt a violent surge of fear and hatred that was so strong it terrified her. No matter how many times she told herself that, given her circumstances, such feelings and thoughts were normal, it seemed as though now all of the violence and hatred she had ever felt were coming to the front, ready to burst out of her. Just like her mother, who after years of abuse had finally fought back, she was going to get even for what had happened to her.

Jesus Christ, just stop it, please! Stop it!

She closed her eyes and pressed her hands hard against her face. Her skin was flushed, as though she had a fever.

What the hell am I thinking?

She didn't dare consider that question honestly because, at least in the darkest corners of her mind, she was afraid that she already knew the answer. Over the last few agonizing months, she had tried her best to deny it, to disbelieve it so much that it just wouldn't be so; but she couldn't stop thinking that, once the wires were out of her mouth, she wasn't going to be the person she had been before her fall off that mountain ridge. She already wasn't! And it was one person's fault!

Oh, God! What the Christ have I become?

She feared that, over the past several months, while her face had been healing and her broken jaw had been mending, she had slowly but inexorably been altered, externally and internally, and now it was just a matter of time before Dr. Collett revealed what she had already become—

A monster!

And she couldn't stop thinking that it was all Edward's fault; and that one way or another, when this ordeal was finally all over—goddamnit!—he was going to have to pay for everything he'd put her through!

Dust swirled in the air as Edward drove the truck into the driveway, but even before he had switched off the ignition and gotten out, he realized he was too late. The car was gone. Muttering a curse under his breath, he started up the walkway to the house, nervously jingling his key ring in his hand. The back door had been left wide open as if someone had left the house in a hurry.

"Holy shit, she must've been really pissed," he said when he entered the kitchen and found Dianne's note on the table.

"Where the hell were you?" he read aloud. Every syllable made his eardrums flutter, and a warm rush went up the back of his neck. "Thanks a lot!"

Sighing, he crumpled the paper into a ball and tossed it into the trash can, then turned toward the doorway. Cupping his hands to his mouth, he called out, "Hey, Brian! You home?"

He waited a moment, but when no answer came, he realized that Brian must also be off somewhere. He thought hopefully that maybe he had gone with Dianne to her doctor's appointment but that wasn't very likely. In spite of all of his best efforts, his son and his new wife still weren't getting along very well.

Not very well at all!

At times, he actually found himself wishing he hadn't arranged for Brian to spend the summer with them. His son's presence certainly was adding extra stress to a situation which he wasn't sure he and Dianne could have handled very well even it had just been the two of them.

A low grumbling in his stomach reminded him that it was well past lunchtime, so he went about making himself a bologna sandwich, got out the bag of potato chips, poured a beer, and sat down at the table to eat. He took a small bite of his sandwich and chewed slowly, thoughtfully. Usually when he had lunch home alone, he found the silence of the house relaxing, but today—for obvious reasons—he felt all keyed up, on edge. He couldn't stop thinking how disappointed and outright pissed off Dianne must be. Stewing over it wasn't going to do him or her any good, but it galled him that, for the first time ever, he had ever let her down like this.

His stomach also twisted with a deeper, colder guilt that had everything to do with his visit with Ray Saunders. Like so many times before, he wished to hell he'd had the courage to confess to his friend what he had

332

done. But again, like all those times before, he hadn't been able to face up to it. He had lived so long with this private torment that he had finally convinced himself that it was all for the best if his secret lived and died with him. Ever since that Saturday morning in the autumn of 1963, he had spent a portion of every day of his life regretting what he had done to Ray. Over the years, he had tried to convince himself that worrying and fretting about it was a ridiculous waste of his time and energy. The past was over and done with, and neither he nor anyone else could do a damned thing about it. Why let it eat away at him like a cancer? He should flush it out of his system and forget about it once and for all!

But like an amputated arm or leg, a "phantom limb" that can still have the sensation of itching, the guilt over what he had done wouldn't disappear, not completely. In fact, over the years, if anything it actually seemed to have gotten worse.

Suddenly Edward shook his head, realizing that he had been just sitting there, staring blankly at the kitchen floor over by the back door. His sandwich was half gone, but he didn't remember swallowing a single bite. He had only a vague memory that it had absolutely no taste. His hand was trembling as he picked up the can of beer, popped the top, and took a swig. The carbonation exploded in his mouth, but there wasn't much taste to that, either—just cold, fizzy water. Even without trying the potato chips, he knew they would taste like sawdust in his mouth.

Yeah, he thought with a shudder, *old sawdust . . . sawdust that's been rotting away on the cellar floor of the old mill for the past thirty years!*

A cold fluttering filled his stomach as he stared blankly at the square of sunlight by the door. Realization dawned on him so slowly, so gradually that he wasn't sure when he had first noticed it or, after he had noticed it, when it first struck him as strange, but at some point, he realized that there was something wrong about the entryway. Pushing his chair back, he stood up and went over to the door, kneeling down to inspect the area around the doormat.

Funny I didn't notice this before! he thought. *Then again, why'd I even notice it now?*

Like a spotlight, the sunlight illuminated the faint trace of a footprint as clearly as if someone had purposely stamped it on the linoleum just so he would see it. Little clumps of dried, black dirt, like miniature mesas, outlined the design of the imprint. Edward traced above the print with a pointed finger, immediately convinced that neither he nor Brian could have made the print. The sole of the shoe—a sneaker, he guessed—was wider than his own, but to confirm it, he placed his foot next to it. The footprint was clearly larger.

"What the hell?" Edward whispered.

He glanced out the door at the back porch, then over his shoulder at the doorway that led into the dining room. Could someone have broken into the house while they were out? He had assumed that either Dianne or Brian had simply forgotten to close the door behind them when they left this morning, but maybe that wasn't what had happened.

With fists clenched tightly, ready for anything, he walked through the dining room and into the living room. He heaved a sigh of relief when he saw that the television and VCR they had brought from their own house were still there. A quick tour of the downstairs confirmed that nothing valuable seemed to be missing, but he couldn't dispel a feeling of uneasiness, as though he could sense but not see an intruder in the house. He leaned over and scanned the living room rugs for more telltale footprints but found none, so he walked back to the kitchen and went outside to have a look around.

The porch and back steps were scuffed and dirty, but there had been so much traffic back and forth that he couldn't clearly discern any more of the footprints he was looking for. In spite of the warm sunshine on his back, he felt a slow, shivery chill track up his spine as he straightened up and looked around the backyard.

Where would someone get their feet that muddy? he wondered.

It hadn't rained in the past few days, so unless there was some large standing puddle nearby, the dirt must have been caught in the grooves of the person's sneakers. He looked down the dirt driveway, then his eyes tracked back to the woods that bordered the backyard. There was no way he could have known with certainty, but he was suddenly positive that whoever had left this footprint in the house must have come from the forest. There was a brook not too far into the woods. The mud easily could have come from there.

He was positive that wasn't his or Brian's footprint, so who's was it? Had someone come out of the woods and broken into the house earlier today?

Who? And why?

Just this morning, Dianne had said that she knew someone was living out at the mill. Could there be someone out there, living nearby without their knowing it?

He took a few steps toward the woods, but then stopped short when he caught a flicker of motion out of the corner of his eye. Turning quickly, he saw that the side door of the shed attached to the garage was open, swinging back and forth in the fitful breeze. Edward knew that door had been locked because, as soon as they had moved into his mother's house, he had cleaned out the storage room and brought over most of his carpentry tools so he would have ready ac-

335

cess to them. He also knew, because he had thousands of dollars worth of tools, that he kept both the front and side doors of the garage locked.

For several seconds, he just stood there, watching as the door swung gently back and forth with a teeth-grinding *squeak-squeak* of rusted hinges. Then, without warning, a sudden rage gripped him. There was no way he was going to tolerate someone snooping around his house, breaking in while he was away and messing around with his personal property. Squaring his shoulders, he walked boldly across the driveway to the shed. He didn't hesitate a moment as he swung open the rough wooden door and stepped into the room. A sickly wash of sunlight shot through the dirt and spiderweb encrusted window, casting an eerie gloom in every corner.

"All right you lousy son of a—" Edward shouted, but his voice trailed away as his eyes adjusted to the dim light inside of the shed, and he saw that there was no one there.

At first sight, anyway, everything seemed to be in order—at least in the semichaotic order in which he remembered leaving it. But as he glanced around, although there was no one thing he could point to, there was a definite feeling that someone had been in here going through the contents of the room, dropping and leaving things wherever they may have fallen: a hammer on the floor, a saw leaning against the wall so the blade was bowed, a bright orange extension cord lying in a tangled knot underneath the workbench. Edward was fairly certain this was not how he had left his things.

He ran his fingers down the door edge to the porcelain doorknob. It was cold to the touch and looked like a spotted bird's egg, but what drew his attention was the latch plate. Scoring the dull, tarnished brass were numerous small lines, like spider webs. They were fresh, glinting with shiny brass. Edward was positive someone had forced the lock to gain entrance to the shed.

But who, and why? What would anyone be looking for?

Although he stored plenty of valuable tools here, there certainly wasn't anything of great value. He walked over to the bench and moved a few things around but soon gave up. Just like in the house, there didn't seem to be anything missing, but he had a disturbing feeling that the place had been violated.

Maybe Brian had been out here, looking for a wrench or screwdriver to fix his bicycle or something before taking off for the day.

He tried to convince himself that's all it was, but the lock had obviously been forced. Edward couldn't get rid of the feeling that there was something else going on here; that someone had been in here rummaging through his tools, looking for something specific.

He decided not to take the time to straighten things up right now and turned to leave. As he did, his foot kicked against something. Looking down, he saw his chain saw, which was on the floor by the door. As soon as he leaned over to pick it up to put it on the bench, he realized what was missing.

"That's it!" he said, snapping his fingers. His voice sounded like sandpaper in the closeness of the shed. "The gasoline can."

He had finished clearing the land for the new house several weeks ago. Because he knew he wouldn't be needing the chain saw again for quite a while, not until it was time to cut firewood for winter, he had put both it and the five gallon gas can on the bench in the shed. Not on the floor! He was positive of that! Knowing that an empty gas can was more likely to cause a fire than a full one, he made it a practice to refill the can

337

after using it, but he couldn't remember if he had done it this time. Because of the fire at his own house and after the hassle of moving into his mother's house, perhaps he had forgotten all about the gas can. Maybe he had left it out at the house site after using up the last of the gas to burn the brush he had cleared.

No, he seemed to remember refilling the can and putting it in here a few weeks ago; but it didn't matter if he had done that or not, the fact was, the gasoline can wasn't here now.

"Shit," he muttered.

He knew he should get back to work this afternoon, at least until Dianne got back from the doctor's office, but he felt much more inclined just to blow the rest of the day off—spend the afternoon in front of the TV watching a baseball game or lying in the hammock out back with a cold beer in hand. He left the shed, making a mental note to look around for the gas can tomorrow when he went back to work.

He closed the shed door firmly behind him and jiggled the doorknob to make sure the lock had snapped shut. He was halfway across the driveway when, from inside the house, he heard the faint ringing of the telephone. He started to run for the back porch, but just as he swung open the kitchen door, the phone cut off in midring. He dashed across the floor and grabbed the receiver anyway, pressing it tightly against his ear as he snapped a quick "Hello."

The line was already dead. It droned in his ear like an angry hornet.

Swearing softly, he hung up the phone and sat back down at the table. He stared blankly at his lunch, then decided to finish it. The beer was probably flat and warm, and the sandwich bread was dried out and crusty, but he ate it anyway. All the while, he couldn't stop wondering if that had been Dianne, calling from the doctor's office to tell him how the operation had gone. By the time he had finished gagging down his meal, the questions of who or if someone had broken into the house and toolshed, and if his gasoline can had been stolen or simply misplaced were out of his mind. The last thought he had about it was, since there obviously wasn't much—if anything—missing, there wasn't much point in bothering the police about it.

Even though she knew Dr. Collett was standing right behind her, watching her, Dianne stared into the mirror on the surgery room wall, unashamed as plump teardrops rose in her eyes and rolled down her face. The doctor had just finished carefully snipping and pulling out the last strands of wire that had held her jaw in place for the last few months. Her hands were shaking as she raised them and began to probe gingerly at the still puffy, pink flesh around her mouth. Her fingertips traced the narrow runnel of scar running down along the edge of her jaw. Gripping her chin, she worked the lower jaw up and down, and back and forth. It was stiff and hurt a little, and it made tiny *click-clicking* sounds inside her head, but—holy mother of God!—she could move it again!

"Of course, it's still going to be sore for a few days," Dr. Collett said, "and your gums are going to bleed for a while. I can prescribe something to prevent infection, but—" He smiled reassuringly and nodded. "I'd say we're pretty much out of the woods on this."

She smiled weakly as she glanced at his reflection over her left shoulder. Although he was smiling back at her, just having him standing there bothered her; she felt threatened, somehow, and mistrustful.

"I can't . . . I just . . . after all this time . . . I can't . . . believe it!" she whispered, pronouncing each word with great care and watching in amazement as her re-structured jaw moved up and down with every syllable. In utter disbelief, she watched as her teeth moved behind her pale lips. The teeth were stained yellow and covered with brownish gunk from months of not being brushed properly, but finally she was able to move them freely.

Oh, God! I can't believe it! I can't believe it!

The tension in her upper jaw was almost unbearable as her smile widened. Her face muscles twitched, and a thick, sour taste flooded the back of her throat. Tiny white spots of light exploded and faded in her field of vision. She was suddenly afraid that she was going to pass out or vomit or something, but she couldn't tear her gaze away from her reflection. There were still hard, bright red scar lines running up the side of her face and cheek, and her skin still looked peeled and raw, but by staring at her reflection hard enough and long enough, she could almost remember how she had once looked. Then she looked closely at the reflection of her own eyes, and a cold jolt shot through her. She remembered that odd sensation this morning that these weren't really *her* eyes. Before she could stop it, the idea took hold again. Her eyes widened with glistening tears, but behind them she thought she detected a cold, almost lifeless stare.

Like a dead person's eyes! she thought.

A freezing shudder raced up her back and gripped the back of her head like a hawk's talons.

That's still not me . . . it's still not my face, whispered a small voice in the darkest corner of her mind. She tried to shut it out, but it struggled to get louder. *Those aren't my real eyes!*

She thought back to that day several weeks ago when Dr. Collett had removed the bandages from her face following the second operation. The elastic bandages had stretched out and clung to her face, and they pulled like adhesive tape as he slowly, carefully peeled them away, unwinding them to reveal her badly swollen face. She shivered, recalling that the sensation of liberation had been so dizzying, so absolutely unbelievable, but also completely terrifying!

She had that same sensation now, only this time it felt like it was her skin, perhaps her very soul that had been peeled away like a snake stripping itself out of its dry, scaly skin.

And what's underneath? she wondered as cold currents of worry and doubt twisted inside her. She pushed at her flaccid skin, fighting hard the impulse to scratch her face away to reveal what was underneath.

Who—or what—have I become?

Chapter Twenty-one
The Portrait

It was almost nine o'clock at night. Strong gusts of wind lashed rain against the side of the house. Brian was sitting cross-legged on his bed, staring blankly at the dark rectangle of his bedroom window, watching as water slid like quicksilver down the glass. Every so often, a whistling shriek of wind would rattle the window, sending a shiver through him.

It never rains like this in Arizona, he thought bitterly, and thinking about Arizona made him think about his mother—his *real* mother, back home in Phoenix—his *real* home. Maybe he should give her a call. Then again, maybe not. He had talked to her less than a week ago, and he didn't want her to think he was acting like a homesick little kid who couldn't handle being away from her. He wished he felt like listening to music or reading or going downstairs to watch TV or *something,* but instead, he just sat there on his bed, waiting . . . waiting.

For what?

He wasn't quite sure.

As much as he didn't like it, thoughts of his mother made him think about Dianne—his stepmother from hell. She had come home from the doctor's office about an hour before supper, still looking just as ugly as before except she no longer looked like she had tried to swallow a ball of barbed wire. For the first time in two months, Brian had heard her speak without the encumbrance of those wires in her mouth. Practically the first thing she had done was start bitching at his father for not being home in time to come with her to her doctor's appointment. His father had tried to apologize, but she hadn't let up, yelling and screaming at him, telling him how scared she had been throughout the procedure and how let down she was that he hadn't made the extra bit of effort to be there for her.

Things weren't improved when, after supper, his father reminded her that he had to go to a meeting with the Cliffords to discuss some changes they wanted to make in their house plans. After an uncomfortably silent and very tense meal, his father had left after helping Dianne clear the table. Complaining of a headache, Dianne had washed the supper dishes and gone straight upstairs to bed.

So two hours later, here he was, sitting in his bedroom, waiting.

Brian realized that one thing he was waiting for was for his father to come home. He never liked being left home alone with Dianne . . . especially at night. The rain and wind beating against the house didn't help his mood any, either. It wasn't as though he was afraid she might say or do something mean to him; it was just that he felt kind of . . . nervous, a little bit spooked whenever it was just the two of them alone in the house.

Another thing—perhaps the *only* thing he was waiting for *really*—was some indication that Dianne had fallen asleep. He certainly wasn't ready to go to sleep yet, but he didn't feel as though he could concentrate on anything—even a mindless TV show—knowing she was still awake. He wouldn't feel quite so uncomfortable about going downstairs and doing something if he was positive she was asleep; but short of peeking into her bedroom, there was no way of knowing.

He shivered at the memory of the first and only time he had gone into that particular bedroom—that night last June when he had helped his grandmother when she was having that heart attack or whatever it was that had killed her shortly thereafter.

Scritch—scritch—scre-e-e-ch.

And what if he looked in there now, and saw Dianne, scarred and mutilated, glaring back at him from the bed?

His mind filled with horrible images of his grandmother, lying there in bed, her eyes blank, her slack mouth open, a thin line of drool running down her chin. He knew he wouldn't be able to handle seeing anything like that again, so he decided just to stay where he was, even if it meant sitting here until well after midnight. He'd wait right here until he was absolutely positive it was safe to come out of his room.

"Yeah, like maybe sometime next year," he whispered, snickering softly under his breath.

But after a while, as the storm continued to slam against the house with hissing bursts of rain, he finally decided that he was going to go nuts if he didn't do *something!* Besides, it was absolutely ridiculous to feel like a prisoner in his own house. And yes, goddamnit, this was just as much his house as it was hers.

Maybe more!

Sighing heavily, he swung his feet to the floor and stood up. The floorboards creaked underfoot as he went over to his door and ever so slowly turned the doorknob until the latch clicked. The old hinges squeaked like a frantic mouse as he eased the door open until there was just enough room for him to squeeze out into the hallway. His breath caught in his chest, as he started down the hall toward the stairway. With every other step, he paused and glanced over his shoulder at Dianne's closed bedroom door. In his fevered imagination, his living stepmother and his dead grandmother blended together, and he began to wonder what kind of horror was waiting for him there inside that bedroom.

Why not go right down there and take a look? he thought as a chill rippled up his back.

What would it hurt?

Did he really think Dianne was some kind of monster? Did he think he might catch her off-guard and see that she was some grotesque parody of what a human being should be? Probably the best thing to do right now, the sanest thing would be to look in there and see that she was nothing more than a woman—a woman who should be pitied, instead of feared, because of what she'd had to deal with over the past few months. Why not face her down and see that there was truly nothing to be afraid of?

But he wouldn't—or couldn't—bring himself to do that.

Why take the chance that she might still be awake and catch him at it. And anyway, he would be going back to Arizona in a couple of weeks to begin the new school year; he wouldn't even have to think about Dianne after the first of September. One thing for sure, he was never going to come and stay in Maine for this long ever again!

So he continued down the hall toward the stairway, step by cautious step. When he was at the top of the stairs, though, he looked back and something else at the far end of the hall caught his attention—the narrow door that led up into the attic.

He drew to a halt and stared at the door, holding his breath until his lungs began to hurt. Ever since they had moved into the house following the fire, he had wondered what might be up there. At least until now, he'd never taken the time to go up there and explore. For all he knew, the attic might contain some unbelievable treasures—old coins, and books or magazines, and other stuff. With Dianne in her room and his father out for the evening, he thought this might be his last chance to get up there and check it out before he went back to Arizona.

Keeping a watchful eye on his stepmother's bedroom door, he started back down the hall until he was standing in front of the attic door. The dim hall light seemed barely able to reach all the way to the door. He tingled with excitement as he snapped the small hook and eye lock that kept the door shut. As soon as the lock was sprung, the door popped and swung halfway open, making a silly horselike whinny.

Brian glanced quickly over his shoulder, but there was no indication from Dianne's room that she had heard anything. Leaning against the edge of the door, he reached into the gloom, feeling around for a wall switch. His hands brushed against bare wall on both sides of the stairway.

"Come on! There's gotta be a light here somewhere," he whispered as he leaned further into the darkness and ran his flattened hands up along the wall. The plaster felt gritty and cool to the touch, but there wasn't enough light to see by. The darkness at the top of the stairs swelled like a living, breathing thing. When he placed his foot onto the first step and leaned forward, the step snapped, sounding like breaking ice. He felt higher up on the walls on both sides of the narrow staircase but still didn't find a switch. When he took another step up, something tapped lightly against his forehead.

He dodged to one side, thinking for a heart-stopping

instant that it might have been a spiderweb or something, but then he realized that it might be a string, hanging down from the attic ceiling—a string that might be attached to the pull chain of a light. He reached out until he found it again and, after feeling it in the dark to make sure it was indeed a string, pulled on it. There was a faint click, and at the top of the stairs, a single, bare light bulb came on, casting a faint, yellow glow.

Brian sucked in a nervous breath as he looked up the steep flight of stairs and counted them.

Thirteen steps. Great!

For a moment he reconsidered what he was about to do. What if he made too much noise and woke Dianne up? What if his father came home and caught him poking around up there? Or what if he found something he wasn't suppose to find? Maybe there was stuff up here that his grandma had wanted to get rid of but couldn't before she died. He hesitated, thinking there probably was nothing but piles of old junk anyway. Why even bother going up there? Why not just go downstairs and watch MTV until his father came home?

Why? Because there's gotta be some cool stuff up here, that's why, and this is probably my last chance to check it out.

Brian was unable to ignore the wave of excitement that swept through him as he stared up at the light glowing at the top of the stairs. It looked so warm and welcoming, and the soft, brown shadows on the stairway seemed to reach out like arms and beckon him forward. Even from where he stood, he could see several stacks of boxes that were tied together with fraying gray twine. Dust coated everything—even the steps—like a thin glaze of snow. Brian realized that for the last several years of her life, his grandmother had probably

347

been too old and stiff to make it up this steep flight of stairs. There *had* to be some really neat stuff up there!

A strong shiver of excitement raced through him as he started up the stairs, taking each step carefully so the dried-out treads wouldn't creak beneath his weight. He could imagine that with every step he took, he was leaving behind the real world and entering an entirely different universe. The yellow light looked as mellow as the setting sun; the air, although dust-dry and almost too thin to breathe, carried with it a rich mixture of age and mystery. The patter of rain against the roof was louder, but it seemed somehow muted, too—more gentle, as though it fell from a different, less angry sky. Even the wind, which had whistled like a banshee outside his bedroom window—*Scritch—scritch—scre-e-e-ch!*—now sounded hushed and seemed almost to carry faint, whispering voices. Brian grew lightheaded with the feeling that he had been magically transported back to a different time and place.

He stopped at the top of the stairs and looked back down. The hall light shining onto the worn carpet made everything in the hallway look somehow thin and watery. The open door framed his view, and for a horrifying instant, he had the impression that the hallway he had just left was nothing more than a flat, dimensionless painting. The angled perspective of the stairs seemed horribly exaggerated, and for a dizzying moment, the staircase seemed to telescope crazily in and out.

Whimpering softly under his breath, Brian backed away from the top of the stairs. He reached out blindly behind himself for something to grab onto, but there was nothing there, and he bumped into a stack of boxes. Thankfully, he didn't knock anything over. All he could think was how lucky he had been not to fall down the stairs and break his neck.

It's just because of how steep the stairs are, and the dim light is playing tricks on my eyes, he told himself, but he found that he didn't dare look back down there again.

He shook his head to clear it and squared his shoulders before moving further away from the top of the stairwell. All around him were piles of old furniture, stacks of magazines, and dozens of boxes, but he didn't dare start exploring them yet. He had to calm down, get a grip on himself. He took a deep, calming breath, but his chest hurt as though it were somehow being restrained.

Suddenly he was filled with a sharp sense of immediate danger. He knew it wasn't because he was afraid of falling down the stairs or of getting caught snooping around up here. There was something else—something in the close, dry air that made every nerve in his body tingle as though electrified. A cold, clammy feeling, like the touch of a dead hand brushing against his skin, made the hairs at the nape of his neck stir. He didn't know how, but he was suddenly convinced that whatever was wrong up here was lurking in the darkness behind him.

Tension bubbled up inside him as he sucked in another breath, held it, and turned around slowly. He wanted to scream but wasn't even able to whimper when he saw the cold, motionless face staring back at him from a darkened corner of the attic.

"It-t-t's-s-s so-o-o c-c-c-cold. Can I l—l-light a f-f-f-fire? . . . P-p-please?"

Michael's teeth chattered, dicing every word into dozens of tiny pieces. Outside, the wind whisked against the mill like a whipsaw. Darkness filled the small room, wrapping around him so tightly that he could easily imagine it was a cold, hungry beast, nuzzling against him for warmth. The cloying aroma of damp earth filled his nostrils, making him think of a freshly-turned grave . . .

My mother's grave!

He whined like a wounded animal, picturing her lying stiff and cold in a darkness that was thicker than this—*much* thicker, a darkness that had no end, no light . . . *forever!* Like a long, steel spike, the thought pierced his stomach and started working its way slowly, inexorably up to his heart.

He sat huddled against the stone wall, his knees pulled up tightly against his chest and his hands clapped over his ears as he rocked gently from side to side. Worse than the wind and rain howling outside, though, were the voices that whispered inside his head, chattering and snapping like the rattle of dry leaves.

"No-o-o-o, I d-d-didn't th-th-think you'd-d-d want me t-t-to," he rasped. "B-b-but I-I-I don't-t-t s-s-see why n-n-not? W-w-why'd you t-t-tell me to g-g-g-et all of my th-th-things out of h-h-h-here?"

Nighttime was the worst—it always had been, even when he was a little boy; but tonight . . . tonight was horrible! The voices were especially strong, and most of them sounded angry and agitated, as though something—the fury of the wind or something else was whipping them, carrying them like storm-tossed leaves up to new levels of fury. Michael didn't like what they were saying or what they were telling him to do, but no matter how hard he pounded his head, he couldn't stop them, couldn't block them out because they had always been strongest here in the cellar of the old mill.

Oh, yes! He had always been able to hear them, ever since he was a little boy, even when he should have been safe in the closet of his bedroom at home . . . even during all those years in that hospital in Massahusetts. He had never gotten away from them entirely, ut *this* was where they came from, this was their ource . . . this was where they muttered and murmured o him, and screamed inside his head when they didn't want to be ignored.

"I ju-ju-just w-w-w-want to sl-sl-sleep," he said, rocking back and forth and moaning deep within his chest. "I c-c-c-can't sl-sl-sl-sleep when I'm-m-m s-s-so c-c-cold. I can't-t-t st-st-stand it an-an-anymore!"

His hands curled up, and he raked his fingernails lown the sides of his face. The pain was like hot wires, ut it didn't change anything; the voices were still there, getting stronger and clearer in his brain. He rolled his ead back and forth, but the darkness was so thick, so ressing that he couldn't tell if his eyes were opened or losed. It didn't matter. Opened or closed . . . awake or sleep . . . alive or dead, those voices were a part of im, and he would never get away from them—*never!* At least not until he did what they were telling him to lo.

Then . . . maybe . . . both he and they would find elease.

"B-b-b-but I—I c-c-c-can't!" he whispered in a voice s raw as a fresh, open wound.

"Oh, yes you can."

"You must!"

"We've waited . . . for so long."

"And now that your mother has left us, we have to lo this."

"You have to do this!"

"To be free."

"But my m-m-m-mother," Michael said, no more than gasp. Tears stung his eyes like acid, and the jackhammer pounding inside his head got louder. "You t-t-t-told n-m-me . . . you said you s-s-s-saw her . . . th-th-that -s-s-she wanted me to d-d-d-do this."

351

"You must!"

"We've waited . . . for so long."

"But d-d-don't you s-s-s-see?" Michael wailed. "I jus
can't!

"Oh, yes you can."

"You must!"

"We've waited . . . for so long."

"In the morning, you can start."

"You have no choice."

"Just as we have no choice!"

Jesus Christ! It's Dianne!

The thought flashed across Brian's mind like a strok
of lightning. He crouched and tensed, waiting for th
deafening crash of thunder to follow. His eyes wer
wide open, and he was unable to look away because th
woman's cold, unblinking gaze held him transfixed, lik
an insect on a pin. He tried to breathe, but the pres
sure collapsed his chest inward. Small, white dancin
dots zigzagged across his vision. The rattling sound o
rain on the roof grew deafeningly loud, roaring i
bursts like a passing train. Still, the face didn't move
Then, with his lungs burning for fresh air, just befor
Brian passed out, a crazy thought hit him—

That's not a person!

Almost against his will, he took a few steps forward
craning his neck as he strained to see the face tha
leered at him from the corner.

It's just a picture . . . just a painting!

He almost laughed aloud, but his throat was still too
constricted to make any more sound than a feeble click
He took a wary step closer, all the while expecting
something to jump out at him, but the woman's fac
remained impassive, immobile.

Of course she won't move! she can't! She isn't real!

But as soon as he thought that, another voice whispered in the back of his mind, *But she used to be real!*

The painting was obviously old. The woman's clothes were old-fashioned—at least a hundred years old—and her face had an aura of antiquity about it. The tarnished gilt frame barely caught and reflected back the weak overhead light. The subject, obviously much older than his stepmother, had been painted with a harsh sidelighting that cast a thin wash of shadow across the lower left side of her face. Loose strands of dark hair curled around her wide, white forehead. She wasn't smiling. Her thin lips were set in a grim line that was not at all pleasant; but it was her eyes that held Brain. They were wide open, shining with a piercing blue, especially the right one, which caught and reflected back the light. With time, the overcoat of varnish had yellowed. The woman looked as though she were staring out from behind a sheet of amber; but even with several year's accumulation of dust covering them, her eyes seemed to hover in the darkness, glowing with their own internal source of light. Brian took a sip of breath and stared at the painting as though expecting to see the woman blink, but her eyes remained frozen open as though caught in a moment of surprise . . . or anger.

"Jesus *Christ!*" he whispered, shaking his shoulders to rid himself of the icy shiver that was dancing up his back. He felt like a fool for being so surprised—and scared—by this; but then again—what did he expect, snooping around in an old attic on a stormy night? Now more than ever he thought he should go back downstairs, but the face and his first impression that it was a real person lingered, irresistibly drawing his attention back to it.

It sure as heck looks like Dianne!

He was unable to repress another cold rush of shivers. The shadow across the left side of the woman's face suggested the hollow depression under Dianne's left eye where her cheek bone had been pulverized in the accident. Squinting and leaning forward to see more clearly, he could almost make out the thin line of scar tissue, running up the inside of the woman's neck along the edge of her jawbone. As impossible as it might be, it was downright uncanny how much this woman — whoever she was — resembled his stepmother.

Or maybe it's her! Brian thought as another, stronger shiver wracked his body. *Maybe it's a picture of the Old Witch Lady!*

He wished he dared to go right up to the portrait, clean the dust off it, and study it closely. It was, after all, nothing more than a painting. What was there to be afraid of? What did he think, as soon as he touched the painting it would bite him or something? No, it was just his overworked imagination and poor lighting that made this woman look so much like Dianne.

But then again, a soft voice whispered inside his mind, *you never know, do you? . . . You never know!*

A particularly strong gust of wind slammed against the house, making the ancient rafters groan with the sudden change in pressure. Outside, something slammed against the side of the house. Brian jumped, but before he could do anything else, the light dangling behind him started to flicker. He turned and looked at it, just in time to see it trail away to dull orange glow and then disappear like a slowly dying ember.

"Oh, *shit!*" he whispered.

His stomach filled with icy tension. He started moving toward the stairwell, but the darkness was too thick to penetrate. Bright afterimages of the fading light throbbed in his vision, confusing him. He resisted the thought that the two bright dots he saw floating in the darkness were the portrait's eyes, following him. Nearly frantic with fear, he reached out blindly, amazed at how

354

dense the darkness appeared. He almost expected to feel resistance from it as he swung his hands back and forth. Outside, the sounds of the storm seemed to magnify. The air in the attic felt suddenly much colder, as if the storm winds had found access and were clawing at him like frantic hands.

Taking short, shuffling steps, Brian moved forward, all the while batting at the darkness with both hands as if he could tear it aside. He kept bumping into things and then feeling his way around them until he was no longer sure if he was heading toward the stairwell or away from it. He considered calling out to Dianne, but as afraid as he was, he didn't like feeling as though he needed her help. No, if he just stayed calm, he could get himself out of here. It wasn't like he was a little kid or anything.

But no matter how much he tried to shore up his courage, the darkness of the attic seemed to generate cold spikes of fear as it pressed in close around him. His breathing came fast and shallow, burning in his chest. He had to force himself to go slowly simply because he didn't want to step out over the edge of the stairwell and fall down the steps and break his neck.

But where are the stairs? Shouldn't I have found them by now?

His pulse throbbed heavily in his neck. Blood whooshed in his ears like heavy breathing. Spinning blue lights still trailed across his vision as he moved slowly forward. The hissing sound of the storm altered, subtly at first, but then more clearly until he thought he heard something else—a light, raspy whisper of a voice—no, several voices, chattering like insects in the dark.

Brian froze, his eyes bugging from his head as he looked around, trying to pierce the solid wall of darkness. The sounds were too faint, maddeningly at the edge of hearing, but they seemed to be coming at him from several directions at once. He couldn't get a clear fix on them, and he couldn't tell for sure what—if any-thing—they were saying because the sound of blood rushing in his ears grew steadily louder with his mount-ing fear.

It's just my imagination! he thought, but the voice inside his mind was nothing more than a trembling whimper. *Just my imagination. Just please . . . please, let me find my way out of here!*

His feet scraped across the old floorboards. The dull voices continued whispering all around him, grating his nerves and sending hot sparks shooting up his spine. He strained to make out anything they were saying, but it was like they were speaking a foreign language. He was frantic, trying to convince himself it was just the wind rattling against the house . . . or the terrified chattering inside his own mind.

They can't be real! It's impossible!

With every passing second, the voices rose and fell, fading in and out of his awareness like rushing storm clouds. He actually thought he could detect individual tones—some that sounded light and feminine, although angry; others that sounded harsher, more masculine. He kept shaking his head to clear it and had to struggle not to scream out loud whenever he caught particular words or phrases.

"*. . . Dark Master . . . unrighteous . . . curse this man! . . . cleansing fire . . . just retribution . . . agony . . . servant of Satan.*"

The words were no more than fleeting, feathery touches in the dark. The sound of the storm battering against the house all but drowned them out. Brian was almost overwhelmed with the urge to run, but the dark-ness held him tightly, like constricting arms. Only with effort could he keep moving forward, searching for the stairway.

He let out a sharp squeal of surprise and almost pitched forward when his foot suddenly slipped out into open air. Lunging backward, he grabbed for something—anything for support but missed and, thrown completely off balance, spun around and fell. His knee slammed so hard against the floor he couldn't contain a barking yelp of pain.

"Hey! Brian! 'S that you?"

His father's voice filled the darkened house like a gunshot. Still too frightened even to call out, the best Brian could do was watch in stunned silence as a dull glow of light filled the darkness at the foot of the stairs. He heard a heavy tread of footsteps. It sounded as if his father had come up the stairs and gone down the hallway to his bedroom.

"Hey! Brian? Where are you?"

"Up here," Brian managed, his voice nothing more than a croak. "In the attic."

The light in the hallway blossomed steadily brighter as rapid footsteps approached the attic doorway. Brian shielded his eyes with one hand when his father directed the flashlight beam up the narrow staircase onto him. He felt foolish, sitting there on the floor with his legs splayed out in front of him.

"What the hell are you doing up there?"

"I was—" Brian began; then he stopped and finished with a lame shrug and quick shake of his head.

"Well get on down here," his father said, angling the light away from Brian's face and waving him down. "We can light some candles until the power comes back on."

Brian was thankful that he caught the trace of laughter in his father's voice, but in his embarrassment, he couldn't share in the humor of the situation. Behind him, in the dark corners where his father's flashlight

357

beam didn't reach, he could still sense, still feel the cold pressure of hidden eyes . . . and whispering voices. His shoulders shook wildly as he stood up, brushed himself off, and started down the stairs. Halfway down, a sudden, choking panic filled him, and he jumped the bottom half of the stairs to the hall floor. Once safely beside his father, he braced his hands on his knees and tried to catch his breath.

"You sure you're all right?" his father asked. Looking at Brian, his face glowed with an eerie underlighting from the flashlight. For a panicky instant, Brian was afraid of him.

"Uh—yeah, yeah. Sure, I—I'm okay," he said, terribly aware of the tremor in his voice. Just then, as if on cue, the lights in the attic and hallway flickered a few times and then came back on.

"Well, yeah—I can see where it'd be a little surprising, especially if you weren't expecting it," Edward said, "but I always thought she didn't look so much angry as—well, I dunno—scared, maybe. At least that's what I used to think when I saw her, back when I was a little kid."

"It's been up there all this time?" Brian asked, shaking his head in amazement as the realization hit home that his father had been a kid, just like him, in this very house.

"Oh, yeah," Edward said. "That portrait's been in the family—" He shrugged. "Forever. I figure two hundred years or more."

"Whew!" Brian said, whistling between his teeth. "Two hundred years!"

He stared in amazement at the antique painting. His father had brought it down from the attic and dusted it off in the kitchen. The abrasion had knocked tiny flakes of old varnish onto the floor. The colors of the woman's face and clothing now seemed pale and dry. Her face, even the glow in her right eye, was tempered by the bright kitchen light. It seemed ridiculous, now, that it had frightened him—that he had *let* it frighten him.

"Although I'll admit, the way the shadow crosses her face there always did bother me—scared the crap out of me, actually," his father went on. His voice had taken on a distant, almost dreamy tone as he stared at the painting.

"If it's so old, do you think it might be valuable?"

"Oh, I don't know. It may be worth something to someone, but it certainly wasn't painted by anyone famous. If you look at it carefully, it's not a very good painting—I mean, technically."

"So what's it doing up in the attic? Why'd your mother put it away up there?"

Edward shook his head. "I have no idea. She probably just plain-old didn't like it." He sniffed with laughter. "Can't say as I blame her. I mean, it's certainly not the most pleasant face to look at, day in and day out."

"Do you . . . know who she is?" Brian asked. He felt all shivery inside. It was late, a little after midnight, and he knew he should be in bed. "Is it just any old painting, or is she like a relative or something?"

"Well, I'm not sure. I told you this picture used to scare the bejesus out of me any time I went up there. Which wasn't very often, believe me. I didn't like going up there because of it, but to tell you the truth, I have no idea who she is. My broth—well, we used to wonder about her, but if my mother knew who she was, she never told me or anyone else. This house has been in my family since before the Revolution, and I always kind of assumed this was some ancestor from back in Colonial times."

"But don't you think she looks sorta like—" Brian cut himself off, hoping his father had been lost in his own thoughts and hadn't been paying attention to him; but he glanced at Brian with raised eyebrows.

"Looks like . . . who?"

Brian withered beneath his father's steady gaze. He folded his hands together and stretched them backward until his knuckles cracked. He had been about to mention his very first impression—that he had mistaken the painting for Dianne, thinking that she had been up there in the attic, watching him as if from a magic mirror in a fairy tale or something. He still couldn't dispel the impression that the portrait was, in fact, a real person, trapped behind the cracking veneer of varnish. Suddenly flustered, he shook his head and said, "No, no—it's nothing."

"You were going to say that you think it looks like your grandmother, weren't you? My mother, right?" his father said, leaning closer to him and frowning deeply.

Brian was still feeling so flustered he misunderstood and thought that his father had said *step*mother. Focusing his gaze on the floor, he considered for a moment, then nodded. "Umm, yeah . . . kind of," he said. "I don't mean anything by it."

He glanced nervously up at the ceiling, knowing that Dianne was sleeping in the room directly above them. Fortunately, even all the commotion hadn't woken her up; but if she was awake now, she certainly would be able to hear everything they were saying, so he lowered his voice. "I just thought—you know, the way the left side of her face is shaded that it sort of—well . . . don't you think she kind of looks like Dianne, at least a little bit?"

"Dianne—?" his father said, sounding surprised.

"Especially around the eyes," Brian added.

His father covered his mouth with his hand and stud-

360

ied the painting in silence for a while longer. Then he sniffed, shook his head, and said, "Well, I certainly never thought about *that* before, but I suppose there's a . . . there's—"

He sighed, then shook his head again and finished, "Naw—I honestly can't see it."

Good! Brian thought, feeling a sudden warm rush of relief. *Then let's pretend I never mentioned it, okay?*

It wasn't until much later, once Brian was lying in bed, listening to the rain still hissing against his windowpane, that another idea struck him.

What if there *was* someone up there in the attic?

And what if it was someone who had nothing to do with Dianne or that old painting?

Several times over the past few days, he had gone out to the mill to look for Uncle Mike but hadn't found any trace of him. The cellar room where he'd been staying had been stripped clean, and there was no sign that he had ever been there. He wondered if he would be breaking his vow if he told his father about Mike now. He was worried for the man and couldn't stop wondering if he had tried to get back to the mental hospital or gone off somewhere in the woods and died or whatever. Now Brian was hit by a new—and scary—idea.

What if, with summer ending and autumn coming soon, Uncle Mike has decided not to leave the area just yet?

What if he'd snuck into the house and was hiding up there in the attic, hoping to stay out of sight and keep at least a little bit warmer than out at the mill?

What if it hadn't been his imagination or the sound of rain on the roof whispering all those crazy-sounding things to him when the lights had gone out? What if it had been Uncle Mike?

He shuddered, remembering that once before he heard Uncle Mike talk like that, out at the mill.

And what if it turns out that Uncle Mike is *really* crazy . . . *dangerously* crazy?

These and other disturbing thoughts shifted and blended in Brian's mind as he finally drifted off to a thin, disturbed sleep. He awoke some time later to the sound of a thick, gurgling scream.

Chapter Twenty-two
True Confessions

There's someone in the room!

Dianne was lying in bed with her eyes wide open. Her heart pounded a thin, rapid drumbeat in her chest. She didn't remember waking up; consciousness had blended slowly from sleep to wakefulness, but now that she was fully awake, she was absolutely convinced there was someone else in the bedroom—someone besides herself and Edward. She tensed, wishing she dared to move but knew she couldn't. A low muscle tremor made her arms and legs vibrate.

Maybe I'm still sleeping. Maybe I'm just dreaming.

She recalled the vivid dream she'd had a few nights ago, when she had been out at the old mill. It had seemed so clear, so real at the time, even when frankly impossible things had happened—like the old Model-A Ford that had been chugging down the dirt road . . . and the blossom of flames that had erupted out of the old building.

Yes, that's it! I'm still asleep . . . I'm dreaming!

But she could hear the steady sawing of her husband's breathing, and she could feel the cool night air that wafted over her face from the open bedroom window.

No, maybe she *wasn't* asleep.

Maybe she had been dreaming, and that's what had awakened her, but she was wide awake now.

She rolled over onto one side and sighed, smacking her lips, pretending to be turning over in her sleep just in case there was someone in the room.

She glanced at the window and saw the fast-moving puffs of clouds streaking across the night sky. She had slept through most of the rainstorm, and now it was breaking up, blowing away to the east. A thin wash of moonlight edged the windowsill like cold silver trimming.

What time is it, anyway? she wondered, but now that she had rolled onto her right side, she didn't dare shift again to look at the alarm clock. Not yet. Give it a few minutes, just in case there *is* someone here!

But how could there be?

She wished to heaven she could force down the rush of tension building up inside her. *If it isn't Brian, who could it be?*

Edward snorted like a pig in his sleep. Dianne wanted to reach out and take hold of his hand, but her fingers were frozen as though paralyzed. She lay there as tense and stiff as a rail, waiting for a sound or some other indication that she was right—that someone had crept into the room while she was asleep and was now standing at the foot of the bed.

As she lay there in the dark, the dream she'd been having came back to her in bright, flashing fragments. It had had something to do with the old mill again. She had dreamed she was out there, like a few nights ago, but this time there had been something else going on: there had been a small group of gray-clad, somber-looking men gathered in a circle around a woman. Yes—an old woman with stringy gray hair and flashing blue eyes that almost looked like—

"No," she whispered in the dark.

364

She had looked a little like the face she had seen in the mill window in her other dream. There had been something wrapped around her neck; it had looked like a thick, coiling snake, but then she realized that it was a rope.

Oh, my God, they're going to hang her!

The thought popped into her mind so suddenly she jumped. The bedsprings creaked, and Edward, snorted loudly again and rolled away from her.

Yeah, thanks a lot! she thought bitterly. *Even when you're asleep you can't help me out!*

But what had the dream been about? she wondered, trying her best to dredge up the fading memory. "What else had happened?" she whispered.

"It was about me!"

"And me!"

"It was about all of us!"

Voices hissed like a chorus in the surrounding darkness, sounding like escaping steam. Dianne didn't know how she knew it, but suddenly she was convinced that there wasn't just one person—there were several, maybe a dozen or more people in the room. Their faces were curtained by the thick shadows, but they were moving closer to her, crowding around the bed, whispering to each other . . . and to her!

Too frightened to cry out, Dianne thought about the group of people she had seen in the woods behind the house, the people she had followed out to the mill a few nights ago.

Had that been real, or part of the dream?

Could these be the same people? Had they come back for her?

Were they here to hurt her and Edward and Brian?

Had they come to burn the house down—with all of them in it?

The soft glow of moonlight seeping in through the

window wavered in and out as clouds scudded by in front of the moon. Dianne thought she could hear soft, subtle motions. Thin washes of shadow shifted against the darkness. A cold, choking fear took hold of her throat and wouldn't let go.

"I wasn't the only one to die out there!"

The voice that spoke this time was louder, clearer. It sounded old and tired, and had a strange, almost foreign-sounding lilt to it. For some odd reason, Dianne now calmly accepted the idea that an old woman and several other people were standing there in the darkness at the foot of her bed. She raised her head slightly and gasped when she made out several dark, slouched figures. One of them had its head cocked at a sharp angle to one side.

"And who else?" Dianne whispered. A prickly rush of fear coursed up her back. "Who . . . who else died out there?"

"We all did!"

"She was the first."

"Rachel was."

"But we others . . . we all followed her."

"And now we've been left alone."

"Forgotten!"

"Abandoned."

"All alone . . . now that she's gone."

"Who?" Dianne said, her voice trembling louder. "Who's gone?"

Her voice seemed to fill the darkness, but it didn't mask the distant wail of a crying baby. Dianne didn't know how long that sound had been going on, but as soon as she was aware of it, the tingling surges that had been playing up and down her back suddenly intensified. Blood rushed into her head, filling it with a hot, pounding pressure. With a loud, keening screech, she suddenly flung aside the covers and, before she

366

knew what she was doing, found herself straddling Edward. She clamped both hands around his throat and was shaking him.

"Did you do it?" she wailed, bouncing his head up and down on the pillow. "Did you? Huh? You lousy *bastard?* Are *you* the one? Out at the mill! *Did you do it?*"

Grunting loudly, he twisted beneath her weight, thrashing like a roped calf. She tried to hold on and pin him down with one hand while raining heavy blows down onto his face with the other; but in spite of her fury, she knew she wasn't strong enough to really hurt him. That only made her rage and frustration rise all the higher because right now she wanted to beat him senseless. With a throat-tearing shriek, she continued to punch at his face.

"You tried to hide it from me!" she screamed. "By pretending! But I *know!* I *know* that you *did* it! That you did it on purpose!"

"Hey, c'mon!" Edward's voice was thick with sleep and confusion. "Jesus Christ, Dianne! Stop it!"

He swung one arm across his body and knocked her aside, breaking the hold she had on his throat. Then he tossed the covers aside and rolled off the bed onto his feet. He staggered, fighting for his balance, and in a flash she leaped off the bed onto his back and started pounding on him again while she screamed into his ear.

"You did this to me! You did it to me on purpose!"

A bright red haze filled Dianne's vision. For a terrifying instant, she had the sensation that she could see in the dark, that she could see every detail in the room as though she were looking through infrared lenses. Behind her, lined up around the bed, she glimpsed several people, all standing there immobile, their faces expressionless as they watched her.

Edward shook her off his back. She hit the floor

with a thump. He spun around to face her and yelled, "What the hell's the matter with you?" His voice was strangled and congested.

"Just leave me alone! Just leave me the Chris alone!"

He moved toward her, reached out for her, but she sidestepped him, backing away so she could keep the double bed between them. The people she had been so convinced were there in the room had vanished, but she hardly noticed.

"Stay away from me! Don't you *dare* try and hurt me again!" she screamed. Her heart was racing high and fast in her chest. "I swear to Christ, I'll kill you if you do!"

"For God's sake, Dianne! Snap out of it, will you? What's the matter with you?"

She heard him but was so caught up in her rage and fear that his words made absolutely no sense. She was swept away with a stark terror of him, and she realized with a terrifying dread that she was no longer even sure who he was. She could see his face, dimly lit by the glow of moonlight, but in some crazy, distorted way, he seemed to be several people all at once. She watched warily as his face shifted into a fast-moving cavalcade of other faces. All of them appeared grim and determined, and she couldn't help but recall the two stone-faced policemen she had seen in the Model-A in her dream and the group of sober-looking men who had surrounded the old woman with a rope tied around her neck.

"You *wanted* to hurt me," she said, her voice low and sputtering with rage. "I think you *wanted* me to die! That's why you let me fall off that cliff!"

"Let you—? What are you—? Why that . . . that's crazy!"

"Oh no it isn't," Dianne said, panting heavily. Her

368

fists were clenched so tightly the palms of her hands throbbed. She wanted to rush at him again and start hitting him, but she knew it would be futile, so she backed away, all the while keeping a wary eye on every slightest move he made.

"Come on, Dianne," he said, dropping his voice low and taking another few steps toward her. "You must've been having one hell of a nightmare or something. Let me—"

"No! It *wasn't* a dream," Dianne said in a low, trembling voice that threatened to break any second. "I know what I saw . . . out there!"

"Out where?"

In answer, she hiked her thumb toward the moonlit window. "Out *there!*" she said, her voice winding up a notch.

"For Christ's sake, calm down, will you? Look, it's almost four o'clock in the morning! Let me just turn on a light and we can—"

"No!" Dianne shouted, but it was too late. Edward moved swiftly to the doorway. There was a faint *click* as he flicked the wall switch, and a sudden burst of light filled the room, stinging Dianne's eyes like a splash of salt water. She covered her face with both hands but, immediately mistrustful of Edward, peered at him through the network of fingers. At first, all she could see was that something was wrong with him; she wasn't sure what. Then a cold pit opened up inside her stomach when her vision cleared, and she saw a network of dark lines and splotches on Edward's face.

Blood!

The word tore through her mind like a bullet.

Oh my God, he's bleeding!

The room suddenly began to spin. Dianne moaned softly as an overpowering wave of dizziness started to tug her down. Her legs felt like wood as she took a single step forward, and then darkness came crashing down around her like a collapsing building.

Edward knew he was bleeding before he wiped his nose with the back of his hand and saw the stringy red streak of blood. Hot pressure throbbed inside his face, and a coppery taste flooded the back of his throat. But he didn't even consider his own injury when he saw Dianne's face go suddenly pale and her eyes roll back in her head just before she fell to the floor. She crumpled beside the bed in a slow-motion pirouette like a stringless puppet. He was beside her in an instant, raising her head and cradling it in his lap as he gently slapped her cheek.

"Come on, honey . . . wake up," he whispered. His voice was all trembly, and he fought hard to keep his panic down. The light hurt his eyes, and he was still disoriented from being yanked out of his sleep so abruptly, but he was nearly frantic with fear for Dianne as he looked at her, wondering and worrying about what was happening to her.

Why had she attacked him like that? What the hell could have made her react so violently?

His stomach was all fluttery as he sat beside her on the floor, gently rubbing her face. Her skin was clammy. Her breathing came in short, rattling gulps. He kept glancing over his shoulder at the telephone on the bed stand, painfully aware that he should get help, but he didn't dare leave her. Should he call to Brian? The commotion must have woken him up.

"Jesus Christ, Dianne . . . Come on . . . Wake up, will you?" he whispered.

She was still breathing, so he knew at least she wasn't dead, but what in the *hell* was wrong with her? She had attacked him for no reason whatsoever. Why would she do something like that? And the things she had said, the accusations . . . she had been talking like . . . like she was out of her mind.

"You tried to hide it from me by pretending, but I know that you did it. It wasn't a dream. I know what I saw out there! You wanted to hurt me. I think you wanted me to die! Don't you dare try and hurt me again! I swear to Christ, I'll kill you if you do!"

What the hell could have made her say such things?

As Edward stared down at her, his vision went suddenly blurry as tears filled his eyes. He wanted more than anything to take away the torment he knew was raging inside his wife, but he also knew that he couldn't do it. Whatever was causing it, he didn't feel confident that he could do anything to change it. How could he when he had to live with his own private torment? Her words, spoken in anger and near delirium, had touched the edges of his own guilt about what he had done to Ray Saunders, and his mind was nearly blank as he thought about how much he wished he could confide in her about it all . . . about everything, but over the years he had convinced himself that he could never tell anyone. It was the one secret he could never tell anyone!

What snapped him back to his senses was a feathery touch against his cheek. He grunted with surprise and shook his head, startled to see that Dianne's eyes were open. She was reaching up to him and stroking his face. Her fingers grazed against his upper lip and came away bloody.

"Oh, honey," she said in a high, whining voice.

"Hey, hey . . . you just take it easy, all right," he said, combing his hand through her hair. "You're gonna be all right now. Just relax."

"But I . . . I tried to hurt you," she rasped.

She looked as though she could barely focus her eyes

as she stared at the blood on her fingertips. Tears poured from her eyes and rolled down the sides of her face. Edward was happy to see a faint blush of color returning to her cheeks, but there was also a disturbing glazed frost in her eyes that almost made her look as if she had been stricken blind. The scar line along the edge of her chin was bright red and looked like a line of fresh blood. For a frozen instant, he wondered if he had hurt her, or if she had cut herself.

"I can't believe . . . I don't know what . . . what I was doing. Oh, God, I hurt you. I—your nose is bleeding."

"No, it's nothing. Nothing at all," Edward said, sniffing as he wiped his nose on the back of his hand. He tried to smile, but the cold ache in his chest filled him with fear—fear both for her and for him.

"Shit, you must've been having one hell of a nightmare."

"No, it wasn't a . . . I was just—I—"

She cut herself off and moaned softly as she ran her hands down over her face. When she looked up at him again, her expression seemed a bit clearer, and a faint fluttering of hope filled him even though he knew there were still plenty of unanswered questions.

But maybe she's going to be all right, he thought. *Maybe . . .*

He helped her swing her legs around and sit up so she could lean against the side of the bed.

"Hang on a second," he said, "lemme get you a glass of water." Before she could say anything, he raced down the hall to the bathroom and returned a few seconds later with a full glass. She took the glass and drank deeply, her throat making tight gulping noises.

"Umm, thanks," she said, snacking her lips as she handed him the empty glass.

372

After a moment of silence, he asked, "Do you want to talk about it?"

She locked eyes with him, and he could see the doubt and confusion still lingering inside her. He wanted to hug her and tell her everything was all right, but something made him hold back.

"I—I'm so *scared*," she said, her voice breaking as she leaned toward him, gripping his upper arms with both hands and squeezing tightly. "I . . . I don't remember what started it. I think I was asleep or something. I must've been, but there was this—this—"

She cut herself off abruptly, and Edward had the distinct impression that she had known exactly what she had been about to say but was holding it back.

"All of a sudden I felt so . . . I don't know, so *threatened* by you . . . by everything. I was having some kind of dream that I had to—to fight you because of something . . . something you did to—to hurt someone."

"You know I'd never do anything to hurt you," Edward said, sniffing loudly. The lingering taste of blood in the back of his throat almost gagged him.

"No, I know—" Dianne said, shaking her head rapidly. The light in her eyes seem suddenly to intensify. "I know you'd never do anything to hurt *me*."

"But you said I did," Edward said softly, lowering his gaze. "I don't know if you remember what you were saying when you were shouting at me, but you seemed pretty damned convinced that I was trying to hurt you. Was that part of your dream?"

"No, I—"

"You don't still blame me, do you—for what happened, when you fell do you?"

"Oh, no, no—of course I don't," Dianne said.

Her voice was clearer now, more forceful, but Edward thought he detected an indecisive edge to it, as though she still only half believed it herself. They sat on the bedroom floor staring at each other until the silence grew uncomfortably long; then Edward took Dianne's hand to help her up to her feet. She resisted, remaining seated with her shoulders hunched up protectively.

"Wait," she said, no more than a whisper. "There— there's something else I want to talk to you about."

Once again a furtive, frightened look filled her eyes. Edward eased himself back down beside her and, still holding her hand, gave it a reassuring squeeze.

"What's that?" he asked.

It took a great deal of effort to keep his voice from cracking, and all he could think was: *goddamnit, she knows! Somehow, she's found out all about what happened out there at the mill with Ray Saunders! That's what she meant when she said that I hurt someone and I tried to hide it from her by pretending! She must know that I'm the one who put Ray into that wheelchair!*

"It was . . . God, I feel so stupid, even saying this, but— you remember when I told you . . . about what happened when I was a kid . . . the time my mother tried to kill my father?"

Edward nodded and forced himself to smile reassuringly.

"It just felt so . . . so— I dunno, so weird that I could block something like that out and not even remember it until I had that first session with my therapist. But ever since then, I've been— been worrying about . . . something."

"So talk to me about it," Edward said. "You know you can tell me anything." He couldn't prevent the accusatory voice inside his brain from asking why he expected complete honesty from her when *he* didn't dare tell *her* everything.

"I was—" Dianne started to say, but then her voice choked off, and she started to cry. Edward pulled her close and held her, trembling until she could speak again. "It's just that it's been eating away at me for weeks, now, thinking how, when she tried to kill him ... how she ... how she looked like—like she was actually *enjoying* it!"

"Well," Edward said mildly, "it must have been horrible, seeing that your mother was living in such an abusive situation, and you couldn't do a damned thing about it."

"No, no! It's not that I, like, blame myself or anything. I think I can deal with that, but I've been worrying that it might be like, I dunno, like hereditary or something, you know? Like I have a black widow gene or something, and just like my mother, I—I have this ... this subconscious drive that makes me want to—want to ..."

Her voice trailed away, but Edward finished for her. "Want to kill me, you mean, right?"

Biting her lower lip, Dianne looked at him, her eyes glistening with tears as she nodded and gasped, "Yeah. I'm afraid that, with all the pressure we've been under, I might completely lose it." She broke down into tears again and, turning toward him, buried her face in the crook of his neck. "Does this mean I'm losing my mind?"

Long after Dianne had drifted off to sleep, Edward was lying awake, bothered both by what she had said to him and by what he *hadn't* said to her.

Certainly, he was worried for Dianne, but he was also convinced that she was still suffering from the trauma of her accident and reconstructive surgery, and in conjunction with the medication, it was really mess-

375

ing up her head. She had complained about it enough times over the past month, and Edward felt confident that it was something she would eventually work out. This talk about a "black widow gene" was, of course, nonsense, pure and simple. Nobody *inherits* a desire or drive to kill their spouse.

His problem, on the other hand, was deeper and, he felt, more difficult to resolve . . . if not impossible. If Dianne's problems were a fresh bleeding cut, then his were decade's thick, knotted scar tissue. For thirty years, he'd been living with the guilt of what he had done, if anything, the scars on his soul grew tougher with each passing year. So many times over the past thirty years, he had wished that he could have told someone—*any*one about what had happened that day, but he never had. He'd never found the courage. His mother had died never discovering the truth even though as a result she had to have her youngest son, Michael, committed to a mental institution. Like everyone else in town, she believed Michael had tried to kill Ray and was too dangerous to have around. It had broken her heart, and the truth that Edward had kept walled up inside him all this time had merely compounded his own pain and suffering by making his mother's misery his.

But why couldn't he tell Dianne about it? Why couldn't he trust his own wife?

The passing storm had stirred up a cool breeze that cut through the summer heat. Tangled emotions filled Edward as he stared out the bedroom window at the slow progression of the waning moon. He thought with deep regret about his first marriage with Sally, and how it had ended in such hatred, such hostility. He was certain much of it was generated by the dark secret he kept bottled up inside him. And now, that same secret was driving a wedge between him and Dianne.

What if Diane was reacting erratically because of his secretiveness? Could what was bottled up inside of him be driving her crazy?

And what about Brian?

It saddened him that they had never had a genuine father-son relationship. Since the divorce, when Brian was four years old, they had treated each other so distantly, almost like strangers. Now that he was remarried to Dianne, he had wanted Brian to stay for the summer so they could try to build bridges between them, but things had gone steadily downhill from the start. Perhaps he should just accept the fact that he was a failure—as a father, as a husband, as a human being!

But was all of this happening simply because he couldn't bring himself to admit—out loud—to someone else—that *he,* not his brother, had been responsible for Ray Saunders's injury? Could an entire life be soured so badly because of one stupid mistake, one foolish accident?

No, it wasn't an accident! I tackled him on purpose, but I did it so he'd leave Mikie alone. I never wanted Ray to get hurt . . . not that badly! I was just trying to help my younger brother, and look what it did! It put him into a mental hospital for thirty years!

He whimpered softly as the sour taste of regret gushed up into his throat from his stomach.

And—Christ—look at what it's done to Ray's life! Just ask him how much he's enjoyed being trapped in a wheelchair for thirty years! His whole life! Look how bitter and resentful it's made him!

But thoughts of Brian kept returning to haunt Edward. He realized that his son was now the same age he had been when he committed the deed that had shadowed his and so many other lives over the past thirty years. What he had done had also ruined his, Mikie's, Rays, and his mother's life, and his first wife's

377

life, and . . . maybe even—*Please, God, no!*—maybe it had even poisoned his son's life. And now that he had a chance to make things better, what was he doing to patch things up between them?

Not a damned thing!

"Christ!" he whispered, clenching his teeth and punching the mattress in frustration.

He realized that Brian must have heard him and Dianne fighting. He was probably lying awake in bed, feeling lost and alone, worrying about his own safety. Why wouldn't he—in a house where both adults seemed to be so out of control?

Huffing with pent-up frustration, Edward eased himself out of bed and tiptoed down the dark hallway to Brian's bedroom—what used to be his own bedroom. The door was closed. He paused outside, his hand resting lightly on the doorknob and shivered wildly, more than half-convinced that, if he opened the door and looked inside now, he would see—not Brian, but himself, a thirteen-year-old boy huddled in bed, clutching the bed covers to his chin and totally consumed by the guilt and fear that what he had done to Ray Saunders would eventually be found out.

So why take the chance of disturbing him? Edward thought. *Maybe it was best just to let him sleep.*

Almost against his will, his fingers tightened on the doorknob and turned it. The hinges creaked, setting his nerves on edge as the door swung slowly open. He leaned his head into the room, watching as his vision vibrated in the thick darkness. After a moment or two, he saw the mounded lump on the bed over by the far wall. He sighed with relief, noticing that the furniture arrangement was different than it had been back when he was growing up in this house. For one thing, there was only one bed. Michael's had been taken away a week or so after he had first been admitted to the mental hospital.

And now where the hell is Michael?

There hadn't been any more news since he had first received notification from the hospital that his brother had disappeared. Nearly every day, he made a phone call to the hospital and to the local and state police in Massachusetts, but they so far had turned up nothing. The authorities had reassured him that they were doing everything possible, but to Edward, it didn't seem like a whole hell of a lot.

For now, as much as he hated it, he had to accept the fact that his younger brother was listed as "officially missing" and there was a missing persons report put out on the wires for him. For a while, he had more than half expected that Mikie—somehow—would show up at the house, but there hadn't been any sign of him. Besides, how could someone who's retarded and who didn't have any money or car make the three hour trip from Danvers to Summerfield, Maine? He sure as hell couldn't have walked that far. Edward knew he had to accept the cold, hollow truth that his brother, probably upset at the news of his mother's death, had wandered off and died . . . somewhere.

What the hell! Just another life I've ruined by what I've done . . . and haven't done!

Edward took one step into the room, straining forward to listen, but he couldn't make out the steady rhythm of his son's breathing above the pulse whooshing in his ears.

Is he faking it? Edward wondered.

He knew from having been that age himself that even if Brian *was* still wide awake, even if he was scared out of his mind and *needed* someone to talk to, he would feign sleeping. The next move, Edward thought, would be for Brian to roll over in bed and smack his lips. Poised and silent, he waited for that to happen, but the lump on the bed remained motionless where it was.

Finally he concluded that, even if Brian had awakened while he and Dianne were fighting and shouting at each other, he must have drifted back off to sleep by now.

"G'night, Bri," he whispered. "Sleep well."

Edward eased back out of the room and closed the door behind him, determined not to disturb Brian right now. In the morning, he promised himself he'd have a serious heart-to-heart talk with his son. Yawning behind his hand, he shuffled down the hall and climbed back into bed. After another half hour or so of staring at the ceiling, he finally drifted off to sleep just as the sky was brightening with dawn.

Chapter Twenty-three
Losing It

The room was bright with morning sunlight, and a warm, sweet-smelling breeze was wafting in through the open window. Dianne opened her eyelids slowly, letting the light shatter into hundreds of dazzling, yellow swirls as she tried to assess how she felt.

Not all that well, she concluded.

Every muscle and joint in her body was stiff, and there was a dull throb of pain centered behind her eyes, keeping time with her pulse. Her right hand—the one she had punched Edward with last night—felt bruised, possibly sprained.

She sighed, feeling the warm buildup of tears in her eyes. Ever since she was a little girl, she had always enjoyed the sensation of waking up, of feeling fresh and ready to face the challenge of a new day; but over the past few months, she had come to dread each new day. After what had happened last night, she was so filled with worry and regret that she was even afraid to open her mouth because she feared all that would come out would be one long, trailing scream. She lost track of time just lying there, listening to the rapid flutter of her pulse in her ears and trying her best to will it to slow down.

Please, dear God, just let it slow down!

She couldn't believe it when, after drifting in and out of wakefulness, she rolled over and looked at the alarm clock. It was already past eleven o'clock. Uttering a low groan, she kicked aside the bed covers and leaped out of bed. As soon as she was on her feet, a wave of dizziness crashed over her, and she had to sit back down on the bed until the heavy pounding in her head gradually subsided.

"Just take it easy . . . take it easy," she cautioned herself, rubbing her forehead with both hands and slowly rolling her neck from side to side. There was no need to hurry, she told herself. There was nothing planned for today—nowhere to go.

As soon as she felt even marginally better, she rose from the bed again—slowly, this time, and took a few hesitant steps forward as she approached the bedroom door. Although she felt an undeniable urge to hurry, she kept reminding herself that she didn't *have* to be getting up. Edward wasn't in bed, and she didn't expect to find him downstairs; he no doubt had left hours ago for the construction site.

And I'll bet he's not even thinking about me, much less caring about how I feel!

She tried to stop herself from thinking it but couldn't; the thought was there almost automatically, and what bothered her even more was the red rush of anger that filled her the instant she thought about Edward.

Yeah, and what about Brian? Halfway down the hall, she paused outside his bedroom, staring blankly at the closed door. Then, sniffing with disgust, she went downstairs.

Why even concern myself with Brian? she thought.

Although over the past few days he hadn't been as openly hostile with her as he had been in the past, she suspected his opinion of her hadn't improved. As far as she could see, he was just biding his time until he flew back to Phoenix next week to be home in time to start school.

And good riddance, she thought with only a slight twinge of guilt.

The truth was, they hadn't connected at all throughout the summer, and the prospect of having him return next summer, although far in the future, was already gnawing at her nerves. She admitted that she might not have made as much of an effort to get to know him as she might have, but—*Christ!*—what did he expect, considering everything she'd had to deal with this summer?

Sweat broke out on her forehead, and her legs felt weak as she walked into the kitchen. An empty cereal bowl and juice glass in the sink, a half-filled carafe of coffee, and a crumpled newspaper and a few crumbs on the table were the last evidence of Edward's breakfast. On the table was a note that read:

HAD TO GET SOME WORK DONE TODAY—SEE YOU TONIGHT.

XOXOXOXO . . . ME!
COME OUT TO THE HOUSE SITE AND SEE ME IF YOU WANT TO TALK OR ANYTHING.

LOVE YAH!!!

"Yeah, sure," Dianne said. She crumpled up the note and tossed it into the wastebasket.

Her emotions were all twisted up inside her, and she wanted just to sit down and cry it all out, but she knew that it wouldn't do any good. Her problems were too big and too deep to put behind her that easily. Choking back her feelings, she grimly set about preparing herself a breakfast of fried eggs, bacon, and toast — something that *should* have given her pleasure after all

those months of not being able to eat real food; bu
when she sat down to eat, everything tasted flat an
colorless. She considered calling to Brian, to see if h
wanted something, but she honestly didn't care if h
was still in bed or if he'd gone off to work with h
father. Over the summer, she had gotten into the hab
of ignoring him, and she decided not to let anyone ir
trude on her privacy.

But as she was eating and then while she was wash
ing the dishes, other, darker thoughts intruded. Thes
thoughts disturbed her because, no matter how muc
she tried to rationalize them away, they didn't eras
what had happened last night. She couldn't believe tha
she had actually attacked Edward, and it scared her t
consider how furious she had felt — so mad at him sh
honestly thought she could have killed him . . . that sh
would have, if she'd had either the strength or som
kind of weapon.

*And maybe he deserves to die . . . for what he di
to me!*

The thought registered in her brain as clearly as i
someone in the room had spoken it. Her eyes were wid
with fear as she glanced around the kitchen, suddenl
terrified by the thought that this sunny, quaint roon
was just an illusion, and that lurking just beneath i
was a whole different world — a world that was dar
and sick with corruption . . . a world of shadows tha
sucked all the energy from the living and used it to fue
a dark, hidden hatred . . . a hatred that churned insid
her every time she even thought about her husband o
stepson.

*Maybe both of them — Edward and Brian — mayb
even me! We all deserve to die-e-e-e!*

The voice whispered in her mind, drawing out the
last word until it faded away.

"No-o-o-o-o."

The word began as a slow, grating whisper that built up to a long, agonized cry as she gripped the edge of the sink and stared blankly out at the morning. She covered her face with her hands and pressed hard against her eyes as a surge of terror swept her away.

"Oh my God! Oh my God! . . . I'm losing my mind!"

The sound of hammering, like rapid gunfire that broke the early morning stillness, was interspersed by the winding grind of a power saw and the clatter of cut-off pieces of wood falling onto the plywood decking. The morning had started out cool, but it had gotten hot and muggy fast. Within an hour of starting work, Edward was sweating furiously as he set about framing up the interior living room walls of the house. He tried not to think how much he was behind schedule and how hard-pressed he was going to be to get the shell of the house finished before cold weather set in.

But Edward tried not to let little things like that bother him as he worked. If he was looking for things to worry about, he had plenty of them waiting for him back at home. What he hoped for was that just for the day—maybe even just for the morning, he could lose himself in his work and forget all about Dianne's and Brian's and even his own problems. They would all be there when he got home this evening. Gritting his teeth and focusing on the length of wood in front of him, he positioned and drove in nails as fast as he could. His hammer left half-moon dimples in the soft pine.

He worked until lunchtime, took half an hour to eat the sandwich and finish off the coffee he had brought along, then got right back to work, hammering and sawing away as the afternoon slid by. The sun began to lower in the west, casting long skeletal shadows of the framing studs across the floor. Other than a bit of stiffness in his shoulders from working so hard and fast, he felt pretty damned good; he'd gotten a lot accomplished for one day.

He didn't notice the first rock when it sailed through the open window space and landed a few feet behind him. His hammering masked the sound of the rock as it clattered across the bare plywood flooring and came to rest beside a stack of two-by-fours. Whistling tunelessly under his breath, he took a few measurements, jotted them down, then went over to the stack of lumber to cut the next several pieces of wood he would need.

The second stone, however, did catch his attention. It came flying from behind him, missing his shoulder by mere inches, and slammed into the stack of wood, leaving a golf ball-sized divot in one of the two-by-fours.

"What the—!" Edward muttered.

He straightened up and looked around, but there was no one there. Moving quickly to the edge of the platform, he looked out at the woods but saw only the dense tangle of trees and brush. Late afternoon shadows stretched out like cat's claws across the bare earth clearing. He listened for some telltale sound, but his ears were still ringing from the sound of his pounding hammer.

"Ha-llo!" he called out, surprised by the sudden loudness of his own voice.

No reply came from the woods. He scanned the area carefully but saw no one. For a moment, he began to doubt what had happened. Maybe the rock had been there all along, balanced on the stack of wood or something, and it had fallen from the vibrations he'd made while working. He walked over to the stack of lumber, put his hammer down, and picked up the rock. Juggling it back and forth between his hands, he went back to the edge of the house and looked out over the yard again.

"Hey! That wasn't very funny, you know," he shouted.

He was slightly surprised by the muffled quality of his voice and attributed it to temporary hearing loss from using the power saw all day without ear protectors. His gaze darted back and forth over the screen of trees, but still he saw no evidence of motion other than the gentle sway of branches in the wind.

It must be either Brian or Dianne, playing a trick on me, he thought.

Cupping one hand to his mouth, he shouted, "Hey! Come on! I can't waste my time playing games with you. Come out, come out wherever you are!"

Then he held his breath and listened.

The area remained perfectly silent, undisturbed except for a gentle puff of wind that rustled the leaves. The humid air seemed to deaden all sound, but then, just at the edge of hearing, he thought he heard a faint ripple of laughter.

" 'S that you, Brian?" he shouted.

The laughter stopped abruptly, leaving the impression that it had never been there at all.

Edward realized he was squeezing the rock too tightly and consciously eased up his grip. None of this was striking him as very funny. Maybe whoever it was—either Brian or Dianne—had thought it would be funny to get his attention by throwing a rock at him, but then must have felt stupid or guilty when they realized how close they had come to actually hitting him.

"Here!" he suddenly shouted. "Maybe you'll need this!"

He cocked his arm back and threw the rock as hard as he could toward the woods. It arced in the air, then ripped like a bullet through the leaves and landed with a dull *thud* somewhere deep in the woods. Edward watched and waited a few more seconds, then, brushing his hands on his pants legs, walked back to the stack of lumber and drew out the pieces he needed to cut. After measuring the first piece, he picked up the power saw, marked the two-by-four and braced it into position, and started to cut.

The whine of the saw was deafening. Sawdust spewed into the air like the fake snow inside a glass, water-filled Christmas ornament. Once the blade had cut through, the wood clattered onto the floor. Edward released the trigger, and the saw quickly powered down. He was just turning around to get the next piece of lumber he needed when a sudden, sharp pain slammed into the back of his head. He grunted as a flash of white light exploded across his vision. Staggering forward, he almost fell but then caught himself on the stack of two-by-fours. His ears were ringing wildly as he dropped the saw to the floor and turned around, doubled over in pain. He clasped the back of his head with both hands.

"Jesus *fuck!*" he shouted.

He shook his head to clear it but was still disoriented. His stomach knotted up when he pulled his hand away and looked at the wide smear of blood on his palm. On the floor to his left, he saw another rock. It took him a few seconds to realize that someone had just nailed him a good one.

Bright bolts of pain speared through his head as he lurched to the edge of the deck and, without breaking his stride, jumped down to the ground. Picking up the first thing he saw—a scrap two-by-four—he brandished it over his head and charged off into the woods. He could only guess at the direction the rock had come from, but ever since he was a boy, he had known all the branching paths that cut

388

through these woods; if he saw him, he could run down whoever had thrown that stone.

His work boots clumped heavily on the packed sod as he jogged along the winding path. He sucked air slowly through his nose so he could pace himself but had to keep shaking his head to clear his vision. He didn't want to miss anyone who might be hiding nearby in the brush, but because of his pain and confusion, everything around him was a swirl of sunlight and shadows that danced like crazy energy through the green canopy of leaves. The heavy throbbing in the back of his head sent a burning spike of pain into his forehead. He ran down the path leading toward his mother's house until the ache in his head and the burning in his lungs was finally too much. At last, he had to stop and, leaning over, panted heavily for breath.

He didn't want to, but finally had to admit that whoever had thrown the rock must have gotten away.

But who the hell would do something like that?

He winced when he touched the back of his head again, and his fingers came away sticky with black strands of clotting blood.

"God*damn*it," he shouted, growling with frustration. "Fuck you!"

He straightened up, swung the two-by-four over his head, and sent it sailing off into the brush where it startled a bird into flight.

"Yeah, and fuck you, too!" Edward said, watching as the dark bird disappeared into the forest, chattering angrily. The bird's cry receded, sounding almost like teasing laughter as it echoed in the distance.

He glanced around one last time, finally convinced that he wasn't going to catch the culprit, then started back to the construction site. With each step, the pounding in his head grew worse until he felt as though his head was an empty oil drum, and someone was pounding on it with a jackhammer. He tried to content himself, thinking about how much he had accomplished on the house today, but he knew he couldn't continue working — not with a headache like this.

What the hell? he thought. It was almost time for supper, anyway. If he didn't get home and take some aspirin soon, this rip-snorting headache was going to last all night.

Still tensed and waiting to catch some sign of his attacker, he followed the trail back to the house. He wasn't ready for what he saw when he got there. On the bare plywood siding, in bright red, spray-painted letters that were still wet and dripping, were three words, written in a huge, childish scrawl. Edward was so taken aback and angry that he barely noticed the misspelling.

FUKC YOU EDDDIE!!!

"I'm really losing it . . . I think I'm going out of my mind!"

"And what makes you think that?"

"I just told you! All the things I've been thinking and feeling lately . . . and the dreams I've been having! God, they're so vivid . . . so real!" Dianne paused and took a breath, a loud sip of air. "And then last night — well, I told you what I did last night!"

"Yes, you told me, but considering all the stress you've been under lately — and I mean *family* stress just as much as physical stress — I think it's slightly more than understandable. I think you have to keep in mind the progress you've made. Look at you! The wires are out, and your face is healing beautifully."

Dr. Murray's voice was soothing and reassuring, but Dianne sat there in the easy chair, feeling wire-tight and ready to explode.

"But how could I—? I mean, why would I do something like that? I—I *love* my husband. I wouldn't want to hurt him—*ever!*"

"I understand that," Dr. Murray said calmly, "but I also recall you telling me last time that, in some ways, you *do* blame your husband for what happened to you. That you—"

"Well not enough to want to hurt him, for God's sake!" Dianne said, her voice almost a wail. "I mean, last night—and even this morning, just thinking about him, I started thinking how maybe what I—I really wanted to do—what I *had* to do was *kill* him. It's like . . . sometimes I feel almost as though something's . . . as though something's—I don't know, *forcing* me to do it."

"Do what? You mean hurt your husband?"

Dianne gave her a quick nod. "Yeah." She took a deep breath and held it. "Especially since we moved into his mother's house, thoughts like that have been so clear, so powerful. It's almost like there's someone *telling* me to do it, you know? Like I'm being controlled or directed to do it! Do you think I—" She snorted and shook her head. "I know you're gonna think I'm crazy for even asking this, but could it be like the house is . . . is haunted or something?"

Dr. Murray laughed softly and said, "I don't think so."

Covering her mouth with her hand, Dianne bit her lower lip and nodded agreement, but that still didn't rid her of the sudden impulse to scream out loud. She took a shaky breath and fought hard against the trembling inside her, but it did no good. Her stomach felt like it was full of Jell-O . . . or something much worse.

"I don't either," she said, shaking her head. "I've been thinking a lot about how—you know, like you said, it's got to be all the stress I've been under lately,

391

and the medication. I think the medication I'm takin
is still messing me up."

"That very well could be," Dr. Murray said. "I don'
think it would hurt if I prescribed you a mild tranquil
izer." She glanced over her shoulder at the clock on th
wall. "I hate to cut you short, but I do have to ge
ready for an appointment in town."

"Well, I appreciate you fitting me in on such shor
notice," Dianne said. She was still thinking about Di
Murray's seemingly casual dismissal of the idea that th
house was haunted. She didn't actually believe it her
self, but the woman's almost condescending reactior
galled her, as if the idea was totally beneath consider
ation. She almost said something about it but stoppe
herself as she watched Dr. Murray scribble somethin
onto a prescription notepad.

"This sedative is very mild," she said, tearing off th
sheet and handing it to Dianne, "but I think it will a
least take the edge off things for you. We should prob
ably schedule for you to see me the first of next week.
She got up and went over to her desk where sh
glanced at the date book. "I have an opening first thin
Monday morning, at nine o'clock."

Dianne nodded shakily. "That'll be fine," she said a
she folded up the paper and slipped it into her purs
before getting up and walking to the door. She still fel
as though she was about to collapse with every step
but before leaving she turned to Dr. Murray and, forc
ing a smile, said, "Thanks for seeing me. I—I really d
feel a lot better just getting to talk about it."

She closed the door behind her and went down th
flight of stairs to the sidewalk. Her car was parkec
across the street, but before she was halfway to it
she took the prescription out of her purse and lookec
at it. Then, glancing quickly over her shoulder to se
if Dr. Murray was watching her from the window, sh

tore the sheet into tiny shreds and sprinkled them onto the road like confetti.

"There! That does it!" she said, her voice crackling with repressed fury as she dug into her purse for her car keys. "I know one thing—I don't need any *more* goddamned medication! Maybe *Edward* does, but *I* sure as hell don't!"

And again, as soon as she said Edward's name out loud, a hot, red surge of fury filled her heart.

The house was empty when Dianne got back a little after three o'clock that afternoon. She sat down at the kitchen table, feeling curiously both energized and agitated by her frustration, and exhausted to the point of near-collapse from the weeks of almost constant worry and confusion.

What she probably needed right now, she told herself, was a nap, but she didn't think she'd be able to settle down. A few times during the drive home she had regretted tearing up the prescription Dr. Murray had given her, but she was determined not to rely on drugs anymore to get her through the rest of this ordeal.

Besides, she told herself, the whole damned thing was all behind her.

If she could just get a few good night's sleep, everything would be just fine. Her face was healing "better than textbook-perfect," according to Dr. Collett, and she felt confident that she and Edward could repair whatever injury their relationship had sustained. Just like their fire-damaged house, their marriage was damaged but certainly not destroyed. She knew she was willing to work at putting it back together again, and she had no doubt that Edward was, too. The bottom line was, although it may have been obscured over the past several months, they still loved each other. They would have plenty of time to patch up everything, especially once Brian went back home to Arizona.

She got up, filled the kettle with water, and put it on the stove to heat up for tea, then sat back down at the table to wait. She folded her arms across her chest and, leaned back in her chair, closing her eyes. She took a deep breath and listened . . . listened as the muffled silence of the house settled around her like cool water. She concentrated on breathing deeply and evenly, letting a soothing calm radiate outward from the center of her body to her hands, her feet, and her face. After a while, the water in the kettle began to hiss as it heated, and she focused on the sound, imagining it was a churning ocean tide, gently lapping over seaweed-clad rocks.

Deeper and deeper she went, letting her thoughts flit lightly over the events of the last few days. Whenever she felt a stirring of regret or anger, she nudged it aside, telling herself just to focus on the silence and calm.

But the sound of the heating water got steadily louder, sounding more and more agitated, drawing and holding Dianne's attention in an iron grip. She listened as the sound wove up and down the scale, shifting along different registers, rising and falling. She wasn't sure when the sound changed or how it happened, but suddenly she realized that for quite some time she had been listening to a voice, soft and lilting, whispering just at the edge of hearing . . . whispering words she couldn't quite distinguish but which—somehow—had made sense until she consciously thought about them.

"Ummm . . . yeah," she said, only distantly aware that she had spoken aloud.

She quieted herself, letting her attention drift with the sound because she knew—somehow—that, if she could remain perfectly still, she would hear more clear what the voice had to say to her. She was no longer aware of her surroundings or that she was waiting for the water to come to a boil. All she knew was the sound as she strained to make sense of the faint, crackling voice—

No . . . voices!

There were several of them, sputtering like the soft hiss of rain on the roof . . . like the crackle and snap of a fire. They rose and fell like a weak radio signal playing tricks in the atmosphere. Nodding her head up and down, Dianne whispered in a dry, rattling voice, "Yes, I know . . . Yes . . . Someone has to do it."

As the voices grew clearer, the sound of heating water got louder. Then, from far off, like the lonely wail of a midnight train, there came a shriek that went quickly up the scale until it was lost in the upper register.

Uttering a strangled cry, Dianne suddenly lurched forward. She banged her knees on the underside of the table and yelped as a bright bolt of pain zinged up her leg to her hips. Her eyes snapped open, and she looked around, momentarily confused as to where she was and what she was doing. When the shrill whistle of the tea kettle drew her attention to the stove, it all came back to her in a dizzying rush. Standing up shakily, she walked over to the stove and turned the heat off. The sound of the kettle died with an abrupt fade, but Dianne didn't reach for it or get a cup and tea bag from the counter. Her eyes were wide open, and her gaze was riveted to the kitchen sink where, for some reason, she sensed that something was out of place . . . something was . . .

"Wrong . . ."

She shook her head as she sifted her memory for a trace of what the voices had been saying to her and realized she must have dozed off, but the voices had been too clear . . . too real to have been just a dream. Raking her fingers through her hair, she concentrated hard, trying to pull it back, but every time she was close to grasping even a fragment of the dream, it slipped away like water through her fingers.

What the hell was it? she wondered. A knot of frantic worry tightened in her stomach. *What were they talking about?*

But it wasn't just the voices she had heard that bothered her; there was something about the sink that struck her as wrong. Had that been part of her dream? Had the voices said something about the sink? Nothing seemed to be out of place. There weren't any dirty dishes in it, and the stainless steel gleamed just as brightly as when she'd left it this morning.

"Shit," she said, snapping her fingers. "That's it!"

That was the problem: there was no mess—no dirty dishes in the sink. The kitchen looked as though nobody had been here all day. She hadn't expected Edward to be home for lunch, but she was positive Brian had still been in bed when she had left the house just after lunch. Could he still be sleeping? Was he okay up there?

Leaving the teakettle steaming on the stove, Dianne went into the hallway. The cold knot in her stomach got tighter as she started up the stairs. Her heels clicked like bone on the wood as she took each step slowly, one at a time. She was suddenly engulfed by confusion as the elusive feeling of the dream came back to her. There *had* been voices talking to her, and they *had* been making some kind of sense—at least while she had been dozing. It was maddeningly frustrating to feel as though it was almost in her grasp, but then the memory eluded her again.

It had something to do with Brian, she thought, as the deep worry wormed its way up from her stomach. *Something's wrong with him! Something's happened to him!*

Her panic was whining like a power drill by the time she had reached the top of the stairs. She hurried to Brian's bedroom and knocked lightly on the closed door, having to resist the urge to throw the door open and call out to him. Suddenly she felt very foolish, wondering how she would explain what she was doing if he was still in there, sitting on his bed listening to music on headphones or whatever.

"Hey, Brian?" she called out, painfully aware of the tremor in her voice.

No answer—no sound came from inside the room.

She grasped the doorknob and twisted it, but the door stuck, and she had to give it a little kick before it swung open with a high-pitched squeak of hinges. The window shades were still drawn. The air was musty, stale. She could vaguely see him—nothing more than a slouched lump underneath the bed covers.

Still, seeing him there in bed didn't allay her surging fear. She was convinced now that the voices had indeed been saying *something* about Brian . . . something either about what he had done or about what had happened to him.

"Brian?" she called out, a bit louder.

The shape on the bed didn't move.

Dianne's heart was racing in her chest as she moved quickly to the bedside, sensing that something was wrong—something was *seriously* wrong!

Holding her breath, she grasped the top of the bedspread and yanked it down. A surprised squeak escaped from her when she saw the two pillows and bundle of clothes that were rolled up and tucked under the sheet to look like a person.

"Oh, Jesus," she muttered.

She tossed the bedspread onto the floor and kicked at it, then turned around, but a quick glance at the room revealed that Brian wasn't there. Shivering wildly, she hugged herself and thought how odd the room looked and felt . . . deserted, almost as if it hadn't been occupied in *years*.

Where the hell is he? she wondered.

Her worry quickly spiked as a vague doubt rose in her mind. Like an onrushing storm front, it started to gather strength, sending shockwaves rippling through her.

What if he was never here?

Her gaze darted frantically around the room, seeking something to anchor her, but the room had turned into a swirl of diffuse light and blurred shadows.

God, what if Brian doesn't even exist?

What if I'm so far gone I've been imagining him all this time?

She recalled how tantalizing those dream voices had been, and she couldn't push aside the thought that they had been ghosts, disembodied spirits, whispering to her—a warning or *something* concerning herself and Edward and Brian.

The pressure exploded inside her head. She covered her mouth with both hands to keep from screaming out loud as the question reverberated in her mind—

Where the hell is Brian? . . . And how long has he been gone?

Chapter Twenty-four
The Mill Again

Dianne had no idea what to do next.

It was fairly obvious Brian had been gone since some time last night, but when had he left? Probably early in the evening. Why else would he stuff pillows under his covers to make it look like he was still sleeping? He had probably heard her and Edward arguing last night and had decided to leave . . . go somewhere.

But where?

He certainly wouldn't be trying to get back home, would he?

Then again, he couldn't just disappear, either. Where would he go? As far as she knew, he didn't have any friends in town where he could go and spend the night.

Dianne had plenty of doubts and anxieties about a lot of things, including her own sanity, but she pushed aside the nagging thought that all along Brian had been nothing more than a figment of her imagination. That idea was ludicrous! She admitted that she might still be pretty screwed up from the accident, the surgery, and the medication, but she wasn't *that* far gone! She hadn't lost her mind.

"Not yet, by Jesus!" she muttered.

Nearly frantic with worry, she rushed back downstairs

and started pacing back and forth across the kitchen floor. She kept glancing out the window and back door hoping to pick up some indication or clue as to where Brian might have gone. The empty silence of the house seemed to mock her.

Was he in some kind of trouble?

Should she go looking for him, or should she go get Edward, first, and tell him what she had found?

Or was she overreacting? Was he off helping his father, and everything was just fine?

If that was the case, why would he leave his bed to look like he was still in it?

She shivered, remembering the voices she had imagined hearing just a little while ago.

Yes, imagined! *They hadn't been real! They couldn't have been real!*

But another doubt she had concerned those voices and what they might have been saying—or *trying* to say—to her.

Why couldn't she remember?

Were they nothing more than elusive dream fragments that wouldn't make sense, no matter how hard she tried to recall them? Or in some way, on some level had they been real, and she simply had not received them. Or— and this thought struck her nerves like lightning—*had* she understood them? At least subconsciously, did she already know what they had been telling her to do?

"Something's got to be done," she whispered, pacing back and forth and slapping her fist repeatedly into her open hand. She stopped short and shivered, feeling as though, in a way, she had just replied to an unspoken, unheard request from someone.

Trembling with panic, she looked around the kitchen, wishing to God she didn't feel so threatened, so vulnerable. She felt suddenly as though she was standing on center stage, with hot, white light burning down on her. Sweat broke out on her brow. Her breath caught in her throat. she could imagine dozens—maybe hundreds—of unseen eyes watching her, stripping her down to her soul as she paced back and forth.

With a low, strangled cry, she turned to the door, flung it open, and raced out into the backyard. The muggy afternoon air wrapped around her like a wet blanket. She was swept up by the intense illusion that she was swimming in slow-motion rather than running. She didn't feel at all in control of herself as she ran, propelled against her will, across the backyard and into the woods. Without even thinking, she started along the path that led to the construction site.

Edward will be there! she kept telling herself. *I've got to find him and tell him what happened! I'll be safe with him!*

As she ran, she couldn't get rid of the unnerving sensation that she was being followed. Afraid of what she might see, she didn't dare chance a look behind. She wasn't entirely sure which path was the right one, so she just kept running, swept up by the pure physical release of doing *something!*

Even in the shade of the woods, everything seemed threatening. Tree branches lashed her face and reached out, clawing at her like skeletal hands. Deep green shadows vibrated with menace, and at every turn she expected something to leap out at her. The slanting sunlight shone red through the afternoon haze and played fiery tracks across her vision, confusing her with wavering afterimages that tripped her up on the uneven ground. In several places where the path branched out, Dianne didn't hesitate even a moment. She just kept running.

Sweat was streaming down her face, glistening on her arms with a cold, clammy touch. Her vision was blurred from the tears that filled her eyes and shattered the light into thousands of dazzling diamonds. Her whole body ached. The thought crossed her mind that she would have to keep running until she either found Edward or else dropped down dead from fear and exhaustion. She wasn't ready for it when she careened around a curve in the path and saw up ahead the slouched roof of the abandoned mill.

"Jesus Christ!" she shouted, drawing to such an abrupt stop that she wrenched her back and neck. Bracing her hands on her knees, she leaned forward and panted heavily, all the while staring up at the gray, battered building and thinking *What the hell? How did I end up out here?* Through the summer heat haze, the building looked like a mirage.

"That's it!"

The voice whispering inside her head didn't sound at all like her own mental voice, but she took another deep, burning breath and focused on the building.

She shuddered when she recalled the vivid dream she'd had about this place—the vigilante crowd, the torchlights flickering in the night, the policemen, and the violent eruption of flames from the mill. It all still seemed so real she felt as though, in some ways, she had somehow lived it.

Nearly blind with panic, she looked around her. The trees seemed to hiss and vibrate in the pressing heat. The afternoon seemed distant, ethereal. In spite of the hot sun beating down on her and the clammy feeling of sweat plastering her hair to her face and neck, she was overpowered by the feeling that this, too, might all be a dream.

Is it? she wondered. *Could it be?*

What if she was still sitting at the kitchen table, asleep?

What if she had never even gone upstairs to check on Brian?

What if she was dreaming all of this, and Brian was sleeping safe and sound upstairs or else he was out at the construction site, helping his father?

Her legs trembled, threatening to fold up under her as she took a few steps out of the fringe of the woods toward the mill. The field was alive with the buzzing of insects. Butterflies and bees darted like comets from flower to flower. The intoxicating scent of high grass and goldenrod filled the air, making it difficult to breathe.

She wanted to keep running but didn't know where to go. She wanted to scream, but her voice felt bottled up inside her. She wanted to shake or pinch herself—do anything to snap out of it, to wake herself up, but she moved forward, step by step toward the mill, drawn as if caught in the irresistible grip of some invisible force . . . a force that was pulling her, dragging her toward the dark, shadowed building.

This can't be happening!

She fought back wave after wave of swelling fear, wishing she could blink her eyes or shake her head and or do *something* to make it all go away; but she couldn't tear her gaze away from the building . . . and from one particular window opening. She remembered what she had seen there that night, and she dreaded what she might see there now!

A body, hanging from the rope! What if it's there again? Like in the dream. Only this time it's . . .

Brian!

She almost choked on her fear as her feet brought her closer to the building. The swelling sound of insects was almost deafening, but beneath it, Dianne thought she could hear something else. She strained to make out what it was, then shivered when she did.

"Please . . . Please! . . . *No!*" she said.

Her voice was nothing more than a low, gravel grind, buried deep beneath the rising, warbling wail of a baby, crying.

* * *

403

When Brian opened his eyes, he had no idea what time it was.

The pain in the back of his head had become a sharp, steady throbbing that made glowing curtains of red light shift across his vision. When he closed his eyes again, squeezing them tightly, he could imagine that the pain was shaped sort of like an octopus, only it was an octopus with at least a hundred arms, all of which were twitching and probing deeper into his nerves, sending messages of burning pain deep into his brain. Again, he opened his eyes and looked around, but the room—wherever the hell he was—was as black as night. He tried to remember what had happened, but his memory—like his surroundings—were shrouded in darkness.

His face felt crusty, but he had no way of knowing if it was crusted with blood or mucus or dust. He wanted to wipe his face, but when he tried to bring his arm from behind his back, it wouldn't move. He let out a yelp of pain as something stung his wrist like a snake bite.

"Hey, what's the matter? You ain't scared, are you? Can't you take a little pain?"

The voice came to him out of the darkness, thick with sarcasm, but Brian recognized it instantly.

Uncle Mike!

Blinking rapidly, Brian looked around, trying his best to focus his eyes, but still everything around him was lost in darkness. Then, off to his left, he heard the dull scraping sound of something being dragged in the dirt. He immediately recognized the sound, and when he did, his breath caught in his throat. A cold tickle of sweat ran down his sides from his armpits.

That scraping sound was Uncle Mike, opening the door to his secret room in the mill cellar. A thin haze of gray light momentarily filled the room, dazzling Brian's eyes; then the light shut off as Mike entered the room and closed the door behind him.

Oh, shit! Brian thought.

He started pulling more frantically with both his arms and legs, unable to admit that it was useless. His wrists and ankles were tightly bound. The rope chafed at his bare arms like sandpaper. He cringed and listened as the shuffle of feet on the dirt floor came closer to him.

"That wasn't you I heard down here, crying like a little baby, now, was it?" Mike asked. His voice was a low, purring growling.

"No," Brian said as unseen hands reached out of the darkness, felt until they found him, and then poked him painfully in the ribs. A hot spike of pain shot through his chest.

"What? You scared, being left all alone down here in the dark? Huh? Is that it, you little crybaby?"

Brian cleared his throat, wanting desperately to say *fuck you!,* but the best he could muster was a feeble, "No."

"Well then, that's good, that's good, because you don't have to be scared, you know," Mike said. His voice dropped to a low, almost rational sounding tone, but Brian knew that this wouldn't last for long.

"Didn't your momma ever tell you that? That you were never *really* alone . . . even here in the dark? *Especially* out here! Well—? Didn't she—?"

Another hard jab in the ribs made Brian cry out.

"I asked you a question!"

Brian licked his lips and shook his head *no,* not caring that the motion was wasted in the darkness. More of what had happened last night was coming back to him, and with it came the cold, sinking feeling in his stomach—the numbed certainty that Uncle Mike was a certified loony, and that he was in very serious danger.

Last night . . . he'd been trying to fall asleep, hoping to forget all about what had happened up in the attic. The storm had passed, and the house had gotten quiet,

405

but the image of that woman's face in the old portrait—and it's haunting similarity to his stepmother—hovered like an unseen bird of prey in the darkness ready to drop on him and rip him apart with razor sharp claws. He'd had trouble falling asleep because he feared the dreams that might come.

And then the argument had started—his father and stepmother, going at it again. He couldn't help but hear everything they said and had silently sided with his father, but their voices had been so loud that he hadn't heard anything else—not until it was too late. Then the feeling he'd had in the attic, that there was someone else in the room with him, returned again. Only this time, he was right!

Before he knew what was happening, much less call out for help, a dark shape had loomed over him as he lay in bed. A powerful hand had clamped down hard over his mouth, almost suffocating him. He had struggled hard but had soon realized, even then, that his father wouldn't have heard any sounds he might make short of screaming at the top of his lungs. He had bucked and twisted on his bed, trying to throw off the weight that was pressing down on him, but the person had taken hold of his arm and had bent it back, forcing him to roll over onto his stomach. Then something—either a fist or a weapon—smacked him hard on the back of the head. White light and a high, ringing buzz exploded in his head, and he was lost . . . lost in impenetrable darkness until he had woken up here . . .

Back in the mill . . . with his crazy Uncle Mike!

"Wha—what do you want?" Brian asked, forcing as much strength as he could into his voice. "I never did anything to hurt you! Why're you . . . why're you doing this to me?"

"Why—? *Why—?*"

Hysterical laughter filled the darkness, drilling into Brian's ears.

"Because I *need* you . . . you're my bait, my lure to lp me finish things off out here once and for all! at's why!"

He expected another poke in the ribs, but a hand abbed him roughly by the shirt and twisted it into a ght ball. He felt himself being pulled forward. Hot, ur-smelling breath blew across his face as Uncle Mike nked him up close and whispered heatedly, "And no e's gonna screw it up, understand? Not you! Not ur father! Not your stepmother! *No one!*"

Pain exploded in the darkness again as something lid slammed into the side of Brian's face. The buzz-g came back, a steady, high-pitched note in the center his head. Dazed and almost unconscious, Brian felt ightless as he was lifted and dragged across the floor, s feet flopping crazily as if he had no control over em. His arms and shoulders screamed in agony, but on all sensation was lost in a single, consuming blaze pain. He heard the rough scraping sound as the or opened. A watery, gray haze of light washed ross his closed eye lids, but he was too far gone to gister much else. The pressure released from his wrists d ankles as the ropes came away, but he was too ak to get up much less to fight back. Then he felt mself being thrown like a limp ragdoll onto the dirt or of the cellar.

From far away, he heard a deep snicker of laughter. en a voice that rumbled like a cascade of rocks roll-g downhill said, "Don't you worry. Someone'll be ong to see you. Real soon. You just get comfortable d wait right here . . ."

"Brian!"

The shout echoed with a strange dullness from inside e cavernous building.

Oh my God! He's hurt! Dianne thought.

407

Almost against her will, she had walked right up to the building and bent down to peer in through the cellar window. That's when she had first seen the motionless form sprawled facedown on the dirt floor at the back of the room against the wall. It had taken her a moment to realize that it was Brian. His arms and legs were stretched out wide as though he were trying to hug the floor. Dianne's first impression was that he had fallen from a great height. His head was cocked to one side, looking away from her, so she couldn't see his face; but she could easily imagine that he was covered with blood, and that his body was already cold and lifeless.

A low whimper sounded deep in her chest as she looked around for some way to get down to him. To her left, was a narrow flight of stone steps leading down into the cellar. Without stopping to consider the situation, Dianne raced over to them and went down. The shadowed darkness vibrated with a subtle energy within the vast room. At first she was nearly blinded as her eyes tried to adjust to the sudden lessening of light. She was frantic to run over to the motionless boy, but she had to pick her way carefully through the debris that littered the cellar floor.

Please don't be dead! Please don't be dead!

She chanted the words in her mind, shivering as each shuffling step brought her closer to Brian. She was unable to tear her gaze away from the boy, and kept stumbling over fallen stones and old lumber, feeling her way blindly. She held her breath and prayed desperately to see some slight motion, some indication of life.

Please don't be dead! Please don't be dead!

And *yes!*

She saw his head move, and she heard a low, bubbling moan accompanied by a soft scraping sound as he shifted about on the floor. His arms slid underneath his chest, and his back humped up as if he were struggling to stand.

"Hey, Brian! Don't worry!" she called. "Just hang on a second. I'll be right there!"

Brian moaned again, louder as he raised his head and looked around, looking for all the world like a turtle, timidly poking his head out of its shell. His face looked thin and pale; it floated like a white balloon in the darkness. His eyes were rolling crazily in his head, unable to focus on anything. For a heart-fluttering instant, Dianne had the impression that he wasn't even there—that he was nothing more solid than a movie projection. Her feet scraped loudly on the dirt floor as she closed the gap between them, not daring to look away from him, not even for an instant, because she was afraid he would disappear.

He continued to struggle to get up and succeeded—finally—in rolling over onto his back. Dianne could tell by the way his head rolled back and forth that he was nearly unconscious. She only hoped that he wasn't hurt *too* badly!

"Hey, hey," she said, as she came up to him and knelt down beside him. She reached out and touched his forehead, surprised by the solid reality of him. "Just take it easy, all right? I'll get you out of here. Did you fall or something? Do you think anything's broken?"

Brian's eyes were still shifting back and forth, looking for something solid to latch onto. At last, when his eyes locked onto hers, the expression of terror that filled them gave her a sharp twist of anguish.

He still hates me! she thought. *He still resents me!*

"Just lie back and relax a minute," she said, fighting hard to keep her voice steady. She continued to rub his forehead gently and could feel a solid lump about the size of a golf ball on the side of his head, just above the left ear. Looking at him lying there in the dirt, obviously in pain, made her remember the horror of her

409

own fall from the cliff last spring. The thought filled her with an icy terror that gripped her and wouldn't let go, but she forced herself to take a steadying breath.

Can't lose it now, she told herself. *Got to stay in control . . . at least until I get him the hell out of here!*

"Are you hurt bad? Do you think you can get up and walk?"

She slid her hands under his armpits to help him if he indicated that he wanted to get up. His eyes were still riveted to her, crazy and unfocused, but they widened suddenly, and his mouth sagged open.

"Behind—"

That was all he got to say before Dianne sensed a sudden flurry of motion behind her. She started to turn around, but it was already too late. Something whistled through the air behind her and slammed into the side of her head with a loud ringing, metal sound. The shattering explosion of white light soon faded along with everything else as Dianne sank down . . . down into the thick blackness of unconsciousness. The last thing she heard was a rough voice say, "Two down . . . and one to go."

Consciousness came back slowly . . . painfully.

For the longest time, Dianne imagined that she was sitting below-decks in a boat as it tossed up and down on huge, rolling waves. She was only vaguely aware that her head was rocking back and forth in time with the swells. A hot line of pain shot from behind her left ear down her neck to her shoulders, but she kept grinding her head against the wall or the floor or whatever the hell it was, trying to pull herself back. The only thing she knew for sure was that she was leaning against something hard, something that felt more like stone than wood.

. . . Can they make a boat out of rock? . . .

Her stomach bubbled with a sour hollowness as she rose and fell. She couldn't stop the sensation that she was tumbling backward head over heels, falling and spinning into darkness. She imagined that she heard voices, whispering and hissing at her from all directions, but she couldn't make out anything they were saying. The pain inside her head kept shifting between faint red tracer flashes of light and a steady, heavy humming sound. It was quite a while, and it took a lot of effort before she could start to remember what had happened. Then fragments of the last few—what? Hours? Minutes?—popped into her mind like fireworks explosions across the night sky.

. . . Brian . . . he was hurt . . . he'd fallen . . . and I was there . . . in the old mill . . . and someone . . . something . . . hit me from behind . . .

She wanted to touch the side of her head, to check for damage, but something restrained her. No matter how hard she tried to move either of her arms, they were locked in place behind her back. Burning pain filled her arm sockets. She wasn't even aware of her legs; there was absolutely no feeling from her waist down.

. . . Did I break my arms . . . or my neck? . . . Am I paralyzed? . . . How did I fall? . . . What the hell hit me? . . .

She wanted to say something, to ask where she was or beg for help, but her mouth was also locked in place, clamped firmly shut. For the longest time she forgot that the doctor had already taken out the wires holding her jaw together. Her tongue felt unusually large, like a bloated slug as it pressed against her teeth, tasting . . . something . . . either the cold sting of metal wires . . . or else blood!

. . . Oh my God! . . . Is my jaw still wired shut? . . .

That thought had a slamming immediacy that in-

411

stantly brought her closer to awareness. Sucking hard through her mouth, she drew in a breath that wheezed and whistled between her teeth. It hurt like hell to do it, but she shifted her jaw from side to side until she felt the satisfying crunch of her teeth grinding together.

Yes, yes . . . I'm okay . . . at least my jaw is!

She came even closer to consciousness and could feel slick sweat on her face and the hard, unyielding rock behind her head. The pain in the back of her head got more acute, shooting like a jet of flame through her. She forced herself to take another deep breath and winced when something sharp jabbed like a knife underneath her ribs

Something's gotta be broken! . . . What the hell happened to me?

"Hey, you're coming around," a voice said. It whispered from the darkness close to her right ear.

Dianne stopped rolling her head and strained hard to see who it was, but she couldn't make out any details of her surroundings, much less who had spoken to her. The darkness was impenetrable.

"Hey, are you all right?"

The voice was clear and seemed to be edged with concern.

". . . Mnnn . . . I don't—"

Dianne cut herself off sharply, startled by the sudden loud sound of her own voice. The ringing in her ears got louder, and she felt curiously dissociated from her body.

The pain increased as she fought to gain consciousness, so why fight?

"I tried to warn you, you know," the voice said, warbling softly.

". . . Uhh-huh . . ." Dianne replied.

She tried again to move her arms but couldn't. Her eyelids fluttered, scraping roughly against her eyes as she forced them open to tiny slits. Thin, watery traces

412

of white light danced in front of her and shattered into hundreds of bright spikes. Overhead, something—probably the ceiling rafters of the mill—glowed like hot metal bars.

. . . Yes! . . . I remember now . . . I came out to the mill! . . . But why? . . . How did I know to come out here?

She craned her neck forward and saw something else—no, someone blocking the center of the light source. The dark silhouette was thick and rounded, and reminded Dianne of a huge purple thunderhead, rolling up over the horizon. *The storm's about to break . . .*

"Don't try to move," the whispering voice said. "It's no use. He's got us."

This time the voice had a trace of familiarity to it. Dianne concentrated hard, trying to place it; then in a flash it hit her.

Brian! Oh, shit! That's right—

"Brian . . . ?"

—it's Brian!

"Shsssh! Be quiet or else you'll—"

"Oh, so you're awake now, are you?"

This new voice came out of the darkness, booming so loud it hurt Dianne's ears. She knew immediately that its source was the dark silhouette she saw squatting in front of the bright light. She heard a high-pitched hiss and realized it was the sound of a Coleman lantern, like the one she and Edward had used camping last spring.

She watched, more than half expecting to see flashing tongues of lightning and hear the steady roll of thunder when the man stood up and stretched to an impossible height.

Who the hell is he?

"And I'll bet you have one hell of a headache, too. Don't ya, little lady?"

Dianne licked her lips, wanting to say something, but

413

she could do nothing but watch in silent horror as the person moved slowly toward her. With the light behind him, he was nothing more than a huge, black blur. From the center of the darkness came a soft chuffing sound of laughter. Dianne could feel the piercing intensity of the man's gaze as he stared at her. A line of white lit up one side of his face, and in a stunned instant, she thought she recognized him.

"Edward . . . ?"

The twisted laughter got louder.

"Oh, my God! Edward! What are you—"

The man's laughter rose even higher, almost masking Brian's voice when he whispered, "No way! That's not my dad!"

Dianne dimly registered what Brian had said, but it was impossible for her brain to process it. Spirals of darkness were shifting and opening up below her. She felt herself falling again . . . falling backward into the cold darkness, away from the hurtful light. She clung desperately to consciousness, but Brian's voice warbled weakly, fading with every syllable. From far, far away, she heard him say, "That's my . . . crazy . . . Uncle . . . Mike."

"That's right!" the other voice said, rising to a sharp, pealing howl. "I'm his *cra-a-azy* Uncle Mike! The nut case! The loony bird!"

His laughter rang out like a chiming bell, drilling into Dianne's ears and making her wince.

". . . Brian? Are you . . . all right?" Dianne asked groggily. She struggled hard to keep her voice from breaking with fear. "He didn't . . . hurt you or anything, did he?"

"No, I'm all—"

"Hurt him? *Hurt him?* Why Jesus Christ of course not! I wouldn't want to *hurt* him!"

He snorted loudly, sounding like an enraged pig.

"There may be *some*body around here who wants to

hurt him, maybe a *lot* of people, but not me! No-siree! Why on earth would I want to hurt my own nephew?"

Mike's voice rose even higher until it was lost in a wild, crazy cackle. Dianne tried hard to block him out so she could focus all of her attention on what she was trying to say to Brian, but the darkness inside her head was luring her, calling to her, telling her just to let go, give it all up and sink back down to where it didn't hurt anymore, where *nothing* would hurt . . . ever again.

"Your father," she said, closing her eyes and gritting her teeth, fighting with everything she had to stay conscious. "Does he . . . know you're out here?"

"No. No one does . . . 'cept you," Brian replied. His voice wavered like he was scared out of his mind, but he was putting up a good front.

"You should have a talk with some of *these* people," Mike shouted. "Listen to what *they* have to say! If you want to know about hurt, *they* can tell you! They know what *hurt* is all about!"

Dianne took a deep, steadying breath and tried to block out the raging voice. "Brian, do you think your dad knows *he's* out here?" she asked.

"I don't think so. I . . . I've known for the past couple of weeks, but I . . . I never told him."

"Jesus . . . Why not?" Dianne said, lowering her head and sighing. She didn't dare say out loud what she was thinking. Even in her pain and despair, she knew, if they were going to have even a slight chance of getting out of this, they were going to have to pull together.

"You've been ignoring them, haven't you? *Haven't you? Goddamn it!* After all this time! After all this time they've been waiting for you or *someone*—for *anyone* to pay attention to them. The least little bit of attention! My mother sure as hell knew they were here!

415

Didn't she *tell* you what you had to do? She was supposed to explain it all to you! To take care of them!"

"Don't worry, Brian," Dianne said. She had to shout to be heard above Michael's nearly incoherent raving. "Your dad's gonna know something's up when we're not around. He'll be worried and he'll—"

"Be worried? Jesus Christ, he's gonna be *worried!*" Michael wailed.

Dianne glanced over and saw him, leaning his head back and shaking his fists wildly at the ceiling. "You bet your fuckin' *ass* he's gonna be worried! He fuckin' well *ought* to be worried! But you and he will have plenty of time to talk about it because I'm gonna go get him for you right now!"

His laughter rose shrilly, but it finally was too much for Dianne. Her grip on consciousness slipped, and she plunged back down into the comforting pitch black inside her mind.

Chapter Twenty-five
Other Voices

It was a little after six-thirty. The sun had already set, and the sky was quickly fading to a deep, bruised purple when Edward pulled into the driveway and stopped the pickup truck. There were no lights on in the house, but he barely gave that a thought as he slipped out of the truck and started up the walkway to the house. In his hand was a small bottle of Tylenol he had driven into town to buy. He had swallowed two tablets dry on the drive home, but—so far—they hadn't even touched his headache. He planned on waiting another few minutes before taking another two.

"Hey, Dianne! I'm home!" he shouted as he entered the kitchen. He let the door bang shut behind him as he swatted on the light switch with the flat of his hand and looked around.

He could tell instantly that no one was home. The house had that weird deserted feeling houses can get when you know they're empty. He glanced over at the kitchen table, which was where he and Dianne left notes for each other whenever they were going out. The table was bare. Frowning, he walked into the hallway, snapped on the light at the bottom of the steps, and called out, "Hey, Brian! You home?"

The house remained perfectly still except for the soft huffing of his breathing.

"What the hell?" he muttered.

He walked back into the kitchen and went over to the sink. Taking a glass from the cupboard, he ran the faucet until the water was nice and cold, then popped another Tylenol into his mouth and washed it down with several gulps of water. After rinsing out the glass, he placed it upside down in the dish drainer, then leaned his elbows on the counter and stared out the kitchen window as evening descended.

It's starting to get dark too early, he thought, wishing to hell that he still had a month or two of guaranteed good weather to get the new house closed in before autumn came. But like it or not, summer was almost over, and cold weather was on its way. He heaved a sigh and gingerly probed the back of his head. The pain seemed to be lessening . . . slightly, and that gave him an opportunity to wonder—*Where the hell is everybody?*

The house didn't *feel* right.

Something was off-key—wrong.

He was pretty sure he had seen the car in the garage, so he knew Dianne couldn't have gone too far. It didn't seem likely that both she and Brian would be out at the same time—certainly not together! For the past couple of days, whenever she wasn't freaking out and screaming at him, Dianne had spent most of her time moping around the house. Brian, playing the role of the alienated preteen to the hilt, spent all of his time in his bedroom, either sleeping, reading, or listening to music. Edward knew his son was just counting the hours until he went back home to Phoenix.

He jumped and let out a startled little cry when the telephone rang.

That's probably Dianne now, he thought as he crossed the kitchen floor quickly and snatched up the receiver in the middle of its second ring.

"Hello—" he said.

A mild little *zing* of pain shot through the back of his head when he pressed the phone against his ear.

"Edward. Good Lord, where the heck have you been all day?"

"Hi yah, Sally," Edward said, cringing at the sound of his ex-wife's voice. "So how are things out there in Arizona?"

"Oh, fine, just fine. You know, I've been calling the house all afternoon and haven't gotten an answer until now. Where has everyone been?"

"I dunno—just . . . out, I guess."

His voice caught for a moment when he sensed a subtle shifting of motion behind him. He turned around, thoroughly expecting to see either Brian or Dianne enter the kitchen, and was surprised to see no one there. He shivered in spite of the heavy heat in the room. Now that he thought about it, the house *did* feel as though it had been closed up all day. Where the hell were Dianne and Brian?

"Well," Sally said, "I was just calling to confirm our plans for next Saturday. You said Brian was flying on Delta, Flight 202, arriving in Phoenix a little after six o'clock my time, right?"

Edward glanced at the note he'd jotted on the wall calendar and read aloud. "Flight 202, arriving six-fourteen P.M. Yup, that's right."

"Great. Say, is Brian right there? I'd like to speak with him."

"Uh—no, no he isn't here right now," Edward said.

There was an uncomfortable pause at the other end of the line; then Sally said, "You sound kind of funny. Is everything all right?"

"Sure, sure. Couldn't be better," Edward replied. "I just—he's over at a—a friend's house and won't be back until after supper."

Pain pulsated like tiny hammer blows in the back of his head.

"But you sound kind of funny to me," Sally said, her voice sharp and probing. "Are you sure you're not—"

"I'm fine! Really, everything's fine!" Edward said. The pain in his head throbbed all the harder. He closed his eyes and pressed against them, wishing to Christ her voice would just go away.

"You know you can't hide anything from me, Edward. Lord knows I lived with you long enough to be able to tell when you're trying to hide something from me. Tell me the truth. Has anything happened?"

"No, no. Everything's just fine out here. Honest!"

But even as the words were leaving his mouth, Edward shivered with the uncomfortable sensation that someone was standing behind him, watching him and listening to everything he said. The hairs at the nape of his neck prickled. He shifted around so his back was against the wall as he scanned the room. The window over the kitchen sink framed almost total darkness outside, and the lights were off in the dining room, but there had definitely been a feeling that something had moved, like the shadow of a cloud passing in front of the sun. But it hadn't come from either of those directions; it had seemed as though, when his back had been turned, the motion had been in the hallway, over by the stairway.

"Edward—?" Sally said, her voice growing heavy with impatience.

"Huh? What'd you say?" Edward asked, realizing that he had completely missed whatever she had just said. Her voice was nothing more than an irritating insect buzz in his ear. Stray thoughts about their relationship and how bad it had been at the end, especially after Brian was born, flashed through his mind. He wanted desperately to end this conversation, and he prayed that listening to her wouldn't make his headache any worse.

"I asked if you'd make sure to have Brian give me a call later—tonight, as soon as he gets home. Because of

420

he time difference, it doesn't matter how late. There
re a few things I have to talk to him about."

"Uh, yeah—sure. No problem," Edward said. "If it's
nything important, you can leave any message with
e."

"No . . . just that."

As they spoke, Edward's eyes kept shifting back and
orth, searching for whatever it was that might have
rawn his attention. It could have been the thin wash
f shadow cast by the kitchen light into the doorway,
ut he couldn't help but think it was more than that.
he house was eerily quiet, as if it were holding its
reath. Sally started going on about something else, but
dward barely paid attention when a heavy thump
ounded from somewhere upstairs.

"What the—?" he said, jumping with surprise and
lancing up at the ceiling. It had sounded like some-
hing heavy—a sledgehammer or something—falling or
ropping to the floor upstairs.

"Uh, look, Sally," he said. A dry lump had formed
1 his throat and wouldn't go down no matter how
ard he tried to swallow. "I—I'd love to talk a bit, but
omebody . . . an old friend of mine just drove up. I
otta go."

"Oh, sure," Sally said. "No sweat. But there's one
nore thing—"

"Yeah?"

"*Please*, Edward, break down and buy yourself an
nswering machine, all right? This *is*, after all, the
wentieth century."

"Yeah, sure," Edward replied. "S'long. Good to hear
rom you . . . and I'll be sure to give Brian your mes-
age."

He didn't wait to hear her say goodbye; he was al-
eady reaching to hang up the phone and moving to-
vard the kitchen doorway. Before he left the kitchen,
hough, he glanced around, looking for something to

use as a weapon, but that struck him as ridiculous.
What the hell was he getting so worked up about? He
admitted that the sound from upstairs had startled him,
but that was no reason to get all worked up. The most
reasonable explanation was that either Dianne or Brian
was up there, perhaps just waking up from a nap or
something . . . or else maybe Brian was in the attic
again poking around and hadn't heard him when he
first called out to him.

"Whatever," Edward muttered as he walked out into
the hallway and started up the stairs, moving quietly on
tiptoes. He was about halfway up and just taking a
breath to call out again when he heard something that
made him stop short. For a fleeting second, he wasn't
sure he had really heard what he thought he had heard.
The pounding in his head got steadily stronger. He
wanted to convince himself that he might have imagined it all, but then the sound came again, wavering
high and low, like some bizarre musical instrument sliding up and down the scale.

Jesus Christ, someone's crying!

His body tingled with a sudden rush of panic. He
took the rest of the steps two at a time, then paused at
the top of the stairs and, holding his breath, cocked his
head from side to side as he listened. For several heartbeats the sound wasn't there, but then, very faintly, he
heard it again—a high, wispy cry coming from the far
end of the hall, from Brian's bedroom.

Oh, Jesus, what's happened?

He took a few steps in that direction, then stopped
short in his tracks as a ripple of chills raced up his
back. His mind filled with a rush of scary thoughts
that echoed hollowly in his mind.

He listened as the crying rose even louder, sounding
clearly through the closed bedroom door. It came in
short, ragged bursts that were punctuated by raw, sniffling sobs.

422

"Hey . . . Brian . . ." Edward called out.

A coldness gripped his chest as he forced himself to ke another few steps forward.

What if he's been hurt? Or what if he and Dianne d another argument, and he finally completely lost ntrol of himself and . . . and did something . . . aybe something to hurt her? Or what if she finally ipped out and attacked him?

The shadowy hallway seemed to stretch outward like arm taffy. The closer he got to the room, the deeper e crying cut into his nerves; it sounded so lonely, so straught he couldn't bring himself to believe that it ight actually be Brian or Dianne. He shivered wildly, inking that the sound reminded him of something se—something he had heard once before.

Where? . . . When?

He searched his memory but came up with nothing. is pulse was slamming hard in his ears when he fially made it to the closed door. His hand was treming as he gripped the doorknob and, licking his lips, repared to call out to whomever was inside the room.

What if I open it, and there's no one in there?

The thought, crazy as it seemed, sent another cold lt through him. At last, unable to stand the winding nsion any longer, he spun the doorknob and pushed pen the door. It creaked on old hinges, setting his eth on edge. No matter what he had thought, he asn't ready for what he saw. Sitting cross-legged on e middle of the single bed, his hands cupping his face s he cried, was his brother, Michael. His shoulders ounced up and down, keeping time with his gutrenching sobs.

"Jesus Christ, Mikie!" Edward was staggered. "What e hell are you—?"

His brother looked up at him, his face glistening with ars.

"Our mommy's dead!" Michael wailed before snorting

423

loudly and wiping his nose with the back of his hand
"She's dead, Eddie! Dead! . . . Dead! . . . Dead!"

"What time was it when you came out here?"

"Huh . . . ?

Dianne's head hurt like hell, but she shook herself,
trying to clear away the cobwebs. It seemed as though
Brian had been talking to her for a long time as she
slowly clawed her way back to consciousness.

"I—I don't know . . . for sure."

A sudden sinking feeling filled her stomach when she
opened her eyes and saw that things hadn't changed;
she was still tied up beside Brian in the mill cellar, still
leaning against the cold, stone wall. The small lantern
was still blazing away, illuminating the room with a
cold, unwelcoming light. But there was one thing different.

"He's gone! Where'd Michael go?"

Brian glanced over at her and shrugged. "Out for
food . . . out for a nature walk. How should *I* know?"
That same old, hateful tone he used with her was back
in his voice.

Dianne almost said something but held herself back,
wondering what possible good it would do. After her
eyes had adjusted to the light, she looked around at the
small room. It was no more than ten or fifteen feet
square. The walls were built of large granite blocks,
mortared together with crumbling cement. Lime
streaked the rocks where moisture had seeped in. The
floor was hard-packed dirt, marred with numerous
scuffs and footprints. Other than the lantern and a di-
lapidated wooden table, the room was bare except for a
threadbare mattress on the ground by the opposite wall.
It was stained and covered with dirt, and seemed like a
perfect haven for lice and maybe a family of rats.

"So what time was it?" Brian repeated, sounding exasperated, as if he'd had to ask for the hundredth time.

"I—I'm not sure. It was getting late." Dianne squinted, trying hard to focus her mind. "I'd just gotten back from the—my appointment, so I guess it was—I'd say around four o'clock, maybe four-thirty."

"So it's gotta be dark by now," Brian said.

His voice sounded deeper than usual, more mature. Dianne looked at him again and was suddenly struck by the realization that she had never really *seen* him before; he looked—different, somehow. The lantern light cast sharp shadows across his face that made him look older, and his eyes reflected the light, shimmering brightly, looking intense and piercing. Even though he was trussed up, his arms, chest, and shoulders looked more muscular, as though he had matured in the last few days—or hours. Brian seemed, in ways, like an entirely different person, and Dianne realized with a deep stirring of regret that she had never really *known* him as a person—not in the least.

"How can you tell? I—I must've passed out or something. How long was I out?"

"Not long," Brian replied. "Five, maybe ten minutes tops."

"Seems a lot longer," Dianne said, wishing to hell she could touch the injury on the side of her head. Whenever she turned, even slightly, dried blood crinkled and pulled at her hair. "But hey! If it's dark now, and we're not home yet, then your dad's gonna have to know something's happened, right?"

"Yeah, but will he know to come looking out *here?*"

Brian's voice was edgy with repressed fear, but Dianne had to give him credit for trying to hang in there. She felt a sudden almost overwhelming fondness for the boy and was filled with regret for how horribly they had treated each other over the summer.

"Brian . . . ?"

"Yeah, what?"

Words of apology and affection cascaded through her mind, but as hard as she tried to phrase what she knew she had to say, everything she thought of sounded phony and inadequate. She couldn't very well say, *You know, it's too bad we hate each other so much, but now that we're both probably going to die soon, I wanted to tell you how sorry I am!*

No, she was the adult here; she was going to have to stay in control, and they were going to have to work together to get themselves out of this . . . or else they were *both* going to be screwed. Hell, maybe they were screwed anyway, but they had to think of *something* to try.

Dianne heaved herself away from the wall and started pushing herself across the floor, her back toward Brian. "Come on," she said, her voice firm with command. "Turn around and slide your butt over here so we can start working free of these ropes."

"Christ All-mighty, Mikie," Edward said.

He was rooted to the spot, standing in the doorway and staring slack jawed at his brother, who sat on the bed, rocking back and forth and crying away, rubbing his eyes and sniffing like a baby.

"You were . . . shit, well, I knew you'd left the hospital. The authorities told me, but I didn't think—well, because I hadn't heard from you, and the police still hadn't found you, I thought you were probably . . ." He ended with a shrug.

"*Dead!*" Michael shouted. Spit flew from his mouth. "You can say it. You thought I was dead, right? Or maybe you *wished* I was dead!" He balled his hands into fists and started pounding the sides of his head as he rocked back and forth. The bedsprings creaked loudly. "No! No! No, Eddie! *I'm* not the one who's dead! *Mommy is! Mommy's dead!*"

"I know, I know," Edward said softly. He had a strong impulse to go to his brother and comfort him, but something held him back. "I went to her funeral. I was here all along, you know, taking care of her—"

"Oh, yeah! Sure!" Michael yelled. His face flushed bright red, and his eyes bugged out of his head, bloodshot and staring. "But you didn't take good *enough* care of her, did you? Oh, no! No fucking way! She wouldn't be dead if you had! She wouldn't be dead!" His voice rose higher and higher, winding up like a siren.

"Hey, everybody dies, you know . . . eventually," Edward said mildly.

Tangled thoughts and emotions warred inside him as he stood in the doorway silently regarding his brother. His resentment boiled when he thought about all the misery and pain Michael had caused the family over the years, all the worry and distress his mother had to endure, trying to cope with raising two boys, especially after her husband died. He wanted to throttle his brother for all the spoiled holidays and wasted weekends they'd had to drive down to Massachusetts to visit him in the mental hospital. He had been in the car driving to the mental hospital when the news came over the radio that President Kennedy had been shot.

But then, it was so painfully obvious that his brother wasn't a fully matured man and never would be. Even after forty years, he was still no more than a shattered, lost little boy, crying his heart out in his old bedroom, perhaps the only safe haven he had ever known. It was pathetic.

And it was then that Edward recognized the sound that had seemed so familiar when he had started up the stairs: it was the same tormented cry Michael had made when his mother had found him hiding in the bedroom closet later that same day after Ray Saunders had fallen—been *pushed*—through the trapdoor and broken

427

his back . . . the last day Michael had ever lived in the family home before being sent off to the mental institution in Massachusetts.

Edward's vision misted over with tears, and his heart twisted with pity and guilt: pity for the mental anguish he knew Michael had had to live with inside his head every single day of his life; and guilt that he—for whatever reason of God or nature or luck—had been the one who had gotten to lead a "normal" life outside of an institution.

Edward took a single step closer to the bed, cleared his throat, and said, "You know, Mikie, that you're going to have to go back . . . to the hospital, I mean."

"Oh, really?" Michael said.

He looked up at Edward. His face was a mask of suffering and pain. His lower lip trembled wildly, and his chest hitched as he took sharp, panting breaths. Tears were running freely from his eyes, shimmering like jewels on his cheeks. Edward found himself actually envying his brother's ability to let go so completely of his emotions. He hated that all his life he had to keep himself so bottled up, so tightly wrapped and had *never* dared let his emotions go. Even when he found out that his mother had died, and when Dianne had been hurt so badly in that fall off the cliff, he had choked off letting the true depth of his feelings show.

He had to!

What would people find out—about him—if he ever dropped his guard? Christ, everything would unravel if he did that! No wonder Sally had left him after three years of marriage, and no wonder his relationship with Dianne was heading toward ruin. He had *never* and he *could* never let himself be reduced to such total emotional vulnerability!

"I don't want to go," Michael said evenly, his voice rumbling deep inside his chest. "And you can't make me go."

428

Edward cleared his throat, crossed his arms over his chest, and took a solid stance. "Of course I can, Mikie. And you know that it's all for the best if you do."

"Why, so you can go on pretending?"

"Pretending?" Edward was taken aback. "Pretending what?"

Michael sniffed with laughter. "You think I don't know, is that it?" His voice now had a calm, almost rational edge to it, but just below the surface, Edward could hear the fuse hissing away; he cringed, waiting for the explosion.

"Know . . . what?"

"What, do you think I am, stupid or something? I know damned right well you were the one who pushed Ray Saunders—when he fell and broke his goddamned back! I was standing right there! You knew that! I fucking saw you do it!"

"Jesus Christ, you're—"

Almost automatically, Edward had been about to say *you're crazy,* but he stopped himself and looked at his brother, wondering just how crazy and just how calculating he really was. At least for the moment, Michael's gaze was clear and direct, and he seemed to be actually relishing this opportunity—finally—of letting his brother know, after all these years, that it wasn't his private secret. It never had been!

"You knew . . . all along . . . and you never said anything."

Edward shook his head in amazement.

"Why?"

"Why? In all this time?" Michael made an obvious effort to keep his voice low and steady. "Why even after they hauled my ass off to the nuthouse? Why did I keep my mouth shut and never tell anyone?" His voice broke and then started to rise again. "Jesus Christ, Eddie! I don't know why! *I* was the one who had to suffer for it, not *you!* I had to pay because you wouldn't admit what you'd done!"

"Mikie, I . . . shit." He shook his head in bewilderment. "I—I don't know what to say."

"You don't have to say anything, Eddie, but you don't have to worry, either. Your secret's safe with me as long as I'm alive." He let loose a snorting burst of laughter. "No, not as long as I'm alive. Even after I'm dead! You're not the only one out there who has a secret, you know. There are plenty of others whose secrets I've kept, too. Plenty of hidden things that people think are buried for good out there!"

"Out . . . where?" Edward said. Michael was talking too fast, and Edward's mind was too numbed to process everything his brother was saying. "What the hell are you talking about?"

"Out at the mill, for God's sake!" Michael shouted. "You know that! They can say whatever the hell they want to say, but I'm not gonna hide it anymore! They can't make me do it! None of it! Not if I don't want to!" He leaned his head back and rolled his eyes up in his head, exposing all white. "No-sir-ee, bobcat! Not anymore!" he screamed; then he let fly another roaring laugh that drilled Edward's ears, making him cringe.

"Mommy's dead, and I don't have to keep any of those secrets to myself anymore! None of them! And I don't have to let you send me away again, either, and ruin what's left of my life! No way! Because it's all gone. It's all over with! All of it! Mommy's dead, Eddie! She's dead, dead, *dead!* She was the last one to know! And when she died, everything else that means jack-shit to me died, too! Can you understand that?"

"Yeah . . . Sure I can," Edward said, forcing a calmness into his voice which he didn't feel at all.

"Jesus! Stop them! Stop them!" Michael suddenly screamed. He started banging the sides of his head again. "Make them stop telling me what to do! Jesus God, make them stop it!"

"I—shit, Mikie, I don't know what to do. I know they can help you . . . at the hospital," Edward's voice cracked with worry. He watched, horrified, as Michael doubled over in a ripping gale of laughter and started kicking his feet and punching the mattress with both fists, raising puffs of dust as he rocked back and forth. The bedsprings squeaked horribly loud, like more insane laughter, but it wasn't loud enough to drown out the winding spiral of Michael's insane babbling.

"Make them stop it! Make them stop telling me what to do, Eddie! Please, Eddie! Please!"

"Look, Mikie," Edward said.

He moved close enough to reach out and place a reassuring hand on his brother's shoulder. "We don't have to decide anything right now, all right? You've got to calm yourself down. Maybe we can work out something that—"

Before he could say anything more, Michael suddenly reached up and took hold of his brother's hand. Gripping the wrist tightly, he bent Edward's arm back and squeezed. Pain shot like fire up Edward's arm.

"Ahh! Stop it," Edward cried out, but before he could react, Michael propelled himself up off the bed and spun him around, gripping his shoulder with one hand and pulling Edward's hand up hard between his shoulder blades with the other. Pain slammed him like a lightning strike as Michael forced him down onto his knees, too stunned to resist as Michael shifted around, grabbed a loop of rope off the bed where he'd been sitting, and wrapped it quickly around his neck.

"Do you like the fit?" Michael said. He snickered and yanked back hard on the rope, as if Edward were a dog on a training leash.

Edward tried to say something but could only make a gagging sound. Michael pulled back even harder. The rope sliced into the flesh of Edward's neck, effectively cutting off whatever he had been trying to say. His vision was swimming with exploding light. He felt himself passing out as the rope cut off what little air he could sip through his mouth.

"I meant what I said, Eddie," Michael whispered heatedly close to his ear. *"No* one—not even you—is gonna fuck up the rest of my life! Not anymore!"

Edward was too dazed to resist as his brother took the end of the rope, tied it around his wrists, and tugged the knots tightly. He was close to passing out, but his mind was clear enough to recognize the knife blade when Michael reached around and flashed it in front of his face.

"And *this* is my insurance policy, to make sure you cooperate," he said as he twisted the blade so the light from the hallway reflected off it. He touched the tip to his brother's throat and pressed down lightly. A biting pain, like a bee sting, zinged along Edward's nerves.

"Com'on! Get up!" Michael commanded. "We gotta get a move on."

With one hand still holding the knife at Edward's throat, he pulled his brother to his feet. Edward was forced to keep his hands held up high behind his back; otherwise the downward pressure would have strangled him.

"We've got ourselves a bit of a walk to take." Michael snorted with laughter, only this time it didn't sound at all crazy. His voice was thick with menace when he added, "Besides, haven't you been listening to what they're saying?"

"Huh? What *who's* been saying?"

"Why, those other people." Michael directed his brother toward the doorway and gave him a shove that almost knocked him off balance. "Can't you hear them? They're telling you that your wife and son are already waiting for you . . . out at the mill. Waiting for you to come out there and die with them!"

Chapter Twenty-six
Into the Cellar

The night was a swirling chaos of darkness and thick shadows as Michael prodded Edward along the path out to the mill. In the time since he'd arrived back home, he had noticed many changes in the landscape. A lot can change in thirty years: trees had gotten bigger while the boulders that lined the path now looked as though they had somehow shrunk.

But the path—ah, the path!

It was still the same as ever, just as he remembered it. Edward kept tripping and almost falling down with just about every other step, but even when the moon was lost behind the thick foliage overhead, Michael instinctively knew the exact location of every gnarled root and protruding stone, every subtle change in elevation. Several times he closed his eyes and had the uncanny sensation that he could see the path just as clearly through his eyelids. The beaten earth glowed like scratched silver in the moonlight. He navigated the dark, winding path as if he had been walking it every day of his life for the past thirty years.

And in some ways, he had. Nearly every day and night over the past thirty years, he'd had tangled thoughts and dreams about this path, these woods, and the abandoned mill. Even when he was far away from home, those people who used to come to his bedroom and talk to him somehow found him. They came usually at night, and told him, things — wonderful things . . . and horrible things that they had done and that had been done to them. He had known that his mother had died long before the phone call from his brother. In a dream, the people from the mill had told him all about it and how they were lost, now that his mother wasn't around to watch out for them, to care for them. They had been the ones who had called him home.

Michael's excitement rose, a tingling rush inside him as they got closer to the old building. The voices inside his head became clearer, too, telling him what he had to do, *demanding* his obedience.

"Don't worry! . . . I've taken care of everything! . . . I just said those things to trick him. Don't worry," he muttered.

You'll have to do it right away!

Right away! No more stalling now.

Now that you've got it started, there's no turning back, you know.

"Mikie!" Edward's voice was high and tight. "Why are you doing this to me?"

You know he wants to send you back.

And he'll do it, too, if you don't do this first!

He'll send you back!

Back to where we might not be able to find you again!

"You've got to stop this, Mikie! You've got to let me go!"

But this is it!

It's all up to you!

You can end it all!

All tonight!

"Hey!" Michael suddenly yelled, shoving hard against his brother's back. "Don't talk! You're confusing me."

Edward stumbled forward a couple of steps before he tripped and fell face first to the ground. He turned around before he hit, but his head or shoulder made a hollow thumping sound that echoed like a drum.

"Stop it!" Michael shouted, his voice whining high as he banged his fists against the sides of his head. "All of you! Just *stop* it! You're just getting me confused! Be *quiet!*"

He grabbed Edward's arm and jerked him roughly to his feet.

"And you, just shut the fuck up too, all right? You'll see them all soon enough!"

They started walking again, but after a while, Michael felt a current of panic.

Shouldn't the path have ended by now?

What if it never ends?

What if we spend the rest of our lives wandering around out here in the dark.

What if we're already ghosts, doomed to wander these woods—forever?

The voices inside his head were silent now, but he could still feel everyone's presence lurking in the dark woods all around him. It was the same feeling he'd always had as a child when he would cry out, *knowing* they were there with him in his bedroom. His mother and brother hadn't believed him, at least that's what they had said; but now . . . soon, at least Edward was going to get his chance to hear them, to see them . . . and *believe!*

Michael walked along behind his brother, following doggedly and forgetting, for a moment, that Edward was his prisoner. When the mill finally came into view, a wide smile broke out across his face as his eyes tracked across the wide front of the building, taking in the flat, moon-washed plane of old wood. The black rectangles of empty windows made a checkerboard pattern across the front. All of the window holes were perfectly black . . . except for one just about in the middle on the first floor. There, a faint blue light glowed, illuminating the dark silhouette of a figure suspended in midair.

"See? There she is, Eddie. See her?" Michael whispered.

His voice was tinged with reverence, but his brother said nothing. He only grunted as he gazed blankly back and forth between the old building and him.

"Why, you should be happy," Michael said. His voice was twisted up high, and he was barely able to contain a wild whoop of joy. "And *look!* There's *mommy,* in the window, see? You ought to be very happy. You're finally coming home, and we're all going to be together again!"

Dianne heard the scuffle of footsteps outside the room. She quickly turned away from Brian, and they both pushed themselves back into position against the stone wall just as the cellar door slammed open. After a brief flurry of activity in the doorway, someone grunted loudly and plunged into the room as though roughly pushed. After a few staggering steps, he wheeled around, fighting to maintain his balance, and then sprawled onto the dirt floor.

"Oh, my God!" Dianne shouted as soon as she saw who it was. *"Edward!* Are you hurt?"

Edward didn't move from where he had fallen. The way the rope was looped around his throat made him pull back, strangling him.

"Jesus! Dad!" Brian shouted. He hitched himself forward in an attempt to stand up as Michael walked into the room, his hands clasped behind his back as he strutted like a self-satisfied sea captain.

"Well, well, well," he said, followed by a twitter of light laughter. "I see we're all here now, aren't we? Have we all been happy?"

"Jesus Christ, do something!" Dianne shouted. In the harsh white light of the lantern, she could see that Edward's face was turning prune purple. "Can't you see he's choking?"

Edward's throat was making a high, strangling sound. His eyes were bulging from his head, but he didn't struggle. Dianne had the impression that he no longer had the

436

strength—or will—to fight back. She made a move to get up but then caught herself short and sagged back against the wall, shaking her shoulders futilely back and forth as though wrestling with her bonds. While Michael had been gone, she and Brian had managed to loosen the ropes binding her hands, but that was all; she knew she couldn't do anything to help, not until her feet were free. If Michael found out she was untied before then, he would no doubt tie her back up . . . if not kill her.

"Shit, he'll be all right . . . probably," Michael drawled. "It's not *my* fault, you know."

He snickered as he produced the knife he'd been hiding behind his back, stepped forward and, leaning down, quickly sawed through the rope. The sudden release of pressure made Edward's head snap forward. Dianne heard the sharp *crack* his neck made as he yelped with pain, then rolled his head to one side and took a long, roaring breath. The purplish blush immediately started to fade from his face.

"You son of a bitch!" Dianne screamed. "How could you do something like this? To your own brother!"

Michael turned and regarded her with a long, languid look. The lantern light caught a wicked gleam in his eyes as he smiled and said, "My brother? Do this? Well, Jesus Christ, Rachel, if you only knew what my *brother* had done to *me!*" Michael laughed again.

"Rachel—?" Dianne was caught off guard. "My name's not—"

She stopped herself and watched as he reached into his pants pocket and took out a small butane cigarette lighter. Cupping it in his hand, he held it up high and flicked the striker wheel until a small orange teardrop of flame danced on top of his clenched fist. He laughed as he brought the flame up close to his face and studied it for a moment. His eyes sparkled in the bright light. Then he released the lever, extinguishing the flame, and whispered, "Why, we're just getting started."

While all of this was going on, Brian was leaning

437

against the wall, wildly kicking his feet in the dirt and screaming obscenities at his uncle.

"You lousy motherfucker! You lying piece of shit! You said you were leaving town! You bastard! If I ever get my hands on you, I—I'll—"

"Oh, but you won't," Michael said calmly. As he looked at Brian, his expression softened for a moment as his shoulders slumped forward. "You know, I hate to spoil the little surprise I have lined up for you, but *none* of us is going to leave this place ever again."

"Oh, yeah? Well *fuck* you! Fuck *you*, you rotten bast—"

With two quick steps, Michael was beside him. He clenched his fist, cocked back his arm, and punched Brian hard on the chin. Brian's eyes rolled upward, and then he sagged back against the wall, unconscious.

Michael's face was flushed. His eyes bulged out as he turned to Dianne and yelled, "Is that what you want? You want that, too?"

Shaking her head, Dianne cowered away from him. The single loudest thought hammering inside her brain was—*I've got to get my feet untied. We're done for if I can't get myself free!*

Edward started to move on the floor, his legs shaking wildly as he scrambled like someone trying to learn how to army-crawl. His head thrashed from side to side. Dianne could see his eyes; they were wide open and staring like a cataract victim's eyes, glazed with distant pain. A cold, sinking feeling of pity and fear filled her as she watched him. Although she tried like hell not to, she couldn't help but think that it didn't matter how badly Edward was hurt. From the looks of things, Michael was right: none of them were going to survive the night!

Michael moved over to his brother's side. For a fleeting instant, Dianne thought he was going to help him up, but then he unlooped the rope from Edward's neck, roughly rolled him onto his back, and tied his feet together in several lumpy knots. With some effort, he got Edward sitting up and leaning against the wall between Dianne and Brian. By the time Michael was through, Edward was out cold. His head hung to one side and his eyes were closed, but Dianne thought—*prayed*—that she could see a slight stirring of his breathing.

"There, there," Michael said, standing up and looking down the line at all three of them as if he were admiring a trio of newborn babies. "I guess we're about set to finish it all off, now, wouldn't yah say?"

"Wha—what are you talking about? What are you going to do?" Dianne asked, her voice scratching like a cat in her throat.

It took a lot of effort, but she stared up at Michael with a hard, steady gaze that, she hoped, would show enough defiance that it might unnerve him. He had obviously completely flipped his lid, and she was desperate to find some way—*any* way to control him or persuade him to stop what he was doing and help them. The way Michael was talking and acting gave her the impression that, in some ways, he didn't want to be doing any of this, almost as if his actions were being controlled.

"Why, if *anyone* should know, *you* should, Rachel . . . You were the one who started all of it . . . way back when . . ." He shook his head and looked dreamily at the ceiling for a moment. "Way back when. You're the one who first *told* me what I had to do."

"But I—"

That was all Dianne managed to say; she was utterly baffled, wondering why Michael kept calling her Rachel, but worse than that were her concerns about what he planned to do next.

"God, we *all* feel sorry that it has to be like this," Michael said. "Especially for you, Rachel . . . I wish you didn't have to die again." His eyes softened as he looked at her with a distant gaze, but she could tell that his resolve wasn't close to breaking. He scrunched up his face as though listening to something he couldn't quite make out, then nodded. Dianne shivered when, just at the edge of hearing, she heard the high, keening wail of a baby.

Michael's expression suddenly hardened again as he looked at her—right through her and said, "Did you hear that?"

Dianne shook her head even though the clear, piercing cry was still ringing in her memory.

"The poor dead," Michael said. "She's in such pain . . . such agony that never ends . . . that *could* never end . . . until tonight!"

Dianne's mouth dropped open, but she had nothing to say.

"Don't you understand?" Michael said, shrugging helplessly. "They *have* to get *even* with us."

"Who has to—? Get even for what? What the hell are you talking about?" Dianne said.

"Don't listen to him," Brian said groggily.

Dianne jumped, surprised to hear his voice. She looked over and saw him watching her with a dazed, cross-eyed expression. A huge bruised lump was forming under his left eye.

"He's out of his frigging gourd. He can carry on a five way conversation with himself. He has no idea what the hell he's saying anymore."

"Oh, I don't, do I? Well, we'll just see about *that!*"

Michael's voice suddenly had a much different pitch to it; it sounded low and threatening, without a trace of the highpitched whine it had had before. Dianne looked back at him, utterly convinced that Michael hadn't spoken at all, that there had to be another person in the room talking to her.

"There, did you hear that—?" Brian shouted. His voice wound up the scale, bordering on hysteria. "That's what he does. He talks in all these different voices, like he's all these different people or something. I heard him do it once before when I was out here with him. He's a frigging schizophrenic."

Michael glared at Brian, then back at Dianne. "He's right, you know! They *are* all here! Everyone who ever died is still here, watching us, listening to us." Michael's eyes opened wide as they darted around the small room. "I've never seen them, you understand, not clearly, but I can hear them all the time. Always could . . . even when I was a kid." His frown suddenly deepened. "What, you mean to tell me you can't hear them!"

Cringing with fear, Dianne let her gaze shift around the room. She couldn't deny the disturbing sensation she had that the four of them weren't alone. All around her, she sensed other people, other presences . . . unseen. Every detail of the room was lit up in sharp relief by the lantern light, and it all seemed so solid and stable, but she was nearly overwhelmed by the disorienting feeling that this room was all somehow nothing more than an illusion. The dirt floor, the hard, stone walls, even her own panic and pain were thin projections, and behind them all was the *true* structure and substance of the mill, maybe of life.

Come on, Michael, do it!

Dianne jumped and let out a tiny shriek when the sharp, feminine voice spoke close beside her. It seemed to come from inside the wall behind her left ear.

Go ahead!

Do it now!

Do what you have to do!

"My father killed some of them," Michael said. His voice trembled and nearly broke as his eyes continued to roll back and forth. "You must have known that! That's why this place almost burned down more than forty years ago. He started the fire, and they all died! They all *burned* to death that time! That's why he died so young. They killed him. They made the truck get that flat tire, and they made the jack slip out so the truck would fall down and crush him. They were strong then. They could make things happen!"

Dianne almost asked who, but instead whispered, almost too softly for him to hear. "I know . . . I saw it all."

"That's right, you *were* here, so you must've seen it all

a thousand times," Michael said. His breath hitched so hard he grabbed at his chest like he wanted to rip his shirt off. "There were five of them that time—a family from Sweden. Their name was Larsen. There was even a baby! Hear her crying?"

He paused and cocked his ear to listen.

"The father, his name was Karl Larsen. He was a stone cutter, working out at Mason's Quarry, in Limerick. He'd been accused of killing his foreman at the quarry, and he and his family were on the run. They were hiding out here in the mill when my mother—oh, God! My *mother!*"

Michael's eyes suddenly widened. He clasped both hands to his head and leaned forward as though desperately trying to contain an explosion. His face was a rippling mask of confusion and agony.

"Oh, my *God!* My mother's dead! *She's dead!*"

Tears filled his eyes and ran down his face as he glanced blankly over at his unconscious brother.

"Did you realize that, Eddie? Did you know she was dead! Dead, Eddie! *Dead! Dead! Dead!*"

"I . . . I know she is," Dianne said in a wildly trembling voice as though answering for her unconscious husband.

"She's dead," Michael continued, "and now—now they can't even *find* her! She was the one who had helped them . . . back when they were hiding out here, in the cellar of her father's mill, and now they want to find her so they can help her."

He swallowed noisily. The twisted, sour expression on his face looked like he had just swallowed poison.

"My mother wanted to believe that Karl was innocent, but either way, she couldn't stand to see the family suffer like that, especially the baby, so she brought them food and clothes, blankets and stuff. But then the police—the police and a whole posse of people from town—a lynch mob, really—found out they were here and came to get them. They were ready to hang them, but Karl Larsen had a rifle, and he threatened to shoot anyone who approached the building. The police arrived and tried to talk him out, but he wouldn't surrender. He shot and killed Dave Lowell, the deputy sheriff. It was my father . . . my *father* who came up with the idea of trying to smoke them out. He was angry at my mother for having helped them. He wanted to see justice done because Deputy Lowell was a good friend of his, so because he knew the mill better than anyone else, he snuck around to the back of the building and started a fire down here in the cellar, to smoke them out."

Michael paused and took a deep breath. His eyes were staring far off, as if he was somehow seeing what he was describing.

"But it didn't work, you know. There were chemicals or something stored in the room above where the family was hiding out. Pretty soon, the fire got out of hand. It was horrible! Oh, Christ! Horrible!"

Michael closed his eyes and doubled over, repeatedly punching his fists against the sides of his head. When he looked up at Dianne, she was absolutely convinced she could see flickering orange flames reflected in his wide, staring eyes.

Was it a memory of her dream, her vivid imagination, or the power of suggestion, she wondered, or could she *really* hear it now, just at the edge of hearing? The raging crackle of flames. A crying baby. The agonized screams of people, dying by fire, and the sharp report of gunfire in the distance.

"They were trapped in here!" Michael wailed. "Trapped! Just like I was. I hadn't even been born yet. I was inside my mother's womb at the time, and I could feel it! I could feel the heat and flames, and I could hear their screams! *Their screams!* Oh, God! The baby was crying, and they were all choking on the smoke, sizzling like bacon in the flames. But they wouldn't come out. Oh, no! They were too proud. They'd rather die, and before anyone could do anything to put out the fire, they were dead . . . *all of them! Dead! Dead! Dead!*"

"But how do you know this?" Dianne asked softly. "If this all happened before you were born, how do you know any of it? Did your moth—"

"Because I felt it! I knew it, even inside my mother's womb I could hear their screams, feel their torment!" Michael wailed, his face going bright red with anger. "And they told me afterward! They told me about it all the time! Ever since I was a little boy! Whenever I'd come out here, like when I was going to build my bomb shelter—in this very same room! I could always hear them whispering down here in the dark, talking to each other about all the pain and agony they've all suffered."

"You must have been . . . terrified," Dianne whispered.

"Oh, yeah—it used to scare me . . . but there are other, scarier things in this world, you know."

Slack jawed, Dianne looked at him and nodded her head.

"And they used to come visit me in my bedroom, too, late at night, usually after Eddie was asleep. He never knew about them. The few times I tried to tell him, he looked at me like I was crazy or something. He and all of his friends used to tease me, saying I was insane—a *retard!* But I'm *not* a retard!" He punched the air with his fists. "And I'm not *crazy!* You know I'm not because you know they're here, don't you? *Don't you?* Because *you—*" He raked the air with his clawed hands. "You were *here* all along! You must remember what they did to you, way back before the mill was even built. They built it right where the old oak stood. Don't you remember?"

Paralyzed with fear, Dianne could only shake her head in denial and mutter, "No, I . . . don't." But after that, words failed her. She was no longer worried about saying the wrong thing to Michael; he was gone—completely insane, and somehow, for whatever reasons, he had plans to make sure she, Edward, and Brian all died . . . died to pay for—For what? For the sins his father had committed over forty years ago? For the deaths of everyone who had ever died even near here?

"Don't you remember the hanging tree? They called it the 'Witch Tree' after you were hanged there, and the house—our house, they called the 'Old Witch House' because of *you!* But you must remember that day in November, the day Judge Talmadge had you hanged? So cold and dreary? Do you mean to tell me you don't remember what you said?"

Had it really been a dream that night? Dianne wondered.

She shook her head and shivered at the memory of the vision she had seen in the mill window . . . of a person, an old woman, suspended in midair as though hanged. *Was it a dream, or did I—somehow—catch a glimpse of something that had happened out here a long time ago?*

She wanted to scream out loud but didn't have enough air in her lungs to do so. Then the voices started whispering again, suddenly swelling much louder.

I curse this man!

We've been waiting for such a long time!

Do it, Michael! Do it now!

Let them and all their kin burn in the agony of hellfire!

None of ye shall escape the cleansing fire of the Lord's judgment!

"None of us!" Michael said. "Don't you understand what you said, Rachel? You said *none* of us will get out!"

"But my name's not Rachel . . . My name's Dianne. I'm married to your—"

"Oh sure, sure" Michael said, cutting her off. He laughed tightly. "That's what *you* say, but *I* know better. You're Rachel Parsons. Your picture's been upstairs in the attic ever since I was a little boy. You didn't think I'd forget you, did you? That I wouldn't recognize you when you finally came back? Hell, I knew it was you from the very first time I saw you, out behind the house last June.

445

I was watching you all the time, you know, just waiting for you to give me some indication of what you wanted me to do." He smiled and shook his head as though he were the victim of a simple practical joke. "That was pretty clever, though, having that surgery done on your face to change it, but did you really think you'd trick me? But you should have known that I can't be fooled. I knew it was you all along. I could see right through your bandages, and even if I couldn't have, I could tell it was you just by looking into your *eyes!*"

"Jesus Christ," Dianne whispered. She slumped back against the cold stone, completely wrung out and feeling as though, after listening to all of this crazy talk, she had absolutely no sense of who she was or what the devil was going on.

"I'm sorry you had to come back like this and die again," Michael said, "but I have to do it. Don't you understand?" He raised his arms and shook them helplessly over his head. "I haven't got any choice!"

He stopped abruptly and glanced over his shoulder at the door that led out into the larger part of the cellar. His shoulders dropped and his face softened. Then, in a much calmer, almost rational sounding voice, he said, "I have to go now. I've got everything just about ready up there, but don't worry. I'll be back just as soon as I can, to be here with you. I promise. After all—" He smiled again, shrugged and slapped his thighs. "I'm only doing what you told me to do!"

Dianne was about to scream that she had changed her mind, that she didn't want him to do—whatever the hell it was he thought she had *told* him to do, but her breath was lodged like a stone in her chest, and her voice failed her. Before she could say a single word, Michael turned, threw open the door, and ran out of the room.

After he was gone, Dianne just sat there. Her mind was so overwhelmed by the confusion of her thoughts that for several heartbeats, all she could do was stare blankly at the white core of the Coleman lantern.

"Come on," Brian said. His voice barely sliced through the maelstrom of confusion and fear in her mind. "Come on, Dianne, get *going!*"

Her gaze drifted over to the unconscious form of her husband and then to Brian. She smiled weakly, her heart aching for them, lost in the hopelessness of knowing that—soon—she and they would all be dead. Her vision went dim.

"Get the hell moving!" Brian commanded, but his voice came from too far away; all Dianne could think was, even if she could move, she would never find him or Edward in the dark and confusion.

The other voices, if they had ever been there before, had stopped now. Faintly, from overhead, she could hear the heavy tread of Michael's feet as he raced about upstairs, doing whatever it was he was preparing to do.

"Jesus Christ, Dianne, *hurry up!*"

With a sudden squeal, the extent of their danger hit her hard, she finally went into action. Leaning forward, she furiously began to undo the ropes holding her feet together. At first the knots resisted her trembling efforts, but soon enough they fell away. The instant she was free, she leaped to her feet, but the blood rushing from her head and into her cramped legs made her feel dizzy and hot. Bright spots exploded in front of her eyes, and her ears whooshed like faulty bellows. Every muscle in her body felt twisted into knots, but she focused her mind on only one thing—she had to act!

Now!

She wasn't sure where to start. She knew she had to get Edward and Brian out of there, but first, shouldn't she try to stop Michael from doing whatever he was about to do. She sucked in a steadying breath and moved stiffly over to the door.

"Come on! Untie me first!" Brian shouted. Struggling with his bonds, he rolled over onto his side, twitching on the floor like a worm on a hot skillet.

Dianne's brain was moving in confused circles. She

looked out into the cellar and realized that Brian had been right; it was nighttime. Thick, impenetrable darkness filled the cellar like inky water. She strained to hear what Michael was doing upstairs, but the night had suddenly dropped down into a steady buzzing silence. Then, like a vision from a dream, a sudden brilliant flash of light filled the night. It was accompanied by a deafening, sucking concussion in the air that almost knocked her over as the night erupted in a swirl of roaring flames.

For a second or two, Dianne just stood there in the doorway, numbed and immobilized by shock. Then, through the blinding glare of flames, she saw a dark shape rushing toward her.

It was Michael, and he was leaping up and down, whooping like a wild animal as he ran, and all the while he was screaming at the top of his voice, *"I did it! I did it! I did it!"*

Chapter Twenty-seven
Up in Flames

The night had become a swirling chaos of flickering light and flame. Overhead, Dianne heard the snap and crackle of dry, ancient wood as it was consumed by the fire. A strong breeze ruffled her hair as air was sucked up and out of the small cellar room, drawn to the heat that pulled like strong lungs, inhaling. Her mind went blank with terror as she stared at Michael racing toward her.

"Come *on,* Dianne!" Brian said, his voice tight with tension as he struggled with the ropes holding his arms. "You can't just *leave* us here!"

She glanced back at him and saw the accusation and fear in his eyes.

He's convinced I really hate him . . . that I want to leave him here to die!

She quickly ducked against the wall, out of the doorway, and scanned the room, hoping to see something she could use as a weapon. Other than the rickety old table, the room had been stripped clean. It was too late to get one of the rough two-by-four legs to use as a club, so she crouched beside the doorway, her entire body tensed, and waited to hear the heavy tread of Michael's approach.

I've gotta time this just right! she thought, flexing her legs and bouncing up and down. *One chance! . . . I'm only gonna get one chance!*

Michael burst into the room. His arms flailed wildly to slow him down, but his momentum carried him several steps forward before he drew to a stumbling stop. As he had rushed past her, Dianne had caught a strong whiff of gasoline, but she gave that no thought as she sprang out the door. Her neck and shoulder muscles bunched up painfully; her arms chugged like pistons as she dashed out into the cellar.

She let out a twisted cry of panic when she looked up and saw through the cracks and holes in the ceiling a wild flicker of flames. Even in the few seconds it took her to get her bearings, the glow grew steadily brighter as the fire quickly spread upstairs, greedily feeding on the old building. She ran to the middle of the cellar, stopped, and just stood there, frantically seeking an escape route. The heat was steadily rising, prickling her skin. She knew it wouldn't be long before the heat grew intolerable. Leaning forward, her hands on her knees, she strained hard to catch her breath, shivering as cold sweat streamed down her face.

"Stop it! Stop right there, Rachel!" Michael shouted.

His voice came from out of the darkness, roaring like the shrieking wind of a tornado. For a moment, Dianne was confused. She was fighting hard against the overwhelming feeling of being trapped. Her only clear thought was, *I have to get out of here! I have to get away from Michael first!*

But where could she go? Where were the stairs? How far had the fire already spread? Where was it safe to run?

All around her, the night was exploding with the gunshot-loud crackle of burning wood. The wild glow of the fire was steadily brightening, but off to her left, back in the direction she had come from, she saw a pile of rocks and rubble. Above it was a wide opening in the floor. Her only chance was to get up there and then out the side of the building before the whole thing collapsed!

But what about Edward and Brian?

The thought drilled into her mind.

I can't let Michael catch me, but I can't leave them down there, either!

"Rachel! You come back here, right now!"

Michael's voice thundered louder. She turned and saw him, shifting out of the darkness, moving toward her slowly with his arms upraised, beseeching.

"Please," he called in a voice broken with misery. "Don't leave me here to do this all alone. It was your idea. You have to see this through . . . just like I do!"

"No! Stay away from me!" Dianne screamed. She shook her clenched fists in front of her face. Somewhere upstairs, something fell with a clatter onto the floor, making her squeal and jump, but she didn't take her eyes away from Michael as he came slowly forward.

"Please . . . Rachel. This is all your own doing. I didn't want to die! It was *your* idea!"

The glow of the burning building made the night all around her pulsate. Dianne's skin felt blistered and tight as the heat of the blaze swirled in a mad dance. When Michael stepped out of the shadows, the firelight flickered madly across his face. He looked like some horrible, twisted demon from hell as he materialized out of the darkness to claim her . . . to claim her soul!

"I'm warning you! Stay away from me!" she shouted.

Her body was trembling as she watched him position himself between her and her intended exit. She desperately wanted to look behind her for an alternate escape route, but she didn't dare take her eyes off him.

"Rachel . . . Don't you remember what you told me—? How we *all* have to be purified by the flames? You called it the 'cleansing fire of the Lord's judgment!' But you realize that *you* have to die, too. Otherwise—" He shrugged and slapped his thighs helplessly. "Otherwise all the rest of them won't be satisfied!"

Feeling her way over the uneven floor and rubble, Dianne started taking little baby steps backward as he

451

tried to close the gap between them. Her gaze was trans
fixed as she watched the hard, white planes of Michael'
face, like cold marble, catch and reflect the flames. Hi
eyes were wide open and stared without blinking, like
snake trying to hypnotize a bird. They seemed almost t
be the source of the fire that swirled around them.

I'm going to die!

The thought hit her with a cold, dread certainty.

*We're all going to die, and there's nothing I can do t
stop it!*

"You're right!" Michael shouted suddenly, his voic
cracking with maniacal laughter. "We're *all* going to die
And you have to come with me, *now!* Back to th
others."

Before Dianne could even blink her eyes, he took a fe
quick giant steps forward and then lunged at her. Purel
on reflex, she spun and ducked to one side. His han
snagged an edge of her blouse, but she pulled away, fee
ing a hard tug followed by a loud ripping noise. Then sh
was free. Staggering for balance, she started running to
ward the rock pile.

"No! Don't!" Michael yelled.

She blocked him and all of her raging fear out of he
mind as soon as she reached the rubble pile and starte
up it. Her hands and feet skittered lightly over the rock
with the curious detached sensation of a dream as sh
quickly scaled the pile and then leaped up through th
opening onto the first floor. Her ribs scraped against th
edge of the floor, knocking the wind out of her, but sh
ignored the pain as she rolled over once and then leape
to her feet.

She screamed when she saw that the doorway was n
more than twenty feet in front, but it was blocked by
wafting sheet of fire. The heat was intolerable. Sh
shielded her face with her arm, but it beat her back
Sweat and tears streamed down her face. When she too
a breath, her lungs felt like they were scorched. Backin

452

way from the opening, she looked for another way out. Above the sounds of the fire, she could hear Michael, puffing like a racehorse as he clambered up the pile of rubble after her.

"*Rachel! . . . Stop!*" he shouted. "*Come back!*"

If she had something to use as a weapon, she would have waited for him and nailed him the second he appeared in the opening; but she was empty-handed, so she didn't wait to see him scramble up onto the floor. She started running toward the far end of the mill where, through a wide, doorless opening, she could see the thick, black curtain of night. The fire hadn't surrounded the entire building yet, but it was spreading fast.

"*Rachel! . . . Please! . . . Wait for me!*"

She started running again just as, with a shrieking groan, a section of interior wall collapsed. Like an explosion of diamonds, sparks corkscrewed wildly into the air, and flames roared all the hotter. Afraid even to take a breath, she started running for the distant doorway. She had no idea how far it was down to the ground through that opening, but she knew she had to try for it. She didn't dare look back to see him, and she couldn't hear anything above the roaring rush of flames, but she could sense Michael as he came after her, calling, "*Please! . . . Rachel . . . Wait!*"

She did this on purpose! That lousy, fucking bitch has left us here to die!

That thought screamed inside Brian's mind as he strained so hard against the ropes binding his arms and legs that he thought his head was going to explode. The rope had long since rubbed his wrists raw. He wasn't sure if it was sweat or blood that was running down his wrists and over his fingers, but he no longer cared.

What was the point?

He pretty much figured out what was going on out

there. Someone—it sounded like Michael, but Dianne, n
doubt, had been the brains behind it all—had set the mi
on fire. She obviously intended to burn down the mi
with all of them in it. Above the crackling roar of th
flames, he could hear Uncle Mike's voice, shouting wildl
in the night, wavering crazily up and down the scale.

"I didn't want them to die! It was *your* idea! . . . We'
all going to die! And you have to come with me, *now*
. . . *Rachel!* . . . *Please!* . . . *Wait for me!*"

It certainly sounded as though he was an innocen
dupe in Dianne's plan. She had probably set the whol
thing up and was using Michael to help her get rid c
Edward and the rest of the family for the insuranc
money or whatever. From the sounds of things, she ha
even convinced Michael to die in the fire. Smart move
That way there'd be no one left to accuse her of anything
She could say the escaped psychiatric patient had bee
hiding out in the mill, had captured them, and ha
planned to kill them all, but she got away—just barely—
before everyone else died in the fire. She probably ha
staged the whole bit about escaping from the room jus
to make it all look good.

"You sneaky, fucking *bitch!*"

Brian could feel the temperature in the small room ris
ing steadily, smothering him like a heavy blanket. Thic
ropes of smoke were boiling down between cracks in th
floor and dispersing into the room to create a dense
foggy haze. The white circle of lantern light looked like
distant sun obscured by storm clouds. Sweat was stream
ing down his face, stinging his eyes. His throat fel
blocked off, and his breathing came in fast, fitful gulp
of hot air. He desperately wanted to deny everything tha
was happening, but he knew that he had to accept the in
evitable—that he and his father were going to die . . .

By fire!

But as much as that thought sapped his mental energy
he never stopped struggling with his bonds. He worke

454

en harder when he glanced over and saw the uncon-
ious form of his father, a motionless, gray blur over in
e corner. Brian tried not to think about all the years, all
e things they had never shared . . . and now would
ver get a chance to share. The years they'd spent apart
ice his parents had gotten divorced—even this past
mmer, as lousy as it had been—everything was lost
wn inside a yawning black chasm. The time he had al-
ays assumed they would spend together—eventually—
as slipping away fast. There were minutes, possibly only
conds left before they would be suffocated by the heat
d smoke. Like the old mill, the promises and hopes
'd had for an open-ended future were being consumed
 flames. Tears started from his eyes, and a cold, dull
he blossomed in his chest as he flashed on the pure
rror of his life ending like this. His mind felt blank,
solutely empty when he tried to imagine what the
orld would be like without him in it.

"Dad," he called out, his voice faint and faltering.
ley, Dad!"

Brian tensed, waiting for a reply. When it didn't come,
 wondered if his father might already be dead. Maybe
at was best. At least his dad wouldn't have to face the
nal, searing agony as the flames consumed them both.

"Jesus Christ, Dad!" Brian wailed, his chest hitching
ith deep, wrenching sobs. Tears carved hot tracks down
e sides of his face. "I—I'm sorry, Dad . . . honest I am.
—"

He jumped when a deafening crash sounded from
omewhere upstairs. The whole ceiling shook as a shower
f blazing embers sprinkled down onto the ground just
utside the opened door. Brian cringed and looked up,
xpecting at any moment to see everything cave in on top
f him. He jerked spasmodically when a scream ripped
rough the night.

"Christ," he muttered, trying to sit up as he stared
ide-eyed at the door. He honestly couldn't tell if that

had been Dianne or Michael screaming, but a voice inside his head told him that it didn't matter. He struggled for few more seconds, then—finally—gave up and leaned back against the cold stone wall.

This is it! he thought. A choking, bitter taste flooded the back of his throat. *I give up! This is the end!*

Knowing that before too long the temperature in the room would rise high enough to bake both him and his father, he laid his head down, closed his eyes, and started praying as hard as he could that—when it came—the pain wouldn't be *too* bad. Sobbing hard, he tried like hell not to think *anything* as he lay there and waited . . . waited for the end to come.

Halfway to the open doorway at the back of the mill Dianne let out a scream and stumbled to an abrupt halt. Not more than three feet in front of her was a gaping black opening. In the wildly flickering light of the fire she could see down into the cellar. Something—a whole lot of dark "somethings"—were scurrying back and forth over a rounded hump of dirt and sawdust. It took her moment to realize that it was rats, driven out of their burrows by the smoke and heat. Their horrible squealing filled her ears.

"Rachel, . . . please! . . . Please wait for me!"

She turned and saw Michael, coming toward her through the billowing smoke. Facing the heat took her breath away and made her skin feel all prickly. The sickly smell of burned hair filled her nostrils. Behind Michael another section of burning wall was slowly pulling away. It collapsed in a spinning shower of sparks, fanning the flames even higher, but Michael kept moving toward her with a slow, measured step as though he was impervious to the heat, not even the slightest bit aware of the danger.

Is he a demon—? Something from hell? she wondered, fighting back crashing waves of panic.

"This was all your idea, Rachel!" Michael shouted in a high, warbling voice. *"You have to see it through . . . to the end . . . with me!"*

She cast a furtive glance behind her, wanting desperately to run, but she was rooted to the spot. Behind her, she could feel the cool rush of night air being sucked into the fire, feeding it, stoking it higher. She knew the open doorway was her last chance for survival, but she remained frozen where she was, watching in utter horror as Michael slowly approached her. His face was a mask of agony and insanity with firelight rippling across his skin like a grotesque, living tattoo.

"Please—" he said. His voice was nothing more than a low moan as he held his arms out to her as though wanting to embrace her. "Come with me . . . Now!"

"No! Never!" Dianne shouted.

She took a step backward, forgetting for a moment that the trapdoor opening was behind her.

"It's not just me they want, you know," Michael said. "At first, that's what I thought, and I tried to convince them that if I died, it would be enough. Oh, God—" He clapped his hands to the sides of his head. "I tried like hell to convince them, but they want all of us! *All* of us, Rachel! *You* must realize that! You said so yourself. You said that we *all* had to burn in the Lord's 'cleansing fire.' Remember? You said it would make us whole again . . . that it would bring the family all together again! Don't you remember that?"

He kept moving forward until he was less than ten feet away from her. Then he stopped. Again, Dianne caught the strong smell of gasoline.

Jesus! she thought, *has he soaked himself with gasoline so he'll burn better?*

Aware that the opening was right behind her, she took a quick step backward and clenched her fists, knowing that he was going to make a grab for her. For several seconds, they squared off, just staring at each other as the

457

fire raged up the inside of the building. The air was as hot as an oven, searing her hair and skin.

Suddenly, a loud, creaking sound from up above drew Dianne's attention. She watched as a loose board slowly peeled away from the ceiling like a burning drape. It dangled for a moment, caught on a nail or something, and then fell, arrowing down at them like a burning spear. It landed behind Michael, but it hit a glancing blow on his shoulder just as he was coiling back to make a leap at her. With a sudden *whoosh,* his clothes burst into flame. He let out an warbling scream as he launched himself at her, his arms outstretched, his hands hooked like claws.

Everything seemed to happen simultaneously and in slow motion.

Michael came at her like a human fireball, his face split by a wild, insane grin. With a shrill cry, Dianne darted away from the trapdoor opening an instant before he caught her, but her foot snagged on something and she fell. She hit the floor hard enough to send a bright bolt of pain lancing through her body. Whimpering like a hurt animal, she rolled away from the opening and got onto her hands and knees just in time to see Michael streak past where she had just been standing and then fall through the trapdoor opening. His face slammed hard against the outside edge of the opening, and then he was gone. His long, agonized shriek ended with a dull thud from down below.

Nearly blind with panic, Dianne scrambled over to the opening and looked down. She was horrified by what she saw. Michael was lying flat on his back, half buried in clots of sawdust. His arms and legs flailed wildly about, clawing helplessly at the air. Rats were scurrying away from him, squealing in panic, but Michael's screams all but drowned out the noises they made. His clothes were burning like an oil-soaked torch as he thrashed about, trying to extinguish them, but his movements seemed only to fan the flames all the higher.

"Get them out of here!" he shouted as he writhed in agony on the cellar floor. "There's still time! I didn't want to do it! They *made* me! *You* made me do it! But maybe it *is* just me they want! Maybe I'll be enough!" He ended with a long, bubbling scream.

Dianne watched, frozen with horror as he stared up at her, his eyes wide open, piercing her as though he could see straight to her soul. Blood was flowing from a gash on his forehead, sheeting down over his eyes like a crooked, black mask.

"Please Rachel!" he rasped, his voice deep and trembling as though the flames had seared his vocal cords. "This is where it all started! . . . Right here! So this is where it has to end! *Go to them!* It wasn't Edward's fault! Tell him I forgive him! Go! Now! You *promised* me that you'd help them!"

He screamed again, his voice winding up higher and higher until it cracked and was finally lost in the roaring rush of other sounds. At first, Dianne thought it was merely the raging crackle and snap of the fire as it spread throughout the building; but then, all around her, she thought she heard voices.

Some were crying out in anger, uttering curses and pleas for help.

Others wailed as though in the midst of unbearable torment.

One was soft and low, cackling with laughter that didn't evidence the faintest trace of humor.

And faintly, just at the edge of hearing, there came the high-pitched wailing cry of a baby that rose and fell as though fanned by the snapping rush of the flames.

But even with the heat of the fire hammering down on her, Dianne couldn't force herself to move. Torn between pity and hatred for Michael, she stared down at him until — at last — he stopped moving. His eyes remained opened, unblinking and glazed as his hands and feet tensed, shivering, and then slowly dropped down to his

459

sides. With a single, deep groan, he settled back onto the burning sawdust pile as though curling up into a comfortable bed.

But even after she was positive Michael was dead, Dianne couldn't find the strength—or will—to move. She guessed that Brian and Edward were already dead as well, so what was the point? Why struggle any more against the inevitable? Why not just give in and let the fire consume her?

She glanced over her shoulder and saw the doorway that opened out onto the clear night sky. A voice whispered in her mind that she had to get up and get moving if she was going to survive, but then, faintly, another voice—Michael's—echoed in her memory:

"This is where it has to end! Go to them! It wasn't Edward's fault! Tell him I forgive him! Go! Now! You promised me that you'd help them!"

She turned around and screamed when she saw the wall of flames between her and the opening that led down to the pile of rubble. Knowing that it was probably suicidal, she poised herself for a moment on the edge of the trapdoor opening and then, before she could think about what she was doing, kicked off and jumped back down into the cellar.

"Hold on, Brian! . . . I'm coming!"

Although Brian could tell that the voice he heard was edged with panic, it drifted over him like a current of cool, fresh air, teasing and fluttering like light fingertip touches in the dark. He stirred and tried to peel open his eyes, but the blackness inside his head, like stretching strands of glue, kept his eyelids firmly shut.

How can there be someone calling to me? Is someone really there, or am I already dead and on my way to heaven?

But even with his eyes closed, he couldn't ignore the

pulsating heat that surrounded him, and he knew that heaven wasn't where it got hot. Memories of the panic and pain he had experienced—when? Mere minutes ago . . . or hours?—welled up like lava inside of him as the intensity of the heat rose even higher. He heard a strangled whimpering sound but wasn't sure if he was making the noise or if it was someone else.

"I'm . . . in . . . here," he said.

He had no way of knowing if he had shouted or whispered. His nostrils flared, making a loud, bubbly sound as he sucked in a breath of air. It was thick with the smell of smoke.

I think I must still be alive!

He was convinced when a coughing fit violently raked his lungs. Pressure squeezed hard against him, sending sharp jolts of pain through his chest as he let his breath out slowly and again tried to ease open his eyes. Through a watery film, he saw the hard-packed dirt floor and the stone blocks that made up the small cellar room's wall.

Oh, shit! I'm still here!

His neck crinkled like cellophane when he turned around and looked at the door. Through the rectangular opening, he could see a wavering dance of bright orange flames, lapping like wicked tongues in the surrounding darkness. A dense haze of black smoke hung above him like a funeral curtain. All sound in the room was curiously muffled.

So I must have imagined that voice.

He shook his head groggily, then suddenly tensed and looked over his shoulder at his father. The motionless form looked like a sad, discarded pile of old rags.

"Dad . . . ?" he whispered in a deep, raspy voice.

There was no answer, but before he could call out again, he heard a heavy pounding sound from outside the room. Turning, he saw a flurry of motion in the doorway.

"Brian!" a voice yelled, so close it sounded like it was

inside his head. A dark figure shifted like a shadow into the room.

At first, Brian didn't even recognize Dianne. Her hair hung over her face in stringy clumps, and her face and clothes were torn and streaked with dirt and soot as she staggered into the room. Her eyes were wide open and staring, as though she had no idea where she was as she looked around. Then her gaze latched onto him.

"Jesus! Brian . . . You're still . . . where's your . . ."

That was all she managed to say before she recognized Edward's motionless body on the floor in the corner. She ran to him and knelt down beside him, leaning over him as she uttered a low cry and roughly rolled him over.

"Edward! Come on, get up! Jesus Christ, Edward!" she yelled, all the while slapping his face. "Get the fuck up! We have to get out of here!"

Brian could see that she was completely out of control as she gripped his father's shoulders and started to shake him. He jostled limply back and forth, but his eyes remained closed.

"Come *on!* Jesus Christ, *get up!*" she wailed. "We can't just stay there! *Get up!*"

"Come over here," Brian said, forcing a calm level of command into his voice. Cold sweat and tears were streaming down his face. "Untie me first."

Dianne looked at him with a crazed expression, almost as if she didn't recognize him. Her lips moved, but he couldn't make out what she was saying—if it was anything intelligible. The thought crossed his mind again that this had all been a setup, and that she had no intention of freeing him before the entire mill came crashing down on top of them.

"Please, Dianne," he said, not caring if his voice revealed the depth of his desperation and fear. "Untie me first! I—I think I know a way out of here!"

As soon as he said that, a thundering boom sounded above them. All around him the stone walls trembled as

462

ancient timbers and floorboards upstairs gave way. They both looked toward the door as a cascade of sparks, flames, and burning timbers collapsed into the cellar. A rolling wave of heat slammed into them. Brian turned his face to the wall, and Dianne screamed and collapsed onto the floor, covering her face with her hands.

"Please, Dianne!" Brian yelled.

When he took his next breath, hot air entered his lungs, searing them like grilled steaks. The wooden door and door frame began to burn, snapping and crackling like a string of exploding firecrackers. Thick scarves of black smoke filled the room and began to lower. Not daring to breathe in any smoke, Brian held his breath until tiny lights exploded in front of his eyes. Waves of dizziness crashed over him, and the darkness opened up below him again. He knew, if he fell into it this time, his fall would never end.

He was so numb with terror that he didn't realize what was happening at first when he felt himself being roughly tossed from side to side. For a moment, he thought it was all in his head, that he had fainted and was falling, spinning backward into the abyss, but the wrenching pain that shot up his arms to his shoulders brought him back, and then he heard a woman's voice—*It must be Dianne!*—muttering . . . something to him. He didn't understand anything she was saying, but then there came a sudden rush of relief as the pressure holding his hands behind his back let go.

"Oh, Christ," he muttered, wanting to burst into tears but holding himself back.

Dianne gripped him by the shoulders and shook him. "Did you mean what you said?" she said, having to yell to be heard above the thundering roar of the flames. "Do you really know a way out of here?"

"Yeah . . . I think so," Brian replied. He was trembling as he worked on the knots that bound his feet. When he was finally free, he scrambled to stand up, but the sud-

den rush of blood leaving his head made him dizz
Again, stars exploded in his vision, and he stagger
backward, almost fainting, until he hit the stone wall.

Dianne started screaming. "Hurry up or else we're
gonna die!"

"Come on, then," Brian said, suddenly bracing fc
action. "Help me."

Crouching low to avoid breathing the thick smo
gathering at the ceiling, he went over to the battered ma
tress. Sitting down, he started to push it aside with h
feet. The mattress and plywood base moved with irrita
ing slowness, grinding on the dirt floor, but Brian lean
back and, grunting viciously, gave it a final, viole
shove. Sweat dripped down and stung his eyes, but h
shook it off as he stood up and looked down into th
tunnel.

Crazy Uncle Mike's "secret entrance!"

The flickering firelight outside the room made the dar
opening look like a doorway down into hell, but he kne
this was their only chance.

"It's real narrow down here," he said, "but I think w
can get my dad through. Take his feet."

Dianne looked at him as if he had completely lost h
mind, but she, too, sprang into action. Brian slipped he
hands under his father's armpits, and together the
dragged the unconscious man over to the opening.

A clutching fear gripped Brian as he put one foc
down into the hole. The air inside was cool and clung t
him like cold, slimy water. A wave of claustrophobi
swept over him; he was almost paralyzed with fear, bu
Dianne shook his shoulder and goaded him on, "Com
on, Brian! We don't have any time left." She sucked in
breath, got a lungful of smoke, and doubled over in a fi
of coughing.

Taking a deep breath as though about to plunge int
brackish water, Brian squinched his eyes shut and lower
himself into the hole, pulling his father's inert body i

after him. He sat down, cradling his father's head in his lap, and started to push himself along the dark, narrow tube, dragging his father after him. He had to fight back a nearly blinding panic as he waited to hear a chorus of soft, chuckling voices begin, but he told himself over and over that it had been Michael he'd heard making those voices down here and nothing more. He pulled his father along, inch by inch, only dimly aware that Dianne was behind him, pushing and helping them along.

"Are you sure this is a way out?" Dianne shouted.

Her voice sounded threateningly close, almost beside him in the dark. Brian was so wound up tight with fear he could only grunt in response. The truth was, he wasn't sure. He had seen Uncle Mike climb out of here, but what if it was just a hiding place and not a tunnel to the outside? He had assumed that it was an exit point, but he didn't know that for sure.

Now all three of their lives depended on it.

Struggling with his father's dead weight, he kept pushing back, inch by tortured inch. The heat of the fire in the building above hadn't penetrated the hole yet, so at least there was a momentary respite from it. The smell of damp earth was thick and cloying. It made him think of a fresh-turned grave. And it *would* be their grave if they ended up trapped down here. Hopefully, it would be mercifully short; maybe they would all suffocate down here in the darkness before the flames roasted them alive. He had read someplace that being burned to death was one of the most horrible, most painful ways to die.

The tunnel closed in on them, growing narrower and tighter. With Dianne blocking his view back, Brian could see only the faintest orange glow of the fire, but he could easily imagine that flames and smoke had by now filled the room they had been in. He wondered why the smoke wasn't funneling out through this hole.

Did that mean there was no exit point? Were they trapped in a dead end?

Brian grunted with surprise when he bumped his head against a solid wall.

End of the line.

"Wait a minute," he called out, his voice raw and tight. He twisted around, feeling blindly with both hands as he tried to figure out what the obstruction was. It took him a moment to realize that the tunnel had a sharp bend upward. Shifting his father's head off to one side, he swung his knees up under him and, stretching slowly, tried to stand. When he had straightened up about halfway, his head bumped against the solid blockage again. By feeling around, he discovered that it was a door . . . or several boards nailed together covering an opening.

Is it the way out . . . or a dead end?

Fear clutched his throat.

"There's something . . . blocking the way," he called out. His voice sounded dense in the darkness. He tensed as he waited for Dianne to answer him. When she didn't, a chilly rush of panic swept through him. He wondered if she had already suffocated. Then an even more frightening thought crossed his mind. What if she wasn't even there at all? Her presence in the room had been so sudden, so utterly strange that he wondered if maybe he had imagined her being there.

What if all of this was an hallucination he was having before he died—or *as* he died?

"Dianne—?" he called out in a trembling voice. "Are you all right?" A cold tightening filled his stomach, but then, after too long a pause, she answered him.

"Yeah. Why'd you stop?"

"I think I might have . . . just a second."

He felt above his head, groping in the darkness until he found one edge of the wood. He wedged his fingers up under it and felt around until he was convinced that some kind of wooden obstruction, like a well lid, covered the opening above him. Tensing his legs, he pressed his shoulder against the blockage and tried to stand up straight, but the weight was too much for him. The effort almost drained what little strength he had left.

"There's a . . . a door or something above us," he said in a voice shaky with panic. "I . . . I'm not sure whether or not I can move it."

"Do you think I could get up there to help you?"

"The passageway's too narrow, I think," he replied. "I suppose you could try."

He heard a heavy scraping sound as Dianne pulled Edward a few feet back and then wedged herself through the narrow throat of the tunnel. She slid into the space beside him, bringing with her a choking smell of smoke and sweat that was almost suffocating.

"It's heavy as hell," Brian said. He fumbled around in the dark until he found one of her hands and then guided it up to the tunnel ceiling. "Feel it?"

Dianne grunted and then shifted around to get herself into position. Their hunched-over bodies were pressed tightly together, leaving very little room to move or even breathe. Brian found the sense of claustrophobia almost overwhelming, but the choking, terrifying sensation was dulled when Diane said softly, "So, Bri, do you think we're going to make it?"

It was the first time she had ever addressed him using a nickname. He snickered and said, "I don't know, but we'll have to give it one *hell* of a shot, huh?"

"Ready?"

"Uh-huh. On three," Brian said.

They both tensed up and started counting in unison.

"One . . . two . . . *three!*"

Brian didn't think he had anything left, but he grunted like a wild animal and pushed up with every ounce of strength in his body. A horribly loud *whooshing* sounded in his ears. He imagined that the slow, grating sound of earth, stone and wood grinding together was, in fact, the sound of his neck and back bones crumbling to dust, but

467

then—unbelievably—the obstruction above them began to lift.

"Heave-*ho!*" he shouted, straining with his effort. His legs and back trembled. He could feel Dianne's heated breath puffing into his face as she struggled with him, and—for some reason—that filled him with a calming reassurance.

At least I won't die alone, he thought, but he didn't let up.

"We—almost—have—it!" Dianne chanted as they kept applying steady pressure. Dirt and rocks rained down on them from above. Although he couldn't look up and see it, Brian knew that the opening was gradually widening to reveal the night sky. It was alive with the raging glow of the fire. Through the narrow gap, slivers of flickering light shined down on them. Then, with a sudden, deafening roar, a hollow concussion filled the tunnel. Brian thought he was inside a cannon as smoke and intense heat from inside the room behind them suddenly streamed past them, finding escape into the outer air.

"Hurry up! Get your father!" Dianne shouted before her voice choked off in a loud coughing jag. Brian felt rather than saw her slide back down into the tunnel to get out of his way.

Blinded by the smoke and terrified of breathing it in, Brian held his breath as he fumbled down inside the dark tornado until he latched onto something—his father's arm. Gripping it with both hands, he pulled until he got a better grip. Then he struggled to lift his father.

"*Go!—Go!—Go!*" Dianne shouted behind him between wracking coughs. "You can *do* it! *Go!—Go!—Go!*"

His father's body felt suddenly feather-light as desperate energy coursed through him. Dianne was lifting and pushing from behind. It seemed to take forever as they prodded Edward's body out through the opening and into the night. Brian cringed back, frightened by the horrible glare of the conflagration above him; but after he got his

468

father out through the opening and rolled him onto the ground, he climbed out of the hole himself, then turned to help Dianne.

"Jesus Christ," she said with a gasp. "I can't believe we made it!"

She smiled grimly as she lurched to her feet and brushed herself off. Her face looked horrible—smeared with dirt, sweat, and soot, but Brian was filled with a sudden urge to hug her.

"Is he—is Uncle Mike still in there?" Brian asked. He shielded his face as he looked at the burning mill, astounded by the intensity of the heat.

"Don't worry about him," Dianne said, her expression hardening. "Let's just get your father the hell away from here."

Together they carried Edward's inert body off into the woods where the cool night air embraced them like velvety water. Once they were within the relative safety of the forest, they gently lowered him to the ground.

Dianne sat down on the ground beside her husband and, sobbing horribly, began to stroke his face as she watched the flames from the building tear up into the sky. Billowing smoke hid the stars, but spinning sparks spiraled like new stars up into the smoke.

"Good Lord," she whispered with an awed hush in her voice. She shivered wildly as she watched the fire with a drained, mindless expression. "It looks just like it did in my dream."

Brian was standing behind her and almost asked her what she meant, but when he tried to speak, he found that he didn't have control of his voice, so he stood and watched silently, hugging himself, unable to stop shivering in spite of the billowing waves of heat coming from the burning mill. Deep groaning sounds filled the night as large sections of the wall collapsed inward and were consumed by the hungry, crackling jaws of the blaze.

When he heard his father moan and then take a deep,

rattling breath, Brian collapsed onto the ground beside him. With a throat-tearing sob, he hugged both his father and his stepmother, drawing them desperately close to him. Then and only then did he allow the tangle of emotions raging inside him to sweep him away. Burying his face into the crook of Dianne's shoulder, he hugged her close and started crying. He found that once he started he couldn't stop.

Chapter Twenty-eight
Aftermath

It was late in the afternoon, the day after the fire out the old mill.

The sky was gun-metal gray and threatening rain as Dianne, Edward, and Brian followed the path out through the woods to the mill. As they got close to the place, they noticed, above the shifting trees, a thin haze of gray smoke, twisting like a worn out sheet against the dull sky. The southerly wind carried to them the singing smell of burned wood as well as the promise of rain.

"We don't have to do this right now," Dianne said.

Her voice was nasally and tight because she was trying hard not to let Edward know just how worried she was about him. After making their escape from the burning mill through the tunnel, they had waited in the woods until Edward had regained consciousness. Once he felt well enough to walk, they had gone back home and called in the fire, then headed into the hospital to get checked over. Dianne and Brian had only superficial cuts and bruises, and were suffering from exhaustion and minor smoke inhalation. Dianne's hair was badly singed, but the nurse assured her that if she cut it short, it would grow back just fine.

Dr. DeFazio had been most concerned about Edward,

whose injuries were the worst. He had wanted to keep him in the hospital under observation for at least a day but Edward had insisted that the lump on the back of his head didn't feel half as bad as it looked. The raw ring of skin around his neck, where the rope had strangled him, looked horrible but would heal with time. When Dr. DeFazio checked the X rays of Edward's skull and didn't find anything broken, he gave Edward a prescription for pain killers and sent him home to sleep after extracting a promise that he'd make a follow-up appointment with his doctor on Monday morning—or sooner, if he began to experience any headache or blurred or double vision. Dianne had far too many vivid memories of serious head injuries and reassured the doctor that she would keep a close eye on him.

But now, with every step that brought her closer and closer to the mill, Dianne felt a cold emptiness growing and tightening inside her. She felt as if she had swallowed a snarl of barbed wire. Although she would never have mentioned it to Edward, she knew exactly why she was so nervous.

"We don't have to do this, you know," she said again, wishing she had the courage to finish the thought—*because I'm scared as hell about what might still be out here!*

Edward stopped and looked at her. Biting his lower lip, he shook his head and said in a broken voice, "I know we don't, but I *want* to." He took a deep breath. "I *have* to!"

"But the police—they said they'd be coming by the house in less than an hour," Dianne said, glancing at her wristwatch. "I'm sure they've still got a ton of questions—for all of us." She glanced back at Brian, who had drawn to a halt behind them and was watching silently. "Shouldn't we be—"

"But don't you understand, Dianne?" Edward said. "I

472

have to come out here to . . . to see where Michael—"

He tried to finish the thought but couldn't. Tears formed in his eyes, making them glisten like wet marbles. Blinking his eyes rapidly, he looked up at the sky and said in a warbling whisper, "Oh, Mikie . . . Mikie . . ."

The cold ache in Dianne's heart was getting steadily worse, but she swallowed deeply and braced herself, knowing that she had to put aside all the irrational fears she had about coming out here so she could be supportive of Edward. She kept reminding herself how good he had been to her after her fall off the cliff last spring, and she was desperately trying to convince herself that, no matter what else might happen to them from here on, whatever had been going on out here at the mill was over now . . . It *had* to be over! No matter what wild dreams or crazy ideas she had about this place, it was over because *Michael* had ended it . . . last night . . . when he had died.

She desperately wanted to believe that; she *had* to believe it!

When they broke out of the woods and saw what was left of the mill, they were surprised by how much activity there still was. Three fire engines and two police cars had plowed up the overgrown dirt road and were parked with their red and blue lights flashing. There were at least half a dozen men in black and day-glow yellow raincoats picking through the charred and still-smoking remains of the mill. Andy Jones, the town fire marshal, noticed them as they started across the weed field and walked over to intercept them.

"Hello, Edward," he said, then nodded to Dianne and Brian. "I'm awfully sorry 'bout what happened . . . to your brother, I mean." He lowered his gaze as though embarrassed. "You know, I haven't got any idea what was going on out here, but I have to say you

473

folks are pretty damned lucky to have made it out of there alive."

All three of them silently nodded their agreement as Andy shrugged and then glanced over his shoulder at the smoldering ruins. "We—uh, we already got your brother out of there," he said, lowering his voice until they could barely hear him. "They took him over to Bissette's Funeral Home, in town. Hope you don't mind. There wasn't much—" His voice caught, and he shivered and looked away nervously. "I mean, I don't think the police will be asking you to identify him."

"No, I suppose not," Edward said, shivering. "It's just as well. I don't think I could handle seeing him . . . not like that."

Andy tipped his head to one side and, stroking the side of his face, said, "You must realize that we couldn't have saved any part of the building. By the time we got out here, it was pretty much a goner. That place was a tinder box, anyway. I'm surprised it hadn't burned down long before this."

"I wish it had," Dianne said to no one in particular.

"We're just damned lucky the sparks didn't catch the woods on fire or anything," Andy said.

Dianne barely heard him. Her eyes were stinging from holding back her tears as she stared up at the streamers of smoke, drifting and blending into the gathering rain clouds overhead. A voice in the back of her mind kept telling her that, no matter what she thought, the smoke didn't *really* look like twisted, tortured human figures, dissolving into the sky. She shivered and closed her eyes for a moment, hoping to compose herself; but try as she might to forget it, she couldn't get out of her mind those voices she had heard, screaming and laughing inside the mill while it had burned. They couldn't have *all* been made by Michael . . . especially not after he was dead!

"Well," Andy said, turning away from them, "I have to get back to work here. If you have any questions or whatever, don't hesitate to give me a call, okay?"

"Sure . . . okay. Thanks," Edward said.

Dianne didn't like the way her husband's voice sounded—so flat, almost robotic. Her heart flipped with a hollow thump when she noticed the tears, streaming down Edward's face. Moaning softly, she went over to him and wrapped her arms around him, pulling him tightly to her. As much as she tried not to, she couldn't stop herself from starting to cry, too. For several seconds, they stood together, holding onto each other; then Edward looked over at Brian and signaled for him to come over to them. He moved forward hesitantly, then melded into their embrace. Before long, all three of them were standing there, crying and holding onto each other desperately.

After a moment, Edward pulled away from Dianne and Brian, and in a raw, scratchy voice said, "He did it on purpose, you know."

"Yes," Dianne replied, forcing the words out of herself. "I . . . I know."

"I mean, he set the whole damned thing up so he . . . so he could kill us all . . . even himself." He snorted and wiped his nose with the back of his hand. "He *wanted* to die, and he wanted to take us with him." He snorted and rubbed his nose. "God*damn!*"

For a moment, he had seemed as though he was gaining control of himself, but then tears started forming in his eyes. "Ever since we were kids, I . . . I never realized how what I did to him ruined him, absolutely ruined his life."

"It wasn't your fault," Dianne said softly.

"Oh yes it was. And I just don't know if I can handle living, knowing how much he must have hated me."

"No," Dianne said softly as she clutched him all the tighter. "He never hated you."

Ringing in her memory as clearly as if he were saying it right now, was the last thing Michael had shouted to her as he died on the cellar floor, engulfed by flames.

"This is where it has to end! Go to them! It wasn't Edward's fault! Tell him I forgive him! Go! Now! You promised me that you'd help them!"

"I . . . I honestly think a lot of what he did was against his will," Dianne went on. "He wasn't in control of himself, and I think that, underneath it all, he genuinely loved you . . . as a brother."

More than anything else in the world, she wanted to tell him, right now, everything that had happened just before and after Michael fell through the trapdoor and died. She wanted to let her husband know how absolutely convinced she was that Michael had been driven to do what he had done; she wasn't exactly sure *what* had driven him, but she was convinced, by things he had said and by things she had experienced in and near the mill, that there was some kind of malevolent force, directing Michael to do what he had done. She knew she would tell Edward everything . . . eventually, but right now she couldn't do it. There was still too much immediate pain to deal with, and too many ancient wounds to heal.

She sucked in a deep breath and said, "But I *do* know that he wanted it all to end—right here, where it all started." Her voice was a wire-tight whisper. "He said as much. And I honestly believe that, no matter what else Michael did before that, at the very end, he sacrificed himself so that—hopefully—all the ghosts and all the terrible memories wrapped up inside that building would be destroyed . . . forever."

Edward licked his lips and regarded her with a long, glassy stare. "But they won't be. Even now," he said.

476

"Not until I have a talk with an old friend of mine."

Dianne looked at him, perplexed.

"My old friend, Ray Saunders," Edward said softly. "There's something I have to tell him before I tell you about it. And then—?" He shrugged and shook his head.

"Well, you have to believe that your brother forgave you," Dianne said, looking back and forth between Edward and Brian. "You'll go crazy if you don't."

She grabbed Edward's shoulders and gave him a vicious shake. "He loved you, goddamnit, and in the end, he made it clear—at least to me—that he had never intended to hurt you—or any of us. Not really! He wanted you to live because I think he was convinced that what he was doing really *would* end it all for good."

"Umm," Edward said, sniffing with tight laughter and forcing a smile as he looked back and forth between his wife and son. "Maybe you're right. Maybe it is all over now." He glanced at the smoldering ruins of the mill and added, "Either that, or else there's just one more angry ghost, lurking around out here somewhere."